Ungodly Injustice

Ungodly Injustice

Theresa A. Campbell

www.urbanbooks.net

Urban Books, LLC
114 Norman Ave.
Amityville, NY 11701

ISBN 13: 978-1-64556-786-8
EBOOK ISBN: 978-1-64556-787-5

First Trade Paperback Printing March 2026
Printed in the United States of America

10 9 8 7 6 5 4 3 2 1

Distributed by Kensington Publishing Corp.
Submit Orders to:
Customer Service
400 Hahn Road
Westminster, MD 21157-4627
Phone: 1-800-733-3000
Fax: 1-800-659-2436

The authorized representative in the EU for product safety and compliance
Is eucomply OU, Parnu mnt 139b-14, Apt 123
Tallinn, Berlin 11317, hello@eucompliancepartner.com

Prologue

Bronx, New York - 1999

"Give me a *P*!" Marisol Fernandez, the pretty head cheerleader, raised her arms high in the air, waving two red-and-white pompoms as she energetically hopped from one leg to the other in her super-short red-and-white skirt.

"P!" The other seven cheerleaders, who looked almost identical, waved their pompoms, jumping and kicking as they spelled out each of the six letters of their high school varsity basketball team's name.

"Pilots!"

The gymnasium pulsed with energy, every seat filled, every voice raised in anticipation. The Cardinal Spellman Pilots and the All Hallows Gaels were locked in a 98–98 tie, the scoreboard's red digits glaring down: six seconds left in the fourth quarter. The crowd was a living sea of red and white clashing against navy and white, the colors of the two Bronx rivals. Teachers, staff, parents, and friends stood shoulder to shoulder, clapping, shouting, their faces alight with hope and nerves.

"All right, it's now or never," Coach Whitman said, his voice low and urgent as his players huddled around him. "We have the ball and only six seconds to win this game, guys."

"We can do it, Coach," said Demarcus Jones, the Pilots' shooting guard and captain, his eyes blazing with confidence.

"Yes, we can," Jerry Mulligan, the power forward, agreed, his voice steady.

The team nodded, a silent pact passing between them.

Coach Whitman's gaze swept over their anxious faces. "Here's what we're going to do," he said, outlining the play that could give the Pilots the victory they so desperately craved.

The referee's whistle pierced the air. The players broke from their huddle and sprinted onto the court. The crowd's roar swelled, the gym trembling with anticipation.

The Gaels' defense was relentless, arms and legs tangling with the Pilots, determination etched into every muscle. The whistle blew again, and suddenly, the world seemed to hold its breath. Silence fell, thick and electric. Alan Galinsky, the Pilots' small forward, took the ball at midcourt. He pivoted sharply, then launched a high pass to Jerry Mulligan, who hovered just outside the three-point line. Jerry leapt, nearly colliding with his defender, and landed in a crouch, back to the basket.

Three seconds.

Jerry's eyes darted, searching for an opening. The Gaels' defenders clung to the Pilots like shadows. Then, in a flash, Jerry sent the ball between his legs, away from the basket. The Gaels were caught off guard. Demarcus Jones lunged low, snatching the ball just before it kissed the hardwood. In one fluid motion, he uncoiled, leaping high, the ball cradled in his left hand. He released it—a perfect arc toward the basket.

Time slowed. Every eye followed the ball as it spun, twirled around the rim, and, after a heartbeat that stretched into eternity, slipped cleanly through the net.

The whistle shrieked. The scoreboard blinked. The Pilots had won.

The gym exploded. Fans leapt, screamed, hugged, and even the Gaels' supporters clapped in admiration. Demarcus Jones had done it again.

"DMan! DMan! DMan!" the crowd chanted, their voices echoing off the rafters.

For Demarcus, "DMan" was more than a nickname. It was a badge of honor, a testament to his strength, resilience, and the legend he was building, one buzzer-beater at a time.

Chapter One

Demarcus Jones – July 2000

"Something smells amazing," Demarcus Jones announced as he stepped into the cramped kitchen, his nose twitching in delight. "Is that ackee and saltfish?"

His mother, Naomi Jones, let out a warm chuckle. "Yup, with fried dumplings to go with it."

"Yes! My favorite." Demarcus slipped behind his mother as she stood over the stove, wrapping his muscular arms around her waist and resting his chin gently atop her head. "Mom, you're the best. You know that, right?"

"And you're my best, baby." Naomi leaned back into her son's embrace, a radiant smile lighting up her face. "What time do you go to work today?"

"I'm on the two-to-eight shift," Demarcus replied, referring to his part-time summer job at JCPenney in Bay Plaza. "And after work, Marisol and I are catching a movie." Marisol Fernandez, his girlfriend, was also working at JCPenney for the summer.

"Good, so you have time to do the laundry and clean up your room before you leave," Naomi said, her tone matter of fact.

Demarcus groaned, "Ah, man."

"Oh, yes, man." Naomi, amused, turned off the stove and spun around to face her almost eighteen-year-old son. His broad, bare chest was a testament to his athleticism, and his pajama bottoms hung low on his narrow waist. At 6 feet 4 inches, Demarcus was the former captain and basketball star of Cardinal Spellman High School. It was during his sophomore year that he earned the nickname "DMan," a title he carried with pride through high school and beyond.

"Do you know how proud I am of you?" Naomi's eyes shimmered with emotion. "Stanford, huh?" She still sounded as if she couldn't quite believe her son was heading to such a prestigious university. Demarcus had just graduated in May, earning a full basketball scholarship to Stanford for the fall.

"God is just so amazing," Naomi continued, carrying a dish of golden fried dumplings to the small wooden table. This time, tears slipped down her cheeks.

"Don't cry, Mom." Demarcus crossed the room, kissed her cheek, and sat across from her. "You know I'm doing this for you, right?" His father had passed away before he was born; his mother was his whole world.

Naomi gazed into her son's striking green eyes. "I want you to do it for *you*, baby. I've lived my life, and I'm fine."

"No, once I become a top-notch lawyer, I'm going to buy you a beautiful house in Westchester and get you out of this little place," Demarcus said, glancing around their tiny two-bedroom basement apartment on Adee Avenue in the North Bronx. He grabbed a fried dumpling and bit into it with gusto.

Naomi smiled, tearing off a piece of paper towel to dab her eyes. "I know you will, sweetheart. Thank you for always thinking of me."

"You've done everything for me, Mom. One day, I'll get the chance to repay you for all you've done."

"Baby, you don't owe me anything. I'm your mother. It's my job to take care of you. I did it the best way I could, with God's help."

"We only have each other," Demarcus replied softly. "It's you and me against the world."

"Yes, it is." Naomi served herself some food. "Are you still off from work tomorrow?"

"Yes, Mom. I'm glad I'm off on Sundays."

"Me too." Naomi smiled sweetly at her son. "Sunday school starts at 10:00 a.m., and we'll be there bright and early."

Demarcus groaned. "Mom, I was planning on chilling tomorrow. You know what I mean?" He stuffed his mouth with food, his eyes fixed on his mother.

"You'll be chilling all right," Naomi replied, her voice firm. "In the house of the Lord. You hear me, Demarcus?"

"Yes, Mom."

"You should always be happy to give God the honor and glory He deserves. He's the one keeping us in this wretched world, and we should always be thankful."

"I am, Mom," Demarcus said quickly, hoping to head off the sermon he knew was coming. When his mother started talking about God, she could go on forever. "I'll be in Sunday school and morning service. Okay?"

"Okay, baby." Naomi's smile was bright. "I want you to have a good relationship with the Lord, Demarcus. There will be times in life when He's the only one you'll have to lean on. It'll be just you and your God. You hear me, son?"

Demarcus nodded, shoveling ackee and saltfish into his mouth.

"And please be home by midnight," Naomi said, her tone leaving no room for argument. "I don't want you out there too late on the streets."

"Mom! I'm eighteen next month."

"Bwoy, I don't care if you're eighty. As long as you live under my roof, you'll obey my rules." Naomi's accent thickened with every word. She had immigrated from Jamaica over thirty years ago, but her Jamaican accent was still strong, especially when she was angry or passionate. “Yuh hear mi, Demarcus?”

“Yah, mon,” Demarcus replied, attempting a Jamaican accent. “Mi hear yuh.”

Naomi rolled her eyes, smiling. “Watch yourself, boy.”

After breakfast, Naomi hurried off to get ready for work. She pressed a kiss to Demarcus’s cheek before leaving around 8:00 a.m., setting off on foot toward the Gun Hill Road station to catch the number 5 train into Manhattan, where she worked as a housekeeper for the Moynihans.

Left alone, Demarcus dutifully tackled his mother’s instructions. He cranked up his headphones, letting hip-hop pulse through his mind as he attacked the chaos of his messy room. Once everything was in order, he gathered his dirty clothes, tossed in some detergent, slung the laundry bag over his shoulder, and headed out into the Bronx morning. The nearest laundromat was just two blocks away on Eastchester Road.

Laundry finished, Demarcus returned home, neatly putting away his clean clothes. He wandered into the living room, grabbed the remote from the entertainment center, and collapsed onto the well-worn brown suede couch. With a click, the television flickered to life, and he tuned in to one of his favorite channels, ESPN.

Minutes later, his cell phone, resting beside him on the couch, began to ring. Demarcus lowered the TV volume and answered, grinning as he recognized his best friend’s voice.

“What’s up, Jerry? How’s Hotlanta?” Demarcus chuckled, teasing. “Having fun down there with the folks?”

Jerry’s laughter boomed through the phone. “Shut up.” Jerry Mulligan and his parents, though Bronx natives, were visiting his grandparents in Atlanta for the summer. “We’re leaving for the airport now. I’ll be home tonight to take Marisol away from you.”

"In your dreams."

The two friends bantered for a while, laughter echoing through the line, until Demarcus glanced at the clock mounted on the wall. "Jerry, I've got to get ready for work."

"All right. You know I start my job at McDonald's on Monday."

"I told you to apply at JCP. You'd get discounts on some nice gear for college, but you prefer the food."

Jerry laughed. "That's right. I'll take a Big Mac over shoes and clothes any day."

"I hope you don't get fired on your first day for eating out Mickey D's."

"Man, shut up." Jerry was a notorious foodie, though you'd never guess it from his tall, slim 6-foot-3-inch frame.

"I'll see you soon, foodie." Still chuckling, Demarcus clicked his cell phone off and went to get ready for work.

Later that night, Demarcus exited the JCPenney building at around 8:30 p.m., dressed in dark blue Levi's slim jeans, a blue-and-white striped Nike t-shirt, and a crisp new pair of white Nike sneakers, his mother's graduation gift. His thick black curls, now trimmed into a low mohawk, framed his light complexion, freckles dusted across his pointed nose and high cheekbones, and his striking green eyes were features that often led people to mistake him for Hispanic.

The JCPenney parking lot buzzed with activity, cars and people coming and going. But Demarcus's attention was captured by the stunning young woman standing a few feet away. She wore a tight, strapless white denim jumpsuit that hugged her slim figure, her 5 feet 6 inches elevated by three-inch platform sandals. Long brown hair, streaked with gold highlights, spiraled around her pretty face and cascaded down her back, settling comfortably atop her full curves.

Demarcus let out a low whistle of appreciation as he swaggered toward Marisol, whose ruby-red lips parted in a wide grin, her brown eyes sparkling with amusement.

"Hola, señorita," Demarcus said, leaning in until their noses nearly touched. "Are you waiting for someone, gorgeous?"

"*Mi novio guapo*, señor," she replied, playing along.

"Oh, your handsome boyfriend, huh? I think he's a lucky guy," Demarcus teased, grinning from ear to ear. "A fine lady like yourself."

"I'll be sure to tell him you said that." Marisol giggled, her laughter light and musical.

"Tell him about this as well." Demarcus kissed Marisol passionately.

When she finally caught her breath, Marisol grinned. "You know what? I just dumped him for you."

Hand in hand, Demarcus and Marisol strolled toward the AMC Bay Plaza Cinema, laughter trailing behind them. The city's evening buzz faded as they stepped inside, the neon lights of the theater flickering over their faces. They bought tickets to the new *X-Men* movie, then loaded up on nachos, popcorn, and sodas, their arms full as they made their way to their seats.

As the lights dimmed and the world of mutants unfolded on the screen, they lost themselves in the action and fantasy. Between mouthfuls of buttery popcorn and tangy nachos, they exchanged quick, secretive kisses, their fingers intertwined. They were young, carefree, and completely in love. Nothing else seemed to matter.

When the movie finally ended close to 11:00 p.m., Demarcus glanced at his watch, a hint of worry in his eyes. "I've got about an hour to get you home, and to get myself home before my mom starts tripping," he said, half-joking, half-serious.

"Oh, so we're on the same curfew now?" Marisol teased, her eyes sparkling. "I reminded my mom this morning that I just turned eighteen, and she told me she's been around since my conception, so she's fully aware of my age."

They both burst out laughing, the sound echoing down the nearly empty hallway.

"They love us and want what's best for us," Demarcus said, his voice softening. "We're lucky to have them."

"Yes, we are," Marisol agreed, squeezing his hand.

Demarcus glanced down at Marisol's high-heeled sandals as they walked outside. "It's probably easier if we walk up the road and hail a cab if you can manage in those shoes."

Marisol rolled her eyes and gave him a playful slap on the arm. "Shut up. I want you to know I can sprint in these sandals if I have to."

As luck would have it, a cab pulled up just then. Demarcus gave the driver directions to Marisol's house on Bainbridge Avenue, and minutes later, they arrived. He paid the fare, then circled around to open her door, offering his hand like a gentleman.

Together, they walked up the flower-lined driveway, the scent of Mrs. Fernandez's garden lingering in the warm night air. Marisol unlocked the door, and they slipped inside the quiet, welcoming house.

"Hi, Daddy," Marisol called out, her voice bright as she and Demarcus entered the living room. Her father was sprawled comfortably on the couch, eyes fixed on the television.

"Hi, sweetheart." Mr. Fernandez glanced over, his face lighting up at the sight of his daughter.

"What's up, Mr. Fernandez?" Demarcus greeted him with a firm handshake.

"Demarcus, how are you, son?" Mr. Fernandez patted the cushion beside him, inviting Demarcus to sit. Demarcus obliged, settling in as Marisol curled up on his other side.

"How's the summer going so far?" Mr. Fernandez asked, his tone warm and genuinely interested.

"So far, so good," Demarcus replied with a relaxed smile. "No complaints, sir."

"That's good. Before you know it, you two will be off to college." He beamed with pride, shaking his head as if still amazed by their achievements. "You at Stanford, and my Marisol at NYU. Full scholarships for both of you." He clapped his hands together, the gesture brimming with disbelief and joy. "Who says you can't achieve what the mind conceives?"

"Yes, you can, by the grace of God," Mrs. Fernandez chimed in, her thick Spanish accent coloring her words as she leaned over the back of the couch. She wrapped Demarcus in a quick hug and kissed his cheek. "Hi, baby."

"Hi, Mrs. Fernandez," Demarcus replied, grinning.

"How is your mother doing?" Mrs. Fernandez asked, her eyes kind. The two women had become fast friends since their children started dating, always keeping a watchful, loving eye on them.

"She's good," Demarcus answered. "Probably home right now, taking out my clothes for church tomorrow."

Everyone laughed at that, the sound filling the room with warmth.

It was around 11:35 p.m. when Demarcus finally told Marisol he had to leave. They were cuddled together on the couch, watching MTV, the house quiet now that Mr. and Mrs. Fernandez had retired to their bedroom.

"Do you want to come over after church tomorrow?" Marisol asked, her voice soft and hopeful. "My parents are going to visit my sister and their grandkids."

Both of Marisol's parents were immigrants—her father from Puerto Rico, her mother from the Dominican Republic. In search of a better life, Mrs. Fernandez had overstayed her visitation visa and lived undocumented for several years, until she met and married Mr. Fernandez. Together, they built a family in the United States, the land of opportunity. Their two daughters, Maria and Marisol, were born here, while Mrs. Fernandez's older son, Carlos, remained in the Dominican Republic with his father until, a few years ago, she was finally able to bring him to New York.

"Okay, I'll come by after dinner," Demarcus promised Marisol. "I have to go now."

"Want me to call a cab for you?" she offered.

"It'll probably take a while for them to get here." Demarcus glanced at his watch. "It's better if I just walk out to Gun Hill Road and flag one down."

Marisol walked Demarcus to the door, and they shared a lingering goodnight kiss.

"I'll see you tomorrow," Demarcus said, stepping out into the warm summer night. He strolled up Bainbridge Avenue, the city's hum softened by the late hour. As he passed Montefiore Hospital heading toward Gun Hill Road, he spotted a number 28 bus idling at the stop.

A quick glance at his watch told him he could still make it home on time if he caught the bus instead of waiting for a cab. He broke into a jog and hopped aboard just as the doors were about to close. Swiping his MetroCard, he found a seat near the front, the city lights flickering past the window.

Ten minutes later, Demarcus stepped off at the intersection of Knapp Street and Gun Hill Road. He walked up Knapp, crossed over to Eastchester Road, and looked up the block. There, outside the deli at Hammersley Avenue, a group of men sat around a small table, playing dominoes, laughing, and talking.

"Yo, DMan!" someone called out.

Demarcus spotted his good friend and former basketball teammate, Trevor Richards, and hurried over, thinking, *I'll just quickly say hello.*

"What's good, Trevor?" he greeted.

Trevor stood and gave Demarcus a man hug. "Just chilling," he replied, settling back into his seat. "It's summer, right?"

"You know that's right." Demarcus grinned, then greeted the other men he recognized from the neighborhood, Mr. Afia, Tom Dunkley, and Jimmy Mason.

Demarcus and Trevor chatted for a little while, laughter and easy camaraderie flowing between them. Then Demarcus glanced down at his wristwatch and sighed. "I've got to run," he said, realizing he was cutting it close to his curfew. Even though his mother might forgive a few minutes, Demarcus always tried to respect her rules.

"Curfew?" Trevor grinned, teasing.

Demarcus smiled back. "Give me a call and let's try to hang out before college sneaks up on us. Cool?"

"Yeah, I'll do that," Trevor replied. He was starting Lehman College in the fall. "Catch you later."

Demarcus took a few steps away, then noticed Ms. Lopez, the elderly woman who lived down the block, struggling across the street with at least three heavy plastic bags and a large, bulging tote slung over her shoulder.

"Let me help you with those, ma'am," Demarcus called, hurrying over. He took all the bags from Ms. Lopez, his strong arms flexing under the weight.

"Thank you, dear," Ms. Lopez said gratefully as they walked toward her house. "That's very kind of you."

"You're welcome, ma'am," Demarcus replied, carrying the bags with ease, his eyes fixed on her house just a short distance away.

Soon they arrived. Demarcus carried the bags through the short metal gate and set them by the front door. Fortunately, Ms. Lopez lived on the ground floor.

"Mama, is that you?" The door swung open, and Ms. Lopez's adult son, Juan, stood in the doorway with a marijuana spliff dangling from his lips. "I'm starving up in here." He made no move to help with the bags.

Demarcus shook his head in disgust. "Goodnight, ma'am," he said, ignoring Juan.

"Goodnight, sweetheart. Thanks again for helping me with my bags," Ms. Lopez called after him.

As Demarcus walked away, he glanced back and saw Juan still leaning in the doorway, watching his elderly mother haul the heavy bags inside.

"Real lowlife," Demarcus muttered, a touch of anger in his voice. "I could never treat my mom like that." He hurried across Gunther Avenue toward Adee Avenue, paying no attention to the small park across the street.

"Help me," the young woman whispered, her voice barely more than a rasp, as she dragged herself across the unforgiving ground. Blood trickled from her split lips, her right eye swollen completely shut, her left eye clouded and stinging with tears and grit. Each word she forced out sounded thunderous in her own ears, but in reality, it was only a faint plea lost in the night.

Hope flickered and faded as she watched the tall young man's silhouette retreat, his back disappearing into the darkness. He hadn't seen her, hadn't heard her desperate call.

"Someone, please help me." A wave of blackness crashed over her, threatening to pull her under. For a moment, she surrendered to it, her battered body limp. But as oblivion beckoned, a stubborn spark ignited within her. She clawed her way back to consciousness, refusing to let go.

I have to reach the road. No, it can't end like this. Not here.

With every inch she crawled, sharp rocks and coarse dirt tore at her raw, bleeding skin. Agony radiated from every limb of her naked body, every breath a struggle, every movement a battle against the pain that threatened to consume her.

Still, she pressed on, inch by agonizing inch, willing herself toward the distant glow of the street, clinging to the hope that someone—anyone—would find her before it was too late.

Chapter Two

Bridget Walsh

"Thank you for calling Ferrari Investment Group. How may I assist you?" Bridget answered the phone with a bright, professional cheer. She listened attentively, then replied, "Certainly, please hold for your transfer." With practiced efficiency, she pressed a button and set the receiver down. Within moments, the phone rang again.

Bridget managed each call with a genuine sense of enjoyment, relishing her summer job at the prestigious hedge fund in Lower Manhattan. She had just graduated from Cardinal Spellman High School and was set to begin her studies at Baruch College in the fall, majoring in finance and economics. While she had dreamed of landing an associate position, she considered herself fortunate to have secured this temporary role while the regular receptionist was on maternity leave.

"Oh, well, I'll get an internship next summer," she had reassured her parents. "At least now I get to meet people in the business and start building connections." Her ambition was clear. One day, she wanted to be a stock trader on the floor of the New York Stock Exchange.

Her parents were delighted to see her so energized by her work. Yet, beneath her excitement, Bridget carried the scars of a difficult past. Though beautiful, she had struggled with her weight and self-image for most of her life. School had been a gauntlet of bullying, relentless teasing, and cruel nicknames hurled by thoughtless classmates. The principal and teachers did what they could, but the damage was done. Bridget had no close friends, rarely spoke unless spoken to, and moved through the halls with her head bowed, eyes fixed on the floor.

It was Demarcus Jones who changed everything during her senior year. Despite living across the street, Bridget and her parents in their stately brick house, Demarcus and his mother in a rented basement apartment, they had never truly known each other. At school, it was always the same. Demarcus, captain of the basketball team and boyfriend to the perfect head cheerleader, moved through the halls with effortless popularity. Bridget, by contrast, was nearly invisible, except to him. Whenever their paths crossed, Demarcus greeted her with a warm smile, never treating her as if she were invisible.

One afternoon, as Bridget stood at her locker, a group of girls suddenly surrounded her, forming a tight, mocking circle. Patricia Harris, the ringleader, sneered, "Hey, Bridget, we heard you're the new poster girl for Jenny Craig." Her words sent the others into fits of laughter.

"We heard you're going to be wearing a bikini for your photo shoot," another girl chimed in, and the group erupted again, their laughter echoing off the lockers.

Bridget stared at the floor, her tears splattering silently onto the tiles.

"Go, supermodel Bridget. You're—"

A deep voice cut through the jeers. "I think that's enough."

All eyes snapped to Demarcus as he strode toward them, his face darkened by a scowl. "It's not cool what you're doing to Bridget." He fixed Patricia with a hard look, then turned to the others. "If you bully her again, I'll make sure everyone at school knows exactly what you're doing."

Fear flickered across their faces. Demarcus's words carried weight, and being on his bad side would make them outcasts.

"I'm sorry, Bridget," Patricia blurted, her bravado gone. "I won't do it again."

Her followers echoed her apology, waiting anxiously for Demarcus's next move.

He reached into his backpack and handed Bridget a pack of Kleenex, something his mother always insisted he carry, though he rarely needed it himself. "Here, Bridget."

"Thank you," she whispered, dabbing her face with trembling hands.

"We truly are sorry," Patricia said again, her voice barely above a whisper.

Bridget glanced up, noticing the fear and shame etched on their faces. They no longer seemed so high and mighty. "Okay," she replied quietly.

Patricia and her entourage scattered, leaving Bridget standing with Demarcus.

"I'm sorry you had to go through that," Demarcus said gently. "I hope it doesn't happen again."

Bridget nodded, unable to meet his eyes.

True to their word, Patricia and her friends never bothered Bridget again. Thanks to Demarcus, her final year of high school became her best.

The summer job at Ferrari Investment Group was the cherry atop Bridget's salted caramel sundae, a rare delight in her life, and it kept getting sweeter. Each morning, she felt a surge of pride as she stepped into the busy office, eager to prove herself.

"Good morning, sir," Bridget greeted Angelo Ferrari, the acting CEO, as he strode through the lobby one day. He was impeccably dressed in a tailored navy-blue suit, his brown leather briefcase swinging confidently at his side. Without so much as a glance or a word, Angelo swept past her, his presence radiating an unmistakable air of arrogance, like a halo that hovered above him, untouchable and aloof.

Bridget felt a sting of disappointment when her boss breezed past her without so much as a nod. Still, she greeted him every morning, just as she did everyone who walked through the door. Some people in the company weren't as friendly, but most employees and visitors returned her warmth.

A week into her new role, the switchboard suddenly lit up with a call. Bridget's heart skipped as she saw Mr. Ferrari's extension flash on the screen.

"Hello, sir. How may I help you?" she answered, her voice steady despite the flutter in her chest.

"Bridget, isn't it?" His voice, deep and husky, sent a shiver down her spine.

"Yes. Yes, it is, sir," she replied, swallowing the lump in her throat.

"Such a beautiful name for a beautiful lady."

Bridget's eyes widened. She glanced around, half-expecting someone to jump out and reveal it was a prank.

"I just wanted to call and apologize," Angelo Ferrari continued smoothly. "The last few days, I've been dealing with some issues at work and wasn't the most sociable. Please forgive me for not returning the warm greetings you share every morning."

Bridget smiled, her nerves easing. "That's okay, Mr. Ferrari. I understand."

"Please, call me Angelo. Mr. Ferrari is my father. I'm sure you see that old goat showing up here time after time."

"Angelo, it is," Bridget replied, ignoring the jab at his father.

Angelo Ferrari was the acting CEO while his father, Alfredo Ferrari, was on an extended sick leave due to a heart condition. Still, Alfredo remained a powerful presence at the firm, always hopeful he'd soon reclaim his role.

"I have to run, Bridget. Have a wonderful day," Angelo said, his tone suddenly brisk.

Bridget spent the rest of the day in a daze of delight, her heart buoyed by the realization that her boss not only knew her name but had called her beautiful.

The following morning, as she settled behind the reception desk, a deliveryman approached, his face nearly obscured by an enormous vase overflowing with pristine white orchids.

"Good morning," Bridget greeted, her voice bright.

"Good morning." The deliveryman set the vase carefully on the edge of her desk. "I have a delivery for Bridget Walsh."

"For whom?" Bridget blinked at him, startled.

"Bridget Walsh?" he repeated, glancing at his clipboard.

She looked from the deliveryman to the lavish bouquet, then back again, incredulous. "Well, that's me. Are you sure?" She had never received flowers before, certainly nothing like this.

"Yes, ma'am. Please sign here." He handed her the clipboard.

Still in shock, Bridget scribbled her signature. As soon as the deliveryman left, she reached for the small white envelope nestled among the elegant blooms. Her hands trembled as she slid the note free and opened it.

"Beautiful flowers for a beautiful flower. A," Bridget whispered, her cheeks flushing as red as ripe beefsteak tomatoes. "Oh my God, they're from Mr. Ferrari. I mean, Angelo."

A dizzy thrill swept through her. Why would that tall, striking, wealthy man send her flowers? Maybe it was just another apology, she reasoned. But the note—this was the second time he'd called her beautiful.

Moments later, the switchboard lit up with a call. Bridget hesitated, her heart fluttering, before she answered.

"Do you like your flowers?" Angelo's voice was smooth and direct.

"Yes, sir," Bridget replied quickly, her words tumbling out. "Thank you. Thank you very much."

"Let's lose the 'sir' and 'mister,' okay? Remember, it's Angelo."

Bridget nodded instinctively, then realized he couldn't see her. "Okay," she managed.

"I like you, Bridget," Angelo said, his tone lowering. "I'd really like to get to know you better. Is that all right with you?"

"Huh? Well, um, I mean, sure," Bridget squeaked, caught off guard.

"But this must stay just between us," Angelo warned, his voice suddenly serious. "You know, with me being your boss and all." He neglected to mention he was also twenty years her senior.

But eighteen-year-old Bridget didn't seem to care, and neither did Angelo Ferrari. For the first time in her life, a man had shown romantic interest in Bridget, and she hadn't even started her new diet yet.

Over the next few days, a fresh bouquet arrived for her every morning. Angelo took her cell phone number and began texting and calling her only outside of work, while at the office, he acted as if she didn't exist.

"This is for our protection," he explained. "Just know I'm always thinking of you, even when I'm at work."

Bridget agreed, swept up in the secret, intoxicating attention.

Bridget's parents couldn't help but notice the transformation in their daughter. She lingered over her hair each morning, coaxing every strand of her long, blonde locks into place. Chapstick was replaced by a delicate sweep of pink lipstick, and she spent far more time than usual selecting her outfits for work.

One evening, as Bridget arrived home, her mother eyed her with gentle curiosity. "Are you seeing someone, Bridget?" she asked, her father's gaze attentive beside her.

"No, Mom," Bridget replied, perhaps a bit too quickly.

Her father pressed, "Are you sure? I mean, I think it would be wonderful if you were dating, sweetheart. As long as he's a good person."

Her mother nodded in agreement. "You're eighteen and about to start college. You should get to know boys your own age."

Bridget's face paled.

"Are you okay?" her father asked, concern etched across his features.

"I'm fine, Dad. I just had an extremely busy day at work," Bridget managed before excusing herself and hurrying to her room, her heart pounding, knowing Angelo would be calling any minute.

Minutes later, her cell phone rang. It was him.

"Hello, baby. You looked so beautiful today," Angelo's voice purred through the line.

"Thank you, Angelo," Bridget replied softly, her cheeks burning.

"I wanted so badly to come over and say hello, but you know . . ." He trailed off.

"Yes. I understand." Bridget knew they couldn't risk anyone at work discovering their secret.

"Listen, I want to see you Saturday night," Angelo said, his tone more commanding than inviting. "What do you say?"

Bridget's eyes widened. Flowers and phone calls were one thing, but a date? "Um, do you mean like a date or something?"

Angelo chuckled. "Well, we can just relax in my car for a few minutes and talk. We'll plan a real date for next time. Okay?"

A heavy silence hung between them.

"Guess what? If and when you're ready to act like a mature woman, let me know," Angelo snapped, his patience thinning. "I thought you wanted to get to know me too."

"Oh, I do," Bridget blurted, her words tumbling over each other. "I'm sorry. I'm just . . . a little nervous. But Saturday night is good."

"I'm sorry I got a little upset." Angelo's voice softened, honeyed once more. "It's just that I really want to get to know you better."

"That's okay. I understand."

"I'll be out of town on business tomorrow and won't be back in New York until late Saturday night. I'll swing by my apartment to freshen up, then get you, say, 11:30 p.m.?"

Bridget's heart skipped. "Sure. That's . . . that's fine."

"And remember, this is just between us," Angelo reminded her, his voice suddenly steely. "No one, not even your parents, should know about us. At least not yet. But I do look forward to meeting them one day soon."

After Angelo hung up, Bridget was left staring at her phone, anxiety twisting in her stomach. She had just assured him their secret was safe, but now a new problem gnawed at her: she'd told her parents she wasn't seeing anyone. How could she possibly explain where she'd be going Saturday night? She had never been out that late unless she was with them.

Sprawled across her bed, clutching her big red teddy bear to her chest, Bridget's mind raced through every possible scenario that might allow her to see Angelo without revealing their relationship. She mulled over it that night and all through the next day. Finally, as she rode the subway home that evening, the answer came to her: she would simply sneak out after her parents went to bed. They were usually asleep by that time anyway.

That Saturday, Bridget's nerves were in knots. She went grocery shopping with her mother, did laundry, and cleaned her bedroom, glancing at the clock every few minutes as if time itself had slowed to a crawl.

At dinner, her father asked, "Sweetheart, how is work?"

"It's great," Bridget replied, forcing a smile. She chatted with her parents but barely touched her food, her appetite lost to anticipation.

As predicted, her parents retired to their bedroom before eleven. Bridget hurried into the bathroom, soaking her voluptuous body in scented bath salts. Afterward, she curled and styled her thick blonde hair until it cascaded down her back in lustrous ribbons.

She had little experience with makeup, so she settled for her usual light pink lipstick and a touch of blush on her pale cheeks. But when she slipped into the black babydoll dress and looked in the mirror, apprehension crept in. The dress was shorter than her usual style, skimming her thick thighs, and the neckline dipped lower than she remembered from the fitting at Macy's. *Should I change?* She tried sucking in her stomach, but at five-foot-one and a little over 250 pounds, it made no difference. Bridget frowned at her reflection.

Just then, her cell phone chimed with a text from Angelo: Parked at corner of Kingsland and Adee.

Now came the hard part, sneaking out of the house without waking her parents. Her cell phone in one hand, Bridget scooped up the black pumps she'd left by the door and eased out of her room. With deliberate care, she pulled the door shut behind her. She froze with the click of the lock, breath held, ears straining for the faintest stir from her parents' bedroom. Nothing.

On tiptoe, Bridget hurried through the living room toward the front door. Two deadbolt locks stood between her and freedom. She eased the first lock open, the metallic snap echoing in her ears like a gunshot. This time, she heard shuffling behind her parents' closed door.

"Bridget?" her father called, his voice thick with sleep.

Bridget swallowed hard, panic fluttering in her chest. She couldn't let her father see her all dressed up. "Yes, Dad. It's me," she replied quickly, forcing her voice to sound casual. "I was just making sure we're locked up before going to bed."

She unlocked the second lock, making sure her voice carried, "There, all set." She spoke a little louder than usual, hoping to reassure him.

"Okay, dear," her father replied. "Good night."

Bridget padded back toward her bedroom door, her feet heavy on the wooden floor. She didn't open it, but waited, holding her breath, glancing anxiously at her parents' room. After a few tense minutes, she crept back to the front door. She eased it open, then slipped through the screen door and out into the night. Not daring to risk another sound, she pulled the door closed behind her, leaving it unlocked.

She hurried down the driveway, shoes still in hand, and slipped through the gate. Only when she was a safe distance from the house did she put on her pumps, walking as quickly as she could toward the corner where Angelo waited.

Bridget told herself she'd be home in a few minutes. Her parents would never know she'd left. But for now, her heart was pounding as she approached the sleek black Jaguar S-Type, its windows tinted so dark that nothing inside was visible.

The passenger door swung open just as she arrived. Bridget awkwardly lowered herself into the car and pulled the door shut.

Angelo let out a low whistle. "Sexy."

Bridget blushed, tugging at the hem of her dress, which had ridden up even further as she sat. "Thank you," she murmured.

"You're welcome, baby. Look at me."

Shyly, Bridget turned to him, her heart doing that crazy dance in her chest again. She met his deep blue eyes, set in a sharply chiseled face. Angelo flashed a grin that reminded her of a young Pierce Brosnan. Her favorite James Bond.

"Thank you for seeing me tonight." His expensive cologne drifted toward her as he leaned in and kissed her cheek.

Bridget nodded, unable to speak, and quickly dropped her gaze to her lap.

"I just wanted to see you for a few minutes. I know you can't stay out too long."

Bridget nodded again, her nerves tingling.

"We could stay here or go for a quick drive. I passed a small park just a block away. Maybe we could talk there?" Angelo's gaze lingered on her, expectant.

"Yes, let's go there," Bridget replied, relief flooding her voice. The close confines of the car with Angelo had her nerves on edge.

"Fasten your seat belt," he instructed, turning the ignition. The engine purred to life, and in a flash, the car surged forward, slicing through the night toward the park.

Angelo parked on a dimly lit street beside the park. Bridget stepped out, feeling the warm night air against her skin. She trembled slightly as he took her hand, leading her off the sidewalk and into the shadows, toward a secluded spot behind a row of silent houses.

They sat on a bench, the darkness wrapping around them. Bridget's nerves prickled as Angelo's thigh pressed against hers.

"I have something for you," he said, turning to face her, his tone low and secretive.

"You do?" Bridget's eyes widened, curiosity momentarily surpassing her anxiety.

From his pocket, Angelo produced a small black box and placed it in her hands. "Open it."

Her fingers shook as she lifted the lid. A gasp escaped her lips. "For me?" she breathed, staring in disbelief at the delicate necklace nestled inside. "It's beautiful."

"Just like you," Angelo murmured. "Here, let me put it on you." He gently took the 14-karat gold necklace with its diamond solitaire pendant, and as Bridget lifted her hair, he fastened it around her neck.

"Turn to me," he commanded. Bridget turned, her heart thudding in her chest. "I knew it was for you the minute I saw it."

"I love it," she replied softly, her voice trembling with a mix of gratitude and nerves. "Thank you."

"You're welcome." Angelo reached out, his fingers brushing her cheek with a practiced gentleness.

Bridget's gaze darted away, discomfort flickering across her face.

"Hey, relax." Angelo patted her bare leg, his touch lingering. "You're safe with me." He winked, a sly glint in his eye, then leaned in and pressed a light kiss to her lips.

Bridget jolted upright as if shocked by electricity. "I . . . I . . . I think it's time for me to go home now." She forced a nervous chuckle. "I don't want my parents to wake up and find me gone."

Angelo's expression twisted, his eyes narrowing into icy slits as he stood up. "Are you playing with me now?" he hissed, his voice suddenly sharp.

Fear prickled down Bridget's spine at his transformation. "No, no, no. I'm not."

He sneered. "You come out here, showing off your fat behind, accepting my expensive necklace, but I can't even get a little kiss?" He unleashed a string of curses that would have made the devil blush, his anger boiling over.

Bridget's mouth opened and closed, but no words came.

"You accept my flowers, day after day, blushing and giggling, but when it's time to show some appreciation, you shy away from *me*? Do you know who I am?" He stepped closer, nostrils flaring, his presence suddenly menacing. "I am Angelo Ferrari."

Bridget turned to leave, her heart pounding and her pride wounded. "I think I'll just walk back home," she said, her voice tight with hurt. She managed only a few steps before Angelo seized her by the hair, yanking her backward until she was pinned against his rigid frame.

Before she could cry out, his hand clamped over her mouth, smothering her scream. Bridget, far from frail, fought desperately to break free, but Angelo's grip was unyielding. She might as well have been struggling against a brick wall.

"You should feel flattered that someone like me wants you, Miss Hippo," he snarled into her ear, his breath hot and venomous. "No one says no to Angelo Ferrari. Especially a fat pig like you." With a violent twist, he spun Bridget around to face him.

She tried to scream again, but his fist crashed into her jaw, snapping her head back. Dazed, Bridget staggered, a shrill ringing echoing in her ears.

"Come here, heifer." Angelo landed another hard punch right between her eyes.

Bridget went down, landing hard on her back in the dirt, one leg bent under her body at an odd angle. She tried to scream, but it came out like a squeak because Angelo was now straddling her, his hands tightly around her neck.

"What Angelo wants, Angelo gets." He folded his fist and sent it with a powerful force into Bridget's right eye.

Bridget felt the blood leaking down her cheek. She looked up through her left eye and saw thousands of multicolored lights dancing above her. It felt like her head was about to explode. "Please," she begged through bloody lips. "Please, Angelo."

Angelo's wild eyes were filled with glee. It was as if the devil himself now possessed the once charming man. "That's right, beg for it, fatty." He landed a few more vigorous slaps and punches all over Bridget's body until she went still.

Bridget now felt like she was underwater and was losing her breath. She caught glimpses of Angelo's face above her, fading in and out, but the beating she was taking was almost unbearable. Then she felt her dress ripped from her body.

"No," Bridget muttered through swollen, bloody lips. "No, no, no." She whimpered when Angelo pulled her panties down to her ankles. She wanted to move, but her body wasn't responding.

"I bet you never had a real man, huh?" Angelo leaned over and bit her left breast. "You're about to get a taste of this Italian stallion."

Bridget's scream seemed to travel from the bottom of her soul, up through her mouth, and reverberated through the air. Angelo responded by pounding her face some more, until she was still again.

Bridget lay frozen beneath his weight, her body unresponsive, her mind desperate to detach. A searing pain tore through her as Angelo forced himself on her, and she drifted, hovering somewhere outside herself, slipping in and out of awareness. The world blurred, distant and unreal.

Please let me die, Lord, she prayed, silent and shattered.

The rape seemed to go on for hours when it was just a few minutes. Her right eye was now swollen completely closed, so she squinted through her left eye and saw Angelo quickly pulling up his trousers.

Angelo ripped the necklace from Bridget's neck. "Give it back. It wasn't worth it." He kicked her in the side.

Bridget had now lost all feeling in her body. The most she could do was groan, pain and shame washing over her beaten body.

Angelo spotted Bridget's cell phone lying in the grass, just inches away. He snatched it up and tucked it into his pocket without hesitation. He then came and knelt by her head, bending close so his mouth hovered just above her ringing ear. "Say a word about this, and your parents will suffer slowly," he whispered, his voice low and venomous. "I'll make sure you watch every second before I carve you up like bacon."

Bridget whimpered softly.

"You know I have the money and means to do it, too," Angelo hissed. "Nod if you understand me," he snapped, calling her every derogatory name under the sun.

Bridget barely moved her head up and down. *Please leave.*

But instead, Angelo was now straddling her, his big hands wrapped tightly around her trachea, pressing and squeezing with all his might.

He's killing me. Someone help me. Bridget wanted to fight and scream, but her body failed her. She struggled to suck oxygen into her burning lungs as Angelo continued to squeeze the life out of her. A thick black cloud descended, surrounding her in darkness where pain no longer reached her.

Bridget gasped as a sharp, electric pain shot through her battered body the moment she dared to move her head. For several seconds, she lay motionless and disoriented, until the memories of the night crashed back over her in a filthy, relentless wave. She tried to open her eyes but was met only with darkness.

Her breath came in ragged bursts. With effort, she rolled onto her stomach. Again, she forced her eyes open and this time, her left eyelid fluttered, granting her a blurred glimpse of the road ahead. *I have to reach the road. I need help.*

But the distance felt insurmountable. Crawling on her belly, slipping in and out of consciousness, Bridget felt like the journey went on forever, a battle against agony and exhaustion. She dragged herself, inch by agonizing inch, toward the edge of the road. Every movement sent fresh waves of pain through her battered body, but she refused to surrender to the darkness threatening to pull her under. As she finally neared the curb, she looked up and spotted a tall figure across the street. The streetlight illuminated his face—Demarcus Jones.

"DMan, help me. DMan," she screamed in her mind, but her lips could only form slurred, broken sounds. Helpless, she watched as Demarcus turned the corner and vanished into the night.

Crushed but not defeated, Bridget summoned the last of her strength and crawled through a wire fence, collapsing onto the asphalt. Her vision blurred, her body screamed in protest, but she pressed on, determined not to give in.

Suddenly, the screech of tires shattered the silence. A car swerved violently, stopping just short of her crumpled form.

"Miss, are you okay?" The driver's voice echoed as if from a distant tunnel. He rushed to her side, fumbled for his phone, and dialed 911. "Yes, I have a bloody, naked girl here in the street. No, she's not moving."

Relief washed over Bridget. *Thank you, Lord*, she thought, fighting to stay conscious as help finally arrived.

Within minutes, sirens pierced the night. An ambulance and a police car screeched to a halt, lights flashing. EMTs rushed to her side. One checked for a pulse, the other slipped an oxygen mask over her face.

"Ma'am, can you hear me?" one asked urgently.

Bridget didn't respond.

"Is she dead?" Detective Hanes demanded, flashing her badge before kneeling beside the EMTs as they worked.

"There's a faint pulse, but we have to get her to the hospital now," the EMT replied.

Detective Hanes stepped back, allowing the team to lift Bridget onto a stretcher and into the waiting ambulance.

"I'll ride with you," Detective Hanes declared, climbing into the back of the ambulance just as it sped off, sirens wailing and lights flashing. Her partner stayed behind to question the driver who had found Bridget, promising to meet them at the hospital.

Inside the ambulance, Bridget mumbled beneath the oxygen mask pressed to her face.

"She's trying to say something," Hanes urged the EMT. "Can you take it off for a second? This could be important."

The EMT shook his head, concern etched on his face. "Detective, this girl is in bad shape. She needs medical attention first."

"But she might be trying to tell us who did this to her. Please, just a few seconds," Hanes pleaded.

With a reluctant sigh, the EMT removed the mask.

Detective Hanes leaned in, her ear close to Bridget's lips. "Sweetheart, can you hear me? Are you trying to tell me something? Who did this to you?"

Bridget trembled, her body contorting with quiet agony. A whisper escaped her lips, "DMan, please. Help me."

"The man?" Hanes glanced up at the EMT, puzzled. "Who is the man?"

The EMT bent closer, listening intently.

"Help me, DMan," Bridget muttered again. "Help."

"I think she's saying *D* man, not the man," the EMT clarified, quickly replacing the oxygen mask over Bridget's mouth.

"Wait—"

"That's it for now." The EMT cut her off. "We're at the hospital."

As the ambulance doors swung open, a medical team rushed out to meet them, whisking Bridget away for urgent treatment. Detective Hanes stood back, the question echoing in her mind: *Who is D man?*

Chapter Three

"They're still working on her?" Detective Rich dropped into a vacant seat beside his partner, Detective Hanes, in the hospital waiting room.

Detective Hanes nodded, her lips pressed together, brows knitted in a deep frown.

"It's a shame what they did to that young girl," Rich muttered, clicking his tongue. "You can tell she was raped. Animal."

"She kept saying D man," Hanes replied quietly. "I think that's who did this to her."

"She talked?" Rich's eyes widened.

Hanes quickly brought her partner up to speed on what had happened in the ambulance.

"What? That's good news." Rich jumped to his feet and began pacing in front of Hanes. "If we find this D man, we find the culprit." His eyes gleamed with sudden hope.

"Wait a minute now," Hanes cautioned, holding up a hand. "We can't jump to conclusions. There's still a lot to investigate."

"Why would she be calling his name and asking for help?" Rich pressed.

"Well, that's what we're going to find out from her," Hanes replied.

The detectives sat in the waiting area for close to two hours, discussing the case and sipping bland, black coffee from a machine in the corner.

"Here comes the doctor now," Hanes said, rising to her feet as a physician approached.

"Detective Hanes." The detective introduced herself, and the doctor shook her hand, then Rich's. "And this is my partner, Detective Rich."

"Dr. Howell." He introduced himself.

"What can you tell us?" Hanes asked, her voice anxious.

"Well, someone hurt her pretty badly," Dr. Howell said gravely. "I believe she was raped and strangled."

"He tried to kill her," Hanes said, glancing at her partner. "She was unconscious, but he thought she was dead."

"Can we speak to her now?" Rich asked. "As you know, the first 48 hours are crucial for us to get a lead to catch the culprit."

"I know and understand your need to speak with her, but I can't allow it at this time." Dr. Howell raised a hand as Rich opened his mouth to protest. "She was savagely beaten, detective. We're still waiting for test results to make sure there's no internal damage. Luckily, the X-ray shows nothing was broken, but her ankle was badly sprained, and she's in a lot of pain. She's now heavily sedated from the strong pain medication I had to give her."

"Okay, we'll have to wait a few more hours," Hanes replied, her tone resigned. "Thanks, Doc. We'll be back in a while."

The detectives strode out of the hospital together. The night air was thick with tension.

"So, what's next?" Detective Rich asked, glancing at his partner as they paused beneath the harsh glow of the streetlights. "We'll have to wait to speak to the victim."

Detective Hanes let out a sharp breath, her jaw tight. "We're going back to the scene," she said. "If we're lucky, we'll find the exact spot, and maybe something the perp didn't mean to leave behind."

Rich nodded. "We should also check if any neighbors are still awake. Someone might have heard or seen something." He checked his watch. It was just after 3:00 a.m.

Without another word, the two detectives crossed the parking lot and climbed into their unmarked car, Rich behind the wheel, Hanes in the passenger seat. Minutes later, they pulled up near the spot where the cab driver had discovered Bridget, right across from the shadowy park.

"I'll grab the flashlights," Rich said, popping the trunk and retrieving two heavy-duty torches. He handed one to Hanes, who clicked it on with a determined snap.

Together, they followed the stark trail of blood that glistened on the pavement, tracing Bridget's desperate crawl from the street into the park. Their beams cut through the darkness, illuminating every detail.

"I think it happened back here," Hanes murmured as they reached the far end of the park, where the streetlights had been knocked out. She pointed to a drag mark in the dirt, smeared with blood. "See that? The struggle must have ended here."

"Yeah," Rich agreed, his voice low. "He picked the perfect spot—isolated, hidden in the dark."

Hanes swept her flashlight over the scene, her brow furrowed. "It had to be someone she knew. She trusted him enough to follow him back here."

"Or maybe he attacked her on the street, then dragged her back here to rape and beat her," Rich suggested.

"Maybe," Hanes replied, stepping toward the bench where Bridget and Angelo had sat. She swept her flashlight across the shadows. "Why was she out here alone at this hour? Sure, it's summer and kids roam late, but I'd expect her to be with a friend, not wandering by herself."

She pointed her beam up toward the backs of the houses bordering the park. "I wonder if anyone heard anything."

"That would be helpful," Rich agreed.

They searched the park for several more minutes, their flashlights slicing through the darkness, but found nothing. Disappointed, they left the park and headed for the nearest house with its lights still burning.

"Good. Someone's awake," Rich said, leading the way up the driveway to the single-family home. He pressed the doorbell, and they waited.

Moments later, a woman's voice called from behind the closed door, "May I help you?"

"Police," Hanes announced, holding her badge up to the peephole. "We'd like to ask you a few questions about an attack that happened in the park earlier tonight."

There was a brief pause before the door opened a crack, the chain still on. An elderly African American woman in a long floral nightgown peered out at them. "You said you're police?"

"Yes, ma'am," Hanes replied, showing her ID again as Rich did the same. "I'm Detective Hanes, and this is my partner, Detective Rich."

Satisfied, the woman removed the chain and opened the door wider. "I'm Mrs. Latty. You said someone was attacked in the park?"

"Yes, ma'am," Rich said gently. "A young lady is fighting for her life in the hospital. She was raped and nearly killed. Did you hear anything earlier tonight?"

Mrs. Latty's face fell. "I'm so sorry to hear that," she said, shaking her head. "You always hear a lot of things in that park. I've learned to keep my door closed and mind my own business."

"We can understand that, ma'am," Hanes said, stepping closer, her tone gentle but urgent. "But anything you can share will help us catch whoever did this. Do you really want such a violent person roaming the streets?"

"Certainly not!" Mrs. Latty replied, looking at her as if she were crazy. "I live here alone since my husband passed away three years ago. My daughter and grandkids visit often, but most nights, it's just me. I hope you catch whoever did this, and soon."

"We're going to do our best," Detective Rich assured her. "Please, anything you remember could help."

Mrs. Latty pursed her lips, thinking. "Well, the lights back there didn't go out by themselves," she said at last. "They always knock out the lights, including the ones I had at the back of my house, so they can do their wrong in the dark. Smoking weed, drinking, fornicating . . ." She shook her head in disgust. "I tell you, I don't know what this world is coming to."

"And earlier tonight?" Hanes asked, her eyes searching Mrs. Latty's face.

"I thought I heard screaming," Mrs. Latty admitted. "It was brief, and I figured it was just those people out there messing around as usual. I didn't pay it any mind."

"What time was this?" Rich asked, rubbing his hands together anxiously.

"I'd just finished watching the eleven o'clock news and went to make a cup of tea," Mrs. Latty said, her brow furrowed in concentration. "I think it was close to midnight, or a little after."

"That's great, Mrs. Latty," Hanes said, her voice brightening. "Anything else? Please, think back and try to remember."

Mrs. Latty hesitated, then nodded. "You know, I heard a man's voice at one point. He was shouting, but I couldn't make out what he was saying because my windows were closed."

"Why did this voice stand out?" Detective Rich asked, leaning in. "You said you always hear things in the park, and I assume that includes voices."

"Well, the voice sounded . . . different," Mrs. Latty said, her brow furrowing as she searched for the right words. "It wasn't like the usual voices you hear around here. The first thing that struck me was it sounded like a white man talking."

The detectives exchanged a quick, excited glance before focusing back on her.

"That's helpful," Hanes replied, scribbling rapidly in her notepad. "Anything else stand out?"

Mrs. Latty thought for a moment. "That's about it. After that, I took my tea and went back to watch David Letterman. He always makes me laugh. I was still up when you rang the doorbell. I don't sleep as well as I used to."

"You've been very helpful, Mrs. Latty," Detective Hanes said, handing her a business card. "If you remember anything else, please don't hesitate to call."

Detective Rich offered his card as well. "You can reach either of us. We really appreciate your help."

Mrs. Latty pointed a stern finger at them. "You catch whoever did this. There are good people living here, but it's always a few rotten apples that spoil it for everyone."

"We're on it, ma'am," Hanes assured her as they stepped back out into the night.

The detectives continued knocking on doors, but most went unanswered, except for one disgruntled man, clearly roused from sleep. "Didn't see or hear a thing," he grumbled. "And don't try to pin anything on my boy. The police are always looking to blame an innocent man just to close a case," he spat, slamming the door in their faces.

"I bet if it was his daughter, he'd have a different tune," Detective Rich muttered angrily as they walked away. "And I'd wager his boy's no angel. I'll have to look into that house number."

"At least we have more than we did before," Hanes said as they returned to the car. "We'll follow up again later today."

"Back to the hospital?" Detective Rich asked, glancing at his partner.

Hanes checked her watch, her brow furrowing. "We should just wait until daylight. The victim is probably sleeping after being heavily sedated."

Rich nodded. "Okay. We'll head back to the station and start writing our report. Hopefully, we won't get another case before then."

The detectives, both seasoned veterans of the night shift when chaos never sleeps, cruised through the hushed streets en route to the 47th Precinct, located on Laconia Avenue. As they discussed the case, both knew the grim truth: the chances of solving it dropped drastically once the first forty-eight hours slipped away.

"We're going to get that bastard," Hanes vowed, her voice low and fierce. "Whether it's 'D man' or some other man, he's going to pay."

Rich's jaw tightened. "I think it's that D man. Trust me, I can feel it in my gut."

Chapter Four

Seventy-eight-year-old Alfredo Ferrari lounged on his luxurious off-white leather sectional in his Upper East Side penthouse, legs elegantly crossed in tailored silk pajamas, the *New York Times* resting between his perfectly manicured fingers. Alfredo stayed buried in the business section, barely glancing up as Polly entered. She posed deliberately in just a thong, her newly enhanced curves front and center. One hand rested on her bony hip, legs parted with intent. At 5 feet 6 inches and barely a hundred pounds, her slight frame was offset by the cascade of blonde extensions trailing down her back.

"Hi, baby," Polly said in the sexy tone she used when she wanted something from Alfredo, mostly his money. At twenty-four, Polly was an ambitious opera singer determined to pursue a career on Broadway. Upon relocating to New York from Idaho at the age of nineteen, she soon recognized the considerable challenges involved in achieving her goal. So, Polly became a high-priced escort to pay the bills until her big break.

"Baby?" Polly was upset, feeling ignored by Alfredo. Six months earlier, Polly had felt incredibly lucky to be sent to her new client's Upper East Side home. After pulling out all the sex tricks she had acquired over the last few years, Polly became one of Alfredo's regulars. Soon, Alfredo wanted Polly to himself, so he told her to quit the escort agency and move in with him.

"Alfredo," Polly said, voice clipped and rising. "I'm talking to you." Her lips curled into a pout.

Alfredo's newspaper lowered, his eyes narrowing into a cold, steely glare. "Who are you speaking to in that tone?" His Italian accent, thick as ever despite decades in New York, cut through the room like a blade.

Polly's bravado evaporated. She swallowed hard, her voice trembling. "I–I'm sorry, baby. I was just trying to get your attention."

"Watch your tone," Alfredo snapped, jabbing a finger at her for emphasis. "Or I'll throw you out of here so fast—" He let the threat hang in the air, heavy and unmistakable.

Polly swallowed nervously. Alfredo could be distant and unapproachable at times, but it was better than being an escort. He also had strong New York ties, and she was relying on his help for Broadway. "It won't happen again. Sorry."

Just then, Alfredo's cell phone rang. He shot Polly another frosty glare before snatching up the phone, glancing at the caller ID, and answering with a clipped voice, "Yes, Angelo."

"Daddy, I . . . I . . . I didn't mean to do it. I'm sorry." Angelo's voice trembled, sounding more like a frightened child than a grown man. "I just snapped. I'm so sorry." His words dissolved into desperate, ragged sobs.

Alfredo straightened abruptly, his grip tightening around the phone. "What did you—" He broke off, noticing Polly's curious stare. "Get out. I need to speak to my son in private," he barked, his tone tolerating no argument.

Polly's lips twisted in disappointment. "Where should I go?" she protested, clearly reluctant to miss what promised to be a dramatic conversation.

"I don't care!" Alfredo's eyes flashed with fear that he refused to let show in his voice. "Take one of the credit cards from my wallet and go to Bergdorf," he snapped, referencing the legendary Fifth Avenue department store.

Polly's face lit up. "Okay." She practically danced from the room, eager for a shopping spree.

Alfredo returned to the call, his voice now a low, dangerous growl. "What did you do this time?"

On the other end, Angelo's wailing grew more frantic. "I think I killed her." His anguish was raw, animalistic. "I killed her, Daddy."

Alfredo felt the phone slip from his trembling fingers, landing with a dull thud on the carpet. The words "I killed her" echoed relentlessly in his mind, pounding with every heartbeat as he staggered across the living room. A migraine coiled at the base of his skull, slithering forward until it pressed against his forehead like a vice.

"Okay, calm down," he muttered, massaging his temples in a futile attempt to ease the pain. "You can fix this. You always fix it."

He retraced his steps, stooping to retrieve the phone. Angelo's sobs still crackled through the line. "Angelo!" Alfredo barked, his voice as cutting as a snapped wire.

"Yes, sir," came the broken reply.

"Get over here. Now. And don't breathe a word of this to anyone. Do you hear me, boy?" Alfredo's tone left no room for argument.

"Yes," Angelo whimpered.

"Take a cab. Get here now!" Alfredo ended the call with a jab of his thumb. Without hesitation, he dialed another number.

"Boss," answered a deep, Russian-accented voice on the first ring.

"We have a big problem. It's Angelo again."

"I'm on my way."

Alfredo poured himself a whiskey, the amber liquid burning a trail down his throat. His hand shook as he set the glass down. “That boy will never learn,” he muttered, voice thick with frustration and dread. “It’s always one thing after another.”

Angelo Ferrari had been a royal screw-up for most of his life, but he was Alfredo’s only child, the sole heir to the vast Wall Street fortune Alfredo had built from nothing. So, Alfredo had spent his life and his wealth cleaning up Angelo’s messes, no matter what the cost.

At Dalton, the elite private school in New York, Alfredo had pulled every string to get Angelo admitted. But privilege didn’t change Angelo’s reckless streak. One day, after claiming a classmate had disrespected him, Angelo nearly ran the boy down with his car, leaving the student with a broken leg and arm. Alfredo moved swiftly. He paid off the boy’s family to keep them from pressing charges and donated a hefty sum to the school to secure Angelo another chance.

Later, at Yale, Angelo’s temper flared again. He punched his girlfriend in the face, breaking her nose. Alfredo covered the cost of an expensive nose job and handed the young woman enough money to last a lifetime, so long as she kept silent and pressed no charges.

Even after college, with an Ivy League degree in hand, Angelo’s troubles only multiplied. He racked up massive gambling debts, millions upon millions, and Alfredo paid them all, time after time. Angelo’s love for fast, flashy luxury cars led to frequent speeding tickets and several charges for driving under the influence. Yet, every ticket and every charge seemed to vanish, as if by magic, erased by Alfredo’s influence and wealth. There was nothing Angelo did that his father’s money couldn’t fix.

But murder?

As Alfredo refilled his glass with whiskey, the intercom buzzed. He barked, “Send him up,” to the door attendant, then moved to open the door, his nerves fraying.

Moments later, a towering figure filled the doorway. The Russian man stood over six feet seven inches and weighed in at roughly 250 pounds, most of it sculpted muscle. His name was Viktor Sokolov, and something about him reminded Alfredo of a young Dolph Lundgren in *Universal Soldier*.

"Problems?" Viktor asked, lowering his massive frame onto the couch. His cold, unblinking eyes locked onto Alfredo with quiet intensity. Officially, he was the personal driver. Unofficially, he handled whatever needed handling, using his muscles and the skills he acquired in the Russian Ground Forces.

"It's Angelo," Alfredo replied, voice tight.

"It's always Angelo," Viktor replied, his smile more a snarl than anything friendly. "Are we alone?"

"Yes, the housekeeper's off today. I sent Polly shopping."

"Good."

"This time it's bad." Alfredo sat beside Viktor, voice dropping. "He said he killed someone."

Viktor's face remained unreadable, as if Alfredo had just told him the weather. "Okay."

"Okay? It's not okay!" Alfredo exploded, leaping to his feet. "He's going—"

The intercom buzzed again. "Send him up," Alfredo shouted, barely holding himself together.

"Remember your heart," Viktor cautioned, calm as ever. "Keep calm."

Alfredo cursed in English and Italian, his anger peaking just as Angelo arrived, looking rumpled and filthy.

Still muttering curses, Alfredo yanked Angelo inside by his wrinkled shirt and slammed the door. He looked his son up and down with utter disgust. "You killed somebody?"

"Boss, lower your voice," Viktor said, steady as stone. "Angelo, come here and tell us what happened."

Angelo slumped onto the couch across from Viktor, his head bowed, eyes glued to the floor. With a trembling voice, he recounted his relationship with the summer intern and described, in halting detail, what had happened in the park the night before.

"*Lui è finito! Finito*!" Alfredo erupted, stomping his feet as he paced the apartment, his hands raking through his thick white hair. "He's finished!"

"Boss, remember your heart," Viktor cautioned, his tone even and unflappable. "We don't want you having another heart attack."

Alfredo, breathing hard, took Viktor's advice and dropped onto the couch beside him, inhaling deep, ragged breaths through his mouth.

"We'll fix this," Viktor assured him. "Just take it easy."

"Fix this?" Alfredo shot back, his voice rising to a fever pitch. "Viktor, this good-for-nothing son of mine, who I've given everything, just told us he raped and killed a young girl. This isn't a DUI or punching a woman in the face. This is rape and murder."

"I'm sorry, Dad," Angelo whispered.

"You're sorry? You'll be sorry in prison for the rest of your pathetic life," Alfredo spat, his face flushed with rage. "My God, what's going to happen to my company? Why did I ever make him CEO? Can you imagine what will happen when the media gets a hold of this? Everything I've worked for is all gone." He snapped his fingers. "Just like that." His tirade continued, more concerned for his company and reputation than the young woman his son had just confessed to destroying, while Viktor and Angelo sat in silence, absorbing the storm.

"Our clients will drop us like stinking garbage. Our investments—"

"Will not be affected." Viktor interrupted, calm and resolute. "As I said, I'll take care of it."

Angelo turned desperate eyes to Viktor. "I don't want to go to prison, Viktor. Please, help—"

"Shut up, Angelo." Alfredo barked, glaring at his son before turning back to Viktor. "Viktor, I want you to handle this. I don't care what it takes. Money is no object."

Viktor nodded. "First, I need to make some calls." He stood, his presence imposing. "May I use your office?"

"Of course." Alfredo turned to his son, his voice low and simmering with fury. "What were you thinking, Angelo? You don't need to force yourself on anyone. Women throw themselves at you—young, handsome, rich, CEO of one of New York's largest hedge funds. Why stoop to this?"

Angelo's earlier vulnerability vanished, replaced by a sneer and a flash of arrogance. "No one says no to me," he spat as he jumped to his feet. "And that fat slob tried to reject me? I'm Angelo Ferrari!"

Alfredo's sigh was heavy, weighted with regret. He looked up at his son and, for a moment, saw the consequences of his own choices reflected back at him. He had created this. Angelo's mother, Isabella, was a beautiful young assistant at his firm, ambitious and eager to climb the ladder by any means. When she became pregnant, she wanted an abortion, but Alfredo struck a deal to have the child, and he'd paid her handsomely. Days after Angelo's birth, Isabella took the money, found another wealthy man, and disappeared to London, never to be seen or heard from again. To fill the void left by her absence, Alfredo spoiled Angelo relentlessly, showering him with everything money could buy and covering up every misdeed instead of confronting the problem.

"What else was I supposed to do?" Alfredo had once confessed to Viktor, after cleaning up yet another of Angelo's messes. "He's my only child."

So, after a heart attack forced Alfredo to step back from the company two years ago, he had made Angelo CEO, relying on his executive team to keep things afloat. It was a selfish move because Alfredo still intended to run things from behind the scenes. Now, with everything on the line, he realized just how much he stood to lose.

Alfredo rose, his fists clenched, nostrils flared, eyes blazing. "You're Angelo Ferrari, huh?"

Angelo recoiled, taking two steps back. Even with his father's age and heart condition, Alfredo's presence was formidable. He could crush Angelo's world with a word.

"That's the problem, Angelo. You're a Ferrari. You carry *my* name, the name on *my* company. Son or not—"

Viktor burst in, cutting the tension. "I have news. My source just told me the girl isn't dead."

Angelo gasped, his face draining of color.

"She managed to reach the street. Someone found her and called for help. She's at Jacobi Hospital, in serious condition."

"She's not dead," Angelo whispered, relief flooding his features. "She's not dead."

"Shut up!" Alfredo shot his son an icy look before turning to Viktor. "This is worse, isn't it?"

Viktor nodded. "Dead men don't talk. Now we have a victim who can identify Angelo as the man who raped and tried to kill her."

Alfredo glanced out the high window above Central Park, barely noticing the vibrant city below. "We need to silence her, Viktor. She can't be allowed to speak."

"Agreed." Viktor then turned to Angelo, eyes sharp, unreadable. "Did you call her? Text?"

Angelo gave a quick nod.

"Then her phone has everything—messages, call logs."

"I took care of it," Angelo replied too quickly.

Viktor's gaze narrowed. "How?

"I grabbed it and tossed it off the bridge on my way back into the city," Angelo said, a note of smug satisfaction in his voice.

"At least he didn't mess that up," Alfredo muttered.

"Okay. Hold on." Viktor stepped closer to Angelo. "Is that blood? Are those the same clothes from last night?"

Angelo nodded, turning aside as Alfredo swore.

Alfredo's eyes drifted to the red smears staining Angelo's clothes, marks he hadn't noticed before. His expression twisted with revulsion. "All those years in private schools, the Ivy League tuition, the endless second chances, and this is what you do with it?"

"Take everything off," Viktor ordered.

Angelo glanced from Viktor to his father, hesitated only for a second, then started to take off his clothes. Moments later, he was standing in front of the men naked, his clothes and shoes at his feet.

"Go shower and clean yourself thoroughly," Viktor said. "Don't miss any spots."

"Use the guest bathroom," Alfredo called after Angelo. "I'll bring clothes soon."

"I'll clean up at his place later," Viktor said. "First, I need to find the girl before the police do. Otherwise . . ." He trailed off.

Alfredo stepped close, meeting Viktor's gaze. "Do whatever it takes to fix this," he said plainly.

Chapter Five

"Hello there, I'm Dr. Howell," the doctor announced as he swept through the blue privacy curtain surrounding Bridget's hospital bed, a nurse trailing behind him. "I've been caring for you since you were brought in last night, or should I say, early this morning."

Bridget, her left eye bloodshot and her right swollen completely shut, managed a cautious glance at the doctor. As she shifted slightly on the bed, a fresh wave of pain surged through her, forcing a deep groan from her throat.

"I see you're still in a lot of pain," Dr. Howell observed, his tone gentle but direct. "I think we can increase your pain medication a bit. Would you like that?"

Bridget nodded, and another sharp jolt of pain exploded in her head.

Dr. Howell leaned toward the nurse at his side, murmured instructions, and she moved to the IV stand, adjusting the morphine drip with practiced efficiency.

"You should be feeling some relief soon," Dr. Howell assured her, stepping closer to the bed. He studied Bridget's battered face that was still badly swollen, mottled with bruises, black and blue like most of her body. He was surprised that, aside from a sprained ankle, nothing else was broken.

"What's your name? There was no ID on you when you were brought in."

"Bridget," she whispered through her puffy, split lips. "Bridget Walsh."

"Bridget. That's a lovely name." Dr. Howell smiled warmly. "It's also a good sign that you remember it. How old are you?"

"Eighteen."

"Okay. Where do you live, Bridget?"

Bridget recited her address, then added in a trembling voice, "I want my dad and mom." Tears slipped down her cheeks.

"What are your parents' names?" Dr. Howell asked gently.

"Larry and Cheryl Walsh."

"We'll call your parents right away," Dr. Howell assured her. "I'm sure they're worried sick. What's their phone number?"

Bridget gave the number, and the nurse quietly left the room to make the call.

Dr. Howell pulled up a chair beside Bridget's bed, his expression both kind and serious. "Now, Bridget, I need to talk to you about what happened last night. Someone hurt you very badly. Can you tell me what happened?"

Bridget turned her head away, silent.

"You don't have to be afraid," Dr. Howell said softly. "The police were here earlier and will be back soon. They'll make sure whoever did this is brought to justice."

A whimper of fear escaped Bridget, but she said nothing.

"Okay, we'll wait until the officers return," Dr. Howell said, his voice reassuring. "I'm glad to tell you nothing was broken, according to the X-rays, and there doesn't seem to be any internal damage. We're still waiting on a few more test results, but I should have those soon. Do you have any questions for me?"

Bridget shook her head, her face still turned away.

"If you remember, we did a rape kit last night. We also gave you medication to prevent pregnancy and protect you from any sexually transmitted diseases."

"I think he used a condom," Bridget mumbled, her voice barely audible.

"Who did, Bridget?" Dr. Howell pressed gently.

But Bridget fell silent, her pain and fear closing her off once more.

Dr. Howell lingered a moment longer, then offered a soft nod. "All right, Bridget. I'll check on you again soon. Your parents should be here shortly."

As the doctor left, Bridget squeezed her eyes shut, desperate to block out the nightmare that still clawed at her memory. But the darkness behind her eyelids was no refuge. She could still feel Angelo's savage kicks and fists, the way he violated her, the suffocating grip around her throat. The terror and shame washed over her anew, and she began to sob into the stiff, white hospital pillow.

She sensed someone standing behind her, but she didn't turn, assuming it was just the nurse returning.

"Hello."

The voice, thick with a Russian accent, made Bridget whirl around. Her one good eye widened in horror at the sight of the large man moving toward her, a sinister grin stretching across his face, pure evil oozing from his eyes.

"Bridget, is it?" Viktor stepped closer, his presence filling the small space.

Before Bridget could scream, his gloved hand clamped over her mouth and nose, cutting off her breath.

"Shhh." Viktor pressed down harder as Bridget thrashed, her legs kicking, her arms flailing despite the agony that shot through her battered body.

"Sorry about this, Bridget." Viktor's other hand pinned one of her legs to the bed. "We can't let you talk about Angelo."

Bridget's strength ebbed away. Her head throbbed as if it might burst. Through the corner of her eye, she caught glimpses of movement and muffled voices beyond the privacy curtain, but no one could see her.

"Just relax and let go, Bridget," Viktor whispered. "You're just going to sleep."

Utterly spent, Bridget's struggles faded. She closed her eyes, feeling her life slipping away.

"Hello, I'm Detective Hanes."

To Bridget, the voice sounded distant, as if echoing from another world, but it was loud enough for Viktor to hear. He jerked his hand away from Bridget's face and sprang to his feet.

"We just spoke to Dr. Howell, and he said it was okay for us to speak to Bridget," Detective Hanes said, her voice growing clearer as Bridget coughed and gulped in precious air.

"We have someone watching your parents right now," Viktor hissed into Bridget's ear, his voice a venomous whisper. "Say a single word about Angelo, and they're dead." With that chilling threat, he slipped away to the far side of the room, ducking behind the curtain into the next patient's area, and then vanished into the active hallway.

Tears leaked from Bridget's tightly shut eyes as she forced herself to breathe slow, ragged gulps of air, desperate to fill her battered body with oxygen.

The curtain snapped open, and Detective Hanes strode in, her voice gentle but urgent. "Good morning, Bri—"

"Are you all right?" Detective Rich rushed to Bridget's bedside, alarmed by her labored breathing and the tremor in her chest. "Get the nurse! Get some water!"

As Hanes dashed out, Rich carefully lifted Bridget's head, supporting her as she struggled for breath. Moments later, the nurse burst in, Hanes close behind. The nurse pressed a cup of water into Bridget's hands, guiding the straw to her lips.

Bridget drank greedily, the water scraping her raw throat like sandpaper. All the while, her eyes darted anxiously around the room, searching for any sign of the tall blond man who had nearly killed her.

"Feeling better?" the nurse asked after Bridget drained the cup.

Bridget nodded, though her gaze continued to flick nervously about, as if Viktor might reappear at any moment to finish what he'd started.

"You're safe now, Bridget," Detective Hanes assured her, her eyes steady and full of concern. "We won't let anyone hurt you again."

Right, Bridget thought bitterly. *I'll never be safe from Angelo Ferrari.*

When the nurse left, drawing the privacy curtain closed behind her, both detectives pulled up chairs and sat close to Bridget's bed, where she now sat upright, still trembling.

"First, I want to say how sorry I am for what happened to you last night," Detective Hanes began, taking Bridget's hand in hers. "As a mother, it breaks my heart and fills me with anger. I know we're supposed to stay objective as detectives, but sometimes, you just can't."

Detective Rich added, "It was a brutal attack. Just seeing you now, and knowing what you've endured, is heartbreaking."

Someone tried to finish the job of killing me, Bridget thought.

"We're here to catch the person who did this to you, Bridget," Hanes said softly. "Do you know who attacked you?"

Bridget shook her head, silent.

"Could you walk us through your evening leading up to the attack, Bridget? Can you do that for us?" Detective Rich's voice was gentle but insistent, his gaze fixed on her.

Bridget stared straight ahead, refusing to meet their eyes. Silence stretched between them, heavy and tense.

"Bridget, we know it's painful to relive what happened, but we need your help. Don't you want us to catch the person who did this?" Detective Rich pressed, his tone urgent.

Bridget squeezed her eyes shut, her body trembling as memories threatened to overwhelm her. The detectives exchanged a glance, a silent understanding passing between them.

"Did he threaten you?" Detective Rich asked, his voice softer now. "Did he threaten your family?"

Still, Bridget said nothing.

Detective Hanes leaned forward. "Who is D man—or 'the man'? Last night, you kept saying that name. Was he the one who hurt you?"

Tears began to stream down Bridget's cheeks. "I want my mom and dad," she whispered, her voice breaking. She rolled onto her side, knees drawn to her chest, turning her back to the detectives.

Detective Rich tried again. "Bridget, we can't help—"

"Your parents should be here soon," Detective Hanes interrupted, giving her partner a quick look. "The nurse told us she called them. We'll also give you the name of a counselor you can talk to, all right?"

Bridget didn't respond.

"We'll check back with you later," Detective Rich said, rising from his chair. "Maybe after you see your parents, you'll feel ready to talk."

There was no answer.

As the detectives turned to leave, Bridget's voice, barely above a whisper, stopped them. "Can you please open the curtain?"

"Of course." Detective Rich moved to the curtain and pulled it back.

The room contained two beds, but the one beside Bridget was empty. Now, with the curtain open, she could see out into the hallway and catch a glimpse of the nurse's station. The partial view brought her a small measure of comfort, just in case the tall blond man returned to finish what he'd started.

Detective Hanes and her partner stepped into the corridor, their conversation low and urgent. "Did you see her reaction when I mentioned D man?" Hanes asked, her voice tight. "She was absolutely terrified."

Rich nodded, his brow furrowed. "I saw it. There's no doubt in my mind that this D man is connected to Bridget's attack."

"I'd bet anything he's the one," Hanes replied, her face contorted as if she'd bitten into a Vidalia onion. "He thought he'd killed her and gotten away with it."

Rich shook his head, frustration simmering. "But why wouldn't she just tell us? It would make things so much easier for her and for us."

"Because she's scared out of her mind," Hanes said, her tone softening. "He threatened to kill her. After what she went through last night, wouldn't you be terrified too?"

Rich sighed, conceding the point. "Sure. But if it were me, I'd want him locked up for life. Telling us what happened is the only way to make sure he can't hurt her again."

"She's dealing with so much, physically and emotionally," Hanes said softly. "Let's give her some time."

Rich asked, "Do you think we should wait for the parents? They could help us fill in a few blanks."

Hanes nodded in agreement, and the two made their way to the waiting area to get coffee. Settling into their seats, they began mapping out their next moves in the case.

Time slipped by until, suddenly, a middle-aged couple came hurrying down the hallway toward them, the woman's face streaked with tears.

"I think that's Bridget's parents," Rich whispered. "What did the nurse say their name was?"

"Walsh," Hanes replied.

As the couple reached them, Rich greeted them with a calm, professional tone. "Good morning. Are you the Walshes?"

"Yes, we are," Mr. Walsh answered, his voice strained. "And you are?"

"I'm Detective Rich, and this is Detective Hanes. May we have a word with you?"

Mrs. Walsh clutched her husband's hand, her eyes red and swollen. "Detective, we're here to see our daughter. Can this wait?"

"I promise we won't keep you long," Rich assured her. "If you could just step over here for a moment." He guided them away from the crowded corridor to a quieter spot by the wall.

"I'm not sure how much you were told over the phone about Bridget's attack," Rich began.

"Not much," Mr. Walsh replied. "The nurse said she was badly hurt and that we should get here as soon as possible. The doctor said he'd speak with us when we arrived."

"We'll let the doctor fill you in," Rich said, "but we're trying to catch the person who hurt your daughter. Do you know anyone who goes by the name D Man?"

Mrs. Walsh shook her head, her grip tightening on her husband's hand. "No, sorry. We really need to see our daughter now."

"We understand," Rich said, stepping back. "We'll follow up with you later."

The detectives watched as the couple moved toward the nurse's station, but suddenly, Mr. Walsh stopped in his tracks and turned back to face them.

Detective Hanes was quick to intercept him. "Is something wrong, Mr. Walsh?"

He hesitated, then said, "I think there's a kid who lives across the street from us with that nickname. I've heard his friends call him DMan a few times."

Mrs. Walsh's brow furrowed in disbelief. "But he always seems like such a nice young man. His mother is always so friendly when we see her. Are you saying he's the one who did this?"

"We're following every lead and examining every angle until we find the person who attacked your daughter," Detective Hanes replied, her tone measured but resolute.

The Walshes nodded, worry etched across their faces, before hurrying away to see their daughter.

As they disappeared down the hallway, Detective Hanes allowed herself a thin, satisfied smile. "Looks like we've found D man," she said, her voice low and determined. "Let's go get this lowlife."

Chapter Six

Demarcus swished the mouthwash around his mouth, savoring the sharp, minty sting before spitting it into the sink. He wiped his mouth with a towel, careful not to splash his crisp, white long-sleeved shirt.

"Demarcus, I'm ready," his mother called from her bedroom, her voice edged with urgency. "Please come out of the bathroom so we can go."

"I'm ready, Mom," Demarcus replied, flashing a grin at his reflection. "Teeth are sparkling white, and my breath is bursting fresh." He sounded like a toothpaste commercial, and the playful tone drew a laugh from his mother.

As Demarcus stepped into the living room, the doorbell rang, slicing through the morning calm.

"I wonder who that could be." Naomi emerged, adjusting the brim of her bold black-and-white hat to match her ankle-length dress. She wore low-heeled black pumps and carried a matching handbag over her shoulder. "Demarcus, I hope it's none of your friends. You're going to church," she said, giving him a stern, motherly look.

"No, Mom. My friends know better," he assured her.

The doorbell rang again, more insistent this time.

"Go and get it," Naomi said, her tone brisk. "And please make it quick. Sunday school is starting soon."

Demarcus hurried to the door, pulling it open just as the buzzer sounded again. "May I help you?" he asked, his voice polite but wary.

A woman with a sharp gaze stepped forward, flashing a badge. "Are you DMan?" Detective Hanes asked, her tone clipped and official.

Demarcus blinked, caught off guard. "Who's asking?"

"I'm Detective Hanes," she replied, holding her badge up to his face. "This is my partner, Detective Rich."

Demarcus frowned, confusion creasing his brow. "What is this about, please?"

Detective Rich stepped closer, his expression stern and unyielding. "Are you DMan?"

"I'm Demarcus Jones, but everyone calls me DMan. How can I help you?"

"We hope you can," Detective Hanes replied, her tone firm. "Where were you—?"

"Demarcus, who's at the door?" Naomi's voice floated from the hallway as she came to stand beside her son.

"These are detectives, Mom," Demarcus answered, his confusion growing.

"Detectives?" Naomi stepped closer, her eyes narrowing as she looked from one stranger to the next. "What's going on here?" She locked eyes with Detective Rich, her posture protective.

"Ma'am, I'm Detective Rich," he said, flashing his badge. "We'd like to speak with Demarcus about an attack on a young woman in the park last night."

Naomi recoiled as if she'd been slapped. "Excuse me?"

"What?" Demarcus blurted, his voice rising. "What attack? Is this some kind of joke?"

"Demarcus." Naomi turned to her son, her voice trembling but firm. "Let me handle this." She faced the detectives again, her chin lifted. "Listen, officers. I don't know what happened in that park, and I'm sorry for whoever was hurt, but Demarcus had nothing to do with it. There must be some mistake."

"We're following up on leads, ma'am," Detective Rich replied, his tone measured. "Demarcus's name came up, so we have a few questions for him."

"My name?" Demarcus's jaw dropped. "But . . . that can't be right."

"No, no, no." Naomi shook her head, her voice gaining strength. "Something's not right here."

"Demarcus, let's go," Detective Hanes said, stepping forward. "We need to take you in for a few questions."

"No!" Naomi cried, her voice cracking with emotion. Her hat slipped off and hit the floor as she stepped in front of Demarcus, blocking the detectives. "You're not taking my son anywhere. He had nothing to do with that attack!"

"Ma'am, we don't want any trouble," Detective Hanes said, her gaze hardening. "Your son is coming with us, one way or another. We can do this the easy way or the hard way. Which do you prefer?"

Naomi's voice broke as she pleaded, "Please, Detective. Please, I'm begging you to listen to me. Demarcus is a good boy. He wouldn't attack anyone. He didn't do this."

"Demarcus comes with us, ma'am." Detective Hanes was unmoved by Naomi's tears. "Let's go, Demarcus."

"No." Naomi sobbed as she turned and protectively wrapped her arms around her son's waist. Her body shook with anguish.

"Mom, I have to go with them," Demarcus whispered, hugging his mother's trembling frame and resting his chin gently atop her head. He took a deep breath, fighting back tears. "I'll go and answer their questions and come back. Okay?"

Naomi's sobs grew deeper, her hands clutching at Demarcus as if she could anchor him to the spot. He tried to pull away, but she held on desperately.

"Mom," Demarcus whispered in her ear, his voice low so the detectives couldn't hear. "If I don't go, they're going to call for more cops and drag me out of here in handcuffs like a criminal. I'll be back soon. This is just a big mistake."

It took a few moments before Naomi loosened her grip. She looked up at her son, her eyes shining with tears. "I love you, baby. God's going to work this out for us. You watch and see."

"I love you, Mom." Demarcus turned to Detective Hanes. "I'm ready to go now."

Detective Hanes took out a pair of handcuffs. "Turn around and put your hands behind your back," she snapped.

"You're handcuffing my son?" Naomi stepped in front of Detective Rich, her voice trembling with outrage. "You're treating him like he's some criminal."

Detective Hanes scoffed. "Turn around and put your hands behind your back," she repeated.

Demarcus did as instructed, flinching as the cold metal snapped around his wrists. The sound echoed in his ears. Despite his efforts to stay strong, tears trickled down his face.

He walked to the police car with his head bowed, his tears leaving an invisible trail behind him, praying none of his neighbors saw him being led away in handcuffs.

As Demarcus sat in the back of the police car, he looked back at his house and saw his mother collapse to her knees, pounding the ground in despair. He turned away, his own tears falling harder, and cried all the way to the 47th Precinct.

Stop crying, and be strong, Demarcus thought as Detective Rich double-parked the car across from the precinct. *You're smart. Don't let them break you.* He forced his tears to subside, sniffed loudly, and drew a deep breath, eyes squeezed shut as he braced for whatever was coming.

The car door swung open. “We’re here. Watch your head as you get out,” Detective Rich instructed.

Demarcus struggled out of the car, his hands still cuffed behind his back. With his gaze fixed on the ground, Detective Rich gripped his right arm, Detective Hanes on his left, and together they walked him across the street and into the precinct.

He kept his head down, tuning out the chaotic noise—the overlapping voices, the clatter of footsteps, the constant movement of officers and civilians. The precinct pulsed with activity, but Demarcus felt utterly alone.

They led him to the back, into a small, dimly lit room with no windows.

“Turn around,” Detective Hanes ordered, and Demarcus complied. She removed the handcuffs. “Have a seat,” she said, gesturing to a metal chair behind a battered wooden table.

Demarcus sat, rubbing his wrists to ease the ache left by the cuffs. Detectives Hanes and Rich pulled up chairs and sat across from him.

“Demarcus, we appreciate you coming with us,” Detective Hanes began, her tone measured. “That was a smart move.”

Demarcus wiped his eyes with the back of his hand, saying nothing.

“Before we begin, I must inform you that anything you say can and will be used against you in the court of law,” Detective Rich told him. “You also have the right to an attorney.”

Demarcus stared at him in silence.

“We’d like you to walk us through your day yesterday,” Detective Hanes said, leaning forward. “Tell us everything from the moment you woke up until you went to bed.”

Demarcus leaned back in the rickety chair, staring at Detective Hanes in silence. The room was thick with tension, arrested in silence.

"We're speaking to you, boy." Detective Rich slammed his hand down on the table, making Demarcus flinch. "Where were you last night between 11:00 p.m. and midnight?"

"You thought she was dead, didn't you?" Detective Hanes's eyes narrowed to slits. "You raped and beat that girl within an inch of her life," she barked.

Demarcus's eyes widened in disbelief. *Rape? Beat?* He swallowed hard, shifting uncomfortably in the chair.

"Oh, yes, she's alive," Detective Hanes sneered. "And guess what? She identified you as her attacker."

"You are going down, boy," Detective Rich said, his voice cold. "For rape and attempted murder. You're looking at a long time in prison, DMan."

"I need a lawyer." Demarcus felt sweat trickling down his face, and it wasn't just from the stuffy, overheated room. A deep, cold fear surged through his body. *Rape and attempted murder.*

"He needs a lawyer," Detective Rich scoffed, glancing at his partner. "That's all he has to say. Can you imagine?"

"Listen up, DMan. It's—"

"My name is Demarcus."

"Listen up, Demarcus." Detective Hanes stood and moved in close, perching on the edge of the table, nearly eye to eye with him. "Things will go better for you if you just tell us what happened and why you did it. Did she reject you, and you snapped?"

"Maybe you didn't mean to do it," Detective Rich added, his tone suddenly softer. "Talk to us, and we'll let the DA know you cooperated. So, why did you do it?"

Demarcus began breathing deeply, his chest rising and falling, his body trembling at the nightmare unfolding around him. But this time, instead of tears, anger flared in his nostrils at the accusations being hurled his way.

"You're not getting out of this, Demarcus." Detective Hanes grabbed the back of his head, forcing him to look at her. "Why did you rape and try to kill Bridget?"

Bridget. Demarcus stared at Detective Hanes as if she were Dracula, his mind racing. *They must be talking about Bridget Walsh, my neighbor. But who would do that to her?*

"I'm beginning to lose my patience with you, Demarcus." Detective Hanes tightened her grip, her voice rising. "I asked you a question." she screamed in his ear.

Demarcus locked eyes with her and said, "I have nothing to say to you until I get a lawyer. I know my rights." His voice was steady, refusing to betray his fear.

"Rights?" Detective Hanes leaned down, her face inches from his, her fingers digging into his scalp. "What about Bridget's rights, huh? She had a right to say no to you."

Spittle rained across Demarcus's face, and his head throbbed from her grip. "I am going to repeat. I do not have anything to say to you until I speak to a lawyer."

Detective Hanes raised her fist. Her face twisted with rage.

"Hanes," her partner warned. "Be careful."

Demarcus raised his voice, clear and strong. "Not only are you refusing to get me a lawyer, even though I have repeatedly asked for one, but you're physically abusing me as well. Is my mother going to get a call that I fell off this chair, hit my head, and died? Or maybe I reached for your gun, we struggled, and it went off and killed me?"

The detectives exchanged a look, and Detective Hanes released her hold, stalking back to her chair. For the next three hours, the detectives circled Demarcus like wolves, taking turns grilling him. One moment, they threatened him with icy voices and cold stares; the next, they tried to coax him with feigned sympathy, playing good cop against bad cop, then switching to two furious interrogators. The air in the cramped, windowless room was stifling. It was already 85 degrees outside, but inside it felt closer to ninety-nine. Sweat soaked Demarcus's white shirt, which clung to his athletic frame. He wiped the salty sting from his eyes with the back of his hand, his throat parched and burning for water. Still, he refused to utter a word.

"We're going to break you," Detective Hanes taunted, taking a long, deliberate sip from her cold bottle of Pepsi, her eyes mocking Demarcus as he stared at it with longing.

Just then, Detective Rich returned from a break. "His mother is out there demanding to see him," he announced to his partner.

Demarcus looked up, hope flickering in his eyes, silently pleading for a chance to see his mother.

"Let her know she's not allowed to see the prisoner," Detective Hanes said, a cruel grin spreading across her face as Demarcus let out a frustrated groan. "She can visit him at Rikers, where he'll be spending the rest of his life."

The two detectives shared a laugh as Detective Rich left to deliver the message, but their tactics didn't break Demarcus. If anything, their cruelty only fueled his anger and resolve. As the day dragged into night, hunger gnawed at his stomach and exhaustion weighed down his limbs. His head throbbed, his throat felt like sandpaper, and his body grew weak.

Help me, Lord. Please, help me, he prayed silently, his head resting on the table as the detectives took another break.

"Why me, Lord?" he whispered. "Why am I being accused of a crime I didn't commit? Why are you letting this happen to me now?" He waited for an answer, but the only reply was the sound of the detectives' footsteps as they returned, determined to send him to prison.

"You're going to be spending the night with us, Demarcus," Detective Rich announced as they reentered the room. "We're taking you to a cell now. Tomorrow, you'll be booked for rape and attempted murder, as we've already informed you."

"Then it's off to Rikers Island for you," Detective Hanes added with a smirk. "A pretty boy like you, oh, you'll be exceedingly popular. Then you'll get to feel what that poor girl felt."

A tremor ran through Demarcus. Rikers Island was said to be one of the ten worst correctional facilities in the country, infamous for violence, mental and physical abuse, and neglect.

"Let's go," Detective Rich barked.

Demarcus tried to stand, but his legs, cramped from hours in the chair, gave out, and he collapsed onto the filthy carpet. The detectives burst out laughing.

"Seems like you're a little weak," Detective Hanes sneered. "Confess what you did, and I'll personally go buy you a bucket of KFC. What do you say?"

Summoning the last of his strength, Demarcus pushed himself up from the floor, gripping the table for support. He met Detective Hanes's gaze, his voice steady and defiant. "After you."

That night, Demarcus lay on the filthy floor of the holding cell, drifting in and out of a restless, haunted sleep. Nightmares clawed at his mind with words like *rape, attempted murder*, and *Rikers Island* echoing relentlessly in his head. Each time he closed his eyes, the accusations and the threat of prison loomed larger, suffocating him with dread. But as bad as this night was, Demarcus sensed deep in his bones that things were about to get much, much worse.

Chapter Seven

Naomi Jones

Ater the police took Demarcus away that morning, Naomi felt utterly hollow, as if all life had drained from her body. She wailed and screamed, her voice echoing through the apartment, then collapsed into desperate prayer, pleading with God to end this nightmare. But reality settled in that her son had been taken for questioning, accused of attacking a young girl.

Determined to fight for him, Naomi splashed cold water on her face, steeling herself for what lay ahead. "Lord, if ever I needed You, it's now," she whispered, reaching for the phone to call a cab. She swapped her pumps for comfortable flip-flops, readying herself for the long day.

Soon, a car horn blared outside. Naomi locked up the apartment and hurried out, her heart pounding. Minutes later, she stood in front of the 47th Precinct, nerves taut as harp wire.

"I'd like to see Detective Hanes, please," she announced to the officer behind the information window.

"Detective Hanes is currently interviewing a suspect. You'll have to wait," came the curt reply.

The word *suspect* hit Naomi like a slap. Demarcus wasn't a suspect. He was a good boy. Why couldn't they see that?

She waited, pacing the lobby, but every time she returned to the window, she received the same dismissive answer. Over and over, for the next two hours, Naomi pleaded to see her son, but her words fell on deaf ears.

"This is not right," she shouted at last, her voice cutting through the room like a blade. Conversations froze mid-sentence. Heads turned. Eyes locked onto her. "I want to see my son. *Now. Now. Now.*" Each repetition struck harder than the last, her voice rising with a fierce, unstoppable rhythm.

"Okay, ma'am, please calm down," the officer said, his tone warning. "You know you're in the right place to get arrested, right?"

A few people snickered, but Naomi was undeterred. "Go ahead and arrest me," she yelled back. "Seems like that's what the police do now anyway, arresting innocent people. I need to speak to Detective Hanes."

The officer shot her a stern look before walking away.

As day faded into night, Naomi refused to leave the precinct. She pleaded with every officer she saw, begging for a glimpse of her son. Finally, as exhaustion threatened to overwhelm her, she looked up and spotted the other detective who had come to her house that morning with Detective Hanes.

"Detective!" Naomi rushed toward Detective Rich, her voice trembling with urgency. "Where's Demarcus? Where's my son?"

Detective Rich barely paused. "Your son is being questioned in connection with the rape and attempted murder of a young lady."

Naomi's knees buckled. She clung to the wall for support, her breath catching. "Rape? Attempted murder?"

Detective Rich smirked. "Your son has been a very bad boy."

"My son would never do anything like that," Naomi shot back, her voice sharp with conviction. "I need to speak to Detective Hanes. I need to see my son."

But Detective Rich simply turned and walked away, leaving Naomi standing alone, arms wrapped tightly around herself, muttering to the closed door where he'd vanished. Minutes dragged by before the door opened again and Detective Rich reappeared.

"Can I please see my son now?" Naomi asked, hope flickering in her eyes.

"Your son will be staying with us tonight," Detective Rich replied coldly. "Tomorrow he'll be charged. But don't worry. You'll get to see him over at Rikers Island."

A scream tore from Naomi's gut, ricocheting off the precinct walls. Two police officers rushed to her side.

"Are you okay, ma'am?" One officer gently guided her to a chair. "Please sit. You look as if you're about to pass out."

Naomi collapsed into the chair, trembling uncontrollably, tears and snot streaming down her face. "Oh, Demarcus. My poor baby."

It took several minutes for the officers to calm her.

"They're charging him with rape and attempted murder," Naomi sobbed, clutching a tissue. "But he's innocent."

"Those are serious charges," the male officer said quietly. "You should try to get a good lawyer for your son."

"Why don't you go home and try to get some rest?" the female officer added, her eyes full of sympathy. "They won't let you see him tonight, but you'll probably get to see him at the arraignment tomorrow."

"I'll write down that information for you." The other officer returned with a slip of paper. "It's going to be at Central Booking on East 161st Street. I'm not sure what time they'll take him over."

"Thank you," Naomi whispered. "God bless you both for the kindness you've shown me." She cast one last, lingering look at the closed door behind which her son was being held, then forced herself to her feet and walked out of the precinct. Outside, she flagged down a gypsy cab and let it carry her home.

Back in her apartment, Naomi wandered from room to room, her eyes lingering on every photograph of Demarcus—his chubby baby cheeks, his first day of kindergarten, the gap-toothed grin when he lost his front tooth, the triumphant leap for a basketball dunk, the tuxedo on prom night, the cap and gown at graduation.

"Now you're off to Rikers Island?" she cried out to the empty walls. "The devil is a liar."

Naomi stormed into Demarcus's bedroom and snatched up the t-shirt he'd slept in the night before, clutching it to her chest as she marched into her own room. She wrapped her hair scarf tightly around her head, a shield for the battle she was about to wage in prayer. In the living room, she pressed play on the small CD player, and CeCe Winans's soulful voice soared through the apartment, filling every corner with one of Naomi's favorite hymns.

The blood that Jesus shed for me, way back on Calvary,
The blood that gives me strength from day to day; it will never lose its power.

Naomi dropped to her knees, Demarcus's t-shirt balled in her fists, and began pounding on Heaven's door. "Lord, I come to You on behalf of my son, Demarcus Jones.

None of this is a surprise to You, but it's breaking me. I'm begging You to give me wisdom, give me understanding. Show me what's really happening here."

It reaches to the highest mountain,
It flows to the lowest valley.

"We can't get through this without You, Lord," Naomi cried, her voice trembling. "We need You. Demarcus needs You." By now, she was swept up in the Spirit, oblivious to the CD skipping and repeating the refrain.

It will never lose—

"No weapon formed against Demarcus Jones shall prosper, Lord," she declared, her voice rising with conviction.

It will never lose—

"I plead the blood of Jesus against anyone and anything that tries to harm my son." Naomi bent so low her face pressed into the carpet, her tears soaking the fibers. "Please, God, Demarcus needs You right now."

It will never lose—

"Satan, I rebuke you in the name of Jesus," she shouted, a river of tears streaming down her face. "Get your hands off my son, in Jesus' name."

It will never lose—

"I bind every person trying to send my son to prison. Lord, You said whatever we bind on earth is bound in Heaven. Open their eyes, God, and let them see the truth. Please, reveal the truth and set my baby free."

It will never lose—

"The blood! The blood that gives me strength from day to day." Naomi pounded her fist on the floor, her heart aching for her son. "It reaches to the highest mountain, and it flows to the lowest valley." She hugged the t-shirt tighter, as if it were Demarcus himself.

It will never lose—

"Lord, do for Demarcus as You did for Daniel. As You did for Shadrach, Meshach, and Abednego and protect my son from every harm and danger."

It will never lose—

"I claim my son's release right now, in the name of Jesus. Release him and set him free," Naomi declared, her voice unwavering.

It will never lose—

"El Roi! The God that sees me."

It will never lose—

She prayed until her voice was hoarse, until she was curled up on the floor, her face buried in Demarcus's t-shirt, eyes squeezed shut as she tried to catch a trace of his scent through her stuffy nose.

It will never lose its power.

Chapter Eight

"Good morning," Lieutenant Gregory Mulligan greeted two officers as he strode into the 47th Precinct, a briefcase in one hand and a steaming cup of Dunkin' Donuts coffee in the other.

"Good morning, sir," one replied. "How was the vacation?"

"Wonderful," Mulligan said, a rare smile flashing across his face. "It was great to spend some time with my parents down south. My wife and son enjoyed it too."

"Welcome back, sir." The other officer gave him a knowing look. "As you can see, it's business as usual."

Mulligan glanced around the bustling precinct. He quickly stepped aside as two officers hustled past, escorting a handcuffed prisoner who was cursing and struggling. "Yup, I can see that," he said, shaking his head.

He exchanged a few more greetings as he made his way to his office. The sight of the paperwork piled high on his desk drew a heavy sigh. He'd only been gone a week, but it felt like a year.

Closing his office door, Mulligan set down his briefcase and settled into his chair, savoring a sip of coffee. He'd barely taken a second sip when a knock sounded at the door.

"Come in," he called, leaning back in his big wingback chair. Mulligan was a tall, broad-shouldered African American man, his presence commanding even when seated.

Detectives Rich and Hanes entered.

"Welcome back, sir," Hanes said with a bright smile. "You look relaxed, even if you were only gone a week."

"Thank you, Detective Hanes," Mulligan replied. "Detective Rich, how's it going?"

Rich gave a weary chuckle. "You know the usual, sir. We're up to our eyeballs in cases. I swear, people commit more crimes in the summer than at any other time."

Mulligan nodded, taking another sip of coffee.

"We've got a bad one, sir," Hanes said, her tone turning serious. "Young girl was raped and nearly strangled to death."

Mulligan's face darkened. "Is she going to make it?"

"Yes, and the good news is she identified her attacker."

"That's something," Mulligan said. "Did you get him, or is he on the run?" He took another sip.

"Oh, we got *DMan* all right," Hanes replied, her voice edged with sarcasm.

At that, Mulligan's hand trembled, spilling hot coffee down his shirt. He shot to his feet, brushing at the stain.

"Here, sir." Rich quickly offered a handkerchief. "Are you all right?"

But Mulligan ignored him, his gaze fixed on Hanes. "Who did you say you arrested?"

"Demarcus Jones," Detective Hanes announced. "His nickname is DMan."

Lieutenant Mulligan's eyes narrowed as Detective Rich pressed, "Do you know him, sir?"

Mulligan closed his eyes for a moment, gathering himself. When he opened them, his voice was heavy with emotion. "Demarcus is my son's best friend. I've known him since he was a little boy."

The detectives exchanged uneasy glances, sensing the gravity in their superior's tone.

"I'm telling you, detectives, there's been a mistake," Mulligan insisted, pacing the office with mounting agitation. "Demarcus Jones was the captain of the basketball team at Cardinal High. He just graduated with honors and earned a full scholarship to Stanford this fall."

Detective Hanes's brow furrowed in recognition. "I knew his name sounded familiar, but I couldn't place it."

Mulligan pressed on, his voice gaining strength. "His mother, Naomi, is a pillar of our church. She's a wonderful woman. There's no way I'll believe that boy"—he jabbed a finger at Hanes—"who's slept under my roof and eaten at my table, would ever rape or try to kill anyone. Not Demarcus."

A tense silence filled the room.

"Where is he now?" Mulligan demanded.

Detective Rich cleared his throat. "He's in the holding cell. We were about to start processing him, then take him to Central Booking."

Mulligan's gaze sharpened. "When was he brought in?"

Rich hesitated, then admitted, "Yesterday morning."

Mulligan's face darkened. "He's been here a day and hasn't been processed? What have you been doing with him all this time?"

"Sir, we were questioning the suspect," Hanes replied, her voice defensive. "We thought we could get a confession."

Mulligan's stare was icy. "And did you get a confession, detective?"

"No, sir."

"What did Demarcus say?"

"Nothing," Hanes answered. "He asked for a lawyer."

Mulligan's jaw clenched. "And let me guess. You refused him one and kept questioning him. Right?"

"The victim identified him, sir," Hanes protested. "If you'd seen what was done to that poor girl, you'd understand why we pushed so hard."

Mulligan's voice was sharp as a blade. "Detective, you cannot continue to question a suspect after he requests a lawyer. You know that." Without another word, he strode out of his office, Hanes and Rich scrambling to follow.

When they reached the holding cell, Mulligan gasped. Demarcus lay curled on the floor, his face to the wall. "Demarcus?" Mulligan called, his voice trembling.

Slowly, Demarcus rolled onto his side. "Hi, Mr. Mulligan," he croaked, his voice weak and raw.

"Open it," Mulligan barked, and Rich hurried to comply, unlocking the cell.

Mulligan rushed in, dropping to his knees beside Demarcus. He gathered the young man into his arms, tears stinging his eyes. "It's going to be okay," he whispered, holding him tight.

It was then that Demarcus began to cry, his tears soaking the shirt of the man he respected like the father he never had.

"I didn't do it, sir. You know me."

"Yes, I know." Lieutenant Mulligan struggled to keep his composure. "Don't say another word." He stood and helped Demarcus to his feet. The boy staggered, weak from hunger and dehydration.

"Here, sit down." Mulligan guided Demarcus to the bench. "Have you eaten anything since they brought you in?"

Demarcus shook his head.

"Anything to drink?"

Again, Demarcus shook his head.

Lieutenant Mulligan shot a furious look at the detectives, his eyes blazing. "I'm going to get you something to eat. I'll be right back." He stood, took a few steps toward the door, then paused.

"Mr. Mulligan?" Demarcus looked up, his face wet with tears. "Do you have . . . I mean, could you please get me a clean pair of pants?"

Mulligan glanced down and saw the small wet spot on the floor where Demarcus had lain.

"I'm sorry, but I had to go," Demarcus whispered, hanging his head in shame.

"That's all right, son. I'll be right back." Mulligan left the holding cell, his voice tight. "Detectives, with me."

Back in his office, Mulligan began to pace, his body vibrating with fury. "Is this how we do things now? Torturing suspects?"

"Sir, it wasn't—" Detective Hanes started.

"Twenty-four hours without food or water," Mulligan thundered. "What do you call that?"

"Sir, if you'd let us ex—" Rich tried to interject.

Mulligan cut him off with a raised hand. "I'm going to get Demarcus something to eat and drink. Then I'm calling his mother to let her know what's going on."

"Lieutenant Mulligan, I'd like to say something," Hanes insisted.

"Detective, I'm not asking you to release him," Mulligan replied, his tone icy. "You said the victim identified him as her attacker. I know why he was arrested and that he'll have to be arraigned. But that's no excuse for treating a seventeen-year-old this way."

Detective Rich finally spoke up. "Well, the victim didn't actually—"

"She said it was him," Hanes interrupted quickly. "So, we thought that was a positive ID."

"I'm going to feed that boy now," Mulligan said, voice clipped. "Then you can do your job." He moved toward the door, then turned to face his detectives. "Just so you know, I'm not going to let Demarcus take the fall for a crime he didn't commit. I don't know why that young lady said he attacked her, but you can trust and believe I'm going to find out."

With that, Lieutenant Mulligan stormed out of his office, his mouth set in a hard line, his eyes narrowed to slits as he strode away. He was halfway to the door when a small voice called after him.

"Lieutenant?"

Without missing a beat or even glancing at the person calling after him, Lieutenant Mulligan replied, "I'm sorry, but now is not a good time."

"It's Naomi."

That stopped him. "Naomi." Mulligan turned and walked back to her. His heart clenched at the sight: Naomi's eyes were swollen and red, stray wisps of her natural hair had escaped her bun and stood up in wild tufts, and her clothes were wrinkled as if she'd slept in them. She wore two mismatched flip-flops. This was not the always well put-together woman he knew. But who could care about appearances when her only son was being accused of rape and attempted murder?

"I thought you were on vacation with your family," Naomi's voice rasped, as if something were caught in her throat.

"We came back last night."

"I wanted to call, but I didn't want to bother you," Naomi said, relief apparent in her voice. "Demarcus is in trouble."

"Yes. I know," Mulligan replied gently. "Come, let's go back to my office for a moment."

He guided Naomi back to his office, grateful that Detectives Rich and Hanes weren't there to witness her distress.

As soon as the door closed, Naomi unleashed a torrent of questions. "Did you see him? Is he okay? Is he scared?"

"Please, have a seat." Mulligan gestured to the chair across from him and sat down. "We have a lot to do, Naomi."

"I know, but I'm so confused. Those officers said last night that I should get a good lawyer, but I don't know who is a good one. Should I try to get one in the Bronx? Maybe I should go to Manhattan. I need one who's really good. One who's going to—"

"Naomi," Mulligan interrupted, his tone firm but kind. "Listen to me. Demarcus is going for arraignment soon at

Central Booking. I want you to go home, get some clothes for him, and meet us there, okay?"

"Arraignment? They're really charging him?" Naomi's lips trembled. "I was hoping they would realize this was a big mistake and let him go."

"They have to. The victim said he did it."

"She's lying, Lieutenant," Naomi insisted, her voice trembling with conviction. "You know Demarcus would never do something like that."

Lieutenant Mulligan nodded, his expression grave. "I know, Naomi. But the detectives have to follow protocol." He leaned forward, locking eyes with her. "You need to be prepared. With a felony charge this serious, and the victim identifying Demarcus as her attacker, there's a strong chance he'll be remanded without bail. That means Demarcus will be sent to Rikers Island."

"Rikers Island." Naomi's voice broke, a deep groan escaping her throat. "That's a terrible place, Lieutenant. Demarcus doesn't belong there."

"No, he doesn't," Mulligan agreed, his voice heavy. "But my hands are tied. We'll have to find the evidence that proves his innocence and get him out as soon as possible."

Naomi straightened, her eyes shining with tears but fierce with faith. "God will keep my baby safe," she declared. "They can't touch a strand of hair on his head."

"As for the lawyer, he'll be assigned a public defender for the arraignment. But we're going to need someone who will fight for Demarcus," Mulligan continued.

"Yes, do you know anyone?" Naomi asked hopefully.

"I have one or two people in mind," Mulligan replied. "I'll make some calls after I get Demarcus something to eat."

"They haven't fed him?" Naomi's composure shattered. Tears streamed down her face as she leapt to her feet, pacing the floor in agitation. "They're starving my son? I bet they haven't even given him a glass of water."

"I've spoken to the detectives about that," Mulligan assured her. "And I'll be following up on it. But for now, let's focus on getting Demarcus out of this mess. It's going to be a tough fight, Naomi. These are serious charges."

"Can I see him, please?" Naomi pleaded, her eyes wide and desperate. "Please, Lieutenant."

Mulligan's voice softened. "Naomi, I want to let you see him, but we have to be careful. Demarcus was arrested, and I'm not the arresting officer. I don't want to break protocol and create a problem for him later. You understand, don't you?"

Naomi nodded reluctantly, her shoulders slumping. "Please get him something to eat for me. And can you bring him a cup of tea? Sometimes his stomach hurts if he doesn't drink something hot."

"I will," Mulligan promised, his eyes full of compassion. "I'll tell him you love him, and you won't stop until he's home."

"Thank you," Naomi whispered. "You know I'm grateful for you."

"Go get his clothes and meet us at Central Booking," Mulligan said gently. "You'll get to see him there for his arraignment. Okay?"

"Okay."

"Come on, let me walk you out. I was just heading across the street to the deli to get Demarcus a sandwich."

As Lieutenant Mulligan moved to stand beside Naomi, she reached out and embraced him. "May God bless you for all you're doing for my son. Thank you."

"You're welcome." Mulligan returned her hug warmly. "Demarcus has a bright future ahead. I won't let it end like this. We're going to fight."

But as Naomi stepped out into the hallway, a chill ran through her. The real battle was only just beginning.

Chapter Nine

Demarcus tore into his turkey pastrami sandwich, taking a massive bite and chewing quickly before swallowing. He grabbed the bottle of water, gulping it down so fast that some spilled down his chin. In just a few more ravenous bites, the sandwich was gone.

He glanced over at Lieutenant Mulligan, who sat beside him in the cell. "Thank you, sir," Demarcus said, then took a sip of green tea and let out a loud burp. "Excuse me." He dropped his gaze to the floor, embarrassed.

"That's all right." Mulligan gave his shoulder a reassuring squeeze. "Listen, Demarcus, things are about to get even rougher for you."

Demarcus managed a wry smirk. "Rougher? You mean it's not rough enough already?"

"I mean it," Mulligan replied, his tone grave. "You're about to be arraigned on charges of rape and attempted murder. In my experience, you'll be remanded without bail and sent straight to Rikers Island."

"Okay," Demarcus mumbled, his voice barely above a whisper.

"I spoke to your mother—" Mulligan began.

"Is Mom okay? How's she holding up?" Demarcus interrupted, worry etched across his face.

"She's struggling, as you'd expect," Mulligan admitted gently. "She'll be bringing you a change of clothes at Central Booking."

"Poor Mom." Demarcus sighed, his shoulders slumping. "I hate that she has to go through this."

"This isn't your fault, Demarcus. You didn't do this, and I'm going to prove it. Your mother and I will do everything we can to get you out. We'll find a good lawyer and fight for bail while we work to uncover the truth."

"Thanks, Mr. Mulligan," Demarcus said quietly.

"Now, I need you to be strong and brave. When you get to Rikers, keep to yourself. Don't get too friendly, but don't act too standoffish either. Understand?"

"I guess," Demarcus murmured, his voice barely above a whisper. Then, after a pause, "Sir, I won't let anyone mess with me. If it costs me my life, I'll go out fighting. I've heard what happens in jail. I know what some of those guys are like, but it'll be over my dead body."

Lieutenant Mulligan swallowed hard, his eyes glistening. "Don't talk like that, Demarcus. You'll be all right."

Demarcus turned and looked at him and asked, "Can you promise me something?"

"Sure."

"Promise me you'll look out for Mom if anything happens to me. I'm all she's got."

"Please stop talking like this, Demarcus. You'll be out soon to continue looking out for her."

Demarcus bit his quivering lip but didn't reply.

Just then, Detective Hanes walked up. "We're ready to take him over for arraignment, Lieutenant. Detective Rich is waiting outside with the car."

Lieutenant Mulligan rose slowly to his feet, as if his knees ached. He held out a hand to Demarcus and helped him to stand. Standing face to face, Demarcus was about two inches taller than Lieutenant Mulligan.

"Remember what I told you?" Mulligan asked.

"Yes, sir."

"God is with you, son."

Demarcus walked out of the cell to Detective Hanes, turned his back toward her, and placed both hands behind his back. He flinched as the handcuffs clicked shut, but he kept his head held high.

Detective Hanes led Demarcus through the precinct and out to the street, with Lieutenant Mulligan following close behind. "Please get in and watch your head," she said, opening the back door of the police car.

Demarcus awkwardly got in the back seat. He briefly made eye contact in the rearview mirror with Detective Rich, who was sitting in the driver's seat, before looking away.

"This is wrong," Demarcus heard Lieutenant Mulligan say to Detective Hanes. "You have the wrong suspect, Detective."

"Lieutenant, you know I have no choice. If he's innocent—"

"He's innocent," Mulligan snapped. He appeared at the door where Demarcus sat, bent over, and tucked his head into the car. "I'm right behind you, Demarcus."

But Demarcus didn't reply. His eyes held a faraway look, and his handsome face was void of emotion. Demarcus was shutting down.

Demarcus stared out the window as the police car threaded through the pulsing Bronx streets. Familiar sights flashed by—corner stores, playgrounds, and a few faces he almost recognized. A quiet question pressed against his thoughts: *Will I ever see these streets again?*

Soon, Detective Rich pulled up in front of Central Booking on East 161st Street. The tall brick building loomed above them, its entrance a revolving door of uniformed officers, handcuffed men and women, and anxious civilians, with one woman openly weeping into her hands. Demarcus's thoughts flashed to his mother. He hated the idea of her seeing him like this, caught in a nightmare he couldn't escape.

"Let's go," Detective Hanes said sharply, opening the passenger door.

Demarcus stepped out, hands cuffed behind his back, and walked between the two detectives into the building. He kept his head down as they led him to the back, where the holding cells waited.

Once inside, a guard removed his handcuffs and shut the cell door with a heavy clang.

"A public defender will be along soon to speak with you," Detective Rich informed him. "He'll represent you until you can get another lawyer, if you choose to do so."

Demarcus moved to the bench and sat down in silence, not looking up as the detectives walked away. Each second ticked by like an eternity. He tried to empty his mind, but the reality pressed in. *I'm about to be arraigned for rape and attempted murder. Me, Demarcus Jones. How did my life come to this?*

Moments later, Lieutenant Mulligan appeared at the cell door, the guard beside him. "Here's the change of clothes your mother brought for you."

The guard opened the door, and Demarcus took the bundle from Mulligan's hands.

"I'll be out here with your mother," Mulligan said gently. "A lawyer will be coming to see you soon. Remember what I told you?"

Demarcus didn't respond. He didn't even flinch as the cell door closed again.

Mulligan sighed, his voice muffled through the bars. "You're going to be okay, Demarcus." Then he was gone.

Demarcus glanced around. Every cell to his right and left was occupied. The guard stood a few feet away, watching. He changed out of his filthy white shirt into the clean beige one his mother had sent. He hesitated, wishing for privacy, but there was none. With his face to the wall, he quickly slipped out of his soiled pants and underwear, pulling on the fresh ones as fast as he could, his cheeks burning with humiliation.

He waited, maybe an hour, before a small, red-haired man hurried toward his cell, the guard trailing behind.

"Demarcus Jones?" the public defender called out, stopping in front of the bars.

Demarcus glanced up at the man, and for a fleeting moment, the comedian Carrot Top flashed through his mind. The resemblance was uncanny. He was about 5 feet 9 inches with a shock of bright red curls and freckles scattered across a pale face.

"Mr. Jones?" the man prompted again, his tone gentle but insistent.

Demarcus nodded.

"Please open the door," the lawyer instructed the guard. The cell door swung open, and the man stepped inside, settling onto the bench beside Demarcus with a battered black briefcase perched on his lap.

He introduced himself. "I'm Carrick O'Connor, your public defender for the arraignment."

"Okay," Demarcus replied, his voice flat.

Carrick studied him for a moment, then grinned. "A man of few words, I see."

Demarcus met his gaze, noting how young the lawyer looked. "Just graduated law school, huh, Mr. O'Connor?"

Carrick's smile widened, his freckles deepening. "Just Carrick, please. Actually, I get that a lot, but I've been practicing for seven years now."

"I didn't do it," Demarcus said, his voice suddenly firmer.

"That's what Lieutenant Mulligan told me," Carrick replied, his tone reassuring. "We'll get into the details soon. For now, we'll enter a not guilty plea. I'll fight for bail, but with the victim identifying you, there's a 99.9% chance it'll be denied."

"I was told," Demarcus murmured, his shoulders slumping.

Carrick leaned in, lowering his voice. "The Bronx District Attorney, 'Silver Fox,' is personally handling your case. Word is, he's running for attorney general soon, and the polls say he's a lock. This is probably his last big case before the election, and he'll want to make an example out of you."

A visible shudder ran through Demarcus.

"I'm not trying to scare you," Carrick said, his tone sharpening with conviction. "I want you prepared. Silver Fox has never lost a case, and he won't want to start now, not with the spotlight on him."

"It's over for me," Demarcus whispered, the words barely audible.

Carrick's eyes flashed. "Not at all. I may not have Silver Fox's years, but I don't back down from a fight. You'll get the best defense I can give."

"Sure," Demarcus replied, sarcasm creeping in. He'd heard the stories about public defenders. They were overworked, underpaid, and quick to cut deals that sent their clients away for decades. Innocent until proven guilty? It always sounded like a hollow promise.

Carrick seemed to read his mind. "You think I don't care because I'm a public defender, right? That I'm just here to move you along?"

Demarcus shrugged, not trusting himself to answer.

"You can always hire someone else after the arraignment," Carrick continued, "but I want you to know that I do this because I care. If you say you're innocent, I'll fight to prove it."

For the first time, Demarcus looked Carrick in the eyes and saw something unexpected: sincerity and fierce determination burning behind those blue eyes.

"Thank you," Demarcus said quietly.

"Jones, they're ready for you," the guard called out, his voice echoing down the corridor.

Carrick leaned in, his tone firm but reassuring. "Don't say a word, Demarcus. From here on, I'm your voice."

Demarcus entered the courtroom in cuffs, flanked on either side by a stone-faced guard and his lawyer. The first face he saw was his mother's. Her expression was devastated, her eyes brimming with tears.

Naomi sprang to her feet and rushed toward her son, only to be stopped by the guard. "No touching, please."

"I love you, baby," Naomi choked out, her voice trembling. "God is going to get you out of this, Demarcus. Please, be strong."

Demarcus blinked rapidly, fighting back tears. "I love you, Mom. Remember that, okay?"

"I will, baby." Naomi sobbed softly. "God be with you."

Standing before the judge, Demarcus tried to steady himself. He glanced at the prosecutor's table and instantly understood why the man was called "Silver Fox." Calvin Wilcox, the Bronx District Attorney, was an imposing figure, tall and powerfully built, with a mane of thick, curly silver hair cascading over his broad shoulders. His deeply tanned face was all sharp cheekbones and steely confidence, and the pinstriped suit he wore was unmistakably expensive. Demarcus recognized the cut from his summer job at Brooks Brothers.

Demarcus's gaze flicked from his lawyer to Silver Fox and back again. The moment felt like David facing Goliath.

"The people versus Demarcus Jones," the judge announced, his voice booming through the courtroom. "How do you plead?"

"Not guilty, Your Honor," Carrick replied, his voice clear and unwavering.

"Prosecutor, your position on bail?" the judge asked.

"Your Honor, this young man viciously raped and nearly strangled a young woman to death after brutally beating her," Prosecutor Wilcox declared, his tone icy. "I ask that the defendant be remanded pending trial."

Carrick stepped forward, his face flushed with conviction. "Your Honor, there is no evidence of this yet. My client just graduated from Cardinal Spellman High School, where he was captain of the basketball team. He's earned a full athletic scholarship to Stanford University this fall. He has no criminal record and is an outstanding member of his community. I respectfully request that he be granted bail until the prosecution can prove its case."

Wilcox sneered. "Bring out the choir. A real angel on earth."

"Your Honor—" Carrick began, but Wilcox cut him off.

"The victim identified Demarcus Jones as her attacker," Wilcox pressed. "That's a positive ID. And I'm confident that when we receive the results of the rape kit, which should be soon, they'll point directly to him."

"The prosecutor said the victim was badly beaten," Carrick countered, his voice steady. "And from what I read in the detective's report, she was slipping in and out of consciousness. If she named my client, and I strongly believe she did not, how reliable is that, Your Honor?"

"As reliable as I am to believe the word of two of my colleagues," Prosecutor Wilcox shot back. "The detectives said she identified him, and I believe them. I am going to make sure that Mr. Jones pays for his crime to the full extent of the law. We will not tolerate the victimization of our young girls." He jabbed an angry finger in Demarcus's direction.

"Oh, save the campaign speech for the campaign trail," Carrick snapped, his patience fraying. "Mr. Wannabe Attorney General."

A ripple of laughter broke out in the courtroom.

"Enough," the judge cut in, his gavel slamming down. "These are very serious charges, and with the identification of the suspect by the victim, bail is denied."

The sound of the gavel echoed in Demarcus's mind like a sledgehammer. He'd been warned bail would be denied, but hearing it pronounced in open court struck him like a physical blow. He doubled over, hands on his knees, struggling to catch his breath.

Carrick leaned in, whispering something urgent in his ear, but Demarcus could only focus on the cold, satisfied smirk on Prosecutor Wilcox's face. The message was clear: this man was determined to see him go down for a crime he hadn't committed.

That thought haunted Demarcus as he was led away, shackled and silent, to the bus bound for Rikers Island.

Chapter Ten

"She's still alive." Alfredo Ferrari's glare could have cut glass. "And soon she'll identify my son as her attacker, and everything will be ruined."

"Maybe not," Viktor replied, his tone cool and measured. "My sources say they've arrested someone else for the crime. He's been denied bail and is already on his way to Rikers Island."

Alfredo's eyes narrowed. "Really? Who?"

"A young man, the girl's neighbor. Apparently, she identified him as her attacker."

A slow, satisfied smile crept across Alfredo's face. "That's excellent. It seems you and Angelo have succeeded in putting the fear of God in her."

Viktor nodded. "We just have to make sure it stays that way. From what I've gathered, there's a lieutenant who's close to this boy and determined to prove his innocence. We need to make sure he doesn't succeed."

"We must," Alfredo agreed, his voice steely. "I want you to retrace this boy's steps that night. Make sure every detail lines up with the attack. He must take the fall for this crime."

"I'm on it," Viktor assured him. "There's something you can start doing on your end."

Alfredo raised an eyebrow. "What's that?"

"I spoke to Angelo. The girl wanted to attend Princeton. She was accepted, but her parents couldn't afford it, and she didn't get a scholarship. She settled for Baruch College."

Alfredo nodded knowingly. "The usual money problems. But wouldn't it be too obvious if we helped? Wouldn't it come back to us?"

"She's one of your employees, and you're very sorry for what happened to her," Viktor said, a cold smile on his lips. "You're just trying to help in any way you can."

Alfredo considered this. "What do you propose?"

"You have contacts at Princeton, and she was already accepted. The admission process is over, but you can pull a few strings," Viktor explained. "Then you'll give her a full scholarship from the company. Well, Angelo should do it since he's the acting CEO."

Alfredo snorted. "Once this is over, I'll fix that."

"Do you know how grateful she'll be to attend the Ivy League college she dreamed of, on a full scholarship?" Viktor pressed.

Alfredo stared at Viktor, then a sly smile spread across his face. "You're a genius. Now I remember why I keep you around. Let's do it."

"We'll wait until she's released from the hospital," Viktor said, "then you'll pay her a home visit with the good news."

Alfredo wrinkled his nose. "Is the home visit really necessary? You want me to go to the Bronx?"

"You'll be fine, sir," Viktor replied. "Our presence will also remind her that we know where she lives and have met her parents. Trust me, this girl will be too scared to say a word against Angelo."

"I guess I can do that for the good of my company," Alfredo muttered, crossing the room to the minibar. He poured a generous measure of scotch for himself and Viktor, then handed Viktor a glass before raising his own. "Cheers."

Their glasses clinked, the sound sharp and conspiratorial. The two men exchanged a look, one of grim satisfaction. Someone else was now behind bars for the crime Angelo had committed. All that remained was to ensure it stayed that way, no matter what the cost.

Two days later, Alfredo Ferrari was huffing and puffing on the treadmill, his face flushed with exertion and irritation. He muttered a string of curses at his doctor, mocking the advice that echoed in his mind. *Alfredo, you need to take better care of yourself, or you'll have another heart attack. Exercise, eat healthy, and please cut down on the drinking*.

Alfredo scoffed aloud, "Eat healthy? I eat rich food. I eat caviar." He swiped his sweaty brow with a towel, dismissing the memory of the personal trainer he'd hired and promptly fired after his last heart scare. "You don't tell me what to do," he'd snapped at the trainer. "Do you know who I am?"

Just then, his cell phone, perched atop the treadmill, buzzed insistently. Alfredo stopped the machine, grabbed the phone, and answered with a brusque, "Yes?"

Viktor's voice came through, cool and direct. "Sorry I'm early, but we have another situation. I'm downstairs in the car."

Alfredo fired off a burst of Italian, annoyance sharpening his tone. "You coming up or what? I'm almost done with this exercise nonsense."

"Why don't we discuss it on the way to the Bronx?" Viktor replied.

Without another word, Alfredo hung up. He'd planned to soak in a long, luxurious bath, but the urgency in Viktor's voice changed his mind. He opted for a quick shower, dressed in record time, and strode out of the penthouse. The elevator ride to the lobby was swift. He barely acknowledged the attendant holding the door as he swept outside.

Viktor stood by the open door of a gleaming black Rolls-Royce, his posture calm, expectant. Alfredo climbed into the back seat with a sharp, restless motion, the tension in his body speaking louder than words.

"What's going on?" Alfredo demanded to know as they pulled away from the curb. "What other situation came up?"

Viktor's eyes met Alfredo's in the rearview mirror. "I've been tracking the activities of that boy who got arrested the night of the assault. I wanted to make sure he didn't have a solid alibi or anything that could prove he was innocent. My people have been talking to folks in the neighborhood, keeping things quiet. They've heard something interesting."

Alfredo leaned forward, tension radiating from him. "What?"

"There's a Hispanic woman, Ms. Lopez, who claims the boy couldn't have committed the crime. She says that at the time in question, he was helping her carry her bags home. She insists he's a kindhearted boy and told my contact she'll be going to the police with the information."

Alfredo unleashed a torrent of Italian curses, his frustration boiling over. "That's it? We're back to square one?"

"That would be up to you, sir," Viktor replied calmly.

"Up to me? Why are we even going to see this woman anyway?"

"Ms. Lopez is in her sixties, works at McDonald's, and lives in a one-bedroom apartment with her drug-addicted adult son," Viktor explained.

Alfredo settled back against the leather seat, his mind racing. "I see. If we offer Ms. Lopez a nice early retirement, maybe she could develop amnesia about that night?"

Viktor's lips curled into a thin smile. "That's my thinking."

"And if she refuses?"

"I'll erase her from the equation entirely. She can take the money and keep quiet, retirement on earth, or retirement in Hell. The choice will be hers."

"Let's do it," Alfredo commanded. "Are we going to see her now as well?"

"No," Viktor replied. "You won't be involved. The Ferrari name must never come up, just in case she changes her mind. I'll handle it."

"Do whatever you must. That boy has to take the fall for this."

Moments later, they crossed the Triborough Bridge into the Bronx. Viktor expertly navigated the car onto Adee Avenue, where Bridget lived.

"Are you sure this is safe?" Alfredo asked, glancing out the window at a group of young Black men lounging on a bench in front of a house.

"You're always safe with me," Viktor assured him, slowing the car as he scanned the house numbers. "I think we're here."

Viktor pulled up in front of Bridget's house and parked. He turned to his boss. "Remember what we discussed."

"Yeah, yeah," Alfredo muttered, rolling his eyes. "Empathy and compassion, blah blah blah."

Viktor smiled faintly and stepped out, circling the car to open Alfredo's door. Alfredo emerged, straightening the jacket of his Hugo Boss suit, casting a wary glance down the block at the young men.

"Okay," Viktor said, pushing open the small metal gate. "No dogs."

Alfredo strode ahead, his steps hesitant, up the short walkway to the front door. He watched as Viktor rang the bell.

The door opened, and a man, presumably Mr. Walsh, looked from Alfredo to Viktor, suspicion in his eyes.

Alfredo stepped forward, flashing a practiced, dazzling smile. “I’m Mr. Ferrari,” he said, extending his hand.

Recognition flickered across Mr. Walsh’s face. “Oh, Mr. Ferrari. You’re Bridget’s employer. I’m Larry Walsh.” He shook Alfredo’s hand firmly.

“This is my driver,” Alfredo added, as Viktor nodded politely. “I heard what happened to Bridget and wanted to pay my respects.”

Mr. Walsh’s expression darkened. “We’re all devastated. We just brought her home from the hospital yesterday.”

“May we come in?” Alfredo asked, his tone smooth.

“I’m sorry. Where are my manners?” Mr. Walsh stepped aside. “Please, come in.”

Alfredo entered the modest living room, where Mrs. Walsh sat on the couch. “Hello, I’m Mr. Ferrari,” he repeated, his voice gentle but commanding.

Mrs. Walsh hurried over and shook his hand. “It’s a pleasure to meet you. Please, have a seat.” She gestured to a couch opposite her own.

Alfredo lowered himself carefully onto the couch, Viktor settling beside him in silence.

“It’s very kind of you to come,” Mr. Walsh said, taking his place next to his wife.

“Of course,” Alfredo replied smoothly. “Bridget may have just started with us, but she’s already part of our corporate family. We’re devastated by what’s happened to her. How is she doing?”

Mrs. Walsh’s eyes filled with tears. “She’s in her bedroom. It’s been four days since . . . since . . .” Her voice broke, and she began to sob.

Alfredo leaned forward, offering his silk handkerchief with practiced sympathy. “That poor girl. I heard they’ve arrested someone?”

"Yes, the boy who lived across the street," Mr. Walsh answered, gently rubbing his wife's back.

Mrs. Walsh blew her nose loudly. "I still can't believe he would do something like that. He always seemed like such a nice young man."

"It's always the ones you least expect," Alfredo said, his tone grave. "I hope they lock him up and throw away the key."

"The prosecutor seems confident in the case," Mr. Walsh added.

"May I speak with Bridget?" Alfredo asked politely.

The Walshes exchanged a quick, uncertain glance. "We're not sure she's up for visitors yet," Mr. Walsh admitted, "but you came all this way . . ."

"I'd appreciate it," Alfredo said, offering a gentle smile. "Please tell her I have news that could change her life. And I won't leave until I see for myself that she's going to be all right."

Mrs. Walsh nodded and hurried off to fetch Bridget. As she disappeared down the hallway, Alfredo engaged Mr. Walsh in small talk. Viktor remained a silent, watchful presence. After a few minutes, the bedroom door opened and Mrs. Walsh returned, Bridget clinging tightly to her arm.

Alfredo's gaze swept over Bridget with a flash of private disdain. *What an ugly little pig,* he thought. *Honestly, there must be something wrong with Angelo for even wanting to touch her*. Yet, outwardly, he masked his true feelings. Springing to his feet, he summoned a look of deep sympathy and said, his voice gentle and practiced, "Bridget, my dear. *Mi dispiace tanto*. I'm so sorry."

Bridget clung to her mother's arm as if it were a lifeline, her grip tightening. She began to tremble, her bruised, discolored eyes wide and fixed on the tall, blond man now standing in her living room.

Alfredo, meanwhile, held his breath, watching her reaction. *Maybe I shouldn't have brought Viktor with me,* he thought, a flicker of unease crossing his mind. *You'd better keep your mouth shut, Miss Piggy.*

Bridget lay sprawled face down on her bed, the familiar comfort of her room offering little solace after her return from the hospital. Every inch of her body ached, but the deepest pain throbbed in her heart. Her pride, too, felt battered and raw. "You're so stupid," she muttered into her pillow, her voice thick with self-loathing. "It's your fault this happened. You're an idiot."

To make matters worse, her parents had told her yesterday that DMan had been arrested for her attack. Confusion gnawed at her because she hadn't accused him, so why was he in jail? The urge to tell her parents the truth surged within her, but the chilling threats from Angelo and the blond man echoed relentlessly in her mind.

What should I do? Bridget wondered, anxiety twisting inside her. *I never told the police DMan attacked me. Why did they arrest him?*

A knock sounded at her bedroom door, but she ignored it, curling tighter around her pillow. The door creaked open, and her mother's gentle voice drifted in. Bridget rolled onto her side, turning her back to the doorway.

"You have some visitors, baby," Mrs. Walsh said, sitting on the edge of the bed and softly stroking Bridget's hair.

Bridget bolted upright, her heart pounding. "Who is it?"

"Your boss."

The room spun. Bridget clutched her pillow to her chest as if it could shield her from the world. "No, no, no," she whispered, shaking her head in panic.

"He said he has some good news for you," Mrs. Walsh continued, concern etched across her face. "Sweetheart, you're trembling. Do you want to go back to the hospital?"

"No." Bridget squeezed her eyes shut, willing the dizziness to fade. *What is Angelo doing here?* she thought, dread pooling in her stomach.

"I'll just tell Mr. Ferrari you're not ready for visitors," Mrs. Walsh said, rising to leave.

"Wait," Bridget blurted, grabbing her mother's arm. Angelo's threat—*I know where your parents live and I'll kill them*—flashed through her mind.

"You don't look well," Mrs. Walsh said, worry deepening in her eyes. "I'll ask Mr. Ferrari to come back another time."

"No, I have to go and see him," Bridget said, her lips trembling. "I don't want you to get hurt."

"Hurt? Who's going to hurt me?" Mrs. Walsh asked, puzzled, her eyes searching Bridget's face.

Bridget hesitated, then quickly added, "I mean, I don't want to hurt his feelings. It was nice of him to visit."

Mrs. Walsh studied her daughter for a moment, concern plastered on her face. "Okay. Come on, then."

Bridget clung to her mother's arm as the door opened. She drew a deep, shaky breath, forcing her legs to move despite the fear tightening around her throat, just as Angelo's hands had once done. Now, she had to face him again. But as they entered the living room, surprise flashed across Bridget's face. Sitting on the couch was not Angelo, but Alfredo Ferrari. She exhaled in relief, releasing the breath she hadn't realized she was holding.

"Bridget, my dear," Alfredo greeted her, just as her eyes landed on the hulking blond man beside him.

Bridget's grip on her mother's arm tightened, her eyes wide with shock. Alfredo's words sounded distant and muffled, drowned out by the pounding of her heart.

He's here, Bridget thought, panic rising. *He's probably here to kill me and my parents.*

Her knees buckled, and she collapsed forward into her father's arms.

"I've got you," Mr. Walsh said gently. "Come, sit down."

Supported by both parents, Bridget allowed herself to be led to the couch, directly across from the man who had tried to kill her in the hospital.

"I'll get some water," Mrs. Walsh said, hurrying to the kitchen.

"Sweetheart, maybe we should take you back to the hospital," Mr. Walsh said with concern.

Bridget didn't answer. Confused, terrified, and overwhelmed, she sat in silence, unsure what to do next. Should she say something to her parents?

"Are you okay, dear?" Alfredo asked, stepping in front of her.

Bridget glanced up and saw the fixed smile on his lips, but his eyes flashed a silent warning. She quickly looked away, her gaze darting to Viktor, who slowly shook his head. The message was clear for her to stay silent.

Mrs. Walsh returned and handed Bridget a glass of water. Bridget's hand trembled as she lifted the glass, taking a tentative sip before handing it back to her mother.

"You'll be just fine," Alfredo assured her, his tone smooth as silk. He reached out and gently touched Bridget's shoulder. She flinched at his touch. Unfazed, Alfredo returned to the couch and settled in, reclaiming his seat with practiced composure.

"Bridget, I know we don't know each other well," he began, his voice warm and measured. "In fact, I haven't been in the office much these past few months, but I always keep up with my company and the well-being of my employees. It broke my heart when I heard about what happened to you."

Bridget kept her gaze fixed on the floor. Her father squeezed her hand, her mother's arm wrapped protectively around her shoulders.

"I'm so proud of you for naming your attacker," Alfredo continued.

At that, Bridget's head snapped up. She glanced at Alfredo, then at Viktor, catching the warning glint in their eyes before quickly looking away.

"I want you to keep being brave and make sure he gets the punishment he deserves," Alfredo pressed, his words carrying a subtle threat. "Don't change your statement, no matter what. Stay strong."

A shiver ran through Bridget at the menace beneath his encouragement.

"You're a smart young lady," Alfredo went on. "I heard you were accepted to Princeton. That's incredible, isn't it?"

"Yes, it is," Mr. Walsh replied. "But unfortunately, Bridget couldn't get a scholarship, and we just couldn't afford it."

"She'll do just fine at Baruch College," Mrs. Walsh added. "It's a great business school."

Alfredo smiled, his eyes glinting. "Why settle for CUNY when you can go Ivy League? An ambitious young woman like Bridget deserves the best. That's why Ferrari Investment Group is awarding her a full scholarship to Princeton." He leaned back, folding his arms with satisfaction.

The room fell into stunned silence.

Finally, Alfredo broke the tension. "Well, Bridget, what do you say?"

Bridget felt every eye in the room on her. She knew this was a crossroads: accept the bribe disguised as a scholarship, or risk everything by telling the truth.

"Make the right decision now," Alfredo said, reading her hesitation. "Look at your parents, so proud. Don't ruin this moment for them by saying no."

Viktor coughed pointedly into his hand.

"Sweetheart?" Mrs. Walsh leaned in closer to Bridget, her voice gentle but insistent.

Bridget's voice was barely above a whisper, tinged with a strange relief. "But the admissions process is already over. It's too late."

Alfredo smiled, the glint in his eyes sharp and unwavering. "Not for you," he assured her. "The president of Princeton is a very good friend of mine. I made a call, and you're back in."

Mr. Walsh's face lit up with astonishment and gratitude. "That's incredible. Thank you, Mr. Ferrari."

"Yes, thank you, sir," Mrs. Walsh echoed, her happiness bubbling over. "My little girl is going to the Ivy League after all. Bridget, isn't that wonderful?"

Bridget felt the decision slip from her grasp, the moment no longer hers. For a fleeting instant, her thoughts darted to Demarcus, and a surge of guilt shot through her like a bolt of lightning. With her eyes fixed on the floor, she surrendered, sealing his fate. "Thank you, Mr. Ferrari. I'm so grateful for the opportunity to attend Princeton. It's a dream come true."

In that moment, Bridget accepted the scholarship and all the conditions that came with it.

Chapter Eleven

"Form a straight line," screamed the correctional officer, his voice slicing through the humid air. The prisoners snapped into formation in front of the bus, hands still cuffed behind their backs. "You're on our turf now. Got it?" He prowled back and forth, his beet-red face locked in a permanent scowl. "We'll tell you when to eat, when to sleep, and when to scratch your behind."

A chill ran down Demarcus's spine. He bit his trembling lower lip, fighting the urge to cry. Instead, he tried to tune out the officer's booming voice, letting his gaze drift up to the looming brick buildings, each one crowned with coils of razor wire. He was at Rikers Island.

"All right, let's go," shouted another armed officer. He led the way, and the line of detainees shuffled after him. Some fell into the familiar rhythm, but a few first-timers, like Demarcus, shook with fear.

Inside, more correctional officers waited. "I'm going to take off the cuffs, and you step to my right," one of them yelled. "Don't try anything, and there won't be a problem."

Demarcus rubbed his numb wrists as the handcuffs were removed, keeping his head low and his eyes glued to the floor.

The group was herded into another room for processing: forms, signatures, fingerprints, and mugshots. Then came the next order.

"I want everyone to step into that room to your right and remove all your clothes."

Demarcus's head jerked up, shock etched across his face.

"Follow the others," another officer shouted, baton in hand. "Now."

Demarcus looked around. He was the last one left. The unsmiling faces of the officers left no room for hesitation. He walked toward the room.

Inside, the other detainees were already naked, standing awkwardly in a line.

"Step up," yelled the officer conducting the search.

One by one, the detainees approached. The officer ordered each to open his mouth wide, peered into their ears, and ran a gloved hand through their hair. The process was brisk, clinical, and demeaning.

"Okay, assume the position," the officer ordered in a loud voice.

One by one, each detainee turned away, bent over with hands on their knees, exposing themselves to the harsh fluorescent light and the scrutiny of the officers. The air was thick with humiliation and tension.

Demarcus stood frozen, still fully clothed, watching in disbelief as the others endured the invasive strip search. Soon, he was the only one left.

"What are you waiting for?" sneered an officer, stepping closer. "The second coming of Christ?"

Laughter rippled through the room, but the officers' eyes were cold and unyielding.

"Strip. Now," the officer snapped.

Demarcus drew a shaky breath. "I didn't do anything. I'm not supposed to be here."

"Oh, he didn't do anything," the officer mocked, turning to his colleagues. He squared up to Demarcus, who towered over him, and hissed, "If I have to tell you again, you won't like it."

Tears stung Demarcus's eyes, but he fought to hold them back. The pressure was too much. As he slowly removed his shirt, wiping his face with it before tossing it aside, the tears escaped, tracing lines of shame down his cheeks.

"Oh, we've got a little crybaby here," the correctional officer announced with a cruel grin. "Bet he'll be calling for his mama next."

Demarcus scanned the faces of the other officers, searching for a glimmer of sympathy, but found only hard stares and hands resting on batons.

"I said, take off your clothes," the officer roared, raising his baton threateningly.

With trembling hands, Demarcus finished undressing. He stood, naked and exposed, his face burning with embarrassment. Without waiting for further instruction, he walked over to the officer conducting the search.

The officer's hands were rough and deliberate, yanking at Demarcus's ears and hair, searching every inch with unnecessary force. Demarcus stood tall, refusing to flinch or cower.

No more tears, he told himself. *You're not weak. You can survive this.*

Then came the final indignity. "Bend over," the officer ordered.

Demarcus complied, his dignity shredded as the officer's gloved hands invaded his privacy. When it was finally over, he straightened, locking eyes with the officer; defiant, unbroken.

Demarcus dressed quickly in the undergarment, institutional brown uniform, socks, and sneakers that were handed to him. Without a word, he fell in behind the officer, the corridor stretching ahead like the road to damnation. As he passed cell after cell, jeers, whistles, and lewd comments ricocheted off the concrete walls, trailing him like smoke.

"Fresh meat."

"Hello, pretty boy."

"Yummy, yummy."

"I'll see you later, baby."

The officer unlocked the cell door and smirked. "Make yourself at home."

Demarcus lingered at the threshold for a few seconds, then he stepped inside. The door slammed shut behind him, the lock clicking into place.

Four bunks lined the wall, three already occupied, leaving one lower bunk vacant. He drew a steadying breath and forced his voice to sound strong, even as nerves fluttered in his chest.

"What's up?" he called out, surprising even himself with the firmness in his tone.

A short white man sprawled on the lower bunk muttered something under his breath. The two Black men on the upper bunks simply stared, their expressions unreadable.

Demarcus crossed the cell and claimed the empty bunk, sitting stiffly on the edge. The cell was a claustrophobic six-by-eight-foot box, its brick walls closing in, the only amenities a stained toilet and a battered sink in the corner. He glanced at his cellmates, then lay back on the bare mattress, his long legs dangling over the side. The reality of Rikers Island pressed in on him, heavy and inescapable.

He tried not to think about his mother because it hurt too much. Tears threatened, but he blinked them away. This was not a place to show weakness. The other men, seasoned by time and routine, seemed at ease, which only heightened Demarcus's discomfort.

Time crawled. Minutes bled into hours as Demarcus remained motionless, fighting the urge to use the filthy toilet. When his cellmates finally left, presumably for dinner, he sprang up, relieved himself quickly, and recoiled from the nauseating stench. He returned to his bunk, resuming his vigil.

"Lights out," someone shouted, and darkness swallowed the cell.

Demarcus's resolve to stay strong faltered as his heart pounded against his ribs. He rolled onto his side, pressing his back to the wall, every muscle tense. *Would they try to jump me? Can I fight off all three?* He stole furtive glances at the others, certain they were watching, waiting.

The other prisoners chatted quietly in the dark, their voices fading as sleep claimed them. The man above Demarcus began to snore, a deep, rumbling sound. However, Demarcus lay wide awake, refusing to let his guard down. He wondered if it was a trick, if they were only pretending to sleep, waiting for him to drift off so they could attack. But he would not give them the chance.

His eyes grew heavy, but he forced himself to stay alert, sitting up on the narrow bunk, knees drawn to his chest, head nearly touching the bunk above. There he remained, tired, wary, and hungry, until the first pale light of dawn crept into the cell. Demarcus had survived his first night in jail. But how long could he keep this up? How long before his strength, and his hope, ran out?

Chapter Twelve

"I'm willing to do everything in my power to get Demarcus out," Carrick O'Connor declared, his voice brimming with conviction. "That's if you'll give me the chance, Ms. Jones."

"Naomi, please," she corrected gently, leaning back in her chair and studying the public defender assigned to her son's case. Everyone, including Lieutenant Mulligan, had urged her to hire a private criminal defense attorney. Demarcus's future was at stake.

"Naomi, a lot of people think public defenders are lazy, that they don't care about their clients," Carrick said, his tone earnest. "Sure, there are some like that. But that's not me. I became a public defender to do the opposite, to help people, especially those who can't afford expensive lawyers."

They sat together in Carrick's cramped cubicle at the County Public Defender's office, the hum of voices and clatter of keyboards all around them.

Naomi fixed him with a searching look. "Why are you so determined to help my son?"

"Because I believe in his innocence," Carrick replied without hesitation. "Look at Demarcus. He has everything going for him. He's bright, he's got a beautiful girlfriend, and he's on his way to a top university on a full scholarship. Why would he throw all that away?"

Naomi's lips trembled. "Mr. O'Connor, I—"

"Carrick, please."

"Okay. Carrick, I'm looking you straight in the eye and telling you that my son didn't do this. I don't know why that girl said he did, but something is very wrong here. It's been three days since they dragged my boy away from his home and sent him to that hellhole. For what? Nothing!" She pounded her fist on the metal desk, the sound sharp and raw.

A few people nearby glanced over at them.

Carrick leaned in, elbows on the desk, his voice low and urgent. "There has to be a reason this girl identified Demarcus. We need to find out why. More importantly, we need to find out who really did this. Why is she protecting her attacker?"

Naomi shook her head, then replied in her native Jamaican patois, "Chobble nuh set like rain."

Carrick's eyes lit up. "Trouble doesn't give signs like the rain," he translated smoothly. "Problems come unexpectedly." He grinned at Naomi's surprise.

"Let me find out you speak patois," Naomi said, a hint of a smile breaking through her worry.

"Tek time mash ant yuh fin im belly," Carrick replied, laughing as Naomi's mouth dropped open. "It's true. If you take the time to investigate, you'll find the answers you seek. That's exactly what I intend to do for Demarcus."

Naomi studied him for a moment, then asked, "Where did you learn to speak patois?"

Carrick smiled. "My wife is Jamaican. I'm not exactly fluent, but after ten years of marriage, I manage. Plus, she's an investigative reporter for the *New York Post*. That's one of her favorite sayings, and it's become one of mine, too."

"You're full of surprises, Carrick," Naomi replied. "I was born and raised in Jamaica. I came to the USA many years ago, but I'll never forget the proverbs my grandparents used to say. I never forget home."

"My wife's the same way. We were just in Jamaica three months ago for our tenth wedding anniversary."

Naomi's gaze softened. "The last time I was there, Demarcus was just a little boy. I've been meaning to go back with him, but time never really allowed. And now..." Her voice trailed off, heavy with despair.

"You'll get to go back with him, Naomi. I promise you," Carrick said gently. "That's if I'm still Demarcus's lawyer."

Naomi closed her eyes for a moment, then looked at Carrick with resolve. Shutting out all the other voices, everyone offering advice and instructions, she decided to trust herself. "I want you to represent my son," she said. "I've been praying and fasting since this happened, asking God for guidance. There's something about you that puts my spirit at peace."

"Thank you, ma'am." Carrick stood and extended his right hand.

Naomi looked at his hand, then back at him. "I guess we're shaking on it." She took his hand and shook it, sealing the deal.

Carrick clapped his hands together, energy sparking in his eyes. "Now, we've got a mountain to move. First, we fight for Demarcus's bail."

Naomi nodded, her resolve clear.

"The prosecutor's playing hardball," Carrick continued, his voice gaining momentum. "He's almost guaranteed to be the next attorney general, and putting Demarcus away for a crime like this would be a trophy for his campaign. But I'm not letting that happen. I'm going to fight Silver Fox with everything I've got, and I intend to win."

Naomi's agreement was silent but strong.

"I'll need to talk to the detectives, dig into the victim's background, retrace every step Demarcus took that night, and track down any possible witnesses. I'll also see Demarcus myself." Carrick's pen flew across his notebook as he spoke, his mind racing ahead.

"What do you want me to do?" Naomi asked, eager to help.

"I need contact information for Demarcus's girlfriend. He said he was with her that night."

"Yes, I'll get that for you."

"I'll also need to speak with his close friends and even his former basketball coach, Anyone who can vouch for Demarcus's character and provide an affidavit."

"I'll gather their information," Naomi promised. "Lieutenant Mulligan is practically family. Demarcus has been friends with Jerry since kindergarten."

"Perfect," Carrick said, clapping his hands again, drawing a few curious glances from others nearby. "Now we're getting somewhere."

"I'm heading to see my son right after this," Naomi added. "Yesterday, they told me he was still being 'processed.'" She made air quotes around the word, her frustration evident.

Carrick frowned. "Hmm. I'll be stopping by to see him soon myself."

"What do you mean he's not allowed visitors today?" Naomi's voice rang out, filled with anger, her eyes blazing.

"Ma'am, please lower your voice," the Rikers Island guard replied, stepping closer. His pudgy face settled into a deep frown. "As I said before, Demarcus Jones is not receiving visitors today."

Naomi closed her eyes, drawing in a shaky breath. "My son was brought here Monday afternoon. I tried to see him Tuesday and was told he was being processed. I came back Wednesday, and they said he was still being processed. I waited all day until dark, only to hear visiting hours were over." She turned desperate eyes on the guard. "Now it's Thursday, and you're telling me again that Demarcus isn't allowed visitors?"

Other guards and visitors in line turned to watch the scene unfold.

"Lord, please help me," Naomi called out, her voice trembling but loud. "I'm trying so hard, but I can't do this without You."

A female guard approached, her face soft with sympathy. "Why don't you come back tomorrow?" she suggested gently.

Naomi shook her head. "I'm told to come back day after day. What's going on? Why am I being kept from my son? Was he hurt?"

The four guards exchanged uneasy glances.

"Well, there's nothing in the system about him being hurt," the female guard said. "It just says he isn't receiving visitors, and we have to follow the instructions in the system. We don't make the rules. Sorry."

"May I speak to the warden or someone in charge?" Naomi's voice was tired but firm. "I need to know why Demarcus isn't allowed visitors when he's entitled to them."

"The warden isn't available," snapped the pudgy-faced guard. "No visitors means no visitors. That's it."

"No, that's not it," Naomi shot back, her tone steely. "You're denying my son his constitutional rights. Unless Demarcus is hurt or did something to lose his privileges, I have a right to see him."

Just then, Naomi's cell phone vibrated in her handbag. She pulled it out and saw Caro Moynihan, her employer's name, on the screen. Stepping away from the line, she moved to a quieter corner.

"Hi, Caro," Naomi answered, her voice heavy with stress.

"Naomi, have you seen Demarcus? How is he holding up?" Caro's voice was anxious.

"I still haven't seen him," Naomi replied. "They said he's not receiving visitors."

"What do you mean, he's not receiving visitors?" Caro demanded.

In the background, Glen, Caro's husband, chimed in, "What? Why isn't he allowed visitors?"

"I'm going to put you on speaker, okay?" Caro said, her tone tense.

"Naomi, what's going on?" Glen's voice boomed through the phone.

Naomi took a steadying breath. She had worked for Caro's parents, Ernest and Jean Templeton, for more than thirty years—first as a nanny, then as a housekeeper. After the Templetons passed away, Caro and Glen kept Naomi on to care for their four-year-old twin boys. The families were deeply intertwined.

"I was told he's not receiving visitors," Naomi explained. "That's all they'll tell me."

"It's bad enough they falsely arrested Demarcus, and now they're keeping him from seeing his mother?" Caro was angry. "Demarcus would never do what they're saying he did."

Naomi could picture Caro running her hands through her short brown hair, a habit whenever she was upset.

"Okay, calm down, sweetheart," Glen said, trying to soothe his wife. "We'll get to the root of this mess. Naomi?"

"Yes, sir," Naomi replied quietly.

"I know you've decided to use that public defender as Demarcus's lawyer, but I think you should reconsider. I have the number for Alexander O'Connor. You may have heard of him. He's one of the best criminal lawyers in the country. I called in a favor, and he said he'll take Demarcus's case."

"And you know we'll take care of his fee," Caro added. "Naomi, please reconsider. Demarcus needs all the help he can get."

Both Glen and Caro were medical doctors—he, a neurosurgeon, and she, a pathologist. Caro's parents had been wealthy real estate moguls, and as their only child, she inherited their fortune.

"I also have that money your parents left me, Caro," Naomi said softly. "I was saving it for Demarcus's college, but he got that full scholarship, and . . ." Her voice trailed off.

"It'll be all right," Caro assured her. "You've been like a mother to me all my life, Naomi. You know I love you and Demarcus. Glen and I won't stop until he's released from that place and his name is cleared."

"She's right, Naomi," Glen said. "You've taken care of my wife, and now you're taking care of our boys. Please let us help you. See Alexander O'Connor. He's the best lawyer for Demarcus."

Naomi's voice trembled with gratitude. "I know both of you are trying to help my son, and it means the world to me. But you also know I'm obedient to the Holy Spirit. I know in my heart that Carrick is the right lawyer for Demarcus. It's not about money."

Glen's voice came through the phone, steady but urgent. "Naomi, listen—"

"This isn't just some ordinary case of mistaken identity," Naomi interjected. "What's happening to my son is a battle against something dark, something determined to destroy him. I need the Lord's guidance for this fight, so I have to follow what He tells me."

Caro's voice softened. "Okay, Naomi. Ever since I was a little girl, you always followed your heart, and you were always right."

Naomi pressed the phone closer, her words trembling with conviction. "There's something else at work here, Caro. I feel it deep in my soul." She paused, glancing at the growing line of visitors, her resolve hardening. "But I promise you, I'm going to get my son out of this place. I will never give up."

"We'll get Demarcus out," Glen replied. "Just give me the number for this lawyer. He needs to find out why Demarcus is being blocked from seeing visitors."

"I was about to call him myself," Naomi said, quickly giving Glen Carrick's number. "Thank you both for everything. I'm sorry I won't be able to come to work until this is over."

"Don't worry about that," Caro assured her. "We have someone filling in, and the twins are fine. You focus on your son."

Naomi thanked them, ended the call, and looked back at the guards. The line had grown even longer. She watched as other families were allowed through, but not her.

With a heavy sigh, Naomi left the building. Outside, she dialed Carrick's office, but it went to voicemail. She tried his cell phone instead.

"Hello?" Carrick answered after a few rings.

"Carrick, it's Naomi."

"Hi, Naomi. I have the Moynihans on the other line."

"Yes, they're my employers," Naomi explained. "They wanted to talk to you."

"I know. Glen was just telling me he thinks Alexander O'Connor would be a better fit for Demarcus."

"He means well, but I told him you're going to keep representing Demarcus."

"Thank you, Naomi. Let me finish with the Moynihans, and I'll call you right back."

Naomi walked toward the bus stop for the Rikers Island shuttle, her mind racing. As she waited, Carrick called her back.

"Naomi, there's something I think you should know," Carrick said, his voice suddenly serious.

"What is it?"

"Alexander O'Connor is my father."

"Oh, you both have the same surname," Naomi replied. "I never made the connection."

"Few people do," Carrick responded. "He's the wealthy, high-profile, well-known criminal defense attorney, and I'm the underpaid, overworked public defender."

Naomi nodded, absorbing the revelation. "I suppose you two aren't exactly on the best terms?"

"You'd be right," Carrick replied. "My father never forgave me for turning down a place at his successful law firm after I passed the bar. But I chose what felt right, and I became a public defender. I love this work, and I'm dedicated to every case I take."

"Thank you for telling me," Naomi said quietly.

Carrick said earnestly, "That said, my father would be a tremendous asset for Demarcus. The Moynihans were right. He's the best. I won't be offended if you decide to go with him. I want what's best for Demarcus."

Naomi shook her head and said, "I know you care, Carrick. That's why I want you to keep representing my son. I think you're an incredibly good lawyer. Maybe just as good as your father."

Carrick laughed, the tension easing. "Thank you, Naomi. Just so you know, I've already told the Moynihans I'm aware of Demarcus's no-visitor status, and I'm working on it. I was turned away this morning, too, and I'm waiting to speak to the prosecutor."

"You're his lawyer," Naomi said, her voice rising with frustration. "How can they refuse you access? This isn't right."

"No, it's not," Carrick agreed, his tone hardening. "I've never seen anything like this. In this country, it's supposed to be innocent until proven guilty, and everyone is entitled to a lawyer. This is pure rubbish."

"What now?" Naomi pressed.

"The prosecutor hasn't returned my call yet, so I'm heading to his office uninvited. I want to know if he's behind this before I file a complaint with the courts. This is just ridiculous."

Naomi shook her head, exasperated. "Carrick, there's more going on here than meets the eye. Something isn't right."

"I'm starting to agree with you, Naomi. This case gets stranger by the minute." Carrick let out a long breath.

Naomi replied, her words purposeful and strong, "I'm binding all forces working against my son, in the name of Jesus. Demarcus must be set free."

But the forces at work had other plans. In fact, every measure was being put in place to ensure Demarcus would never leave Rikers Island again.

Chapter Thirteen

Carrick barged through the half-open door and closed it behind him.

"Well, hello to you, too." District Attorney Calvin Wilcox leaned back in his chair and propped his feet on the desk. "Why don't you come in?" he said, sarcasm dripping from his voice.

"This is a low move, even for you, Mr. Prosecutor." He leaned forward, his face flushed with anger. "You're denying my client the right to see his attorney now?"

Silver Fox frowned, his gaze sharpening. "What are you talking about?"

"Demarcus Jones. Don't pretend you don't know," Carrick shot back. He sprang to his feet and began pacing, agitation radiating from every step. "You're out to get my client, and you know it. But blocking me from seeing him? Do you really think I'll let you get away with that?"

Many lawyers feared Silver Fox, both in and out of court. His reputation for toughness and his magnetic presence in the courtroom won over jurors and judges, while intimidating his opponents. Carrick O'Connor, however, was not so easily cowed.

Carrick had faced Silver Fox twice before. The older, decorated lawyer had won both times, but Carrick had made him fight for it. Their last battle, defending a man accused of drug trafficking, had been so fierce that Silver Fox had actually offered Carrick a plea deal, an unheard-of concession. If Carrick's main witness hadn't taken the Fifth out of fear, he might have handed Silver

Fox his first loss, something the DA had neither forgotten nor forgiven.

"You're not going to let me get away with anything because I don't know what you're talking about," Silver Fox replied, his tone hardening. He lowered his feet and sat up straight. "And don't ever barge into my office uninvited and try to threaten me again."

Carrick paused, meeting the DA's glare.

"Sit down or get out," Silver Fox snapped.

Carrick hesitated, then sat. He knew that pushing the prosecutor any further would only make things worse for Demarcus. His wife always reminded him that you catch more bees with honey than vinegar, though sometimes, vinegar was necessary.

"Fine. I'm upset. I shouldn't have accused you before hearing your side. Can we talk about Demarcus Jones?"

Silver Fox studied him for a moment, his eyes still blazing. "What about him? He raped and nearly killed a young woman. If you want to make a plea, I might be able to offer him twenty-five to life."

"Twenty-five years to life in prison," Carrick repeated, tilting his head as he studied the DA. He offered a smile that didn't reach his eyes. "That's very generous, but I'm not here to bargain. My client is innocent, and I'll prove it."

"Here we go again." Silver Fox smirked. "My last dance before I become attorney general will be with you. I'm actually looking forward to it."

Carrick felt a chill run through him but shook it off. "I went to visit my client at Rikers Island and was told he's not receiving visitors. Was that your office's doing?"

"I've been practicing law for many years," Silver Fox replied. "I have never bent or manipulated the law, and I'm not about to start now. I stand for justice. Got that?"

Carrick nodded in understanding.

"Everyone is entitled to legal representation," Silver Fox continued. "Why would I want to prevent you from seeing your client?"

Carrick studied him, searching his eyes for any sign of deception. He saw only sincerity. "Then who is responsible? I tried to visit Demarcus earlier at Rikers Island, but they turned me away. Even his mother can't get in to see him."

Silver Fox shook his head. "I don't know, but I intend to find out. This is my case, and I don't appreciate anyone interfering. All this is doing is delaying the process, and I want to resolve it as soon as possible."

"I'm filing a complaint with the courts," Carrick replied firmly. "Now that I know you're not behind this, I hope the ban will be lifted and I'll be able to see my client soon."

Silver Fox nodded, shuffling papers on his desk, signaling that the conversation was over.

Carrick remained still, then leaned in, his voice calm but deliberate. "While I'm here," he said, "I'd also like to discuss bail for Demarcus."

Silver Fox's expression hardened. "No bail. I will oppose it and fight you every step of the way."

"You claim to stand for justice," Carrick told him. "Demarcus didn't commit this crime, and pushing forward with prosecution isn't justice. It's a mistake."

Silver Fox narrowed his eyes. "Then prove it," he replied. "I play to win, but not at the cost of an innocent man. Justice means convicting the person who actually did it."

Carrick leaned in. "I will prove it, to you and to the court. But in the meantime, there's no reason Demarcus should sit behind bars. Let him out on bail while we build the case."

"No bail," Silver Fox said, his voice like ice.

"Come on. This kid has never been in trouble with the law. Where is he going to go?"

"I don't know, and frankly, I don't care to find out."

"Then put an ankle monitor on him," Carrick suggested. "Have him report to the precinct every morning. Surely, he deserves bail."

"He deserves nothing," Silver Fox snapped. "Actually, he deserves to stay at Rikers Island until I send him to prison for the rest of his life. That's what he deserves, and that's what I intend to make happen. Now, I'm busy."

Carrick let out a heavy sigh, realizing just how tough this fight would be. "I'll see you in court," he said, rising and leaving the office.

As he hurried out to the parking lot, Carrick's mind raced. He climbed into his car and drove off, already planning how he would draft the complaint about Demarcus's visitor restriction for the judge.

As he navigated the city streets, Carrick's thoughts churned. If Silver Fox wasn't the one blocking Demarcus from receiving visitors, then who was? Who had the power and audacity to manipulate the judicial system so brazenly? And, most importantly, why?

"No visitors for DBoy, huh?" Alfredo chuckled, crossing his legs in the back seat of his town car as it glided down Fifth Avenue toward Lower Manhattan.

"DMan," Viktor corrected from the driver's seat.

"Whatever. I'm glad our contact came through for us," Alfredo replied, a cunning grin tugging at his lips.

"For a hefty price," Viktor added, glancing at Alfredo in the rearview mirror. "The boy's lawyer will fight it, but it'll take a few days to straighten out this little mistake." He smirked, his eyes sharp. "That gives me some much-needed time to track down all possible witnesses."

Alfredo's gaze narrowed. "It may also arouse suspicion."

"Maybe, but nothing will come back to you," Viktor assured him. "We can't allow him to speak to his lawyer yet. He's going to tell him about the men in front of the deli that night, and I still haven't contacted all of them."

"They could provide an alibi for him," Alfredo said, his voice low.

"Yes, according to my source. I need to get to them first."

"Make it happen," Alfredo told him. "That Lopez woman is packing up and will soon move into her new house. Little Miss Piggy is starting at the Ivy League soon, free of cost, and scared out of her mind. Only these four men are a threat to the plan."

Viktor's tone turned cold. "You don't need to worry too much about them. If they refuse the money, they won't live to say a word."

"Good." Alfredo nodded, satisfaction gleaming in his eyes. "We have too much to lose. That boy must go down for this."

"And he will." Viktor pulled up in front of the Ferrari Investment Group building and double-parked. He stepped out and opened the back door for his boss.

Alfredo climbed out and strode briskly into the building, his cane in hand more for show than support. He passed security without a word and headed straight for the elevator. Moments later, he was on the top floor.

"Good morning, Mr. Ferrari." The new receptionist greeted him with a bright smile.

Alfredo didn't respond or look her way. He continued down the hall, moving past rows of cubicles and employees without so much as a glance, until he reached Angelo's office.

"Hi, Mr. Ferrari. He's on a call," Angelo's assistant said from her desk outside the office. "If you'll allow me, I'll—"

Alfredo seized the door handle, swung the door open, and strode in, slamming it behind him.

Angelo looked up in surprise, the phone pressed to his ear. "That's right," he said into the receiver, then held up a finger to Alfredo, signaling for a minute.

"Get off the phone now," Alfredo ordered brusquely. He strode to the leather couch and sat, facing the floor-to-ceiling window, his gaze drifting toward the New York Stock Exchange building.

"That was one of our biggest clients," Angelo said as he joined his father, crossing his arms and scowling.

"If I were you, I'd lose the attitude," Alfredo snapped. "If our client finds out you're a rapist, he won't be one of our biggest clients for long."

Angelo uncrossed his arms, his face softening. "I said I was sorry about that."

"Sorry?" Alfredo's voice rose. "Do you have any idea how much it's costing me to clean up your mess? Do you realize how vulnerable you've made *my* company?" He jabbed his finger into his own chest for emphasis.

"I appreciate your help, Father." Angelo turned to the window, his voice subdued. "I can't go to prison. I'd rather kill myself first."

Alfredo's head jerked back as if he'd been slapped. "Kill yourself? You'd better watch your mouth, boy." Despite all his son's failures, Angelo was still his only child. "You're not going to prison. Viktor and I are handling it. Just make sure you stay out of trouble." He pointed at Angelo, his glare unwavering.

"I will. Nothing like this will ever happen again."

"You make sure of it," Alfredo said. "Viktor is parking the car and will be up soon. We're going to update you on where things stand. Since that girl was your employee, the police may eventually come to you. It's important you do exactly as we say."

"Thank you, Father," Angelo replied humbly. "I'll do as you say."

"Do you know what it took for me to build all this?" Alfredo swept his hand around the room. "To become one of the most profitable and powerful hedge fund companies in New York?"

Angelo wisely stayed silent.

"This is my sweat and blood," Alfredo shouted. "I won't let anything or anyone destroy my company." He stood and walked to the window, eyes scanning the heartbeat of Wall Street below. "We belong here," he said quietly but firmly. "And here we'll remain."

Behind him, Angelo nodded in agreement.

Desperate times called for desperate measures, and Alfredo's determination to save his company, and his son, knew no bounds.

Chapter Fourteen

Demarcus lay flat on his back, staring at the ceiling of his cell, utterly alone. His cellmates had already left for breakfast, leaving him in silence. It was his third day at Rikers Island, and he hadn't stepped outside his cell since arriving.

He timed his use of the toilet, brushed his teeth, and washed his face only when the others were gone. He drifted in and out of restless naps, but he hadn't eaten a single meal since he got there. The deprivation was taking a heavy toll. His body felt weaker with every passing hour, and his mind was beginning to fray.

Why hasn't Mom come to see me? Where is my lawyer? How long am I going to be trapped here?

These questions circled endlessly in his mind. His stomach rumbled, a sharp pain stabbing his side. His mother would have called it gas, blaming it on the emptiness gnawing at him from within.

"I can't stay in this cell forever," Demarcus muttered, his voice barely more than a whisper. "I need to get something to eat. I need a shower." But as soon as he said it, memories of the taunting and jeers from the other inmates echoed in his mind, and he changed his mind.

"Maybe I'll get sick, and they'll have to send me to the hospital," he whispered, almost hopefully. "Anywhere away from this place would be a blessing."

Another sharp pain twisted in his gut. He pressed his hands against his stomach, his mouth so dry he could barely swallow. “Lord, please . . .” Demarcus paused, the words catching in his throat.

He remembered how he’d been ready for church the morning the detectives came and dragged him away in handcuffs. He’d been going to church since he was a baby, sometimes two or three times a week. His mother had taught him to pray, to read the Bible, to believe.

“God has you in the palm of His hands so no harm can come to you,” his mother had always told him.

“I believed you, Mom,” Demarcus whispered, tears trickling down his face. “So why am I here? Why did God let them take me out of the palm of His hands?”

He rolled over, burying his face in the thin pillow, and wept. His body shook as he pounded his fist on the bed in despair. His wounded sobs were muffled in the pillow as he cried for being jailed for a crime he didn’t commit, for a future that might be spent in prison, for his mother and the hell she must be going through. But he also cried for feeling betrayed and deserted by a God he had always believed in—a God who, he thought, had helped him earn a hard-won scholarship and a promising future, only to snatch it away in the most brutal way. What kind of God would do something like that?

Demarcus didn’t finish his prayer. He wiped his wet face with the back of his hand and tried to ignore the rumblings and hunger pains in his stomach.

“What’s up, man?”

Startled, Demarcus looked up. He was so deep in thought that he hadn’t heard his cellmate returning. Not good.

“What’s good, Ray?” Demarcus replied. The man had introduced himself to Demarcus the day before.

Ray sat on his lower bunk, facing Demarcus. “I can tell you’re a first timer, and this is hard. But you have to eat to keep your strength, or you’re no use to yourself.”

Demarcus sluggishly sat up and looked over at Ray without a word.

"Plus, you're starting to smell." Ray grinned, showing tiny, crooked, yellow teeth. "You're going to need to take a shower."

Demarcus's face remained blank, hiding the storm of emotions inside. Ray was smiling, but his little beady eyes were cold and unsettling. Demarcus felt a chill run down his spine. "Thanks for the lookout."

"No problem. Make sure you get some lunch, and if you want to tag along when I go for my shower, you're welcome. You'll be all right."

Demarcus sized up Ray's frame, about half his size. *I can easily take him if he tries to mess with me,* he thought.

He nodded and replied, "Appreciate it."

Ray got up and left the cell as quietly as he had entered.

As the rest of the morning dragged on, every minute seemed like an hour. The other cellmates returned and were locked in with him. Demarcus was conflicted about what to do. Should he go out and get something to eat and have a shower, or just stay in the cell? When lunchtime came, Demarcus could tell. The cell doors opened, and the prisoners poured out into their different boisterous groups, chatting and laughing as if they were heading to a Christmas feast.

Two of Demarcus's cellmates dashed out, leaving only him and Ray behind.

"You coming or not?" Ray paused by the cell door, glancing back at Demarcus.

Just then, Demarcus's stomach growled, a sharp jab of hunger twisting beneath his ribs. He got up, stumbled forward a couple of steps, then regained his balance and joined Ray at the door.

As they walked side by side down the long hallway—the same one Demarcus had used when he first arrived—he kept his head straight, refusing to look left or right. Curious glances, hard stares, a few smirks, and even some mocking air kisses followed him as he passed.

The dining hall resembled a school cafeteria, with rows upon rows of wooden tables and benches and a sea of brown uniforms. But that's where the similarities ended. Armed correctional officers stood at various posts around the room, their faces set in deep frowns and stony expressions.

Ray joined the long food line, and Demarcus followed, his head still held high. Soon, a brown plastic tray was pressed into his hands, holding two baloney sandwiches, a bag of corn chips, and a flavored drink.

Ray found a seat at a table and patted the space at the end of the bench beside him. Demarcus sat down as indicated, briefly glancing at the faces around the table. He noticed they were all white, except for him. Out of the corner of his eye, he saw other tables grouped by race—Black, Latino, Asian. The same pattern repeated to his left and right. Demarcus took a deep breath. He had heard about the different gangs in jail.

The baloney sandwiches were so hard they could probably chip a tooth, but Demarcus devoured them as if they were gourmet burgers. The juice sliding down his parched throat almost brought tears to his eyes. He ignored the looks he was getting from some of the prisoners, especially those at his own table, where no one spoke. Instead, he felt like the main attraction, the new exhibit on display. The attention made Demarcus even more uncomfortable.

"Excuse me," he mumbled after finishing his meal. He jumped to his feet, wove his way around the tables, and hurried out of the dining room.

In the hallway, Demarcus broke into a jog to get back to his cell. Once inside, he sat down on his bunk, breathing deeply through his mouth, his heart racing. He looked at his hands and noticed they were shaking. There was something deeply unnerving about having all those men staring at him.

Ray returned to the cell about an hour later. "Now you see I was right. You had your meal, and no one bothered you."

Demarcus nodded.

Ray grabbed his towel and soap, then stood in front of Demarcus. "I'm going to take a shower. Are you coming?"

Demarcus hesitated, feeling a nervous flutter in his chest. The thought of showering in jail filled him with dread. He'd heard all the horror stories.

"No one is going to mess with you," Ray assured him. "As long as you're with me and my friends."

That's the problem, Demarcus thought. *I don't trust you or your friends. In fact, I don't trust anyone here.*

"All right, you can shower when you're ready," Ray said, shrugging.

"He's ready now," interrupted a coarse voice.

Demarcus looked up to see his big, burly Black cellmate, the one who slept in the bunk above him. The man had never spoken directly to Demarcus before, but he'd heard the others call him "Blacks."

"You need a shower, dude," Blacks said in a hard, unyielding tone. "Stop acting like a baby and go wash yourself."

Ray chuckled lightly. "Easy, Blacks. You can tell he's new at this."

Anger simmered inside Demarcus, but he kept it in check. He was trapped in this small space with Blacks and didn't want to provoke the older man. Grabbing his towel, Demarcus left the cell.

He paused in the hallway, waiting for Ray to catch up.

"Don't worry," Ray said, giving Demarcus a playful slap on the back.

As they stepped into the communal bathroom, laughter boomeranged off the tiled walls. Steam mingled with the stench of rust and sweat. Naked bodies crowded the space, water gushing from corroded pipes, voices rising in casual chatter. A few inmates turned to stare at Demarcus. He didn't flinch. His face was locked in a scowl, his "don't mess with me" look worn like armor.

Ray peeled off his jumpsuit and underwear in one fluid motion, standing bare without a hint of hesitation.

Demarcus lingered. Black's voice echoed in his head. *Stop acting like a baby and go wash yourself.* He tugged off the jumpsuit, letting it slump to the floor like Ray's, but kept his underwear on. That was the line he wouldn't cross.

He strode to an empty shower, his tall, muscular frame towering above most of the others. The catcalls started. Conversations dimmed. A jittery energy churned in his chest, as if a frog were somersaulting inside him. His hand trembled slightly as he reached up to turn on the shower, but his face stayed hard.

Demarcus scrubbed his hair fast, determined to get in and out. Still, the water, cool, clean, and long overdue, felt like a blessing. As it streamed over his lean, mocha-colored skin, he felt the weight of eyes on him. The man at the next shower didn't bother to look away. His stare was bold, unblinking. Demarcus rinsed off in a rush, the heat of humiliation crawling up his spine. He grabbed his uniform, dressed quickly, and glanced at Ray, who was already pulling on his clothes. They didn't speak, just walked out, side by side, and returned to their cell, the tension of the moment still clinging to Demarcus like a second skin.

"I bet you're feeling better." Ray grinned at him, then went to sit on his bunk.

Demarcus nodded and replied, "Yes, I am. Thanks, man."

"It's all good," Ray said. "You just have to try to make the most of it until you get out of here."

"Yeah."

"Well, I'm going to meet up with my friends for a few minutes. You're welcome to join us."

"Thanks, but I'm going to chill here."

"Maybe next time," Ray said, then left the cell.

Demarcus lay back on his bunk, a heavy sadness settling over him. *Where are you, Mom? I know you wouldn't leave me here to rot. What's going on?* He stared at the ceiling, the silence pressing in, his thoughts swirling with worry and longing.

Unbeknownst to Demarcus, his mother was locked in a battle beyond his comprehension.

Chapter Fifteen

"Your Honor, I have no knowledge whatsoever of any visitor ban placed on Demarcus Jones," District Attorney Calvin Wilcox declared, settling back in his chair and shooting Carrick, who sat beside him facing the judge, a frosty glare.

"Your Honor, I never accused the prosecutor," Carrick responded, turning to the judge. "In my complaint, I made it clear that the prosecutor and I spoke, and he denied any involvement."

"That's correct, Counselor," Judge Mambo replied, nodding. "That's also why I made time for this meeting so quickly. I'm extremely interested in discovering who issued this order to violate Mr. Jones's constitutional rights, and for what reason."

"Mr. Wilcox," the judge continued, addressing Silver Fox, "you're here as the prosecutor on this case to help us find the underlying cause of this. I'm preparing an order for the warden at Rikers Island to investigate this situation as well. Mr. Jones must be allowed visitors, especially his attorney, without delay."

"I agree, Your Honor," Silver Fox replied. "I'll work with the counselor to resolve this matter as quickly as possible. I'm eager to move this case forward and secure a conviction."

"Your Honor!" Carrick leapt from his seat. "The prosecutor is already declaring my client guilty, and we haven't even gone to trial."

"Counselor—" Judge Mambo began.

"He's even denied my client bail," Carrick pressed on, his voice rising.

"Counselor." Judge Mambo leaned forward, his face showing clear disapproval at being interrupted twice. "Let's address these issues one at a time."

Carrick, still fuming, sat down at the edge of his chair.

"Now, let's remember we are in session," Judge Mambo said, glancing at the court stenographer.

"Apologies, Your Honor," Carrick said, regaining his composure. "If it pleases the court, I'd like to discuss bail for my client."

"Your Honor, the prosecution strongly opposes bail," Silver Fox declared, his tone unwavering. "Defense counsel may believe I'm simply chasing another victory or boosting my political ambitions, but my commitment is to justice. That has always been the core of my career." He fixed Carrick with a long, pointed stare.

"This was a heinous crime, and the victim deserves justice," he continued. "The reasons for my opposition to bail were made clear at the arraignment and are on record. The defense has not presented any new evidence that would warrant reconsideration."

Carrick interjected, frustration sharpening his words. "Well, perhaps if I'd been allowed to see my client, I could have gathered the evidence you need. But—"

"Enough," Judge Mambo interrupted, raising a hand to halt the exchange. "Mr. O'Connor, you are to visit your client at Rikers tomorrow morning. I'll ensure the warden receives the court's order. If there are any further issues, notify us immediately."

"Thank you, Your Honor," Carrick replied, his voice more measured. "To prevent this from happening again, the best course is to grant Mr. Jones bail. House arrest or any other restrictions you deem necessary would be acceptable."

"I stand with the prosecutor," Judge Mambo responded. "Please submit an appeal for bail when you have sufficient evidence for the court to reconsider. Is there anything else?"

Both Carrick and Silver Fox shook their heads.

"Very well," Judge Mambo concluded. "Enjoy the rest of your evening."

As Carrick and Silver Fox exited the judge's chambers and stepped into the hallway, they faced each other, Carrick looking up, Silver Fox looking down, both locked in a silent battle of wills.

"I can't wait to wipe that smirk off your face when I beat you," Carrick said, his voice low and fierce. "Do you think you're God?"

Silver Fox's grin widened, revealing perfect white teeth. "That's a matter of opinion."

"Don't worry. You'll get my opinion soon," Carrick shot back, storming off as Silver Fox's laughter echoed down the corridor behind him.

"I told you," Lieutenant Mulligan exclaimed, clapping his hands together. "Trevor Richards said he saw Demarcus that night, just a few minutes before midnight. After that, he helped Ms. Lopez, his neighbor, carry her bags home. Isn't that right around the time the girl was attacked?"

Detectives Rich and Hanes, seated in the lieutenant's office, exchanged glances before turning their attention back to him.

"And guess what?" Lieutenant Mulligan continued, pausing for effect as he looked from one detective to the other. "There were three other men playing dominoes with him who also saw Demarcus."

Detective Rich cleared his throat. "We'll go talk to Trevor, and we'll speak with the other three men as well."

"I have Trevor's information right here, along with the names of the other men," Lieutenant Mulligan said, holding out a piece of paper. Detective Rich reached over and took it. "I knew Demarcus was innocent. I just knew it."

"We have a meeting now with a possible witness on another case, but we'll follow up on this right after," Detective Rich said, holding up the paper.

"I'm not trying to tell you how to do your job," Lieutenant Mulligan added, his tone earnest. "I hope you know that. But I'm going to do everything I can to help Demarcus. I have that much faith in his innocence."

"We appreciate your help, Lieutenant," Detective Rich replied. "Right, Hanes?"

Detective Hanes nodded, stood up, opened the door, and walked out of the office.

"She's upset that I'm involved," Lieutenant Mulligan remarked to Detective Rich.

Detective Rich closed the door and replied, "I've worked with you for many years, Lieutenant. I've learned a lot from you, including when to trust your instincts."

Lieutenant Mulligan nodded thoughtfully.

"There's something I meant to run by you," Detective Rich continued, holding up the paper his boss had just handed him. "And with this, I think now is a good time."

Lieutenant Mulligan folded his lips and fixed his gaze on Detective Rich.

"The victim didn't exactly say Demarcus attacked her," Detective Rich pointed out.

"Excuse me?" Lieutenant Mulligan said, his voice rising in surprise.

"She was mumbling 'DMan' when she was being taken to the hospital. Hanes asked her if he was the one who attacked her, and she kept saying 'DMan.' She repeated it a few times, or so I was told."

"When you interviewed her at the hospital, she didn't confirm what she said in the ambulance," Lieutenant Mulligan observed, his tone sharp.

"No, she refused to talk to us," Detective Rich admitted.

"I read the report, and it stated the victim identified Demarcus Jones as her attacker," Mulligan pressed, his eyes narrowing.

"Hanes wrote up the report and is convinced that's what she meant," Rich replied, glancing away.

"Let me see if I understand this correctly," Lieutenant Mulligan said, his voice rising with incredulity. "You have a traumatized, brutalized victim, slipping in and out of consciousness, muttering a nickname before anyone even asked her who attacked her. Then, when she was finally asked to confirm who did it, she refused to answer. Is that right?"

Detective Rich nodded, the weight of the mistake settling between them.

"You and Hanes charged Demarcus with this crime without a positive identification from the victim once she was coherent. Yet, you told me and the prosecutor that the victim said he was the one who attacked her."

"Hanes said she asked her a few times in the ambulance, and she kept saying that nickname," Rich explained, his voice growing quieter.

"She was just beaten and raped," Lieutenant Mulligan exploded, his fist slamming onto the desk. "You need her to confirm after she's received medical attention, and she didn't."

"I know you're upset, but—" Rich began.

"Upset? An innocent boy was charged with a crime he didn't commit. And for what? Because you're trying to close a case?" Mulligan's voice thundered through the office.

Just then, a knock interrupted the tension.

"Not now," Lieutenant Mulligan barked.

"It's Hanes," came the voice from outside.

Detective Rich opened the door, and Detective Hanes stepped in, her face tense with apprehension.

"What's going on?" she asked, glancing between the two men. "I was waiting for Rich and heard loud voices in here."

"Detective Hanes, I want you to tell me again how and when the victim identified Demarcus Jones as her attacker," Lieutenant Mulligan demanded, his tone icy. "I want every single detail, right now."

Detective Hanes looked at her partner, then sighed heavily. "She was saying his nickname," she admitted quietly. "I asked if that was the person who attacked her, and she said his nickname again."

"I see. And she confirmed that at the hospital, didn't she?" Lieutenant Mulligan's voice was sharp.

"No, she didn't," Detective Hanes replied quietly, lowering her head.

Detective Rich turned to Hanes. "He deserves to know, especially now that we have this latest information. As the senior detective, I take full responsibility for how this case has been handled."

Lieutenant Mulligan's anger faded into disappointment. "Is this what detective work has come to?" He shook his head. "And don't think I've forgotten your interview tactics. There will be a full investigation into that as well. For now, let's focus on the facts. Follow every lead until we find the person responsible."

"We're on it, boss," Detective Rich assured him.

Lieutenant Mulligan nodded. "I hope we can gather enough evidence to give Demarcus's lawyer grounds to appeal his bail while we continue investigating. He doesn't belong in Rikers, not for this."

***

Detectives Hanes and Rich exited the office, their faces clouded with concern.

"Officers Thomas and Henry will handle that interview for us," Hanes told him. "We can head straight to Trevor's house now."

Rich glanced at his partner. "I know you're upset, but he deserves to know the truth."

Hanes let out a shaky breath. "Honestly, I feel sick to my stomach. Did we just send an innocent boy to Rikers? Was I so focused on closing this case that I ignored the possibility we were wrong?"

Rich's voice softened. "It's on me, too. I've been doing this for years. I should have insisted we trace Demarcus's actions right up to the time of the incident."

"I told you she said he did it. So, it's on me," Hanes replied, her voice barely above a whisper.

Rich shook his head. "When she didn't confirm it again in the hospital, when she was fully coherent, I should have realized something was off. But let's not play the blame game. We have a chance now to uncover the truth. Let's focus on what we do best." He paused by the car door, looking Hanes in the eye.

"We kept that boy for hours without food or water. Even after he asked for a lawyer, we kept drilling him." Hanes's voice trembled, her eyes glistening. "I'll probably be suspended for this. Honestly, I'll be lucky if I'm not fired."

Rich nodded grimly. "We're in hot water, especially since he's so close to the lieutenant. Maybe if we solve the case, it'll help our cause."

"Maybe," Hanes muttered, worry etched across her face. She walked around to the passenger side, opened the door, and slid into the seat.

Rich climbed in behind the wheel. "Right now, our priority is to catch a rapist and an attempted murderer. We'll deal with the fallout later."

He started the engine and navigated the Bronx streets with practiced ease, taking shortcuts only a native would know. Within minutes, they arrived at Trevor Richards's house, where a teenager stood waiting at the gate.

Rich parked, and the detectives approached.

"Detectives Rich and Hanes?" the boy called out, anxiety in his voice.

"Yes. Trevor?" Rich replied.

Trevor nodded. "Yeah. The lieutenant just called and said you were coming. This is really messed up. How could you arrest DMan for something like that?" His voice rose, anger and disbelief mixing. "DMan would never do something like that. I saw him that night, coming from his girlfriend's house."

"Okay, let's calm down," Rich said, holding up a hand. "I know you're upset, but can we talk inside?"

Trevor's eyes narrowed with anger, his jaw clenched tight. Without a word, he stormed into the house, the detectives trailing behind. He dropped onto the couch, fists balled in his lap, while the detectives settled across from him.

"You sent my boy to Rikers?" Trevor's voice trembled, thick with emotion. "DMan was headed to Stanford on a full scholarship. You've destroyed his life, and for what?" Tears welled in his eyes, and his hands shook as if he might strike out at any moment.

Detective Hanes let out a heavy sigh. "If we made a mistake, we're going to fix it. That's why we're here."

Trevor shot her a glare. "If? You did make a mistake," he shouted. "Demarcus could have any girl he wanted, but he loves Marisol. He'd never rape anyone."

"The victim called his name, and when we asked if he did it, she repeated it," Hanes replied, her tone measured. "We took that as a positive identification."

Trevor shook his head, incredulously. "If Bridget Walsh said that, she's lying. I talked to Ms. Naomi, and she told me it was Bridget. Why would she lie about DMan? He even helped her at school."

Detective Rich leaned forward, curiosity piqued. "Demarcus helped Bridget? How?"

Trevor's voice softened as he explained, "Some girls used to bully her. One day, DMan saw it and made them apologize. He told them if it happened again, he'd tell everyone what they were doing to Bridget. They never bothered her after that."

The detectives exchanged a meaningful glance.

"Does that sound like someone who would rape and try to kill her?" Trevor pressed, folding his arms and leaning back, defiant.

Detective Hanes cleared her throat and flipped open her notebook. "We certainly have a lot to look into. Trevor, can you walk us through the night of the crime when you saw Demarcus?"

Trevor recounted the events of that night. "We all saw him—Mr. Afia, Jimmy, Tom, and me. We chatted for a bit and made plans to get together soon. Then he noticed Ms. Lopez struggling with her bags. DMan went over, took them from her, and walked her home. Tell me, when did he have time to rape and beat someone, huh?" Trevor leaned forward, arms crossed, challenging them. "You tell me that."

Detective Rich asked, "You said this was around 11:55 p.m.?"

Trevor nodded. "Yeah. I remember because DMan checked his watch and said he had five minutes to get home. His mom had him on curfew."

Detective Rich's tone shifted, more respectful now. "This is useful information, Trevor. Thank you. Do you know the full names of the other three men, and where we can find them?"

"Jimmy Mason's my friend. I've got his number," Trevor replied, pulling out his phone. "Tom, I don't know his last name or number, but he works at Golden Krust on Gun Hill Road, right by the five train. Mr. Afia's always on the corner. We play dominoes there most weekends." He scrolled through his contacts and read off Jimmy's number as Detective Hanes jotted it down.

Trevor's voice grew urgent. "Are you going to get Demarcus out of that place? You heard me. He didn't do it. Bridget is lying."

"We're working on it, Trevor," Detective Rich assured him. "Once we speak to the other three men, we'll take this back to Demarcus's lawyer, and he'll handle it from there."

"You've ruined his life." Trevor shook his head, his voice tight with disbelief. "A brother on his way to doing big things, and you just messed that up. It's a shame."

"We were just doing our job," Detective Hanes replied, her tone edged with irritation. Having her investigative skills questioned by her boss was one thing, but hearing it from a teenager stung in a different way.

Trevor's eyes flashed. "Oh, yeah? Then why are you only talking to me now, after I contacted the lieutenant when Jerry called me crying about what happened to DMan?"

"We'll get to the bottom of this, Trevor." Detective Rich stood up, his voice steady. "Thanks for the information. We'll be in touch." He walked out, with Detective Hanes and Trevor following him to the gate.

At the car, Detective Rich paused and turned back to Trevor, who lingered at the gate. "Just so you know,

Demarcus's lawyer may want to speak with you and the other men too."

"Is he the Asian dude my mother said was here earlier this morning to see me?" Trevor asked.

Detective Rich frowned, stepping closer. "What Asian dude?"

"I don't know. I thought he was probably a detective or something."

Rich glanced at Hanes, concern showing on his face. "That's definitely not Demarcus's lawyer," he said to Trevor. "And we are the detectives assigned to this case."

"He told my mother he wanted to speak to me about DMan's case. But Jerry and I were over at DMan's house, checking up on Ms. Naomi."

"Did he leave a name with your mother?" Detective Hanes asked.

"No, just that he'd be back," Trevor replied. "My mom said she left for work shortly after he drove off, and as she was stopped at the red light by Golden Krust, she saw him coming out. Looks like he was trying to find Tom, too."

"Say what?" Detective Rich's face tightened with apprehension.

"She said he went to a white sports car parked out front, and a huge blond man got out and started talking to him. My mother said he looked like that actor from *Universal Soldier*. You know, the big dude."

"Huh?"

"Anyway, she figured that was his partner and assumed they were investigating the case."

Detective Hanes leaned in, her tone sharp. "You're sure you don't know these men or why they were looking for you?"

Trevor shot her a defiant look. "You're the investigators, so investigate, like you should have done before you locked up my friend." With that, he spun on his heel and stormed back into the house, slamming the door behind him.

Detective Hanes exhaled, tension crackling in the air. "Something is off. Why is this man so determined to track down our witnesses?"

Detective Rich met her gaze, his voice low and urgent. "That's a very good question and one we need to answer immediately."

"I only made contact with one of the men at his apartment," Viktor said, glancing from Alfredo to Angelo. "His name is Baako Afia."

The three men gathered in Angelo's luxurious SoHo apartment, the city's energy humming just beyond the windows.

"Afia is an illegal immigrant from Ghana. I also found evidence he's dealing drugs, nothing major, just some marijuana," Viktor continued, scrolling through notes on his phone.

"Is that enough to make him take our deal?" Angelo asked, his voice tight with anticipation. "Will he say he never saw that boy that night?"

Viktor's lips curled into a thin smile. "Even better. Mr. Afia is already on his way to Arizona, carrying a generous sum to keep him comfortable for a long time. If we ever need him to testify, he'll be more than willing to say whatever we want."

Alfredo nodded, though his tone remained unimpressed. "That's a start, but there are still three too many alibis left."

Viktor scanned his phone. "Tom is off work today, but my contact is tracking down his home address. Jimmy is working construction upstate with his uncle, and I have someone waiting for him to return to the Bronx. The last one is Trevor Richards, the boy's close friend and former teammate. He wasn't home this morning, and his mother refused to give us his whereabouts or his cell number. We'll try his house again this evening."

Angelo's frustration flared. "What if the police get to them before we do? Why did it take so long to reach these people?" He fell silent as Alfredo shot him a withering glare.

Viktor's voice sharpened. "We're moving as quickly as possible, and as thoroughly as we can."

Alfredo fixed Viktor with a hard stare. "None of these people have seen you, and nothing will trace back to either of us, correct?"

Viktor nodded, his expression resolute. "Absolutely. There will be no loose ends."

Alfredo folded his arms, letting out a guttural grunt. His displeasure was unmistakable. The lack of progress in silencing Demarcus's potential alibis gnawed at him.

Suddenly, Viktor's phone vibrated. He glanced at the screen, answered with a curt "Yes?" and listened intently for a few seconds. Without another word, he ended the call.

Alfredo's eyes narrowed. "What now?"

Viktor checked his watch. "A judge just issued an order that Demarcus is to be allowed visitors immediately. Visiting hours are over for today, but I'm sure his lawyer will be there first thing tomorrow."

Alfredo erupted, cursing in Italian. The outburst echoed through the room.

"We knew this was coming," Viktor said, his tone even. "I was hoping for another day or two, but this public defender is more persistent than I expected."

"Find out everything you can about him," Alfredo snapped. "If it comes to it, see if he can be bought. You know how little those public defenders make. Most don't really care."

Viktor nodded, but his voice was measured. "I'll look into it, but that should be a last resort. If he refuses, he'll have enough to take to a judge, and he could claim someone tried to bribe him to betray his client. That might be enough to create reasonable doubt, and then they'll start looking for the real culprit." Viktor's gaze flicked to Angelo, who shifted uncomfortably on the couch.

"You're right," Alfredo conceded with a heavy sigh. "What about that Lopez woman?"

"She's already left her apartment," Viktor replied. "She's staying at a small hotel in Yonkers for now, but she'll be moving into the house soon. As you know, the house is in the name of one of my people. He bought it for cash a few years ago and is selling it to us for a hefty profit."

Alfredo scoffed. "At least twice what it's worth."

Viktor continued. "He'll wait until the case is closed, then transfer the title to Ms. Lopez for her help with this little matter."

Alfredo nodded his approval. "Now you just need to reach those men before the lawyer or the detectives do."

Viktor clapped his hands together, stood up, and declared, "I'm on it."

Chapter Sixteen

"How are things going?" Ray asked as he and Demarcus sat together in their cell. "Much better, huh?"

They had just returned from breakfast, where Demarcus sat with Ray's group, eating his oatmeal, milk, and two slices of bread in silence.

"I just need to get out of here," Demarcus replied, his voice low.

"You will. But until then, stick with me and my people, and no one will mess with you. You see that, right?"

"Yes," Demarcus said. He still attracted some unwelcome attention, but no one had dared approach him directly. "Thanks for looking out."

"It's nothing," Ray replied. "My second son is about your age. If he were ever in a place like this, I'd want someone to watch his back, too."

"Appreciate it." Demarcus closed his eyes, ending the conversation and retreating into his thoughts. He daydreamed about his glory days on the basketball court, fun dates with Marisol, his mother's delicious Jamaican cooking, and the future he hoped for at Stanford. Those memories were all that kept him sane in jail.

The day dragged on, just like the ones before. Demarcus barely moved from his bunk until Ray came to get him for dinner. Again, he sat with Ray and his friends, eating the bland meatloaf in silence.

That evening, the cell block buzzed with loud, animated conversations as Demarcus headed to the showers.

He and Ray found two empty stalls beside some of Ray's friends, and Demarcus began to wash, still wearing his underwear.

The noise and laughter faded into the background as Demarcus closed his eyes, letting the warm water carry him away from his grim reality. A few tears slipped down his cheeks, but the running water quickly washed them away. He wasn't sure how long he stood there, lost in thought, but when he finally opened his eyes, he realized the shower room was eerily quiet. He glanced around, but he was alone.

A chill ran through him. Where was everyone? Where was Ray? He quickly shut off the water and rushed to where he'd left his uniform, only to find it missing. Panic tightened in his chest, and he felt as if a ball had lodged in his throat.

Demarcus hurried toward the exit, heart pounding, then stopped abruptly. Standing before the exit, Ray and five of his friends blocked Demarcus's path. The oldest of the group, clearly the leader, stepped forward. He was of medium height, with short, salt-and-pepper hair receding at the sides.

"Demarcus, is it?" he asked, his tone sly. "Or do you prefer DMan?"

Demarcus stayed silent, his eyes moving over the hardened faces around him, each glance tightening the knot in his gut as he weighed his odds.

"I'm Cyclone," the leader announced, moving closer. His prominent brown front teeth gave him a mean bunny-rabbit look. "You're a very handsome young man, Demarcus."

Demarcus instinctively stepped back, fists clenched. "Stay away from me," he growled, voice tense. "Ray, what's going on?" His gaze pleaded with Ray for an explanation.

Ray only grinned, moving to stand beside Cyclone. "Looks like the boss has taken a liking to you. He wants you," Ray said, spreading his hands as if the situation were perfectly ordinary.

Cyclone's grin widened, his eyes glinting with malice. "And whatever Cyclone wants, Cyclone gets. I want you, Demarcus." The threat in his voice was unmistakable.

"Over my dead body," Demarcus shot back, retreating further.

Cyclone laughed, the sound echoing off the tiled walls. "Well, that can be arranged." The others joined in, their laughter bouncing around the room. "One way or another, I'm going to have you, Demarcus. The choice is yours."

Panic surged through Demarcus. "Help! Help!" he shouted, his voice reverberating through the showers. "Somebody help me!"

Cyclone and his men only laughed harder.

"No one can hear you," Ray sang mockingly. "And even if they do, they know better than to interrupt the party. So, let's get it on." He rubbed his hands together, anticipation sparkling in his eyes.

"You're sick and disgusting," Demarcus spat, pressing his back against the cold tile. He raised his fists, ready to fight.

Cyclone closed the distance, stopping just inches from Demarcus. "You think you can escape all of us?" he sneered.

"Stay away from me. I'm warning you." Demarcus's fists trembled, but he held them high.

Cyclone's gaze roamed over Demarcus's wet, muscular frame. He licked his lips, then turned to his men. "What do you think?"

"I'm after you," Ray replied.

"I'm next," another man chimed in.

"Says who? I'm up before you," a third argued.

Demarcus squeezed his eyes shut as the prisoners argued over who would take their turn with him. He realized with chilling clarity that he was utterly alone, surrounded by predators, and running out of options. *Is this really how it ends?* he wondered, despair flooding his thoughts. *What did I do to deserve this? What did my mother do to deserve this pain? Why, Lord?*

Without realizing it, Demarcus began to pray silently, bracing himself for the worst. There was no way he would let these men violate him while he was alive. No way.

Suddenly, Demarcus felt a hand where it shouldn't be, and his eyes snapped open, alarm flashing across his face. Instinct took over, and he landed a punch squarely between Cyclone's eyes, then followed with a powerful kick to the groin.

Cyclone collapsed like a bag of rocks.

Ray and the others, enraged, rushed at Demarcus like a pack of wolves. Fueled by anger and disgust, Demarcus's fist connected with Ray's mouth, sending blood spraying as Ray stumbled backward. But then a sharp pain exploded in Demarcus's head as another prisoner struck him, followed by a brutal kick to his side.

Hurt but undeterred, Demarcus fought back, punching and kicking wildly. Sometimes he landed blows, sometimes he missed. But five against one was never a fair fight. The barrage of fists and feet began to overwhelm him. Blood filled his mouth, and his vision blurred, but he refused to give up.

Ray jabbed Demarcus twice in the stomach, doubling him over in pain. Another prisoner seized the moment and slammed a fist into the back of Demarcus's head, sending him crashing to his knees. Agony shot through his body, sharper than anything he'd ever felt.

"Get him up," Cyclone snarled, dragging himself off the floor, fury blazing in his eyes.

The men yanked Demarcus to his feet and slammed him against the wall, pinning his arms and legs wide.

"You hit me," Cyclone growled, baring his teeth as he advanced. "Nobody hits Cyclone." He slapped Demarcus hard across the face, drawing a scream. "Yeah, scream. I'm about to make you scream even louder." Cyclone yanked down his jumpsuit and underwear, exposing himself.

Demarcus struggled desperately, but the men held him fast, pinning him against the cold tile wall. He was trapped, powerless against Cyclone and his crew.

"Turn him around," Cyclone hissed. "I'm going to teach you a lesson you'll never forget."

Rough hands yanked Demarcus's underwear down. He screamed through his split lips, the sound echoing off the shower walls.

"Yeah, keep screaming," Cyclone taunted, slapping Demarcus hard across his bare skin.

Demarcus's voice rose, raw and desperate. "No! No!"

"Oh, yes," Cyclone growled in his ear, pressing his chest against Demarcus's back.

Demarcus felt Cyclone's arousal brush against him and, in that moment, closed his eyes in defeat. This was it.

Chapter Seventeen

Cyclone's foul breath hovered over Demarcus's face as he sneered, "Ready or not, here—"

A thunderous voice erupted, slicing through the tension like a lion's roar. "Enough!"

Instantly, the entire room froze. Cyclone's heavy breathing shifted from anticipation to fear. Ray and the other prisoners dropped their hands and stepped away, releasing Demarcus as if he were suddenly radioactive.

Demarcus, legs trembling like overcooked spaghetti, collapsed to the floor, sobbing in relief and exhaustion. Footsteps thundered across the tiles, and Cyclone was yanked away from him as if he weighed nothing.

"You like to rape young boys, huh?" demanded the same commanding voice.

Turning his head, Demarcus caught a glimpse through one swollen eye. A group of at least fifteen Black Muslim prisoners, each wearing a crisp white taqiyah, had surrounded Cyclone and his crew. Despite the leader's small stature, his presence filled the room, his voice booming with authority and righteous fury. Cyclone and his men, moments ago so menacing, now visibly shook with fear, their bravado shattered.

The Muslim leader squared up to Cyclone, his presence commanding the space despite his being slightly shorter. "It's scumbags like you I detest," he declared with contempt. "You prey on young men who are already in a bad situation, instead of protecting them or teaching them the right way."

His followers glared at Cyclone and his crew, their eyes burning with moral anger.

"Allah frowns on the corruption of mankind," the leader continued.

Cyclone, suddenly sounding like a chastised child, tried to protest, "Listen, I don't—"

"Shut up," the leader thundered, delivering a sharp slap across Cyclone's face that snapped his head back. "I am speaking now."

Cyclone rubbed his cheek, glaring but remaining silent.

"Get yourself decent and cover up that little thing," the leader ordered, casting a look of disdain at Cyclone's exposed body.

Cyclone's face flushed crimson, not just from the slap. He shot the leader a venomous look but quickly pulled up his jumpsuit.

Despite the pain and humiliation still throbbing through his body, Demarcus managed to make a small, satisfied smile as he watched the scene unfold.

"We crush our enemies, knowing that Allah stands with the righteous," the Muslim leader announced. He strode toward Demarcus, then paused, turning his back to Cyclone and the others. With a snap of his fingers, chaos erupted in the shower room.

Demarcus's mouth dropped open as the Muslim prisoners descended on Cyclone, Ray, and the other four men. Their cries of pain echoed off the walls, a twisted music to Demarcus's ears after being the one suffering only moments before.

"Murder!" Ray screamed from the floor as kicks rained down on him.

"You're dead," Cyclone shouted, pinned against the wall as blows landed from every direction. "I swear—" His body went limp, and he collapsed, unconscious.

Just as suddenly as it had begun, the beating ended. Cyclone and his men lay battered on the floor, three of them knocked out cold.

"Here, let me help you up," the leader said, extending a hand to Demarcus.

Demarcus looked up, saw the outstretched hand, and accepted it. The leader pulled him to his feet. One of the men handed Demarcus a jumpsuit, and only then did he remember his nakedness. Embarrassed, he quickly slipped into the jumpsuit, wincing as pain flared with each movement.

"I'm Salaam Alihammad." The Muslim leader introduced himself, his voice steady and authoritative. "These are my brothers in the faith." The men around him nodded in silent solidarity.

Salaam hesitated, biting his lip as he glanced at Demarcus. "Did he . . .?" he began, unable to finish the question.

"No," Demarcus replied quietly, his voice rough but grateful. "Thank you."

Relief washed over Salaam's face. "I was afraid we were too late. We give Allah praise." He nodded to two of his companions, who each took hold of Demarcus's arms and gently helped him toward the exit.

As they stepped into the main area, Demarcus noticed the eyes of many prisoners fixed on them. He wondered if everyone had known what was about to happen to him, and if so, why no one had intervened.

Suddenly, three correctional officers rushed over, their faces tense. "Salaam, what happened?" one demanded, clearly flustered.

"Why don't you tell me?" Salaam shot back, his tone sharp. "Where were you when my young brother here was being beaten and nearly raped?"

Another officer turned to Demarcus. "Are you okay?"

Salaam answered for him, his gaze icy. “Does he look okay to you? Wait until I speak with the warden.”

“Come on,” a correctional officer said, reaching for Demarcus. “Let me take you to get checked out.”

“I’m fine,” Demarcus snapped, anger rising in his chest. Where had these correctional officers been when he was screaming for help? He didn’t trust them to take him anywhere.

“The filth in there,” Salaam said, gesturing toward the shower room, “needs your help. My brother here will be all right.” With that, he led the way, Demarcus flanked on both sides by the men who had saved him.

They reached Salaam’s cell, and Demarcus hesitated for a moment before stepping inside. He reasoned that if these men had wanted to hurt him, they wouldn’t have just rescued him.

“Go and lie down over there,” Salaam instructed, pointing to a lower bunk. “My brother Ebrahim was a registered nurse. He’ll look at you.”

Ebrahim approached, concern etched on his face.

“I’m really fine,” Demarcus insisted, trying to sound convincing. “Nothing’s broken. Well, except my pride.” He sat down on the bunk, exhaustion settling into his bones.

Salaam sat across from Demarcus, studying his bruised and bloodied face, his split lip, and his eyes, which were nearly swollen shut.

“Okay, but at least take some aspirin.”

Demarcus didn’t ask how they had obtained painkillers or bottled water, but he gratefully swallowed the pills and drained the bottle. It was clear that Salaam and his brothers held a certain status within the jail.

“Go on and get some sleep,” Salaam said gently. “You’ll be safe here. I promise.”

Without another word, Demarcus lay down and closed his eyes. For the first time since arriving at Rikers Island, he slept—a deep, dreamless sleep, finally free from fear.

Carrick handed the guard the judge's written order. "I'm not leaving until I see my client, Demarcus Jones."

The guard barely glanced at the paper before handing it back. "There's no problem with you seeing your client, sir."

Carrick was taken aback. He had expected a fight to gain access, but clearly the judge's order had reached the right people.

"I just need to see your ID," the guard said.

After being processed, Carrick was led outside to a bus. He boarded with other visitors, and the bus rumbled across the grounds before stopping in front of another building. Carrick stepped out and entered, following the flow of people through a metal detector. Soon, he was led into a vast visiting room filled with rows of tables and benches, correctional officers stationed at intervals, their eyes watchful.

Inmates sat across from their loved ones, voices low and faces tense. An officer pointed Carrick to an empty table, and he sat down to wait for Demarcus.

Moments later, Demarcus entered, escorted by an officer. Carrick leapt to his feet, his face darkening with anger as he took in Demarcus's battered appearance. "What in the world happened to you?"

"It's cool," Demarcus said, wincing as he sat. His face was swollen and bruised, the aftermath of the previous night's beating still fresh.

Carrick's voice rose. "Cool? You were beaten."

"Sir, please lower your voice," an officer warned.

"Lower my voice? I want to speak to the warden right now!" Carrick's foot stomped on the floor.

Demarcus glanced around, noticing the attention they were drawing. He reached across the table and tugged Carrick's arm. "Please," he whispered, "just sit and let me explain."

Carrick glared at the officer for a moment, then dropped onto the bench. "Who did this to you?" he demanded.

Leaning in, Demarcus spoke in a low voice, recounting the harrowing experience in the showers.

Carrick's eyes widened in horror. "Oh, my goodness. I must get you out of here, Demarcus."

Demarcus's voice was strained. "Where have you been all this time? Where's my mother? Has she seen you?"

Carrick explained what had happened, how both he and Naomi had been blocked from visiting.

"Who would do that?" Demarcus asked in surprise.

"I don't know yet," Carrick replied, his tone steely, "but I intend to find out."

"Please help me, Carrick. I think I'm safe for now with Salaam and his men, but I need to get out of here."

"I'm working on it," Carrick assured him. "But I need your help to make it happen. Tell me everything you did that day, from the moment you woke up to the second you went to sleep. Leave nothing out."

"Okay," Demarcus agreed, his voice steadying as he prepared to recount every detail.

"I got home at 12:05 a.m. I remember because my mother was waiting on the couch, and she pointed at the clock on the wall. I was five minutes late."

Carrick leaned in. "And you didn't see Bridget that night?"

"No. I swear, Carrick," Demarcus replied, his voice earnest. "If I had seen someone hurting her, I would have helped. I've helped her before."

Carrick's eyes narrowed with interest. "You have?"

Demarcus explained how Bridget had been bullied at school and how he had intervened. "I even asked my girlfriend to talk to her and be friendlier whenever she saw her. That helped Bridget a lot, because Marisol was popular, and many of the girls respected her."

Carrick's face brightened. "This is good, Demarcus. I'm going to speak to Trevor and those three men as soon as I leave here."

"And Ms. Lopez," Demarcus added. "I carried her bags to her front door, then I went home. That's why I was a few minutes late."

Carrick nodded enthusiastically, lowering his voice as he glanced at the officer. "You have at least five alibis—six, counting your mother. Plus, you took the bus after you left Marisol's house."

Demarcus sighed. "I wish I had taken a cab. It would have dropped me right in front of my house."

"That's all right," Carrick replied, his excitement growing. "You still have your MetroCard, right?"

"Yes. It's in my wallet at home."

"Good. It will show you used that card that night on the bus, and the exact time. Maybe just as the attack was happening. I'm going to nail Silver Fox's behind."

Demarcus looked up, frustration apparent in his eyes. "Why does he hate me so much? I've never done anything to him. I don't even know the man."

Carrick shook his head. "Maybe not, but he wants to sacrifice you to catapult himself into the attorney general's office."

Demarcus nodded, his voice quiet but resolute. "Make an example of me by sending me to prison for something I didn't do."

"But not on my watch," Carrick said firmly. "I truly believe I have enough to get you bail while I tie the pieces together and work to get these charges dropped."

Demarcus lowered his head, pressing his fingers into his eyes to hold back tears. "That's . . ." He swallowed hard, his voice trembling. "That's good to hear. I needed some good news, Carrick."

Carrick nodded, his tone softening. "I know. I have more good news. Your mother is coming to visit you later as well."

A tear slipped down Demarcus's cheek, and he quickly wiped it away.

"Although," Carrick added, "we probably shouldn't let her see you like this."

Demarcus let out a heavy sigh. "It'll break her heart, but I need to see my mom. I really need her. You understand, don't you?" He looked at Carrick with pleading eyes, the little boy in him shining through.

Carrick offered a gentle smile. "Yes, I think I do."

"It's just us," Demarcus said quietly. "We only have each other."

Carrick shook his head. "I think Naomi would probably beg to differ. I'm sure she'd say it's you, her, and the Lord."

Demarcus opened his mouth to protest but closed it again as an image of Cyclone, just before Salaam and his men burst in and saved him, flashed in his mind. It had come down to the last second.

Are you there, God? Demarcus wondered. *Even in this mess, are you really there?*

He would get his answer . . . eventually.

Chapter Eighteen

"Speak," Jimmy answered, his voice brisk as he picked up his cell phone.

"Is this Jimmy?" Detective Rich asked, sitting in the car with Detective Hanes beside him.

"Yes. Who's this?"

"This is Detective Rich. Trevor gave me your number. I'd like to ask you a few questions about Demarcus Jones."

Jimmy let out a frustrated sigh. "More questions? Man, I just told another detective everything. If you think I'm going to change my mind, think again. You've got the wrong guy."

"Jimmy, please calm down," Detective Hanes interjected gently. "What other detective are you talking about?"

A tense silence followed, broken only by Jimmy's heavy breathing on the line.

"Jimmy?" Rich pressed.

"I'm talking about that little Asian detective. He was just here. Said he drove all the way upstate to see me because it was important and urgent."

Rich shot Hanes a look. "An Asian man went to see him," he said, then returned to the call. "Did he say he was a detective?"

"Not really, but he asked me what happened that night, if I saw DMan, when I saw him, all that. So, I figured he was a detective. I told him everything, but he kept asking if I was sure. It was like he wanted me to say I wasn't."

"What happened next?" Detective Rich asked, his tone sharpening.

"My uncle and two other workers were right there, so the guy asked me to come talk privately in his car. I told him I wasn't going anywhere with him. I wanted other people to hear me say DMan didn't do it."

"And then?" Rich prompted.

"He looked pissed, his face all twisted up. Then he said he'd catch up with me later and left," Jimmy replied. "Now you're calling. But I'm telling you the same thing I told him, and I won't change it because it's the truth. You arrested the wrong person."

"Jimmy, I'm working this case with my partner, Detective Hanes, who's right here beside me. I don't know who that man is, but you'll see my cell number on your caller ID. If he ever approaches you again, I want you to call me immediately."

"Say what now? So, why'd that dude come all the way up here to ask about the case?"

"I don't know," Rich said, his voice steady. "But I'm going to find out. Can you just tell me again what happened that night? This is going to help Demarcus."

Jimmy sighed but described his encounter with Demarcus on the night of the crime, his voice steady as he stood by his story.

"You're sure about the time?" Detective Rich pressed.

"I'm positive," Jimmy replied. "I left not long after DMan and got to my girlfriend's house a block away around 12:10 a.m. This is some nonsense, trying to pin this on him. DMan is a good guy, talented too. Ms. Naomi goes to the same church as my mom. They're good people."

"What time are you getting back to the Bronx?" Detective Hanes asked. "Trevor said you're upstate?"

"Yeah, I'm in Albany for a job with my uncle. I'll be back in the Bronx around seven or so."

"Great. Can you come to the precinct to give a formal statement?" Hanes asked.

"No doubt," Jimmy said. "Actually, I'll ask my uncle if I can leave earlier to get there. You have to get DMan out of jail. He didn't do it."

"We're working on it, and your statement will help a lot," Detective Rich assured him.

"I'll be there as soon as I can." Jimmy ended the call.

Rich frowned, glancing at his partner. "That Asian man again. He traveled all the way to Albany to see Jimmy. This case is starting to stink like rancid cabbage water."

"We need to reach Tom and Afia before he does," Hanes replied.

"Let's stop by Golden Krust and see if the manager can give us Tom's number or address. After that, we'll circle back to the deli to check for Mr. Afia."

Just then, Rich's phone rang. He answered, "Rich."

"I have Demarcus's lawyer here and he'd like to speak to both of you as soon as possible," Lieutenant Mulligan said, his voice tense. "How far away are you?"

"We're close by. Did something else happen? You sound upset."

"Demarcus was attacked last night in Rikers," the lieutenant said, barely containing his anger.

Rich closed his eyes. "I'm sorry to hear that. Is he . . . is he going to be okay?"

"He will be when we get him out. Get here now." Lieutenant Mulligan hung up.

Rich turned to Hanes. "That was the lieutenant. Demarcus was attacked last night."

Detective Hanes groaned, her eyes suddenly glassy. "That's awful. From what we're finding out, Demarcus shouldn't even be in there. Now he's been attacked."

"Let's work fast and get him out," Rich said, starting the car. "We'll go speak to the lawyer, then circle back for Tom's info at Golden Krust."

"Why don't you drop me at Golden Krust and go see the lawyer?" Hanes suggested. "If I get Tom's number, I'll call him and ask him to meet us at the precinct. I'll take a cab back."

"Sounds good." Rich drove off, letting Hanes out in front of Golden Krust before quickly continuing down Gun Hill Road, turning right onto Laconia Avenue. Within minutes, he was double-parked in front of the 47th Precinct and almost jogging inside to Lieutenant Mulligan's office.

"Come in," Lieutenant Mulligan called as Detective Rich knocked and entered, closing the door behind him.

A small man with a shock of bright red hair stood up and extended his hand. "Carrick O'Connor, Demarcus Jones's attorney. You must be Detective Rich. Where's your partner?"

Rich shook his hand firmly. "My partner is following up on a lead for the case."

"A lead? Interesting." Carrick sat and crossed his legs, a hint of sarcasm in his tone. "So, we're finally doing some investigating. That's good to know."

Rich bristled. "Listen, I'll admit we may have acted a little too quickly in arresting Mr. Jones. But—"

"You think?" Carrick cut him off. "And don't think I haven't heard about how you tortured him in what you call an interview. Once I get this bogus case dropped, I'm going to make sure Demarcus sues your drawers off."

Lieutenant Mulligan interjected, steering the conversation back on track. "Let's focus on getting Demarcus out for now. Rich, Demarcus confirmed he saw those men playing dominoes that night and helped Ms. Lopez with her bags. Have you spoken to Trevor?"

"Hanes and I spoke with Trevor and Jimmy," Rich replied, detailing the conversations.

"This Asian man, whoever he is, went to see Trevor at his home and drove all the way to Albany to see Jimmy?" Mulligan asked, his brow furrowing.

"Yes, sir," Rich confirmed. "According to Trevor, his mother saw the man leaving Golden Krust, where Tom works. It's safe to say he was looking for Tom, who happened to be off work that day."

"This man is trying to get to Demarcus's alibis," Mulligan said, leaning back in his chair, concern on his face.

Rich nodded. "Hanes is getting Tom's address from his workplace so we can pay him a visit. Later, we'll head back to the deli to see if we can find Mr. Afia."

Carrick uncrossed his legs and turned to face Rich. "Let me get this straight. Trevor and Jimmy both confirmed they saw my client around the time the crime is believed to have been committed?"

Rich nodded again.

"And now there's another person, not a detective, trying to contact our witnesses?"

"That's what I just said," Rich replied, still irritated by Carrick's earlier threat of a lawsuit.

"If I were you, Detective, I'd lose the attitude," Carrick said, pointing a finger at him. "You're the one who sent an innocent young man to Rikers Island, where he was assaulted. Do you get me?"

Lieutenant Mulligan cleared his throat loudly, redirecting the conversation. "Have you contacted Ms. Lopez, Detective?"

"Not yet. She's next on the list after we contact Tom."

At that moment, a knock sounded at the door.

"Come in," Lieutenant Mulligan said, and Detective Hanes entered the room.

Detective Rich quickly gestured to his chair, but Hanes shook her head, so he sat back down.

"I was able to get Tom's cell number from his manager, but she wouldn't give out his address," Hanes reported. "Anyway, I spoke with Tom, and he basically confirmed what Trevor and Jimmy said. His cousin is giving him a ride, and he'll be here soon to give a formal statement."

"That's three of the four people corroborating Demarcus's account," Carrick added. "Including his mother, who waited up for him that night, I now have four witnesses. I also got a call from his girlfriend, Marisol. She and her parents will provide a formal statement confirming the time Demarcus arrived and left their house."

"We were planning to speak with them as well," Detective Hanes said softly.

"Of course you were." Carrick offered a tight smile.

"We'll speak to Ms. Lopez right after taking Tom's statement," Detective Rich added quickly.

"Do you have enough to take to the prosecutor and the judge for Demarcus's bail?" Lieutenant Mulligan asked Carrick.

"I believe so. I just need copies of the formal witness statements, signed and dated."

"We'll have Jimmy, Tom, and Trevor soon," Rich noted.

"Hanes, why don't you wait here and handle that?" Lieutenant Mulligan instructed. "Rich and I will go speak to Ms. Lopez. I've confirmed the address Trevor gave me for her." He flipped a page in his notebook. "Ms. Carmen Lopez. She's posted bail for her son, Juan, a few times."

"I'll make some calls and wait for the witnesses to arrive," Carrick said. "I also have a few questions for Detective Hanes about her interrogation of my client." He gave Hanes a forced smile, his expression quickly turning serious.

Detective Hanes sighed and glanced at her boss.

"Counselor, as I said before, let's work together to get Demarcus out and these charges dropped. Then we'll take it from there," Lieutenant Mulligan said, looking at Carrick. "The detectives are working hard to help us. We need to cooperate, especially with other people interfering in the investigation."

Carrick shot Hanes a sharp look and replied, "All right, I can do that. Actually, this probably has something to do with Demarcus being denied visitors."

"Then we're dealing with some powerful people," Rich said.

"People determined to make things harder for Demarcus," Carrick replied. "The question is, why?"

"And who?" Lieutenant Mulligan added.

Carrick's eyes narrowed. "I'd bet anything if we find these people, we'll find our real rapist." He glanced from Hanes to Rich. "The true criminal."

Lieutenant Mulligan nodded. "You can stay here and catch up on your calls, Carrick. Hanes will come to get you when the witnesses arrive. Rich and I are heading out to speak with Ms. Lopez."

As the detectives and the lieutenant exited, Carrick was already dialing his phone, determination fixed on his face.

Rich glanced at his boss as they moved down the hallway. "He's going to make this difficult for us, isn't he? I'm probably going to lose my job, right?"

"Let's not jump to conclusions," Lieutenant Mulligan replied, his voice steady. "I meant what I said in there. Right now, it's all about Demarcus. That's it." He strode off, leaving Rich to follow.

Detective Rich pressed Ms. Lopez's buzzer again, waiting as the seconds ticked by. No answer. He turned to Lieutenant Mulligan. "I don't think anyone's home."

"She's probably at work. Come on, let's try there," Mulligan replied, leading the way through the gate.

Suddenly, an elderly woman next door called out, her voice carrying across the yard. "I think she moved out."

Lieutenant Mulligan approached her. "Moved? When did she leave?"

"About two days ago," the neighbor replied. "She didn't even bother to take the furniture. Yesterday, the landlord told me she's not getting her security deposit back because he'll have to clean out the apartment and throw out her stuff. She just left a message saying she's no longer living there."

Rich, standing beside Mulligan, frowned. "Seems like she left in a hurry."

The neighbor nodded. "That's what it looked like. I only saw her and that no-good son loading bags into a cab that morning. They came back and did the same thing that evening. And that was it."

"Any idea where they went?" Mulligan asked.

She shook her head. "I can't say. I wasn't that close to her. Sorry."

Rich handed her a business card. "If you see her again, please give me a call."

The neighbor eyed the card, then asked, "What did that boy do now? That drug has him in all kinds of trouble."

"He didn't do anything, ma'am," Rich assured her. "We're actually looking to speak with Ms. Lopez."

"Okay. If I see her, I'll let you know, but honestly, I doubt it."

After thanking the neighbor, Detective Rich and Lieutenant Mulligan made their way back to the car. Rich was about to slide behind the wheel when he paused, then turned and walked back to Ms. Lopez's neighbor.

"By any chance, did you notice an Asian man around here recently?" he asked. "Maybe you saw him talking to Ms. Lopez before she moved?"

A bright smile spread across the woman's face. "I told my husband he looked just like that Kung Fu guy. What's his name? Oh, yes. Jackie Chan."

A spark of excitement lit up Rich's eyes. "So, you did see him?"

She nodded, lowering her voice and glancing around as if sharing a secret. "I'm not one to spy, but I happened to see that Asian man leaving Ms. Lopez's apartment late one night. He parked right where you're parked now. He drove a flashy car, looked extremely expensive."

"Really?" Rich grinned. "Do you remember what color it was?"

The neighbor looked almost offended by the question, then replied with certainty, "It was a white sports car." She lifted her chin with pride.

"Thank you, ma'am. You've been a tremendous help."

She beamed. "Always happy to help the police."

Detective Rich returned to the car, got in, and turned to Lieutenant Mulligan, who sat in the passenger seat. "Looks like that same Asian man met with Ms. Lopez."

"Say what?" Mulligan exclaimed, his voice rising. "What's really going on here, Rich?"

Rich pressed his lips together, staring at Mulligan for a long moment before starting the car and pulling away.

"She works at the McDonald's on White Plains Road and 233rd Street," Mulligan said quietly as they drove.

Both men fell silent, each lost in thought as Rich made his way through the Bronx streets toward White Plains Road. He turned into the McDonald's parking lot and eased the car into a space. They got out and stepped inside, greeted by a wave of noise and the greasy scent of frying oil hanging thick in the air.

"Excuse me," Rich called out, raising his voice above the chatter to a teenager behind the register. The woman placing her order shot him a sharp look.

"I'm Detective Rich, and I'd like to speak with Carmen Lopez." He flashed his badge.

"She's not here today."

"What about a manager? This is important."

"Sanchez," the cashier shouted. "Cops are here for you."

A few curious customers glanced over. Rich stepped aside as a short Hispanic man hurried over, his eyes full of questions.

"Is there somewhere we can talk privately?" Rich asked. "Maybe you could step outside with us for a minute?"

Sanchez's face paled as he stammered, "Wh–what did I do?"

"Oh, nothing, sir," Rich replied quickly, his voice carrying above the din and loud enough for the eavesdropping customers to hear. "We just need to ask about one of your employees."

Sanchez exhaled in relief. "I'll come around." He whispered something to a woman working the fries, then hurried out to meet Rich and Lieutenant Mulligan. Together, the three men stepped outside and walked over to the police car.

Leaning back against the car, Lieutenant Mulligan began, "We're looking for Carmen Lopez. We understand she's not working today?"

"That's right," Sanchez confirmed. "She's on an extended vacation."

"Extended vacation?" Rich arched an eyebrow, folding his arms. "For how long?"

"She said a few weeks, maybe a month or so." Sanchez's gaze flicked between the two officers. "What did she do? Or is this about her son?"

Lieutenant Mulligan ignored the questions and pressed on. "Was this vacation scheduled in advance, or was it more of a spur-of-the-moment thing?"

Sanchez shook his head. "It wasn't planned. She said she had a family emergency and needed some time. Honestly, I think it's her son again. Probably overdosed . . . again."

Rich exchanged a knowing look with Mulligan.

"She's been working here a long time, so the boss doesn't mind. Most of it is unpaid time off anyway."

"Here's my card," Rich said, handing over a business card. "Please call me as soon as Ms. Lopez comes back to work. It's important."

"Sure. Anything else? As you can see, we're a little swamped right now."

"Thanks for your help," Lieutenant Mulligan said, and Sanchez hurried back inside.

Rich frowned as he watched Sanchez disappear into the restaurant. "Now Ms. Lopez is gone too. What is going on here?"

Mulligan's jaw tightened. "Maybe there's a conspiracy to make Demarcus the fall guy. But not on my watch. We're going to find Ms. Lopez, and she'll tell the truth about what happened that night."

He was about to find out that it was easier said than done.

For the love of money is the root of all evil: which while some coveted after, they have erred from the faith and pierced themselves through with many sorrows.

1 Timothy 6:10

Chapter Nineteen

“No, no, no.” Naomi shook her head from side to side, arms wrapped tightly around her petite frame, tears streaming down her cheeks as she watched Demarcus approach. “Oh, dear Lord. Have mercy.”

“It’s okay, Mom,” Demarcus said softly, stepping in front of her in the Rikers Island visiting room. “It looks worse than it really is.” His eyes were still swollen, the left one bloodshot, his lips puffy, and his face mottled with bruises.

“Oh, baby.” Naomi threw her arms around his waist, pressing her tear-stained face against his chest, ignoring the no-touching rule. “What have they done to you?” she sobbed, her voice breaking.

“Oh, Mom.” Demarcus hugged her close, squeezing his eyes shut to keep his own tears at bay.

“What . . . what did they do to you?” Naomi lifted her head, searching his battered face. She reached up, gently touching his bruised cheek.

“Ma’am, no touching,” interrupted a correctional officer who stepped beside them. “Both of you, please have a seat.”

Naomi turned, her eyes blazing with fury. She hissed, barely above a whisper, “So now you’re trying to do your job, huh?” She took a step toward him, but Demarcus’s hand tightened on her arm. “Where were you when they were brutalizing my son?” she shouted. “*Answer me*!”

The room fell silent. Conversations stopped as every eye turned toward Naomi.

"Jesus, have mercy." Naomi raised her hands to the ceiling, her body trembling with pain. "Oh, my poor son," she wailed.

"Mom." Demarcus gently pulled her back, guiding her to a seat. "Please, Mom, they'll ask you to leave. I want to talk to you, okay?"

Naomi met his pleading gaze, but it took a while for her sobbing to subside. She glanced over her shoulder at the officer, shooting him a look of pure disdain. With trembling hands, she pulled a tissue from her skirt pocket and wiped her face.

"They hurt you," she finally managed, her voice thick with emotion. "Did they . . .?" Her words trailed off as she stared down at her hands, folded in her lap. "I've prayed so much. I've been fasting since they took you. I begged God. I—"

Demarcus leaned across the table and whispered, "No, they didn't, Mommy."

Naomi's mouth opened, but no words came. She searched his face, then lowered her head to the table and began to cry again, her shoulders shaking.

"I think we're going to cut this visit short," announced the officer, now joined by another stern-faced colleague. "This is disruptive to all the other visitors."

Naomi's head snapped up, her eyes blazing as she turned to the officers. She wiped her face with a crumpled tissue, leaving tiny white flecks clinging to her cheeks. "My son was attacked, and all you can say to me is that I'm disruptive?"

"I'm sorry for what happened to your son, ma'am. But—"

"Please, just give us a few more minutes," Demarcus interjected, his voice steady but pleading. "This is very hard for her."

The two officers exchanged a look. The one with the perpetually sour expression finally relented. "One more outburst and she's out of here."

Naomi opened her mouth to respond, but after glancing at Demarcus's face, she closed it and nodded. "I got it. Thank you."

"It will be okay," Demarcus repeated softly, trying to comfort his mother, though it should have been the other way around.

Naomi gazed at her son, marveling at his bravery. "You're so brave, sweetheart. Please, tell me what happened to you." Her eyes pleaded for the truth.

Demarcus hesitated, wanting to spare her the worst of it, but he knew she wouldn't rest until she heard everything. So, in a low voice meant only for her, he told her the whole story.

When he finished, Naomi squeezed his hand, then quickly pulled away, glancing at the officer. "'Though I walk in the midst of trouble, thou wilt revive me: thou shalt stretch forth thine hand against the wrath of mine enemies, and thy right hand shall save me,'" she quoted, her voice trembling. "That's Psalm 138:7." She looked at Demarcus, her eyes shining with gratitude. "I thank God for sending you help. I'm glad they . . . I mean, it wasn't worse. I'm so sorry you're going through this, my son."

Now it was Demarcus's turn to rest his head on the table. He wiped his tears away with the back of his hand. "Why is this happening to me, Mommy?"

Naomi's heart broke even more. When he was a child, he called her Mommy, but as he grew older, it became Mom. Hearing that word now told her just how vulnerable he felt. "Baby, the only answer I can give you is God knows best. I know it might not be what you want to hear right now, but He's with you, Demarcus." She longed to wrap her arms around him, but the officers watched them like hawks. "Do you see how He sent help for you when you were attacked?"

Demarcus nodded, his head still resting on the table, eyes fixed on his feet.

"Demarcus, please look at me," Naomi said softly.

It took a few moments, but Demarcus finally lifted his gaze to meet his mother's.

"God is going to get you out of here," Naomi told him, her voice steady with conviction. "You're going to come out better than you went in. Mark my words."

"Okay, Mommy," he replied quietly.

"I want you to stay strong. Tomorrow, when I come to visit, I'd like to meet Salaam Alihammad and thank him personally. Can you let him know for me?"

Demarcus nodded again.

"Please remember, we're doing everything we can to get you out of here. Carrick and the detectives are talking to the eyewitnesses. Trevor has already spoken to the lieutenant. They're all working hard to get you bail."

Naomi continued, her voice gentler, "Marisol has spent almost every night with me at the house. She's coming to visit tomorrow with her family."

"No," Demarcus said quickly. "I don't want her to see me like this."

"Why not? She'll be even more devastated if you keep her away."

"I only want to see you and Carrick for now. Maybe later, all right?"

Naomi hesitated, then agreed. "Okay. I suppose that goes for Jerry and Trevor, too. They were at the house this morning."

Demarcus looked away. "I'm glad they're there for you," he said, his voice catching in his throat. He fell silent for a few seconds. "Tell them I'll let them know when they can come visit."

"Of course." Naomi looked at her badly bruised son, both physically and emotionally battered, and made a silent vow in her heart. She would do whatever it took to get him out of jail. Soon, she would discover that the path to his freedom would unearth secrets she had buried long ago—secrets that would change many lives forever.

Chapter Twenty

"The boy was assaulted last night," Viktor reported to Alfredo, his tone grave. "A group of rednecks beat him badly and tried to rape him, but the Black Israelites intervened and saved him."

Alfredo showed no remorse. He leaned back in his large executive chair, his gaze fixed on Viktor across the conference room at Ferrari Investment Group. "Better him than Angelo," he said coldly.

"His lawyer was there this morning, too," Viktor added.

Alfredo waved a hand dismissively. "I'm not worried about a public defender."

Viktor leaned in, lowering his voice. "This might worry you, though. The detectives spoke to three witnesses who saw the boy at the time of the crime. They all said he didn't do it."

Alfredo shot to his feet, his face flushed with anger. "What? I thought your people were supposed to reach them before the cops!" He struggled to steady his breathing, chest rising and falling rapidly.

"My guy did make contact with Jimmy," Viktor replied, glancing at his notepad. "But Jimmy was surrounded by a group of men and refused to speak privately. There was nothing my guy could do with so many people around."

"That's it?" Alfredo demanded, glaring.

"Of course not," Viktor assured him. "We plan to visit Jimmy again later. As for Tom, no one at his workplace would give out his contact information, but they did when the detectives showed their badges. We'll be speaking with Tom as well. It's never too late to convince someone to recant their statement." Viktor gave Alfredo a sly wink.

Alfredo sat back down, taking deep breaths to calm his racing heart. "What about the Lopez woman?"

"The cops went by her apartment and workplace, but she wasn't there," Viktor said. "I think we're safe with her."

Alfredo stared past Viktor, lost in thought for a moment. "Who's the prosecutor on the case?"

Viktor smirked. "District Attorney Calvin Wilcox."

Alfredo clapped his hands, a sharp smile spreading across his face. "Ah, the great Silver Fox. You know he's married to Bradshaw's daughter?" he said, referring to William Bradshaw, the former governor of New York and one of his old friends.

"Yes, and I read he's running for attorney general," Viktor replied.

"I'm sure Silver Fox would appreciate a sizable donation to his campaign," Alfredo mused. "I should pay him a visit, reacquaint myself. It's been a while."

"Is that wise?" Viktor cautioned. "We don't want any of this to trace back to you or Angelo."

Alfredo waved off the concern. "It'll be fine. I'll arrange a visit with Bradshaw, and I'm sure he'll mention his son-in-law's campaign. I'll pay Silver Fox a visit, make a contribution, and casually mention the case since the girl was an employee of mine. We'll get a sense of where he stands."

Viktor nodded, but warned, "Just don't ask too many questions. You don't want to raise his suspicions."

Alfredo folded his arms, satisfied. "If there's anyone I'd want prosecuting this case, it's Silver Fox. This is good news. Really good news."

***

"Sorry, but I still oppose bail." Silver Fox extended the witness statements toward Carrick, his expression unreadable. "Here, you can have these back."

Carrick's face flushed with disbelief. "Are you serious?" he exploded, standing rigid in front of Silver Fox's desk. "I've given you not one, not two, but four signed witness statements, each one confirming my client's whereabouts at the time of the crime. He's in jail for something he didn't do, and you're still refusing bail?" His voice trembled with frustration. "Really?"

Silver Fox leaned back in his chair, crossing his legs with a dismissive air. "Those are friends of the suspect and his mother. What else would they say?"

Carrick jabbed a finger at him. "What about the fact that the victim never positively identified my client? You spoke to the detectives. You know what happened in that ambulance."

"She repeated his nickname a few times," Silver Fox replied, his tone flat.

Carrick's patience snapped. "I'm filing a motion for a bail hearing and taking this to a judge," he declared. "You're being completely unreasonable."

Silver Fox's eyes hardened. "You and I both know that if the prosecution opposes bail, it's going to be difficult for you to get one."

"But not impossible," Carrick shot back, his voice sharp. "We have enough for reasonable doubt, and you know it." He pointed at Silver Fox, his anger barely contained.

"We'll see about that," Silver Fox replied, the glint in his eyes icy. "As I said, I'm still against bail, and I'll fight you on it." He tossed the witness statements at Carrick, two landing on the desk, two fluttering to the floor. "This discussion is over."

Carrick glared at him for a long moment, then spun on his heel and stormed out of the office.

Outside, Carrick's frustration boiled over. His tires squealed as he peeled out of the parking lot, narrowly missing another car. In his rearview mirror, he caught the other driver flipping him off. He nearly returned the gesture but stopped himself at the last second. He was too angry to care.

"What am I supposed to tell Naomi and Lieutenant Mulligan now?" Carrick muttered as he sped back to his office. As if on cue, his phone rang in his jacket pocket. He fished it out with one hand, steering with the other.

"Lieutenant, I was just about to call you," Carrick said as soon as he answered.

"I couldn't wait," Lieutenant Mulligan replied, his voice tense. "Did Silver Fox agree to bail for Demarcus?"

"No, sorry."

"What?" Lieutenant Mulligan's voice rose in disbelief. "Didn't you show him the witness statements?"

Carrick rolled his eyes. "That's exactly why I went to see him."

A heavy sigh echoed through the phone. "Sorry, Carrick. I'm not frustrated with you. What's our next move?"

"I'm still going to petition the court for bail, even though the prosecutor objects," Carrick said, his tone resolute.

"And our chances?"

Carrick's silence spoke volumes.

"We need Ms. Lopez," Lieutenant Mulligan said at last. "We have to find her."

"And don't forget Africa's," Carrick added. "The more witnesses, the better."

"Afia's," Lieutenant Mulligan corrected. "Jimmy gave us an address for him, but we were told he hasn't lived there for about two years. The detectives plan to look for him later at the deli."

"Good. We knew this was going to be a tough fight, right?"

"Yes, but I'd feel a lot better if Demarcus were out of Rikers while we fight," Mulligan replied, his voice trembling slightly. "I worry about what they'll do to him next."

"He said he's staying with the Black Israelites," Carrick informed him. "I think he's safe for now."

"Hopefully they're not just pretending to befriend him, only to betray him later."

"Ah, man." Carrick slapped the steering wheel in frustration. "Please don't say that."

"We'll keep praying, Counselor. I have to believe Demarcus is in God's hands. It's too painful to think otherwise."

Unfortunately, there was a lot of pain coming.

Chapter Twenty-one

"What a pleasant surprise," Silver Fox said, gripping Alfredo Ferrari's hand in a firm handshake. "Mindy just mentioned your name at dinner the other night." He gestured toward the visitor's chair.

"How is that beautiful wife of yours?" Alfredo asked as he settled into the seat. "And Samuel?"

"My wife and son are both doing great, thank you," Silver Fox replied. "Just the other day, Mindy was asking her father how you were doing after your little scare a few months ago."

"Tell her to call me herself and find out," Alfredo replied with a wink. "I'm doing absolutely wonderful. My heart is back to good health, and I'm even spending more time in the office."

"Ready to take the reins back from Angelo, huh?"

"Ready to share the reins with Angelo," Alfredo said, laughing heartily. "He's doing such a great job with the firm. I'm incredibly pleased with how he stepped up when I had to take some time off." It was still difficult for Alfredo to say aloud that he'd suffered a massive heart attack.

"Who knew, right?" Silver Fox smiled. "Everyone thought Angelo was just a playboy, but look at him now. Mr. Wall Street, CEO of a multimillion-dollar hedge fund."

"He just needed a reason to step up," Alfredo agreed, seizing the opening he needed. "He really loves the company, especially our hardworking employees who keep us at the top. That's why it was so devastating when we heard what happened to poor little Bridget."

Silver Fox gave him a questioning look.

"Bridget Walsh. The beautiful young lady who was beaten and raped in the park a few days ago."

"Oh." Silver Fox's eyes widened. "She worked for you?"

Alfredo nodded. "She just started as a receptionist for the summer, but she had great potential."

"Wait a minute." Silver Fox shuffled through some papers on his desk until he found what he was looking for. "Here it is." He tapped the paper with his finger. "It only says here she was a receptionist for a Wall Street company, without giving the name. What a coincidence."

"Isn't it?" Alfredo replied smoothly. "I was so pleased when I heard you're the prosecutor on the case and that you have a suspect in custody. I know you'll get justice for Bridget."

"You can bet on it. I plan on meeting with her and her parents soon so I can start building my case against Demarcus Jones."

"Any chance he'll get off?" Alfredo asked, his tone suddenly anxious.

"Not on my watch." The anger in Silver Fox's voice was unmistakable. "What he did was despicable and evil, and I'm going to make sure he pays for it."

"Awesome!" Alfredo clapped his hands, then quickly caught himself. "I mean, that's good news for that poor child. Plus, you need to end your DA journey on a high note, right?" He leaned in and winked. "A little birdie told me you're on your way to becoming the next attorney general of New York."

"That little birdie is right." Silver Fox's grin stretched from ear to ear. "I almost have it in the bag."

"I've got a little something to help you with that." Alfredo reached into his jacket pocket and pulled out an envelope. "You know, you, Mindy, and Samuel are like family. Your father-in-law is one of my best friends." He handed Silver Fox the envelope.

Silver Fox opened it, pulled out the check inside, and gasped. "Really?"

"Oh, yes," Alfredo replied smoothly. "This is just a little something to help with your campaign. And please, let me know if there's any other way I can assist. I know a lot of important people." He tapped his chest with pride. "I'm Alfredo Ferrari."

"Yes, you are." Silver Fox stood and extended his right hand, but Alfredo swept around the desk and pulled him into a hearty embrace.

Stepping back, Alfredo repeated, "As I said, we're like family."

"I appreciate it," Silver Fox replied, his voice warm with gratitude. "Just wait until I tell Mindy."

"I'll invite you all over for dinner soon," Alfredo said cheerfully. "It's been too long."

"We look forward to it. I hope Angelo will be there too. I haven't seen him in a while."

Alfredo nodded. "He will be. He'll also be happy to hear you'll be giving our employee the justice she deserves."

"Happy to do my job," Silver Fox replied, his face glowing like a July Fourth fireworks show.

The men said their goodbyes, both feeling on top of the world—Alfredo, because Demarcus's fate seemed almost sealed, leaving his son off the hook; Silver Fox, because of the generous donation he'd just received and the privilege of having such powerful, wealthy allies.

"The prosecutor still opposes bail for Demarcus." Carrick reached over and gently touched Naomi's hand, which gripped the edge of the couch. "I'm sorry, Naomi."

Naomi stared straight ahead, her eyes fixed on a photograph of Demarcus as a six-year-old, dressed in a blue-and-white jogging suit, white sneakers, and a white baseball cap. The most striking feature in the picture was Demarcus's radiant smile.

"I still remember the day I took that picture," Naomi said softly. "He was six going on sixteen. Do you see that beautiful smile?" She glanced at Carrick, who nodded. "I want to see my son smile like that again. I want to see his eyes light up with the joy he had before it was stolen from him. I want my son to be free. Do you hear me, Carrick?"

"Yes, ma'am. I want you to know I'm still going to request a bail hearing for Demarcus. However, I must warn you, with Silver Fox fighting us and still claiming the victim identified Demarcus as her assailant, our chances are very slim."

"But I spoke to the detectives. They explained what happened in the ambulance. She muttered my son's nickname, which could mean anything."

"I agree with you, but that's the report Detective Hanes filed with the DA's office, and the prosecutor still considers it a positive ID by the victim."

"You saw what they did to my boy, Carrick. It was only the grace of God that saved him from being—" Naomi bit her bottom lip, still staring at Demarcus's picture.

"I know," Carrick said gently. "We're not giving up."

"Wait a minute." Naomi turned slightly on the couch to face Carrick, her eyes suddenly wide, as if she'd just discovered the key to the case. "This just came to my spirit. Demarcus said he took Gunther Avenue after dropping off Ms. Lopez's bags. That's opposite the park. What if Bridget saw him that night and was trying to call out to him for help?"

Carrick's freckled face furrowed in thought. "Hmm."

Naomi pressed on, "She was probably calling out to Demarcus, but he didn't hear her." Her wide eyes met Carrick's. "That's why she kept saying his name. She saw him coming home that night."

Carrick shook his head, a spark of realization in his eyes. "Naomi, I never even considered that possibility." He took her hand in his. "That's another strong point for reasonable doubt. Silver Fox claims she was identifying Demarcus as her attacker, but what if she was actually calling his name because she saw him heading home that night, desperately trying to get his attention for help?"

Naomi's gaze lingered on a nearby photograph, her voice soft but determined. "Do you think the judge will see it that way?"

"We'll find out," Carrick replied. "It would make a huge difference if we could get Ms. Lopez's statement. That would confirm Demarcus walked that route home and help establish the timeline. Ms. Lopez isn't related to Demarcus, nor is she a friend. Her testimony would carry weight."

Naomi's eyes returned to the picture, her hope flickering. "If only the prosecutor would agree to bail, my son could come home while you and the detectives work to uncover the truth."

"That's the plan, Naomi. But Silver Fox is stubborn, and he's determined to make an example out of Demarcus."

Naomi stared ahead, unblinking. "Still, as you said, God will show us a way to get this done."

Carrick nodded. "I agree with you. We're going to get Demarcus out, even if—"

Suddenly, the doorbell rang, cutting him off.

"That's probably Marisol," Naomi said, rising from her seat. "She's been staying with me and just went home to get some clothes. Give me a moment." She hurried to the door.

"Hola, Señorita Naomi." Carlos greeted her with a big hug and kisses on both cheeks as soon as she opened the door. "Carlos is here to end this nightmare, okay? No more worries. I'm going to help you get my boy out of jail, okay?"

Naomi managed a small, weary smile. "Thank you, dear. Please, come in." She stepped aside, allowing Carlos to enter, followed by Marisol, who paused in front of Naomi.

"He was at the house and insisted on coming with me," Marisol whispered. "You know he and Demarcus have become good friends."

Naomi nodded, a hint of humor in her voice. "I know. God help us with Carlos on thc case." The two women followed Carlos into the living room, where he had already claimed Naomi's seat beside Carrick. They settled on the opposite couch.

"So, Counselor, what's the plan?" Carlos asked, his Spanish accent thick with determination. "My sister said you lost Señorita Lopez. She vanished into thin air."

Carrick glanced at Naomi, raising his eyebrows in question.

"This is Carlos, Marisol's brother," Naomi explained. "He's also a good friend of my son."

"Demarcus is *mi familia,"* Carlos declared. "He's going to college to become a big-shot lawyer. Carlos will not allow anyone to send him to prison. He didn't do this, okay?"

"Okay," Carrick replied, matching Carlos's conviction. "I agree with you."

"*Excelente,"* Carlos exclaimed, giving Carrick a friendly slap on the shoulder. "That's what Carlos needs to hear. Now, my boys and I are going to find Señorita Lopez for you. Sí?"

Naomi interjected, her tone gentle but firm. “Carlos, I think we should let the police handle this. They’re already searching for her.”

Carlos shook his head, undeterred. “The police? They put Demarcus in jail, remember?”

Marisol chimed in, “He has a point. They put Demarcus in jail, and now they’re trying to get him out? Sorry, I’m not buying it. I agree with my brother.”

Naomi sighed, her voice weary but resolute. “Carlos, I don’t want you or your friends getting into trouble. We don’t need any more problems.”

Carlos placed a hand on his chest, feigning innocence. “Not Carlos.”

Carrick and Marisol laughed, while Naomi simply rolled her eyes.

Carlos leaned back, stretching out his legs with a mischievous grin. “Don’t worry. We’ll find Señorita Lopez and call the counselor with her location. Carlos won’t be dealing with any police, okay?”

Carrick handed Carlos a business card. “We really need to find Ms. Lopez as soon as possible. Do whatever you have to do.”

Naomi shot Carrick a look of disbelief.

He quickly added, “Within the law, of course.” He winked at Carlos.

Carlos winked back. “Of course. Carlos is a law-abiding citizen.”

Naomi groaned inwardly, making a mental note to increase her prayers. With Carlos playing detective, anything could happen.

Carrick trudged into his Bronx apartment, exhaustion weighing on his shoulders. As he fumbled for his keys, his cell phone buzzed in his pocket.

"This is Carrick," he answered, his voice weary.

"Counselor, this is your partner, Carlos," came the energetic reply. "*¿Cómo está?*"

"I'm hanging in there, Carlos," Carrick replied, ignoring the "partner" comment. "What's going on?"

"We found Señorita Lopez for you."

Carrick stopped in the middle of his living room, stunned. "Say that again? Where?"

"She's living in a nice big house on North Broadway in Yonkers."

Carrick dropped his battered briefcase onto the sofa. "Wait a minute. Last I heard, Ms. Lopez worked at McDonald's and lived in a one-bedroom apartment with her son. Now she's in a big house in Westchester?"

"Something's not right, Counselor. But Carlos didn't approach her, just like you said."

"How did you find her?"

"Her son is a crackhead. My boys know where he likes to score, so we staked out the area. Earlier, he came through, and we grabbed him."

"You grabbed him?" Carrick sat on the edge of the sofa, alarmed. "What do you mean, you grabbed him?"

"Relax, Counselor. Carlos didn't hurt him. We just asked a few questions."

"And he told you where they're living now?"

"No, señor," Carlos replied, amusement in his voice. "With a little . . . persuasion, he let us give him a ride home." Carlos chuckled.

"Carlos, are you and your boys going to need a lawyer?"

Carlos burst out laughing. "Carlos is a law-abiding citizen, Counselor." Then, in a more serious tone, he added, "Please take the address and give it to the detectives. They'd better speak to Señorita Lopez soon, or Carlos will. Demarcus must get out of jail now."

"All right, Carlos. Please don't approach Ms. Lopez," Carrick urged. "That could cause more harm than good for Demarcus. Wait, let me find something to write the address down." He rummaged through his briefcase.

"Here." Simone, Carrick's wife, appeared beside him, handing him a pen and notepad.

"Thanks, babe." Carrick took them and said, "Okay, go ahead." He jotted down the address as Carlos dictated it. "Thank you. I'm going to call the detectives right now and give them this. Remember what I said. Please don't speak to Ms. Lopez. Also, stay away from her son now that we know where—" Carrick stopped mid-sentence as he realized Carlos had already hung up. "Geez."

"Who was that?" Simone asked, settling beside him and glancing at the notepad.

"*My partner*, Carlos."

"Oh? I didn't know you had a partner." Amusement sparkled in her eyes. "Whose address is this?"

"Ms. Lopez."

"What?" Simone jumped to her feet, staring at the address. "She's living on North Broadway now? *Wha gwaan yah*?"

"What's going on here is a good question." Carrick shook his head. "I'm sure the detectives will want to ask her when they speak to her."

Simone's voice trembled with conviction as she paced the living room, her small frame taut with energy. "This has been sitting heavy on my heart," she said, eyes locked on her husband. At 5 feet 3 inches and barely a hundred and ten pounds, she was all fire and fight. "A young Black man earns a scholarship to a top-tier college, trying to lift himself and his mother out of struggle, and they slap a rape charge on him? Just like that? Throw him behind bars?" She spun on her heel, pacing faster. "And now the one woman who could clear his name suddenly moved from her tiny Bronx apartment to some fancy Yonkers house overnight. That doesn't smell right, Carrick."

She dropped onto the couch beside him, her voice low but fierce. "We need to dig. We need to find out what is going on.

Carrick leaned back, studying her. "We? Sweetheart, I'm not sure—"

"No, no, no." Simone sprang to her feet again, cutting him off. "The *Daily News* and a few TV stations did their little surface-level stories, but it's time for the real story to come out." She raised a finger, silencing Carrick before he could protest. "You told me to wait before writing about it, but now it's time. The *New York Post* is going to run a full feature on this injustice. Naomi Jones is my island sister, you hear?"

Carrick grinned. "Out of many, one people?" He quoted Jamaica's motto.

"You better believe it. Demarcus Jones is like a brother to me now," Simone declared. "Let the war begin."

"Sweetheart, it's not exactly a war. I mean—"

Simone cut him off with a gleam in her eye. "In the words of the great Bob Marley, 'Get up, stand up: don't give up the fight.' Call the detectives, Carrick. Let's get ready to rumble!"

Carrick groaned, shaking his head. "Oh, man."

Chapter Twenty-two

"Listen, don't pay any attention to what they're saying," Salaam Alihammad said, giving Demarcus a reassuring pat on the back. "The news is full of made-up stories."

Demarcus glared at the small television mounted on the wall, arms crossed tightly. "They're telling the whole world that *I* raped and tried to kill someone."

It was the first time he'd watched TV since his arrest. Now, in the recreation room with the Black Israelites, the 6 o'clock news blared. Suddenly, his own image flashed across the screen, soaring through the air in his basketball uniform, about to dunk. His stomach twisted.

"This is an update on the story we brought you a few days ago about Demarcus Jones," the anchor announced. "He's the former Cardinal Spellman High School basketball star, still being held at Rikers Island without bail for the rape and attempted murder of a young woman. Here's Daisy West with more."

The camera cut to a poised young reporter standing outside the DA's office, Silver Fox at her side. "I'm Daisy West in the Bronx with District Attorney Calvin Wilcox. DA Wilcox, can you give us an update on this case?" She thrust the microphone toward him.

"I can tell you it was a vicious crime, and I'm working hard to get justice for the victim," Silver Fox replied, his voice cold and resolute. "We have to make sure criminals know we will not tolerate these acts of violence in our community. They will be punished to the full extent of the law."

"You're sure that Demarcus Jones committed this crime?" Daisy pressed.

"He's in jail, isn't he?" Silver Fox stared straight into the camera, his eyes sharp as blades. "I'll only say that I'll make sure justice is served in this case. Thank you." He turned and strode away, the camera lingering on his retreat before returning to Daisy.

"There you have it from the prosecutor himself," she concluded. "I'd like to remind you that Jones was on his way to Stanford University this fall on a full basketball scholarship. We tried to contact the university, but they refused to comment. I'm Daisy West, ABC News."

Demarcus hung his head, shame burning through him. He could feel the eyes of everyone in the recreation room, some locked up for even darker crimes, boring into his back.

"It will be all right, my brother," Salaam said, his hand steady on Demarcus's shoulder. "Once your name is cleared, that slimy DA will be the first to apologize to you. Mark my words."

Demarcus nodded, but the words barely registered. He shot to his feet and hurried from the room, shoulders slumped, eyes stinging with tears. He made his way back to Salaam's cell, the only place that felt remotely safe since the attack in the bathroom.

He collapsed onto the bed, his long legs dangling over the edge, face buried in the thin pillow. *My teachers, friends, and schoolmates just saw that*, he thought, his mind spinning with the humiliation of the broadcast. *Oh my God. What do they think of me now? How can I ever face anyone again? My life is over.*

Tears leaked from the corners of his eyes, soaking into the pillow. The cell door opened and closed, and his body tensed. He sniffed, trying to stifle his sobs, his face still pressed into the pillow.

The bed across from him creaked as someone sat down. "You're upset by what you just saw people saying about you," Salaam Alihammad said, his voice steady and strong. "I know it hurts even more because you're innocent of what they're accusing you of."

Demarcus turned to face the small man with the powerful voice. "You believe me?" he asked, his words barely above a whisper.

"I do," Salaam replied with hesitation. "After you've spent enough time in a place like this, you develop a sixth sense about people."

Demarcus sat up straighter, wiping his damp face with the back of his hand. "What are you in here for?" he asked. "How long have you been locked up?"

Salaam pressed his lips together and leaned back against the wall, his eyes drifting to a distant memory. "Where do I even begin, my brother?"

"It's all right if you don't want to talk about it," Demarcus said quickly. "Honestly, you don't seem like you belong here."

"This time, I don't," Salaam admitted. "But for some people, once you're labeled a criminal, you'll always be a criminal."

"I know," Demarcus mumbled.

Salaam shook his head. "That doesn't apply to you. Your case is different."

Demarcus tilted his head; curiosity filled his eyes.

"I grew up in the Monroe Houses," Salaam began, referring to the notorious housing project at 1779 Story Avenue in the Soundview section of the Bronx. "It was a dangerous place, gangs everywhere, violence on every corner. When I was ten, I came home from school and found my mother dead on our filthy living room floor, a needle still stuck in her arm."

"Man," Demarcus breathed, shaking his head. "I'm sorry."

Salaam's gaze drifted above Demarcus's head, his eyes clouded with the past. "My father was never around. Sometimes he'd stop by, but most days he was at the bar or crashing at some girlfriend's place. I had to fend for myself, begging, stealing, doing whatever I could to survive. By thirteen, I dropped out of school completely and started hustling."

Demarcus listened in silence, drawn in by the raw honesty.

"I started running drugs for a small-time dealer. He'd give me a little money for food, just enough to keep me going. Then, one day, I made the worst decision of my life." Salaam's eyes met Demarcus's, the pain clear. "I decided to sample the product. I was seventeen."

Demarcus groaned, feeling the weight of Salaam's confession.

"Yup. Back then, people were practically killing each other for a hit of coke or crack. It must have been doing something powerful for them. At that point in my life, I had nothing and no one. So, I didn't care. I sniffed some coke, and the feeling was out of this world. Nothing else compared."

Salaam offered Demarcus a sad smile. "It didn't take long before I became a full-fledged dope fiend. I was begging, stealing, fighting, and nearly killing just to get that monkey off my back."

He continued. "Eventually, I got kicked out of the rat hole in the projects, so the streets became my home for years. One day, I was in this rundown drug house getting high when the cops raided the place. I probably had less than a quarter ounce of cocaine on me, just for personal use, which I'd stolen from a small-time dealer. They scooped me up and hauled me off to jail. Hours later, when I finally sobered up, I realized where I was, right here in this lovely place."

Demarcus scoffed.

"I was charged with possession of five ounces of cocaine and distribution of an illegal substance," Salaam said. "By that time, no one would trust me to sell drugs for them because it would end up in my nose or my veins, and it certainly wasn't five ounces. My public defender was a joke. He told me to take a plea deal for twenty-five years. I told him exactly where he could stick that deal."

He shifted on the bed, his voice steady. "So, I decided to take my chances in court. Twelve men and women of my so-called peers found me guilty of possession and distribution, and I was sentenced to fifteen years in prison for having less than a quarter ounce of cocaine."

"For personal use," Demarcus said, shaking his head. "The system did you wrong. You didn't need prison. You needed a rehabilitation center."

Salaam nodded. "I was locked up with some white guys who had committed murder," he emphasized, "and they were doing less time than I was. There was this racist white guy who had wiped out his wife, mother-in-law, and father-in-law. Do you know how much time he got for that triple murder?"

Demarcus shook his head.

"Seven years. They gave him a plea deal."

"What?"

"Oh, yes. The Black crack addict got more than twice that time for having a small amount of drugs for personal use. That's the system, my brother. Sentences for Black men are double or triple those of white men, many of whom are there for drug offenses. Especially here in New York, where you have those wretched Rockefeller Drug Laws. Do you know anything about them?"

"Not much," Demarcus admitted.

"The laws were named after Nelson Rockefeller, the state governor at the time. He signed them on May 8, 1973. They set the penalty for selling two ounces or more of heroin, cocaine, cannabis, or other illegal drugs at a minimum of fifteen years to life in prison, and a maximum of twenty-five years to life."

"That's crazy," Demarcus exclaimed. "This law is outdated and needs to be revised."

"You're preaching to the choir," Salaam replied. "But the one good thing that came out of my fifteen years in prison was that it got the monkey off my back. I got clean. Thank Allah for that."

"So, you got out, but why are you back here?" Demarcus asked.

"After doing my bid, I came back to the Bronx, the place I'd known since birth. Some things had changed, but much remained the same: gangs, violence, all of it. I'd converted to Islam in prison and was on a different path. I didn't want to get caught up in all that again. You know what I mean?"

"Yes," Demarcus replied.

"I decided I was going to leave the next day. I wasn't sure where I'd go, but I knew I had to get out and start fresh somewhere else. With nowhere to go, I slept under a bus stop that night. I woke up the next morning surrounded by cops and at least ten guns pointed at me."

"For what?" Demarcus nearly shouted.

"They said I robbed a grocery store in Staten Island and fled to the Bronx," Salaam said, shaking his head sadly. "I tried to tell them I'd only been to Staten Island once as a kid. I had just gotten out of prison and came straight to the Bronx. It wasn't me."

"They still arrested me," Salaam continued, his voice heavy with resignation. "They said there was an eyewitness, and I fit the description of the perpetrator."

"Eyewitness, huh?" Demarcus replied, skepticism in his tone.

"I was brought here almost two years ago and still haven't heard a thing. No bail, no public defender, nothing. They just left me here in Rikers like I'm nothing."

"You're innocent too," Demarcus said, his Adam's apple bobbing as he met Salaam's eyes. "When I get out of here, I'm going to do everything I can to help you. I promise."

Salaam smiled, a glimmer of hope in his tired eyes. "Thank you, but first, I want you to take care of yourself. Clear your name and get your life back. You hear me?"

"Yes. You know, I'm supposed to start college this fall, and I was still a little unsure of my major at times, but now, I'm certain. I want to become a lawyer."

"There you go." Salaam grinned. "You're going to make a very good one, too."

"I want to help people like you—and me, come to think of it. Innocent people, locked up for crimes they didn't commit, especially people of color," Demarcus said with conviction. "You know what I believe?"

"What's that?"

"I would rather see a guilty man go free than an innocent man go to prison."

Salaam stood and gave Demarcus a high five. "That's the spirit I want to see in you. That fighting spirit, my brother."

"Thank you," Demarcus replied, his voice steady. "Hey, my mom is coming to see me later. She told me again yesterday that she wants to meet you."

"No, no, no," Salaam said quickly, shaking his head. "That's not necessary."

"She won't stop until she thanks you personally for helping me," Demarcus insisted. "You might as well just get it over with."

Salaam hesitated, then shrugged. "Okay, sure."

***

"Look at this." Alfredo slammed a copy of the *New York Post* onto the conference room table in front of Viktor. "*Arresting the Wrong Man*," he read aloud, his voice brimming with disbelief.

Angelo, seated beside Viktor, snatched up the paper. The front cover was dominated by a striking photo of Demarcus, soaring through the air in his high school basketball jersey, about to dunk, a moment of triumph now twisted by the headlines. Angelo flipped the page and found another image, Demarcus in his graduation gown and cap, his signature megawatt smile shining out.

"Demarcus Jones is not only very talented," Angelo read, "but he's also brilliant, earning a full basketball scholarship to one of the preeminent institutions of higher education in the United States, Stanford University. Why is someone trying to rob this young man of such a promising future by falsely accusing him of rape and attempted murder? Why is the Bronx District Attorney so determined to convict an innocent man? We'll explore that some more later. However, based on where this investigation is going and where the evidence is pointing, I strongly believe the police have arrested the wrong man, and we will prove it."

"An incredible piece," Alfredo muttered, pacing furiously on the far side of the table. "After watching that news broadcast last night, I thought we were finally sealing that boy's fate. Now, here comes Ms. Simone with a cover story that turns everything upside down." The veins in his neck bulged as he shouted, "What is happening?"

"Dad, calm down," Angelo urged, "Remember your heart."

That only fueled Alfredo's rage. He erupted in a torrent of curses, switching between English and Italian, his anger echoing off the walls. Angelo and Viktor sat in silence, watching him rant and rave.

At last, Alfredo gripped the table with both hands, his chest heaving as if he'd just run a marathon. Sweat poured down his face. "I'm about to lose my company and everything I've worked for all my life, and you're telling me to calm down? You little rapist, no good—" He cut himself off, yanked out a chair, and collapsed into it, breathing heavily through his mouth.

Angelo lowered his head in shame.

"Boss, it's not over yet," Viktor finally told him. "It's just two sides telling different stories. We still have the DA on our side."

Alfredo shot Viktor a glare. "It would help even more if we had all the witnesses on our side as well."

Trevor Richards, Jimmy Mason, and Thomas Dunkley had all given signed witness statements to the police, confirming that they had seen Demarcus at the time he supposedly committed the crime, statements that supported Demarcus's claim of innocence.

"Afia has disappeared," Viktor reminded him, "and Ms. Lopez just moved into her new house. I know she won't talk to the cops."

"That's two more in our favor," Angelo added quietly, stealing a glance at his father before looking away.

Ignoring Angelo, Alfredo turned to Viktor, his eyes blazing with frustration. "Find out everything you can about the woman who wrote this garbage," he snapped, stabbing his finger at the newspaper. "I want this to stop. No more!"

Chapter Twenty-three

Carrick pulled up in front of the elegant house on North Broadway in Yonkers, his eyes sweeping over the manicured lawn and the neatly trimmed shrubs lining the driveway. "You've certainly come a long way in a short time," he muttered, parking along the curb. After locking his car, he strode purposefully up the driveway and rang the doorbell, taking a moment to admire the row of stately, well-kept homes that made the neighborhood feel almost storybook quiet.

He waited a few seconds, then pressed the bell again. Just as he was about to try a third time, the front door swung open.

"Ms. Lopez?" Carrick asked, addressing the elderly Hispanic woman who appeared in the doorway.

"Who wants to know?" she replied, her tone sharp and defensive.

"I'm Carrick O'Connor, Demarcus Jones's attorney," he said, extending his hand in greeting.

A flicker of surprise crossed Ms. Lopez's face, but it vanished as quickly as it came. "What do you want?" she snapped, ignoring his outstretched hand.

Carrick lowered his hand, keeping his voice calm. "There's no need for hostility, Ms. Lopez. I'm here to talk about a young man who once helped you and now needs your help in return. I hope you'll hear me out."

"I have nothing to say to you." Ms. Lopez stepped back, preparing to close the door, but Carrick gently but firmly pressed it open.

"Please, just a few minutes of your time," he insisted, stepping closer. "This is important."

Ms. Lopez glared at him, her patience clearly wearing thin. "I said I have nothing to say. Leave me alone."

Carrick tilted his head, studying her. "Why did you suddenly move from your Bronx apartment to this beautiful house?" he asked, gesturing to the impressive surroundings.

Ms. Lopez muttered something in rapid Spanish under her breath and tried again to shut the door, but Carrick held it firmly.

"I'm not leaving until you answer my questions," he said, his tone firm. The situation was getting more suspicious by the minute, and Ms. Lopez's evasiveness only fueled his determination.

Realizing she wouldn't get rid of him so easily, Ms. Lopez sighed in frustration. "What do you want?"

Carrick took a steadying breath. "Perhaps we could talk inside?"

Ms. Lopez glanced at her silver wristwatch, then shook her head. "No, we'll talk here. What do you want to know?"

"Do you know Demarcus Jones—DMan?" Carrick asked.

"I think so," she replied, folding her arms. "Why?"

"He was arrested a few days ago for attempted murder and sexual assault."

"So?" she shot back.

Carrick met her gaze. "Last Saturday night, close to midnight, Demarcus says he helped you carry some bags to your apartment. Can you confirm if that's true?"

"That's not true." Ms. Lopez uncrossed her arms and placed one hand on her hip.

"Excuse me?" Carrick's eyebrows shot up. "I have two other people, plus Demarcus himself, who all say he helped you that night. Ms. Lopez, this is extremely important. The timing matches when that young woman was attacked in the park. Your confirmation could help prove my client's innocence. So, I'm asking you again: can you confirm that Demarcus helped you carry your bags that night, around that time?" He held his breath, waiting.

"I never saw that boy that night." Ms. Lopez's eyes drifted to a spot above Carrick's head, refusing to meet his gaze.

"Ms. Lopez, look me in the eyes and repeat what you just said."

She bristled. "Listen, I've answered your questions," she said loudly. "Now leave, or I will call the police."

"You're lying." Carrick's voice trembled with anger. "You suddenly moved out of a one-bedroom apartment in the Bronx into this house just days after the incident. Now you're lying to send an innocent young man to jail, the same one who helped you."

Ms. Lopez jumped back, startled.

"I'm going to prove you're lying, and then I'll sue you for everything I can," Carrick shouted. "Don't get too comfortable in this house. Demarcus Jones is going to own it soon."

Ms. Lopez slammed the door shut in his face.

"She said what?" Naomi stared at Carrick in disbelief as she sat in his cubicle. Carrick had just finished telling her about his visit to Ms. Lopez.

"Yup, she said she never saw Demarcus that night," Carrick replied, his hands clasped together as if in prayer.

"She's lying," Naomi said, her voice rising. She quickly glanced around and lowered her voice. "Why is she doing this to my son?"

"Maybe for the same reason she was able to move into a big house in Yonkers. A house even I couldn't afford."

Naomi's face filled with horror. "That means we won't be able to get bail for Demarcus."

"It certainly works against us, but I'm still going to try with Tom's, Jimmy's, and Trevor's statements. Lieutenant Mulligan is also going to provide a character statement, and he's an officer of the court."

"But it would help if Ms. Lopez had told the truth and given us a statement, wouldn't it?"

Carrick nodded. "Tremendously."

"And it would be even better if the prosecutor didn't oppose bail?"

He nodded again, leaning forward. "Naomi, do you see what's happening here? I've been thinking about it, but now it's clear. There's another party working against your son, someone with money and power, trying to frame the wrong man."

"Carrick," Naomi leaned in, her voice low and urgent, closing the distance between them until only a few inches separated their faces. "There's another force at work here, one far more powerful than any person, one who owns all the wealth in the world, who is fair and just, who rebukes evil. That's the side I'm most concerned about. The Almighty God will give my son the victory."

Carrick offered a gentle smile. "I believe with you."

"Thank you," Naomi replied. "Can you do me a favor?"

"Of course."

"Please wait before you go to the judge about my son's bail."

Carrick frowned. "Why? I know the odds are against us, but we should still try."

"Oh, we will," Naomi assured him. "I just need to take care of something first."

"Naomi, are you going to see Ms. Lopez?"

Naomi gave a sad smile. “Ms. Lopez. I declare she will never have a good night’s sleep in that house until she tells the truth. That’s from my mouth to God’s ears.” She stood up. “I have to go see my son now.”

Carrick rose as well. “Are you sure you want me to wait to file the bail request?”

“Yes, please,” Naomi said. “Get everything ready, and we’ll do it soon. Thank you, Carrick.” With her head held high, she strode out of the room, leaving Carrick watching her until she disappeared.

Salaam drew a slow, steady breath as they stepped into the visiting room. “All these years behind bars,” he murmured, “and this is my first time here. Never had anyone come see me.”

Demarcus scanned the room. “Looks like my mom’s not here yet. Let’s wait at that table.”

They sat, and Salaam’s eyes wandered, taking in the unfamiliar space with quiet curiosity. Moments later, Demarcus spotted his mother approaching, her stride brisk, her presence radiant. He rose, a wide smile breaking across his face despite the bruises that lingered, the swelling that hadn’t yet faded.

“My son.” Naomi’s voice brimmed with joy as she reached him. She wrapped him in a warm embrace, then quickly let go before the nearby officer could intervene.

“Mom, this is Salaam Alihammad,” Demarcus said, gesturing to the man now standing beside him.

Naomi’s eyes brimmed with tears as she stepped forward and gently took both of Salaam’s hands. “Salaam,” she said softly. “The man God used to help my son.”

Caught off guard by the attention, Salaam shifted his weight and murmured, “It was just the right thing to do.”

"Done by the right person," Naomi replied softly, "with a heart strong enough to do it." She pulled him into a warm embrace and whispered, "Thank you."

A nearby correctional officer cleared his throat, sharp and deliberate.

Naomi quickly stepped back, allowing Demarcus to guide her to a seat.

"How are you feeling, baby?" she asked once they were settled, her eyes scanning his face, taking in every bruise and shadow.

"It's a little better," Demarcus said, "now that I'm with Salaam and his men."

Naomi turned to Salaam, her smile radiant, her eyes glistening again. "What you've done for my son," she said, "you've done for me."

Salaam nodded, his voice steady. "He's like family now. I just wish I could've stopped it all before it happened."

"You got there just in time," Naomi said, leaning over to gently pat Salaam's hand. She quickly withdrew, glancing up at the nearby officer. "How long have you been here, if you don't mind me asking?"

"Not at all," Salaam replied, then offered a condensed but powerful glimpse into his life, both the years before his incarceration and the long stretch behind bars.

When he finished, Naomi's eyes filled with sorrow. "I'm so sorry," she said softly. "You were wrongfully accused, just like my son. And to think you've been here all this time without even standing before a judge. It's heartbreaking."

"That's exactly what I told him," Demarcus added. "The system's broken."

Naomi turned back to Salaam, her voice steady with purpose. "I'm going to help you. Once I get my son out, I'll start working on your case."

Salaam's eyes dropped, emotion tightening his throat. "No one's ever tried to help me before," he whispered.

"I truly believe God places us in each other's lives for a reason," Naomi said with conviction. "You were there for my son, and now I'll be there for you."

"And me too," Demarcus added, his tone full of quiet loyalty.

Salaam's face lit up, a rare smile breaking through.

"Time's up," the officer said, stepping beside their table.

"Thank you again for helping my son," Naomi said quickly to Salaam. "I'll—"

The officer rapped the table and barked, "We have to go. Now."

Salaam stood up and looked at him. "We need another minute, my brother," he said in a low, dangerous voice.

The officer stepped back a few paces. "All right. Make it quick, Salaam."

Salaam sat back down, eyes locked on Naomi, silently urging her to finish.

"I was going to say I'll be back to see you," Naomi told him. "And I promise I'll do everything in my power to help you. Please look after my son until I get him out of here. Hopefully very soon."

"I promise I will," Salaam said sincerely. "My heart is full right now. Allah is the greatest."

"Salaam?" The officer's voice cut through the moment as he returned to the table.

Salaam, Demarcus, and Naomi rose together.

"Take care of yourself," Naomi said, stepping forward and wrapping Salaam in a firm embrace, ignoring both the rule and the officer's presence.

Salaam hugged her back and quickly hurried from the room.

"I'll see you soon, baby." Naomi also hugged Demarcus. She let him go when the officer loudly cleared his throat but didn't say anything. "You're going to get bail soon."

"Really, Mom?" Demarcus locked his hopeful eyes with hers. "For real?"

Naomi replied, "I know what I have to do. It's time to bring you home, my son."

There is a time for everything, and a season for every activity under the heavens.

Ecclesiastes 3:1

Chapter Twenty-four

Naomi turned the key in the lock just as a car screeched to a halt in front of the house. Carlos leapt out, rushing through the gate to join her.

"Señorita Naomi, I just spoke to Counselor, and he told me about Señorita Lopez. *Increíble*! That woman is a liar." Carlos's face twisted with fury, his thick black eyebrows nearly meeting in the middle. "*Mentiroso*. Liar."

"Come inside, dear." Naomi pushed the door open, stepped aside to let Carlos enter, then closed it behind them. She followed him into the living room, sighing as she lowered herself onto the couch and patted the space beside her. "What a day."

Carlos perched on the edge, his fingers tapping his knees as if playing a frantic piano. "I knew something was wrong when she moved to that big house." He shot Naomi a look. "Señorita Lopez was paid to lie on *mi familia*."

"Yes, she's lying, Carlos," Naomi replied, her voice steady. "There's something very suspicious about her sudden move to Yonkers. God will reveal everything soon and take care of her."

"God? Oh, no. Carlos is going to help God on this one."

"Now, Carlos, I don't want you talking like that." Naomi straightened, giving him a stern look. "I already have a son in jail. I don't need you to join him. Right now, I must get bail for Demarcus."

"Señorita Lopez is making that even more difficult." Carlos flashed an evil grin. "Okay, let the games begin, Señorita Lopez. Carlos has something for you." He sprang to his feet.

"Carlos." Naomi stood quickly and grabbed his hand. "Please stay away from Ms. Lopez. The detectives are investigating. They'll get to the bottom of this."

"Those detectives are fools. *Tontos*." Carlos gently pulled his hand free, took three quick steps toward the door, then paused and turned back. "Carlos is going to give God a little help with Señorita Lopez. Justice for Demarcus."

"Carlos. Wait—" Naomi called, but he was already gone.

She stood in the quiet, shaking her head. "Lord, this thing is just getting more complicated each day. Please continue to see us through." Naomi walked into the small kitchen, opened the refrigerator, and took out a bottle of Gatorade that Demarcus had left there.

She took a long drink, then made her way back to the living room, the bottle still in hand. Just as she settled in, her cell phone rang from her handbag on the couch. Naomi dug it out and saw Carrick's name on the caller ID.

"Hi, Carrick," Naomi answered, her voice weary but hopeful.

"Naomi, how is Demarcus holding up?" Carrick asked, referencing her earlier visit to Rikers Island.

"As best as he can under the circumstances," Naomi replied. "I promised him we're going to get bail for him soon."

Carrick groaned audibly. "I'm standing outside the prosecutor's office right now. I decided to try speaking with him again while I wait for you to give me permission to file the bail hearing request. Silver Fox won't budge, Naomi. He seems more determined than ever to block Demarcus's bail."

"Carrick, I have to run, but I'll call you later," Naomi said, grabbing her handbag and rushing out of the apartment as if it were on fire.

She hurried up Adee Avenue toward Eastchester Road, her mind a tangle of anxious thoughts. As she walked, a familiar gypsy cab passed by in the opposite direction. She flagged it down, and the driver made a quick U-turn, stopping at her feet.

Naomi climbed into the back seat and gave the driver the address. As the cab drove through traffic, she sat with her hands trembling in her lap, eyes squeezed shut, lips moving in a silent prayer. "Please give me the strength, Lord."

Doubt gnawed at her. She considered asking the driver to turn around and take her home, but the image of Demarcus's battered, bruised face flashed in her mind. "This is for my baby," she whispered. "This has to be done."

The cab pulled up in front of the building, but Naomi remained oblivious, her eyes still tightly closed.

"Ma'am, we're here," the driver said, turning in his seat.

Naomi opened her eyes slowly, handed him some money with a trembling hand, and stepped out. The cab peeled away as she stood on the sidewalk, clutching her handbag to her chest. Apprehension twisted in her gut as she gazed up at the building. She drew a deep breath, steeled herself, and walked inside.

The lobby buzzed with activity, but to Naomi, the world seemed to move in slow motion. After clearing security, she was directed down the hall where someone would further assist her.

When Naomi reached the reception desk, she found it unattended. Her eyes drifted to the closed office door behind it, where the name she sought was displayed. Without hesitation, she strode over and knocked.

"Come in."

Naomi entered, closing the door softly behind her.

"Who are you?" District Attorney Calvin Wilcox asked, straightening in his chair as he watched her approach. "I don't have an appointment on my schedule."

"I'm Demarcus Jones's mother," Naomi replied, standing tall and unwavering.

"Ma'am, I can't discuss your son's case with you," Silver Fox said, his tone clipped. "He has an attorney who can contact me if needed. And he does, by the way."

"My son is innocent." Naomi sat down in one of the visitor's chairs, uninvited but resolute. "He's being wrongfully accused."

Silver Fox threw his head back and laughed, the sound echoing off the office walls. "Of course he is. You're his mother. Naturally, you don't want to believe the worst of him."

"You're right. I am his mother, and I know my child," Naomi snapped, her composure slipping as her voice sharpened. "He's a *good* person."

"He's a rapist," Silver Fox retorted, his voice cold and final.

"You don't know him!" Naomi shot to her feet as if the chair had burned her. She leaned across the desk, her eyes blazing, and Silver Fox leaned back, a smirk playing on his lips.

With her finger pointed directly at him, Naomi's voice rang out, "Tell me, Mr. Prosecutor, why are you so determined to send your own *son* to prison?"

Chapter Twenty-five

New York City

Almost Nineteen Years Ago

"That low-down, dirty dog," Naomi spat as she stormed down Seventh Avenue in Manhattan. "Good-for-nothing drug addict. Crackhead. Cokehead. Nasty john crow." She hurled a string of Jamaican curses into the night, wincing as she dabbed her swollen lip with a white handkerchief now speckled with blood.

"You think you can beat me?" she muttered, pausing at a red light, her anger simmering. "Because I'm a woman, right? I showed you, though. You piece of—"

A couple waiting beside her at the crosswalk exchanged uneasy glances and hurried away, but Naomi barely noticed. Her fury blazed hotter with every step. "I used to help you, you idiot. You have the nerves to put your hand on *me*? Naomi Jones? Yuh mussa mad."

Naomi kept cursing, her long, blonde weave whipping behind her as she picked up speed, three-inch platform sandals clicking against the pavement. Her tight red dress clung to her petite frame, riding up her thighs as she marched on.

Earlier that evening, Naomi had dressed to the nines for a rare night off from her job as a live-in nanny for the Templetons. She'd planned to window shop in Midtown, treat herself to dinner, maybe even catch a movie, simple pleasures for someone with no close friends or family in the city. The moment Naomi stepped out of her employer's building, a disheveled man lunged from the shadows and snatched at her handbag. Instinct kicked in. She held tight and yanked it back. Enraged, he struck her across the face before she had a chance to defend herself.

Naomi stood frozen at first, dazed as the man's fists found their mark again. But then, fury ignited in her chest. She lashed out with everything she had, refusing to be anyone's victim. Her fists flew, sharp, relentless, driving him backward until he broke away and fled.

Panting, with her weave whipping around her face, blood trailing from a cut above her eye, and her dress rumpled and askew, Naomi looked around and realized she was still standing outside her employer's home.

"I'll get you another time," she shouted after his retreating figure. She straightened her dress, smoothed her hair, and strode away, her anger undiminished.

Now, after what felt like miles of walking, Naomi's aching feet finally carried her into the Meatpacking District. She spotted a small, nondescript bar called Memories and marched inside, not bothering to glance left or right. With determined steps, she made her way straight to the bartender.

"Whiskey, neat," she ordered, rummaging through her handbag until she found a fifty-dollar bill, which she placed firmly on the counter.

As the bartender poured her drink, Naomi slid onto a high barstool, her dress riding up her smooth thighs. She ignored the curious and interested glances from a few men nearby. Taking the glass, she threw her head back and swallowed the whiskey in a single gulp.

"One more," she demanded, slapping the glass down and pushing the bill toward the bartender, who nodded and poured her a second.

That drink vanished just as quickly as the first. Naomi, now feeling lightheaded from drinking on an empty stomach, slowed down for her third, sipping more cautiously.

A deep voice beside her broke the silence. "Looks like someone else is having a rough day."

Turning, Naomi noticed for the first time the tall, handsome white man sitting next to her.

"Vodka, neat," he said, raising his glass in a mock toast. "My fourth one, I think." He took a long sip, his green eyes locking with hers.

Naomi grinned. "Guess I need to catch up with you," she replied, quickly finishing her drink. She tapped the counter for the bartender's attention and began searching her bag for more cash.

"Put her drink on my tab," the man told the bartender as he approached.

"You didn't have to do that," Naomi said, her tone softening. "I can pay for my own drink."

He shrugged. "I figured as much. Calvin Wilcox." He extended his right hand, which trembled slightly.

"Naomi Jones," she replied, shaking his hand, her own a little unsteady as well.

Calvin glanced at her face, noticing the swelling. "What does the other guy look like?" he asked, taking another sip.

Naomi gave him a puzzled look until he gestured to her bruised eye.

She smirked. "Hopefully worse than me. That little crackhead."

"Crackhead? You were attacked? Did you call the cops?" Calvin looked at her with genuine concern.

Naomi shook her head. "No. He ran away."

"You still should have reported it," Calvin replied sternly. "He had no right to put his hands on you. He should be arrested."

"You're probably right. I beat his behind, though. I bet he won't try it with me again if he sees me." She took a sip of her drink, then tapped her temple. "Plus, it looks like he's not too right up here. Probably on drugs."

"Even more reason to get him off the streets."

Naomi studied Calvin for a moment, then asked, "What's got you drinking yourself into a stupor?"

Calvin's face darkened as he stared straight ahead, his hand tightening around the glass. "I left work early to surprise my fiancée. I knew she was at work, so I had time to make my famous lasagna, her favorite, and have it ready for her when she got home. I used my key and let myself into her apartment. As I made my way to the bedroom to change, I heard sounds coming from inside."

"Oh, man." Naomi shook her head, knowing what was coming.

"I reached the door, which was partially open, and observed her presence." Calvin glanced toward Naomi, his expression composed, though his emotions were evident. "My fiancée having sex with her ex-boyfriend. *Surprise.*" He tipped his glass back and drained the last of his drink, then caught the bartender's eye and signaled for another.

"What did she say when she saw you?" Naomi asked, her voice laced with sympathy.

"She didn't see me."

Naomi blinked in surprise. "What do you mean?"

"I turned around and left the apartment before they saw me," Calvin replied, his tone flat.

"She has no idea you know?"

"Nope." The waiter set a fresh drink in front of him. Calvin raised his glass in a silent toast and took a long swallow.

"You're better than me," Naomi said, shaking her head. "I'd probably have killed them both. When I was done with them, they'd know not to cross me."

Calvin looked at her, then burst out laughing. Naomi joined in, their laughter bubbling up and filling the bar, the alcohol in their veins making everything seem even funnier.

"Buff, baff." Naomi's folded fists punched wildly in the air, her head moving left to right, as if she were in the boxing ring. "Upper cut, lower cut."

Calvin laughed so hard he nearly toppled off his barstool. "You're something else," he told Naomi, shaking his head in disbelief.

Their conversation flowed easily, laughter and stories filling the air until Calvin admitted he was starving. Naomi's stomach grumbled in agreement. After settling the bill, the two slipped out of the bar, arms wrapped around each other's waists, weaving through the city's neon-lit streets on unsteady feet.

They giggled like mischievous teenagers, glancing around for a late-night bite. As they passed the Liberty Inn, they stopped abruptly, eyes locking, desire flickering between them. The world seemed to pause. Without a word, they surrendered to the moment, drawn together by a magnetic pull.

Calvin pressed his lips to Naomi's, and she responded with equal fervor. Wordlessly, he took her hand, and together they crossed the lobby to the registration desk. Moments later, they entered a modest hotel room, hands still entwined, hearts pounding.

Clothes fell away in a flurry of laughter and clumsy movements. Calvin nearly tripped over his pants, sending Naomi into another fit of giggles. In seconds, they were tangled together on the bed, losing themselves in each other, letting the night's disappointments dissolve in a rush of passion and reckless abandon.

***

Early the next morning, Naomi groaned as she rolled onto her back. It felt as if a sumo wrestler was sitting on her head. She opened her eyes and scanned the room, the memories of the night before slowly returning. Ignoring the throbbing pain in her head, Naomi quickly sat up and glanced at the empty pillow beside her. Calvin was gone. Her eyes darted to the small digital clock on the bedside table, widening in alarm.

"Work, work," she mumbled, hopping off the bed and hurriedly pulling on her wrinkled dress.

Moments later, she exited the motel. Raising her right thumb, she tried to hail a yellow cab. One screeched to a stop in front of her. She hopped into the back and gave the driver the address.

As the cab weaved its way uptown, Naomi's thoughts drifted to Calvin Wilcox and the night they had shared. "You're a real little skank," she muttered under her breath, then giggled. The truth was, Naomi didn't regret spending the night with the handsome stranger. She had broken up with her high school sweetheart long before leaving Jamaica and had been single ever since arriving in New York. To keep loneliness at bay, she threw herself into her work, focusing on the two children she cared for. It felt good to share a moment of intimacy with someone, even if it was just for one night.

But eight weeks later, when Naomi ran to the bathroom to throw up her breakfast, she realized that her one-night stand would become a lifelong reminder. That afternoon, her doctor confirmed it. She was pregnant.

Naomi returned home from the doctor, her mind in turmoil. It was one thing to have slept with a stranger, but neither she nor Calvin had thought about protection.

"You're lucky it's not some sexually transmitted disease," Naomi scolded herself. "Especially AIDS."

What am I going to do? Naomi wondered, sinking into the couch, her mind swirling with anxiety. She reached for a copy of the *Wall Street Journal* that Mr. Templeton had left on the coffee table, hoping for a distraction. Instead, her eyes landed on a headline that made her gasp,

THE GOVERNOR'S DAUGHTER WED BRONX'S ADA CALVIN WILCOX.

There, in full color, was a radiant wedding photo of Mindy and Calvin Wilcox.

Naomi's hand instinctively pressed against her stomach as she stared at Calvin's familiar, beaming smile. The reality hit her with a jolt. Her baby's father was now a married man.

Right then and there, Naomi decided no one would ever know the identity of her child's father, not even Calvin himself. She quietly rented an apartment in the Bronx and, with the support of her employers, continued working until just days before her son, Demarcus Jones, was born.

Naomi raised Demarcus alone, telling him, when he was old enough to ask, that his father had died before he was born. It was a secret she guarded fiercely, a truth hidden from the world. Now, that secret was on the verge of unraveling. The prosecutor—District Attorney Calvin Wilcox, known as Silver Fox—was, in fact, Demarcus Jones's biological father.

Everything was about to become far more complicated.

Chapter Twenty-six

"You . . . you're Naomi?" Silver Fox's eyes nearly popped from his head. "I've only ever been with one—"

"Black woman," Naomi finished for him. "Yes, I'm Naomi Jones."

"I was going to say I've only been with one other woman since meeting my wife in college. Oh my gosh." Silver Fox sprang to his feet, staring at Naomi as if she were a ghost. "Naomi? You look so different."

"I am different," Naomi replied, her tone steady. "Second Corinthians 5:17: 'Therefore if anyone is in Christ, he is a new creation. Old things have passed away; behold, all things have become new.'"

Naomi had shed the long, blonde weave for her natural hair in short, elegant twists. The heavy makeup and bright lipstick she once wore had given way to a soft gloss and a light dusting of face powder. Her once tight, short dresses had given way to modest, graceful attire. It was a complete transformation from nearly nineteen years ago.

"But . . . but . . ." Silver Fox paced in front of her, words failing him for once. "My son?"

"Yes, Calvin. Demarcus is your son."

"Why didn't you tell me?" Silver Fox demanded, stepping close, his shock quickly morphing into anger. "All this time?"

"First of all, we never exchanged numbers," Naomi snapped, her voice sharp. She drew a deep breath, then sat down and gestured for him to do the same. "Please, sit. I'll explain."

"You'll explain? Explain how you kept something like this from me?" he shouted.

"I did what was best," Naomi shot back, her voice rising to match his.

"Best for whom?" Silver Fox slammed his fist on the desk, making Naomi flinch.

"You were a married man," she shouted. "Married to the governor's daughter. Did you want me to show up at your doorstep and announce to you and your new bride that you were about to be a father? That you'd fathered a child with a Black woman? A child conceived when you cheated on your fiancée?"

It felt as if the air had been sucked out of the room. Silver Fox slumped into his chair, suddenly looking years older. "You saw the article in the newspaper," he murmured.

Naomi nodded. "It was everywhere, on the news, in print. I suppose you forgave her for cheating on you?"

Silver Fox nodded slowly. "I cheated too. Yes, her infidelity drove me into that bar, and that's how we ended up together. Two wrongs don't make a right, but I thought it best to forgive her and move on."

"I understand," Naomi replied gently. "But can you see why I chose not to tell you about the baby? We would have become a media circus. I can just imagine the headlines. 'ADA cheats on governor's daughter and fathers a Black child.' I couldn't face that."

"It's not about Black or white, Naomi," Silver Fox said, his voice firm.

"For you and me, maybe not. But to everyone else . . ." Naomi gave him a knowing look. "We would have had no peace, and I didn't want to live like that. I didn't want my child to suffer for it."

"It wasn't just your decision to make, you know." Silver Fox's expression softened, though the hurt lingered. He turned his chair to face the window, his back to Naomi. A heavy silence settled between them, each lost in thought, both aware that their lives had just changed forever.

At last, Naomi broke the quiet. "I need you to help me get my son out of jail. Carrick said if you don't oppose bail, it will make things easier."

"Your son." Silver Fox still faced away from her.

"Once he's out and I have a chance to tell him about you, we can get a DNA test done."

Silver Fox turned to look at her. "I only spent a few hours with you, Naomi, but you don't strike me as a liar. For the other people this will affect . . ." His voice trailed off.

"Your wife and son," Naomi said, her gaze drifting to a framed photograph of Silver Fox's family on his desk. "You have a very handsome young man there."

"Samuel," Silver Fox replied, his voice softening. "He's fifteen, but he acts like he's twenty-five."

Naomi offered a gentle smile. "Demarcus was always an old soul, even as a child. And then he shot up like a weed. He's about six-foot-four now."

"He gets that from me," Silver Fox said, meeting Naomi's eyes. "But I want you to know, I would never have turned my back on my son. No matter what anyone said or did, I would have been there for him."

A wave of shame washed over Naomi. She looked down at her lap, her voice trembling. "I know. What I did to you, and to Demarcus, was probably wrong, but at the time, I thought it was best. It's the one thing I ask God to forgive me for every day. It's the one thing that's kept me from being totally free. It's ironic, isn't it? After all this pain, the truth has to come out to fix a lie. I just hope you'll find it in your heart to forgive me."

Silver Fox's eyes glistened with unshed tears. One slipped down his cheek before he quickly wiped it away. "Forgiveness," he murmured. "There's going to be a lot of that needed, from many people, including me."

Naomi looked into the green eyes her son had inherited. "He's going to be so angry with me," she whispered, thinking of Demarcus. "I just hope, in time, he'll understand. But right now, I need to get him out of that place. He was attacked, you know?"

Silver Fox lowered his head, his voice barely audible. "I know. His lawyer told me." He looked up, pain etched across his face.

"Will you help us?" Naomi pleaded, her voice raw with hope.

"I'll have to recuse myself from the case," Silver Fox said, his tone resolute. "But first, I'll call Carrick and let him know I won't oppose bail."

Naomi burst into tears. "God bless you," she managed, her gratitude overflowing. "If you only knew how much this means to me."

Silver Fox shook his head, a dazed smile flickering across his lips. "For some strange reason, I feel like I'm dreaming and about to wake up. Don't get me wrong, I'm not saying this is a bad thing. It's just . . . a lot. To find out I have an almost eighteen-year-old son, a boy I thought was a criminal, someone I was preparing to prosecute and send to prison. Is this the Twilight Zone?"

Naomi tilted her head, a bittersweet smile on her lips. "It feels that way, doesn't it? But as I said, I take full responsibility for this mess."

"No, no, no. It takes two," Silver Fox told her. "I'm probably going to feel slighted for a while for missing so many years, but we can't go back. I'm going to try and move forward, and hopefully we can figure things out."

"I would like that."

Silver Fox looked at Naomi and said, "Let me give Carrick a call, then I want you to tell me everything you can about Demarcus."

"Oh, thank you, Lord." Naomi planted kisses all over Demarcus's face. "You're a great God." Kisses and more kisses.

Demarcus pulled his mother into his arms and held onto her tightly, the tears flowing down his face. "I'm home, Mom. I'm really home."

From where he stood across the room, Carrick struggled to hold back the tears as he watched the reunion of Naomi and Demarcus in her living room. He had just returned from picking up Demarcus at Rikers Island after his bail was granted.

Naomi pulled away slightly and looked up into her son's face, and said, "You've lost weight," as if she hadn't seen him two days ago.

Demarcus laughed out loud, happy to be home. He had spent ten days at Rikers Island, and it felt like ten years.

"I'm so glad to have you home, sweetheart," Naomi replied.

"Thank you for bailing me out as you promised," Demarcus said. "I knew you and Carrick would get me out."

Naomi and Carrick exchanged a quick look before she looked away.

"I want to talk to you," Naomi told Demarcus. "This is very important."

"Okay, but in a few minutes, Mom." Demarcus gave her a kiss on the cheek. "I need to take a shower and change. Carrick, I'll be back, okay? I know you said you also wanted to talk to me." He rushed off toward the bathroom.

Carrick went and sat down on the couch. Moments later, Naomi joined him. "I still can't wrap my mind around what's going on," Carrick said to her. "Silver Fox is Demarcus's father?"

"Yes. It was a long time ago," Naomi replied. "I was a different woman back then."

"Naomi, I'm not judging you," Carrick said, reaching over to gently touch her hand. "Honestly, I'm just stunned by how everything has unfolded. I wish you could have seen Silver Fox in court when he told the judge he didn't oppose bail, but recommended Demarcus be released immediately into his mother's custody." Carrick let out a chuckle.

"I can just imagine the judge's face," Naomi replied.

"Judge Mambo stared at him as if he'd just seen Bigfoot. Then he asked Silver Fox what had changed his mind so suddenly. Silver Fox explained he'd received new information that might prove Demarcus's innocence, and that it wouldn't be fair to keep him in jail while the case was being investigated. The judge pressed for details, and I was holding my breath, since I'd just learned about Silver Fox's connection to Demarcus. I thought he might reveal it right there. Instead, he told the judge about the men who'd given signed witness statements, confirming they saw Demarcus at the exact time the crime supposedly happened, and about him helping Ms. Lopez that night. Thankfully, the judge reviewed everything and agreed to bail, though it was set at two hundred thousand dollars."

"I'm grateful, even if that's a steep amount," Naomi said. "And I'm especially thankful to Calvin for paying the bond."

"The man just wrote a check for twenty thousand dollars," Carrick said, snapping his fingers. "Just like that."

"He promised he'd help Demarcus," Naomi added.

Carrick nodded. "You know, I was really looking forward to going up against Silver Fox in court. But I have to admit, I feel much better working with him than against him. The man is a beast of a lawyer."

"I've heard," Naomi replied. "We need all the help we can get, don't we?"

"Yes, we do. Unfortunately, the fight isn't over until the case is dismissed, or we win at trial."

"God won't let it go to trial," Naomi said firmly. "The truth will come out, and the real culprit will be revealed. Mark my words."

However, there were people determined to keep the truth hidden—at any cost.

Chapter Twenty-seven

Ms. Lopez peered anxiously through her bedroom window, her eyes wide with fear. The yellow sports car was still there, parked in front of her house, its presence haunting her for two days, coming and going like a threat that refused to leave.

"They're not going away," her son Juan muttered as he shuffled into the room and perched on the edge of her king-sized bed. "Last night, they told me you'll never have any peace until you tell the truth. But what truth?" His bloodshot eyes, wild and restless, fixed on her.

Ms. Lopez bristled, stepping away from the window. "I don't know what they're talking about," she snapped. "Those thugs won't intimidate me."

Juan scratched at his arms, the effects of his last hit already fading. "Can I have twenty dollars? I want to get some cigarettes."

With a heavy sigh, Ms. Lopez replied, "I don't have any money."

Juan scoffed, glancing around the lavishly furnished bedroom. "You had enough to buy this big house. All this time you said we were broke, and now look at this place. This room is bigger than our whole apartment in the Bronx."

"I've been saving for years to buy this house for us, Juan," she lied, her voice tight. "I used every cent I had."

Juan scratched harder. "When are you going back to work? We need money."

"Maybe you could try getting a job for once in your life," Ms. Lopez shot back, marching out of the bedroom and into the kitchen, Juan trailing behind. "All you do is lie around and get high. And who pays for it? Me."

Juan glared at her for a moment, then stormed out, slamming the door so hard the walls rattled.

Ms. Lopez flinched, then lingered in the kitchen, lost in troubled thought. Juan was right. The money Alfredo had given her wouldn't last forever. She needed to get back to work, but the men stalking her house filled her with dread.

"This house is a blessing," she whispered to herself. "I've worked hard my whole life, and I'd never be able to afford something like this otherwise. No one is going to take it away from me." With renewed determination, she returned to her bedroom and retrieved her handbag from its hiding place beneath the mattress.

Moments later, she locked the front door and set off down the street toward the bus stop, her steps slow and stiff.

"Ms. Lopez," Carlos called out, spotting her as he leaned against the car, two friends flanking him. "That's a nice house you've got there."

She ignored him, quickening her pace.

"Where'd you get the money to buy that house, Ms. Lopez?" Carlos shouted, his voice echoing down the quiet street as he and his friends followed. "Did you win the lottery? I didn't see you on TV collecting your prize."

Panic surged through Ms. Lopez. She tried to move faster, but her aching knees betrayed her. Her heart pounded as she glanced around, desperate for someone, anyone, to appear, but the neighborhood was still and empty except for the occasionally passing car.

"You think you can get away with lying on my family, Ms. Lopez?" Carlos's voice grew sharper, angrier. "Send him to prison for a big house? No way."

Suddenly, Ms. Lopez screamed as someone grabbed her from behind. "Let me go," she cried, struggling in their grip.

Carlos spun Ms. Lopez around to face him, his two friends closing in behind her, boxing her in. She was trapped.

"What do you want?" Ms. Lopez's voice trembled. "I'm going to call the police."

Carlos's lips curled into a snarl. "That's exactly what you should do. In fact, it's why we're here." He stepped closer, so near he could see every wrinkle and freckle on her face. "You're going to call the police and finally tell them the truth about Demarcus Jones."

Ms. Lopez's eyes widened, her whole body shaking. "I–I don't know what you're talking about," she stammered, clinging to her lie.

Carlos's eyes narrowed to slits. "Don't play games with me, señorita," he hissed. "You know exactly who I mean. The young man who helped you carry your bags home a few nights ago. The same one you told the police you never saw. The one now facing charges of attempted murder and rape because of you. The one you're trying to send to prison."

"No, no, no." Ms. Lopez shook her head frantically. "No one helped me carry my bags. That's a lie."

The veins in Carlos's neck bulged. He stepped even closer, their bodies nearly touching. "So, you want to do this the hard way? Fine—"

"What's going on out there?" The strong voice boomed from behind the high gate of the house they stood in front of.

"Help me!" Ms. Lopez screamed, her voice cracking. "Help! Help!"

"Leave her alone! I'm calling the police," the man shouted.

Carlos shot Ms. Lopez a furious glare and leaned in, his breath hot against her ear. "This isn't over. We'll be back."

Ms. Lopez watched, heart pounding, as Carlos and his friends jogged back to their car and sped away. She let out a shaky breath, then hurried back inside, too rattled to continue her errands. It took several minutes for her trembling to subside. The encounter had shaken her to her core. She wandered from room to room, touching the walls, reminding herself of the house's importance to her and Juan.

"This is my house," she told herself. "I did what I had to do. There's no turning back now."

Suddenly, the doorbell rang, slicing through her thoughts. Ms. Lopez froze, fearing the men had returned. The bell rang again.

"Ms. Lopez, we're the police."

Moving as quietly as she could, Ms. Lopez crept to the front door and peered through the peephole. Her heart skipped. Two police officers stood on the other side.

"Oh, dear," she whispered, realizing the man from earlier had indeed called the cops.

The doorbell rang again, more insistent this time. Ms. Lopez hesitated, her nerves fraying. The last thing she wanted was to talk to the police about the incident. Too many questions would follow, and she had no good answers.

"Ms. Lopez," the female officer said loudly. "We know you're in there. Please open the door."

"We're not leaving until we speak with you," added her partner.

Reluctantly, Ms. Lopez cracked the door halfway. "Yes?"

"Ms. Lopez, I'm Detective Hanes, and this is my partner, Detective Rich. We're from the 47th Precinct in the Bronx. We'd like to ask you a few questions."

"About what?" she snapped, her tone defensive.

"Demarcus Jones. May we come inside, please?"

"That won't be necessary," Ms. Lopez replied sharply. "I already spoke to that lawyer."

Detective Rich stepped closer, his voice calm but persistent. "Ma'am, we've received new information since then and would really appreciate a moment of your time. I promise we won't take long."

"I told you I didn't see that boy that night. He never carried my bags," Ms. Lopez insisted, her voice rising. "I don't know what else to tell you."

The detectives exchanged a knowing glance.

"So, our witnesses and Mr. Jones are all lying?" Detective Hanes pressed.

Ms. Lopez shrugged, refusing to meet their eyes.

Detective Rich glanced around the entryway. "This is a really nice house. Must have cost a pretty penny, huh?"

"I have to go," Ms. Lopez snapped, her patience gone. "I said I never saw that boy that night." She shot them a nasty look before slamming the door shut.

That was her story, and she was determined to stick to it.

Chapter Twenty-eight

"Demarcus, please open the door and talk to me." Naomi's knuckles rapped gently but insistently on her son's bedroom door. "It's been two days since you locked yourself away. We need to finish talking about your father."

Demarcus's eighteenth birthday had come and gone, passing like any other day. What should have been a milestone was overshadowed by the chaos that had engulfed his life. Just when he thought things couldn't possibly get worse, his mother dropped a revelation that shattered his world.

"I thought my father was dead," Demarcus shouted from behind the door, his voice raw. "Isn't that what you've been telling me all these years?"

"Baby, I made a mistake. Please, come out so we can talk about this. Please, Demarcus. We still have a criminal case hanging over you."

The door swung open abruptly. Demarcus stood in the doorway, bare-chested in gray jogging pants, his glare sharp and wounded. "How could you lie to me like that, Mom?" His eyes brimmed with pain.

"I thought I was protecting you, baby."

"How convenient. And you call yourself a Christian." His words dripped with bitterness. "What a hypocrite."

Naomi stepped closer until she was inches away from Demarcus. Tilting her head back to meet his eyes, she hissed, "Let me tell you something, boy. Watch your mouth. I'm still your mother."

"My mother who told me my father was dead!"

"That was wrong." Naomi's voice softened, but her gaze remained steady.

"That was a lie." Demarcus's voice rose, each word sharper than the last.

"Yes, it was. Listen—"

"I'm tired of listening to all this crap," he snapped.

"Demarcus."

"I don't care, Mom. This is messed up."

"I know it is," Naomi agreed. "Please, let me explain everything."

"You mean tell me more lies, right?"

Naomi drew a deep breath. She knew Demarcus had every reason to be angry, but his tone was crossing a line she never condoned. "No, and again, please watch your mouth. Okay?"

Demarcus rolled his eyes, refusing to back down.

"Every saint was a sinner, Demarcus. And every sinner has a past. I'm not proud of what I did, and if I could go back, I would probably handle things differently. But I did what I thought was best."

"Best for whom?" Demarcus shot back, his anger simmering.

"Best for you." Naomi gently poked his stomach with her finger. "Everything I've done, from the moment I became pregnant with you, has been for you." She sighed, rubbing her hands over her face. "I know—"

The shrill ring of her cell phone cut her off mid-sentence. She pulled it from her skirt pocket and glanced at the unfamiliar number on the caller ID.

"Hello?"

"Hi, it's Calvin," Silver Fox said, his voice as weary as hers. "I . . . hmm . . . I was wondering if we could get together today and talk some more about Demarcus."

Naomi glanced at Demarcus, then quickly looked away. "Of course. I've taken some time off work until this whole mess is resolved. I'll—"

"Is that him?" Demarcus interrupted, raising his voice so Calvin could hear.

"Yes, Demarcus," Naomi replied, then turned her attention back to the call. "Calvin, I'll have to call you back."

"You told him?" Calvin asked, his voice tense. "You told him about me?"

"Yes, and as expected, he's not taking it well," Naomi admitted.

"I can imagine," Calvin said quietly. "This has been hard on everyone, Naomi."

"I know. I'm sorry," she replied. "Let me finish talking with my son, then I'll call you back, okay?"

Calvin agreed, and Naomi ended the call.

"What does he want?" Demarcus demanded.

"*He* is your father," Naomi answered, stepping around Demarcus and entering his bedroom. She took in the chaos, the unmade bed, clothes strewn across the floor, even a dirty sock hanging from the dresser. Normally, she would have insisted he clean up immediately, but the last few days had been anything but normal.

She sat on the edge of his bed and patted the space beside her. "Come sit with me, please. I've been trying to explain everything, but you haven't let me."

Demarcus hesitated, then sat beside her, arms crossed over his chest, his face clouded with frustration.

"You know, it was unfortunate circumstances that brought Calvin and me together. It wasn't planned," Naomi began, her voice gentle. "It just happened."

Demarcus uncrossed his arms and looked at her. "What unfortunate circumstances?"

Naomi lowered her head, as if weighed down by shame. "We were only together once."

Demarcus stared at her, surprised.

"It was my day off from work," Naomi said, then began to recount her chance encounter with his father.

Demarcus listened in silence, emotions flickering across his face like the neon lights of Times Square.

Naomi's voice trembled as she looked at Demarcus. "After I saw the news that he'd just gotten married, I didn't know what to do." Tears welled in her eyes. "I wish I'd had someone to talk to, but I was all alone."

Demarcus's anger softened, his own tears slipping down his cheeks. "I'm sorry, Mom."

She shook her head gently. "I'm not. You are the best thing that ever happened to me. My only regret is not telling Calvin about you, and for lying to you."

He squeezed her hands. "I think I can understand why you did it then, but you could have told me when I got older, Mom."

Naomi nodded, her tears flowing freely now. "I know, baby. Would you believe that I honestly intended to tell you? I kept telling myself I'd wait until you turned eighteen, right before college started, because I felt that would be the perfect moment." She reached out, wiping away his tears. "You know, it's the one thing I had to repent for every day—this lie that hovered over my head."

"I'm sorry I called you a liar." Demarcus pulled her into his arms. "I'm just so mad about everything, Mom. My life is spinning out of control, and I don't know what I did to deserve this." He rested his head on her shoulder and wept.

Naomi held him close, her own tears mingling with his. "We're going to get the victory, my son." She rubbed his back, her voice steadying. "Don't you see God is already at work? Who would have thought that someone who could have been our biggest enemy is now our ally?"

"My father," Demarcus whispered, tightening his embrace.

"Yes. The man who was prosecuting you just posted your bail to set you free. Do you think it's a coincidence that the DA turns out to be your father? It's all part of God's plan, Demarcus. None of this is a surprise to Him, baby."

Mother and son clung to each other, crying and talking until their tears were spent. Drained but comforted by the honesty between them, they lay down together, Demarcus's head on his mother's chest, her arms wrapped protectively around him. Before long, exhaustion pulled them both into sleep.

But the nightmare was not yet over.

Chapter Twenty-nine

"The Ocean Club, Bahamas. How may I help you?"

"Room 409," Alfredo barked, impatience sharpening his tone.

"One moment, sir. I'll transfer your call."

A pause, then "Hello?" Mr. Walsh answered, his voice relaxed and content.

"Mr. Walsh, I trust you and your family are enjoying your vacation?" Alfredo's words oozed with false warmth.

"Yes, we are, Mr. Ferrari. This is exactly what Bridget needed after everything she's endured. We can't thank you enough."

"Speaking of Bridget, let me say hello to her." Alfredo took a leisurely sip of scotch, reclining into his leather chair.

A moment later, Bridget's voice came through, barely above a whisper. "Hello?"

"Bridget, it's Alfredo Ferrari. Your father tells me you're having a wonderful time in the Bahamas."

Silence. Bridget didn't answer.

Alfredo's patience snapped. He sat up, voice cold and commanding. "I'm talking to you, girl."

"Yes, sir," Bridget replied softly. "It's very nice here."

"I don't like your attitude," Alfredo said, his tone turning icy. "Imagine how you'd feel if your parents had a little . . . accident down there. Something to make them disappear forever."

"Mr. Ferrari—"

"Quiet. I know your parents are probably right there with you."

"Yes, sir."

"Now, you remember our deal, don't you? Yes or no."

"Yes, sir."

"When you get back, the DA and the police will want to talk to you. Stick to the plan."

"Yes, sir."

"That Black boy was the one who attacked you. Understood?"

"Yes, sir."

"Bridget, don't make me hurt you or your parents. This is a win-win for everyone. Do you understand?"

"Yes, sir."

"Good." Alfredo took another sip of his drink, his voice smooth as silk. "Now go enjoy your vacation. I'll see you soon." He hung up.

Behind him, Viktor's voice cut through the silence. "Is she still on board?"

"Viktor! How many times must I tell you not to sneak up on me like that?"

"Apologies, boss." Viktor eased himself into the chair across from Alfredo, his tone cool and unruffled. "Old habits die hard."

Alfredo's eyes narrowed, scrutinizing Viktor for a long moment before he spoke. "She's still on board. I just called to remind her exactly what's at stake if she dares to open her mouth."

"If only that reporter from the *Post*, Simone O'Connor, would take the same hint," Viktor replied, holding out a newspaper.

For the first time, Alfredo noticed the paper in Viktor's hand. He snatched it, scanning the bold headline splashed across the front page.

JUSTICE FOR DEMARCUS JONES: THE QUEST TO FIND THE REAL CRIMINAL

"Looks like she's on a mission," Viktor observed, his voice edged with irony.

Alfredo scoffed, waving a dismissive hand. "Let her dig. She has no proof. In the end, it all comes down to the victim's word, and she's on our side. DBoy is headed for prison."

"DMan," Viktor corrected quietly.

Alfredo shrugged, unconcerned. "Man, boy, whatever. His fate is sealed."

Viktor's gaze sharpened. "And Angelo? How many more of his disasters are we expected to clean up?"

Alfredo fell silent, the weight of Viktor's question hanging in the air. After a moment, he admitted, "This one nearly cost me my company and my reputation."

"And it's about to cost an innocent young man his freedom," Viktor said, his voice low.

Alfredo's glare was icy. "Whose side are you on?"

"Yours. Always," Viktor replied, unwavering. "My job is to protect you. But if this happens again, we're in real trouble. You need to keep a tighter leash on Angelo. This time, he went too far."

Alfredo's lips curled in distaste. "Rape and attempted murder. Don't worry, I have a plan for Angelo. I'm taking back control of the company. He'll stay on as my second-in-command." He raised a finger, silencing Viktor's protest before it began. "He's still my son. My heir."

"Yes, I know. But I suggest we have someone keep a close eye on him, at least for a while."

Alfredo nodded, conceding the point. "Good idea. Make it happen."

"I already have the right man for the job."

"Speaking of the right man for the job, we need to visit DA Wilcox again soon. He must understand just how crucial it is to ensure that boy ends up in prison."

***

"We'll now go on record," announced Assistant District Attorney Carter, the new prosecutor assigned to the case. She nodded to the stenographer seated across the room. "Thank you for coming in, Bridget, Mr. and Mrs. Walsh. I know this is an incredibly difficult time for your family, and I'm terribly sorry for what you've endured."

"Thank you," Mrs. Walsh replied quietly.

ADA Carter turned to Bridget, her tone gentle but direct. "Bridget, I hate to put you through this, but we need an official statement as we move forward. To begin, are you absolutely certain that Demarcus Jones was the person who attacked you?"

"She already told you it was him," Mr. Walsh snapped, his voice tight with anger. "My daughter has suffered enough."

"I understand, sir," ADA Carter said, her voice calm but firm. "As the new prosecutor on this case, it's important for me to review every detail with the victim. We must be certain we're prosecuting the right person for such a heinous crime."

Mrs. Walsh frowned, glancing toward the back of the conference room where Silver Fox sat, his face shadowed by a deep frown. "I'm still not sure why DA Wilcox stepped down from the case."

True to his word, Silver Fox had recused himself, citing a "conflict of personal interest." He'd handed the case to one of his brightest protégés, Joyce Carter, confident in her reputation for toughness and fairness, and certain she would eventually uncover the truth. Although it was highly unusual for a former prosecutor to sit in on a victim interview, Silver Fox remained in the room, silent and watchful, determined to observe for himself as the father of the accused.

"You know you're not supposed to be here, right?" ADA Carter had asked him earlier as he entered the conference room where the interview was about to begin. "This is my case now."

"I know, Joyce," Silver Fox replied, his tone measured. "Just give me a few minutes to observe. I promise I'll sit quietly at the back and won't say a word."

ADA Carter studied him, curiosity flickering in her eyes. "Are you going to tell me what's really going on? First, you recuse yourself from a case you said could have sealed your bid for attorney general, and now you're still inserting yourself into it. I don't get it."

Silver Fox let out a heavy sigh. Nearly three weeks had passed since he'd discovered Demarcus Jones was his biological son. Aside from Judge Mambo, who had demanded the real reason for his recusal, he hadn't told a soul—at least, not yet.

"This has become very personal for me, Joyce." He raised a finger as she started to speak. "I promise you'll know soon enough. Just do me this one favor. Let me listen in and observe the victim while you interview her. It's important."

ADA Carter stared at him for a long moment, then nodded sharply. "Just this once. You gave me this case because you know I'll get to the bottom of things. Let me do my job, all right?"

Silver Fox nodded and quickly took a seat at the back of the room.

Turning to the family, ADA Carter addressed them with calm authority. "DA Wilcox is no longer on the case for personal reasons. However, I assure you that I will seek justice for Bridget with equal dedication. We all want the truth. Now, as I said, I hate to do this, but Bridget, can you please walk me through your day on the day of the crime?"

"She's not going to relive that horrible day again," Mr. Walsh interrupted, his voice rising.

ADA Carter paused, glancing down at her notes before looking up at him. "It's important for me to get an official statement from Bridget for the record. The detectives are also waiting to do the same."

"Why do—"

"Mr. Walsh," ADA Carter cut in, "do you want the person who hurt your daughter to pay for his crimes?"

"Of course I do," Mr. Walsh replied in a tight voice.

"Then please allow me to do my job. We haven't had a chance to interview Bridget since the attack, and you've just returned from your vacation. A vacation you didn't inform our office about."

"We didn't know we had to tell you that," Mr. Walsh said defensively.

"Speaking of vacation, you said you were in the Bahamas?"

"Yes. Mr. Ferrari was kind enough to send us away. He knew Bridget needed that time," Mr. Walsh answered.

ADA Carter checked her notes. "Mr. Ferrari is Bridget's employer, correct?"

"Yes. He's a nice man," Mrs. Walsh added.

"Wait a minute. Which Ferrari are we talking about? The father or the son?"

"The father," Mrs. Walsh replied.

"I thought it was the son, Mr. Angelo Ferrari, who is now running the business?" ADA Carter pressed, her pen poised above her notepad.

"Well, that's correct," Mr. Walsh replied. "But Mr. Ferrari—the father, I mean—heard what happened to Bridget and came by the house to see her."

"Mr. Alfredo Ferrari visited Bridget after the attack?" Carter's pen moved swiftly as she spoke, even though the stenographer was already recording every word. "When did he come by?"

"The day after Bridget was released from the hospital," Mrs. Walsh answered. "I thought that was very nice of him."

"Very nice indeed," Carter murmured, jotting down notes. "And he paid for the entire vacation, correct?"

"Correct."

"Very nice indeed," Carter repeated, her tone thoughtful. "Well, I'm glad you had a chance to get some rest, Bridget. Now, please walk me through that day."

Bridget's voice was barely above a whisper. "I was home most of the day doing chores, except when my mother and I went to the supermarket." She hesitated, glancing at the prosecutor before quickly looking down again. "After dinner, I went to my bedroom to watch television."

"Please continue," Carter encouraged. "I'll have some follow-up questions for you after."

Bridget's hands trembled in her lap. "I wasn't sleepy, so later that night I decided to go for a walk after my parents went to bed. I walked around the block, and when I was heading back home, I saw DMan. I mean, Demarcus." Her voice broke, and she made a small, wounded sound in her throat. She bent her head until it was almost resting in her lap, her shoulders shaking as tears began to fall.

"That is enough," Mr. Walsh said, rising from his seat.

"Mr. Walsh, please sit down," ADA Carter said firmly, but kindly. "I know this is difficult, but I need Bridget to recount what happened that day, in her own words. Remember, she may have to testify in court."

Bridget's sobbing intensified, her body trembling as Mrs. Walsh wrapped her arms around her daughter, holding her close. The room fell silent, heavy with tension. As Mr. Walsh reluctantly returned to his seat, he fixed his glare on the ADA.

At last, Bridget's tears subsided to a shaky whisper. "He said we were just going to the park to sit and talk," she managed, still clinging to her mother. "Then he just snapped and started to attack me." She buried her face in the crook of her mother's neck, her entire body quaking.

"That's enough!" Mr. Walsh shot to his feet again. "No more."

"Thank you, Bridget," ADA Carter said gently. "I'm sorry to make you relive this. We'll pause here and continue another day. But before you go, I need you to confirm for the record—is Demarcus Jones the person who raped and tried to kill you that night?"

Bridget nodded, but ADA Carter pressed. "Please answer verbally for the record."

"Yes," Bridget replied, her voice barely audible.

"Let the record show that Bridget Walsh has identified Demarcus Jones as her attacker," ADA Carter announced, nodding to the stenographer. "We'll conclude for today and schedule a follow-up interview soon."

Mr. Walsh's face flushed with anger. "You should be ashamed of yourself," he spat. "There will be no more interviews. *That's it.*"

ADA Carter leaned back, meeting his glare with calm resolve. "Mr. Walsh, I urge you to take some time to reflect on what's at stake. We'll conduct as many interviews as necessary to ensure every detail is clear. We have multiple witness statements that contradict Bridget's claim."

"They're lying," Mr. Walsh insisted.

"That's why I need Bridget's help to clarify the truth," ADA Carter replied. "Next time, we'll need more details—when she left the house, who she saw, who she spoke to, where she went. These are questions the defense will certainly ask."

Mrs. Walsh stroked Bridget's back, her voice trembling. "They're treating her like she's done something wrong. She's the victim."

"She is," ADA Carter agreed softly. "However, I must prosecute based on facts and evidence. Let's end for today. I'll contact you to arrange the next interview." She gave Mr. Walsh a pointed look as he muttered under his breath.

After the family left, Silver Fox approached ADA Carter, settling into the chair beside her. "She's lying," he said quietly.

ADA Carter turned to him, eyebrows raised. "Really? What makes you say that?"

He shook his head, his gaze steady. "Just watch her. Look at her body language, the way she answers. Something's off."

"She's traumatized. She was raped and beaten. Don't forget that," ADA Carter reminded him.

Silver Fox nodded, his expression somber. "I know, and believe me, I feel for her. That's one of the reasons I recused myself from the case. Demarcus isn't the one who attacked her. I intend to prove it."

ADA Carter's eyes narrowed, her curiosity piqued. "Hold on. Aren't you off this case?"

"I am," Silver Fox replied, rising from his chair. "I'm still interested in what's going on.

She started to protest, but he cut her off. "I'm not interfering, I promise. This is your case now. I'll stay out of your way."

ADA Carter pressed. "What do you mean, you intend to prove Demarcus Jones is innocent? Last I checked, we're the prosecutors."

He paused at the door, glancing back. "You're the prosecutor on this case now. I'm not." With that, Silver

Fox exited swiftly, leaving ADA Carter alone with her thoughts.

She watched the door swing shut, her mind racing. "I need to find out what's really going on here," she murmured to herself. "Something isn't adding up."

The lip of truth shall be established forever: but a lying tongue is but for a moment.

Proverbs 12:19

Chapter Thirty

"Her father refused to let us speak to her," Detective Rich burst out, striding into Lieutenant Mulligan's office and dropping heavily into a chair. Frustration radiated from him as he continued, "Can you believe it? He claims she's still too traumatized and needs more time. How are we supposed to get a complete statement about her attack? We need to talk to her about identifying Jones."

Lieutenant Mulligan regarded him with a deep, thoughtful frown. "I need to bring you and Hanes up to speed on some new developments in the case. By the way, where is she?"

"She stopped to speak to someone—" Rich began but was interrupted.

"I'm right here," Hanes announced, entering quietly and closing the door behind her before taking a seat beside her partner.

"What's going on?" Rich pressed, leaning forward, his gaze locked on the lieutenant.

Just as Mulligan opened his mouth to respond, a sharp knock sounded at the door.

Rich let out a heavy sigh. "Let them—"

Mulligan silenced him with a raised finger. "Come in."

The door swung open, and Silver Fox stepped inside, his commanding presence shrinking the already cramped office. "Good morning," he intoned, his voice deep and authoritative.

Mulligan, Hanes, and Rich immediately rose to their feet.

"To what do we owe the honor, sir?" Hanes asked, her expression puzzled.

"He's probably here to tell us he's dropping the case against Jones," Rich said, eyeing the district attorney intently.

Silver Fox closed the door firmly and moved farther into the room. "Not exactly." He glanced at Lieutenant Mulligan.

"I haven't had a chance to tell them yet," Mulligan admitted.

"Tell us what?" Rich demanded.

"Let's all have a seat," Mulligan suggested, rolling his chair closer to Silver Fox before perching on the edge of his desk. The four of them formed a tight semi-circle.

Silver Fox cleared his throat, loosening his silk tie. "There have been some new developments," he began, his tone measured. "As a result, I've turned the case over to ADA Carter."

"What new developments?" Hanes asked with curiosity.

Silver Fox and Lieutenant Mulligan exchanged a loaded glance before Silver Fox spoke, his words deliberate. "Demarcus Jones is my biological son. I believed Naomi when she told me, and the lab called this morning with the DNA result to confirm."

A stunned silence gripped the room.

"Say what now?" Rich finally blurted, his eyes wide with disbelief. "You're Jones's father?" He turned to Mulligan, searching for answers. "Boss, what's going on?"

Lieutenant Mulligan nodded. "Naomi called me this morning before I got here. That's what I wanted to tell you."

Silver Fox continued, his voice steady but heavy with emotion. "It's a long story," he admitted, then gave a concise account of his chance encounter with Naomi that led to a child he never knew existed until just weeks ago.

Hanes shook her head in amazement. "I've never seen anything like this. The boy you were so determined to send to prison turns out to be your own son? Unbelievable."

"I was prosecuting a brutal rape and attempted murder case," Silver Fox snapped. "One, I must remind you, in which the investigating detectives informed me the victim positively identified her attacker. So, I was doing my job. Nor did I know who Demarcus was."

"Let's just calm down," Lieutenant Mulligan interjected, glancing at Silver Fox's flushed face. "Now, we're all working toward the same goal of finding out who's truly responsible for this crime and bringing them to justice."

"Agreed," Rich replied. "How's Demarcus taking all this?"

Silver Fox's expression darkened. "He's refused to see or speak to me. He went with his mother for the DNA test, but only on the condition that I wasn't there. That's where things stand."

"He's still upset with his mother, too," Lieutenant Mulligan added gently. "Understandable, considering his entire life as he knew it has been turned upside down."

Silver Fox's eyes softened, a flicker of sadness passing through them. "It won't just be his life that changes. Later, I'll have to tell my family about Demarcus. Many lives are about to be upended."

For a moment, no one spoke. Then, Silver Fox clapped his hands together, determination returning to his voice.

"However, our focus now is clearing Demarcus's name. We have a lot of work ahead."

"We?" Hanes shot him a pointed look. "As the father of the accused, you can't work this case, sir. My partner and I are handling it."

Silver Fox started to protest. "Listen—"

"She's correct," Lieutenant Mulligan interjected. "As far as the investigation goes, you can't be actively and publicly involved. I have reason to believe there's a conspiracy at play here. For instance, who blocked Demarcus from receiving visitors while he was at Rikers?"

"It must be someone with serious influence," Silver Fox replied thoughtfully.

"Exactly," the lieutenant said, locking eyes with him. "A man with your connections can dig a little behind the scenes, quietly, discreetly."

"Boss, with all due respect, I don't think that's a good idea," Hanes objected, her brow furrowed. "He's—"

"The father," Silver Fox finished for her. "That's why I'm going to do everything I can to help my son, because now I believe he's innocent. There's also another reason. I agree with the lieutenant. There's much more going on here. Someone is framing Demarcus." His green eyes darkened with anger. "I've spent my entire career bringing criminals to justice. This will be no exception. Everyone involved in this will be brought to justice and punished to the full extent of the law," he said with such strong emotion that no one in the room doubted him.

Later that afternoon, Silver Fox sat in his office, gazing out the window, though his eyes didn't register the cityscape beyond. His mind churned with the conversation he knew he'd have to face at home.

"How is she going to take it?" Silver Fox muttered. "Yes, she's going to be angry," he answered his own question. "What about Samuel?" he said of their son.

A knock at the door pulled him from his thoughts. "Come in," he called, not turning from the window.

"Calvin, how are you?" Alfredo Ferrari swept into the office, his presence as grand as ever.

Silver Fox drew a deep breath, then turned to face him. "I'm well, Alfredo," he replied, his tone flat. "How are you?"

"*Magnifico!*" Alfredo declared, settling into a chair without waiting for an invitation, legs crossed with practiced elegance.

"That's good. What can I do for you?"

Alfredo's dramatic smile faltered as he picked up on the mood. "Are you all right? You sound a little down."

Silver Fox offered a half-smile that never reached his eyes. "Just work stuff. You know how it is."

"Is it about Bridget's case?" Alfredo asked anxiously. "Actually, I was in the area and wanted to check in with you about it."

Silver Fox regarded him coolly. "Did you?"

"Yes. As I mentioned before, that poor girl was an employee of mine, and I want that Black—hmm . . . that boy to pay for what he did to her. I was shocked to hear he got bail. Bail? After raping and nearly killing an innocent girl?" Alfredo's words tumbled out, unchecked now that Viktor wasn't there to rein him in.

Silver Fox caught the slip—"that Black boy"—and felt a surge of anger and protectiveness. *That Black boy is my son.* Outwardly, he remained composed, a skill honed over years in the courtroom.

"I've never lost a case, and I don't intend to lose this one either."

"I know it. I told Angelo not to worry," Alfredo blurted out.

"Angelo?" Silver Fox tilted his head, his gaze sharpening. "What is he worried about?"

Alfredo faltered, searching for words. "He . . . well, he's not worried, exactly. I mean, he's concerned because Bridget worked with him. Remember, he's the acting CEO, so she was also his employee. We care about all our employees."

"Of course," Silver Fox replied, his tone unreadable.

"I was just reassuring Angelo that you would get justice for Bridget," Alfredo continued, still scrambling to regain control of the conversation.

"I'm no longer on the case," Silver Fox informed him. "It's been reassigned to ADA Carter."

"You can't do that," Alfredo protested, his composure slipping.

"Excuse me?" Silver Fox's frown deepened.

Alfredo closed his eyes tightly for a moment, then fixed Silver Fox with a determined stare. "I meant to say I don't think you should be off the case. I want you to take it back immediately."

"With all due respect, that decision isn't yours to make," Silver Fox replied in a cool voice. "I'm off the case, and that's final. For the record, ADA Carter is one of the sharpest prosecutors in this office. She will not rest until she uncovers the truth and brings Ms. Walsh's attacker to justice."

Alfredo's face contorted, as if he were battling a sudden wave of discomfort. Silver Fox leaned back in his chair, his gaze fixed on Alfredo, unblinking and steady.

"Very well," Alfredo muttered at last, his voice low and tight. "I trust your judgment. But may I ask why you reassigned the case?"

Silver Fox hesitated, then swallowed hard. "Personal reasons," he said quietly. "Trust me, it's the best decision for everyone involved. You and Angelo have nothing to worry about."

Alfredo's face flushed a deep, angry red, even his ears burning with frustration. "I see." He rose from his chair, every muscle tense, and forced a thin smile. "Well, thank you for your time," he hissed through clenched teeth, then stormed out of the office, his head held high, his posture rigid.

For a long moment, Silver Fox stared at the empty chair Alfredo had vacated. His brows knitted in deep concentration, his green eyes narrowed to slits, and his lips pressed into a hard, thoughtful line.

Could it be?

Chapter Thirty-one

Demarcus sprawled across his bed, lost in his own thoughts, when the front door creaked open and then shut. Footsteps echoed down the hallway, pausing in the living room. Silence settled.

"Mom?" he called out, his voice cutting through the quiet. When no answer came, he pushed himself up, swung open his bedroom door, and started, "I thought you went to the super—" but froze mid-sentence.

Standing in the center of the living room was Silver Fox, his expression pleading. Demarcus glared, saying nothing.

"I know you said you didn't want to see me, but you can't avoid me forever," Silver Fox said, his green eyes, so much like Demarcus's, shining with emotion. "We need to talk, son."

"Son?" Demarcus spat the word as if it tasted bitter. "Now I'm your son?" He walked over to his father until they were standing eye to eye. "A few weeks ago, I was a rapist, and you were ready to make sure I spent the rest of my life in prison. Now I'm your *son*?" Grief welled up, and tears streamed down his face despite his efforts to hold them back.

Silver Fox took a step forward, reaching out. "Listen, there's a lot we need to discuss—"

"Don't touch me." Demarcus recoiled, fists clenched. "Do you have any idea what I've been through? What I'm still going through? My life is ruined."

"No, it's not." Tears glistened in Silver Fox's eyes as he took in his son's pain. "I'm going to help you if it's the last thing I do. Please, Demarcus, don't shut me out. At least give me a chance to explain."

Demarcus stared at him for a long, tense moment, tears still falling, then stormed off to the bathroom. Fifteen minutes later, he emerged, face washed but still red from crying. Silver Fox sat patiently on the couch, waiting.

"I thought you left," Demarcus muttered, dropping onto the far end of the couch.

"No, I still want to talk to you."

Demarcus shrugged, as if to say, "Whatever," but he didn't move.

"I didn't know about you," Silver Fox began quietly. "Please believe me, I would never have turned my back on my child. I would have been a father to you, Demarcus."

Demarcus's eyes filled again, and he bit his lip to keep from crying.

"Your mother said she told you everything, but I'd like to share my side, too. Is that okay?"

Demarcus shrugged again, staring straight ahead.

Silver Fox recounted his encounter with Naomi, just as he had for his wife, his other son, and finally, his parents three days earlier. "You can imagine how shocked I was when Naomi came to see me and told me you were my son," he finished. "All this time, I thought I had only one son, never knowing I had two."

"How old is he?" Demarcus finally asked, referring to his brother.

"He's fifteen. His name is Samuel. Now that I look at you, I see the resemblance."

"He's white."

"You're half-white. And he still resembles you."

A quiet moment passed before Demarcus asked, "Is your wife angry with you? I bet she doesn't want you to have anything to do with me."

"That's absolutely not true," Silver Fox said firmly. "She was just as stunned as I was. This has undoubtedly changed our lives, but she's taking the time she needs to process everything. I've made it clear that I fully intend to get to know you and be part of your life. That's if you'll let me." He turned to Demarcus, his gaze steady.

Demarcus stared ahead, silent.

"Try to forgive your mother, Demarcus," Silver Fox said. "She meant well, even if I disagree with her choices. I get angry about the lost years, but my own mother reminded me everything happens for a reason. I'm focusing on that."

"Your mother?" Demarcus asked.

"Yes, your grandmother. She and your grandfather want to meet you."

"Meet me?"

"Yes, and your brother too."

Demarcus looked away, the apprehension still etched in his eyes. "I wonder if they'll even want to meet me once I go to prison."

"Stop it," Silver Fox said a little sharper than intended. "Listen, Demarcus." His tone softened. "Detectives Hanes and Rich are digging and uncovering a lot of things about this case. Also, I just hired one of the best private investigators I know to pursue another angle that I think may just blow this case wide open."

"You did?"

"Of course I did. I don't want you giving up. I need you to fight with us to clear your name and reclaim your life."

Demarcus nodded slowly. "That's what Carrick said, too."

"Well, Carrot Top's right."

Demarcus smirked. "That's what I thought when I first met him. Carrot Top and Silver Fox. You two make quite the team."

"Demarcus, I was just doing my job—"

"You told me to focus on the positive, right? I'm going to try." His voice wavered. "I won't pretend it's easy because it's not. I still don't understand why this is happening to me, and maybe I never will. But I don't want to go to prison for something I didn't do."

"You won't."

"I've lost so much . . . including a full college scholarship." His lips trembled. "Maybe I'll still get the chance to go to another college."

"Stanford can't revoke your scholarship unless you're proven guilty," Silver Fox assured him. "And if they try, I'll sue them. Either way, you can still go, Demarcus."

Demarcus turned to him, his eyes filled with silent questions.

"I'll pay your tuition," Silver Fox said gently. "It would be an honor."

Demarcus swallowed hard, emotion tightening his throat. He couldn't speak.

"We'll cross that bridge when we get there," Silver Fox added with quiet understanding. "But there's something else I hope you'll let me do for you."

"What's that?"

"I want you to talk to someone about what you've been through, and what you're still going through."

"You mean a shrink?" Demarcus asked, eyebrows raised.

"Yes. A psychiatrist," Silver Fox replied. "Believe me. It'll help. Will you give it a try?"

Demarcus paused, thinking. His mind was a whirlwind of memories and fears, nightmares of Cyclone's attack, sleepless nights haunted by the thought of returning to Rikers Island. Sometimes, it all felt too heavy to carry.

"Yes," he said at last. "I'll do it. I need all the help I can get."

"I think it's the right decision," Silver Fox said warmly. "I'll make the arrangements and call you with the details, okay?"

"Thank you."

"Now, I've got a meeting with your lawyer, Counselor Carrot Top."

Demarcus caught the wide grin on his father's face and gave him a small smile. "Okay, DA Silver Fox."

Silver Fox threw his head back and laughed heartily. "See? You're just as funny as your old man."

They shared a look, one that spoke of the long road ahead but also of a new beginning. No longer prosecutor and defendant, they were now father and son.

Ms. Lopez lay curled on the couch, trembling beneath a blanket pulled tightly to her neck. Her weary, dark eyes, shadowed by heavy bags, darted around the lavishly furnished living room, searching for something—or someone.

It had been days since she'd slept soundly. Every time she closed her eyes, Demarcus Jones appeared. Sometimes, it was as a red devil, pitchfork in hand, whispering that he'd come to drag her to Hell. Other times, he wore white, a glowing halo above his head, pleading with her to tell the truth. And then there were the nights he came cloaked in black, a vampire with hollow eyes, murmuring that he'd come to claim her soul. No matter where she turned, he was there haunting her dreams, twisting them into waking nightmares.

"I can't lose this house," she muttered through cracked lips. "I can't tell the truth. I just can't." Her body shivered violently, though it was the middle of summer.

A sudden pop shattered the silence. A car backfired as it passed the house. Ms. Lopez screamed and tumbled off the couch. On all fours, she scrambled across the floor to the light switch. Her chest heaved, heart pounding like a drum. She pulled herself up and flicked the switch, plunging the room into darkness, then collapsed back to the floor.

"They're trying to kill me," she whispered. "They're shooting at the house."

She wished Juan were home, but he hadn't been back in two days, not since the TV vanished from his bedroom. Crawling to the coffee table, she reached for her phone with trembling hands and dialed.

"Nine one one. What's your emergency?"

"They're trying to kill me," she whispered.

"Who's trying to kill you, ma'am?"

"They're shooting. They're coming for me."

"Ma'am, did you say someone is shooting at you? What's your location?"

She almost gave her old Bronx address before catching herself and blurting out her new one in Yonkers.

"Police are on the way," the dispatcher said calmly. "Where in the house are you now?"

A breeze stirred the branches of the large maple tree outside. One scraped against the kitchen window with a soft, eerie scratch. Ms. Lopez screamed again and dropped the phone.

She was still screaming when two police cruisers screeched to a halt in front of the house, sirens wailing, red and blue lights flashing across the walls.

She was still screaming when the doorbell rang.

"Police. Open the door."

A heavy pounding followed. Ms. Lopez finally fell silent. She crept to the door, heart still racing.

"Police."

With a shaky breath, she stood, flicked on the light, and opened the door. "Thank God you're here," she said frantically. "They were shooting. Then they tried to break in through the kitchen window. They came to kill me. They won't stop until I'm dead."

"Ma'am, please try to stay calm," one officer said gently. "Two officers are checking the perimeter. May we come in and look around?"

She nodded and stepped aside, arms wrapped tightly around herself.

As the officers moved through the house, Ms. Lopez perched on the edge of the couch, mumbling under her breath. A few minutes later, the officers returned from upstairs.

"Everything looks secure inside," one said.

"All clear outside, too," another added as he stepped in from the porch. "No signs of gunfire or forced entry."

The four officers exchanged glances, then turned their attention to Ms. Lopez. Her hair was disheveled, her body still trembling.

"Ma'am," one asked gently, "are you okay?"

"How can I be okay when someone's trying to kill me?" Ms. Lopez cried out.

"Who's trying to kill you?" one of the officers asked softly.

"It could be those thugs watching the house," Ms. Lopez replied, her voice trembling. "Or maybe it's the devil. He said he wants to take me to Hell."

"Ma'am, are you currently on any medication?"

Ms. Lopez ignored the question. "Or maybe it's the vampire," she whispered. "He wants to bite me . . . take my soul."

The officers exchanged a knowing glance.

"Would you like to go to the hospital for a checkup?"

“I’m not sick,” she snapped. “I need protection. I need sleep. I need to feel safe in my own home.”

“There was no sign of gunfire tonight,” one officer said calmly.

Ms. Lopez shook her head, refusing to believe it. She insisted they were out there waiting. Despite their efforts, she refused to go to the hospital.

“We’ll increase patrols in the area,” one officer assured her before they left.

Alone once more, locked inside the house she was desperate to keep at any cost, Ms. Lopez whimpered from where she huddled on the wooden floor. Her eyes grew heavy, but she fought the pull of sleep. She was terrified of what waited for her in the dark: another visit from the devil, or the vampire.

Chapter Thirty-two

"Gentlemen, thank you again for coming in and speaking with me," ADA Carter said, closing her notebook.

"No problem," Trevor Richards replied. "We just told the truth."

"Demarcus didn't touch that white girl," Tom Dunkley repeated. "Y'all just trying to hold a good brother back because he's going places."

Tom had been just a kid when a white cop shot and killed his brother. The loss left a scar that deepened into a quiet mistrust, especially toward white authority figures.

ADA Carter let out a long sigh. "This isn't about race, sir. It's about justice, and justice doesn't have a color."

"Justice?" Tom snorted, eyes narrowing. "You talk about justice like you've ever had to beg for it." He stood abruptly, chair legs screeching. "I'll wait outside," he said and walked out without looking back.

"He's right, you know," Jimmy Mason said, turning to ADA Carter. "If you really wanted justice, you'd be prosecuting the real criminal."

"That's exactly why I took your statements myself," she replied, her tone steady. She had interviewed each of the men, one by one, while the others waited in the hallway. "I'm not here to prosecute innocent people, black, white, blue, or green. I'm here for the ones who break the law. You feel me?"

Trevor grinned. "Now you're talking, ma'am."

ADA Carter smiled. "I appreciate you all coming in."

Trevor and Jimmy headed toward the door.

"Oh." ADA Carter's voice halted their steps, and they turned to look at her. "Just so you know, I've been dating a fine African American man since college, and I've a strong feeling he's about to pop *the* question." She gave them a wink.

Trevor and Jimmy chuckled as they exited.

The smile faded from ADA Carter's face as she looked down at the witnesses statements. She reached for her phone but paused when the door opened and someone stepped inside.

Silver Fox closed the door behind him. "We need to talk."

"Okay," she said, setting the phone aside.

Moments later, the two prosecutors sat across from each other in silence. ADA Carter opened her mouth to speak, then closed it again.

"Mind-boggling, isn't it?" Silver Fox asked. "I'm sorry I didn't tell you about Demarcus sooner. I had to talk to my family first."

"Demarcus Jones is your son."

He nodded.

"Wow. Now I understand why you reassigned the case. It would've helped to know earlier, but I get it. You had a lot to process."

"He's innocent, Joyce." Silver Fox raised a hand as she began to respond. "You do your job, and I'll do mine. I'm betting we'll reach the same conclusion."

"Says the prosecutor, or the father?"

"Right now?" He leaned forward. "I'm the father. And my son needs me."

ADA Carter nodded, her expression firm. "Fine. But stay out of my case." A faint smile tugged at the corners of her mouth. "Until I either dismiss the charges against your son or take this to trial, I don't need your interference."

Silver Fox raised both hands in surrender. “Yes, ma’am.” He stood, crossed the room, and extended his right hand. They shook.

“I have a feeling we’ll reach the same conclusion soon,” Silver Fox told her before he turned and walked away.

Meanwhile, across town in the Soundview section of the Bronx, Detectives Hanes and Rich stepped into Saab, a modest African hair-braiding shop.

“Good afternoon,” Rich announced, his deep baritone cutting through the hum of conversation. The shop fell silent. Three stylists were mid-braid, working on two women and one man.

“I’m Detective Rich. This is my partner, Detective Hanes.”

Suddenly, one of the stylists, a short, plump, dark-skinned woman, bolted toward a door at the back and vanished through it. Rich gave chase.

“No one else move,” Hanes commanded. “We’re just here to ask a few questions. That’s all.”

Rich returned moments later, gently guiding the woman, now trembling and in tears.

“Please don’t deport me,” she whispered.

“We’re not immigration,” Rich assured her. “What’s your name?”

“Ode.”

“Ode, are you Baako Afia’s sister?”

Her eyes widened as she glanced between the two detectives. “Yes.”

“We’d like to ask you a few questions about your brother,” Rich said. He gestured toward the back. “I saw a room back there. Can we talk in private?”

Ode nodded and led them to a cramped space behind the shop. A worn brown couch sat against one wall, a microwave perched on a rickety table, and a tiny refrigerator hummed in the corner.

"Where's your brother?" Hanes asked directly.

"In Arizona," she replied.

"Arizona?" Rich raised an eyebrow. "Like I said, we're not immigration. I don't care about your legal status. But if you lie to us, I'll make a call."

"No, no," Ode said quickly. "He told me someone gave him a lot of money to leave the Bronx. He even sent some to our mother in Ghana."

Rich and Hanes exchanged a glance.

"Do you have an address for him?" Rich asked. "Be honest. We're not here to hurt your brother. We believe he can help us with an important investigation."

Ode hesitated, uncertainty flickering in her eyes. "He left some important documents at our cousin's house. I mailed them to him."

"Let me have the address," Rich said gently.

Ode slipped her phone from the pocket of her dress, scrolled quickly, then handed it to Detective Rich.

"Thanks. Can you give us a moment?"

Without a word, Ode turned and walked back into the shop, leaving Rich and Hanes alone in the back room.

"Phoenix, Arizona," Rich said, passing the phone to Hanes to show her the address.

"How do you want to play this?" Hanes asked, handing the phone back.

"I'll call Phoenix PD. We can either have them take his statement there or arrange to bring him back to New York. We need to know exactly what Afia saw that night, and who paid him to disappear before we got his testimony."

Rich dialed.

***

"Yes! Yes!" Hanes slapped the dashboard as they drove back to the precinct. "Now we're getting somewhere."

"He was paid a lot of money to get out of the Bronx," Rich repeated. "Wait until the lieutenant hears this."

"Someone's working hard to frame Jones."

"No question. But who?"

They talked through the case all the way to the precinct.

"Phoenix, Arizona?" Lieutenant Mulligan paced his office, eyes darting between Rich and Hanes. "You've got to be kidding."

"Phoenix PD is en route to pick him up," Rich said.

"I want him back here in New York," Mulligan replied. "Let me make a few calls and get that moving."

Rich and Hanes stepped out to give him privacy. In the hallway, they nearly collided with Silver Fox.

"Maybe we should find you a desk here," Rich joked.

"Funny," Silver Fox said, nodding toward Mulligan's closed door. "Is he in? I need to speak with all three of you."

"He's on some important calls," Hanes replied.

Silver Fox's eyes lit up. "Is this about Demarcus's case? What happened? Fill me in."

"Sir—"

"There you are." Carrick hurried down the corridor, his battered briefcase swinging at his side. "Glad I caught you all. Can we talk somewhere?"

"I'll run across the street and grab coffee," Rich offered. "That'll give the lieutenant time to wrap up."

A few minutes later, the five of them gathered in the precinct's break room. Hanes and Rich brought Carrick and Silver Fox up to speed on Afia's location.

"He'll be back in New York tomorrow," Mulligan informed everyone.

"It's just like we've been saying," Carrick said, leaning back in his metal chair, eyes wide with disbelief. "Someone's trying to make my client the fall guy."

"Someone with deep pockets," Hanes added, her expression sour.

"Someone with a lot to lose," Rich said quietly.

As the men delved into the peculiarities of the case, Carrick noticed Silver Fox had gone quiet.

"You okay, man?" he asked, turning toward him. The others paused mid-conversation and followed his gaze.

Silver Fox cleared his throat. "I've hired a private investigator. Just following a gut instinct."

"You did what?" Hanes barked.

Rich scowled. "We told you to let us handle this."

Carrick leaned forward. "Silver Fox, you need to—"

"Enough." Silver Fox's eyes blazed. "He's my son. I barely know him, but I care deeply. I'll do whatever it takes to help him, and I don't need anyone's permission."

Silence fell over the room.

"You're all doing great work," Silver Fox said, his tone softening. "But I had an encounter recently that set off alarm bells. This person has serious money"—he glanced at Hanes—"and a lot to lose." His eyes flicked to Rich.

"He's also very invested in the case," Silver Fox continued. "Got visibly upset when I told him I'd reassigned it. Insisted I take it back."

Carrick's eyes narrowed. "Who is this?"

Silver Fox hesitated, lips pressed together. Then he looked away and said, "He's someone I've known for years. A close friend of my father-in-law. His name is Alfredo Ferrari, Bridget Walsh's former boss. His son, Angelo Ferrari, supposedly runs the company now."

Lieutenant Mulligan's jaw dropped. Rich and Hanes stared, stunned.

"Well, well, well," Carrick murmured. "The plot thickens."

Silver Fox pulled a slip of paper from his jacket. "The PI just called. He found the Asian man that witnesses mentioned. That's why I came. I've got his address."

"I'll take that." Rich snatched the note and looked at it. "East Tremont."

"We need to tread carefully," Mulligan warned. "If this guy's tied to the Ferraris, he's well-funded and won't hesitate to protect their secrets."

"My investigator also said he's chasing a hot lead," Silver Fox added.

"We've got a little wannabe detective to bring in," Hanes said, her eyes gleaming.

"Yes." Carrick pumped his fist, his baby face nearly as red as his hair. "Finally, this case is moving in the right direction."

But would it reach the destination they were hoping for?

Chapter Thirty-three

"A few of my contacts say there's a man snooping around, asking questions about the case," Viktor informed Alfredo and Angelo.

Alfredo took a long, deliberate gulp of his whiskey.

"You mean like a private investigator?" Angelo's hand trembled, causing his glass of tequila to rattle. He quickly set it down on the coffee table.

"Seems that way." Viktor sat across from them on the couch. The moment he got the unsettling news, he'd called an emergency meeting at Alfredo's penthouse.

"Why hire a PI when there are detectives already working the case?" Alfredo asked, frowning. "And who's footing the bill?"

"Good question," Viktor replied. "I'm still digging. I'll let you know as soon as I find out."

Alfredo placed his nearly empty glass beside Angelo's and rubbed his eyes, weariness evident on his face. "This just keeps getting messier by the minute."

"Father . . . what are we going to do?" Angelo looked at him, eyes pleading. "I thought we had—"

"Shut up!" Alfredo shouted, his body trembling with rage. "I want this buried." He jabbed a finger toward Viktor. "I've paid you a fortune to handle this. There's more where that came from."

"Boss, I've been trying—"

"Trying isn't good enough. Get it done." Alfredo's breathing quickened, his chest rising and falling like waves in a storm.

"Please, remember your heart," Viktor urged gently. "Try to stay calm."

"Don't tell me to stay calm," Alfredo hissed, then downed the rest of his drink in one swift motion. He handed the glass to Angelo, who hurried off to refill it. "First, the boy gets bail. Then we've got three witnesses we can't silence, still swearing he's innocent. The top prosecutor in the Bronx drops the case, and now a PI is sniffing around? *Cosa sta succedendo*?"

"You're asking what's going on, but it's not as simple as we thought," Viktor told him. "I'm doing everything I can, but things keep slipping out of control."

"Then we need to escalate," Alfredo growled. "Make those witnesses disappear if you have to. And that PI, handle him."

Viktor stared at him. "I can do that. But we're crossing a line. It's going to get even more tangled."

"It's already tangled," Alfredo said, snatching the drink Angelo handed him. "If we don't act fast, I'm going to lose everything."

"I can't go to prison," Angelo muttered, reclaiming his seat beside his father, avoiding his piercing gaze.

"Anyway, boss," Viktor continued, ignoring Angelo, "I'll apply more pressure. Do what needs to be done. It wouldn't hurt if you spoke to the DA again."

At the mention of Silver Fox, Alfredo exploded. He cursed furiously, his hand shaking so violently that some of his drink splashed onto the floor.

"I'm godfather to his wife, for heaven's sake. Practically family. And he still reassigned the case after I told him how important it was?" The veins in his neck bulged. "He said it was for personal reasons? He betrayed me!"

"Maybe you should stop asking so nicely." Viktor's lips curled into a vicious sneer.

Alfredo inhaled deeply, steadying his breath. For a few tense seconds, he stared at Viktor in silence, then calmly raised his glass and took a slow sip.

"Let's remind him of the importance of loyalty," Viktor said, his voice low and deliberate.

Around 10:00 p.m., Silver Fox eased his Mercedes into the driveway and parked. He leaned back against the leather headrest, gazing up at his elegant two-story brick home nestled in Riverdale, Bronx. The soft glow of the exterior lights shimmered across his wife's pride and joy—the pink pearl roses and fragrant stargazer lilies lining the long drive. He closed his eyes, the weight of recent events pressing heavily on his chest. His thoughts raced, tangled in uncertainty.

I have to help my son, no matter what.

Minutes passed before he finally opened the door and stepped out, his movements slow, burdened. He had barely taken a few steps toward the house when a voice cut through the night.

"Excuse me, Mr. D.A."

Silver Fox turned around and saw a tall figure approaching the gate, his silhouette stretching under the streetlamp's glow. For a moment, unease flashed in his eyes, until recognition settled in.

"What do you want?"

Viktor stopped just short of the gate, hands casually at his sides. "Why so aggressive? I'm only here to deliver a message."

"I'm not interested," Silver Fox snapped. "And don't ever come to my house again." He turned, heading for the front steps.

"Mr. Ferrari would like a word. It's important."

Silver Fox halted, then pivoted slowly. "Tell Alfredo to come to my office if he wants to talk. Nothing's changed. I'm off the case."

"That's exactly what he wants to discuss," Viktor replied smoothly. "Why don't you come with me?"

"I'm not going anywhere with you." Silver Fox's composure cracked, his voice rising. The last of his doubts about Ferrari's involvement in Demarcus's case vanished. This visit confirmed everything. Fury surged through him, loosening his tongue.

"He thinks he can do whatever he wants and get away with it, huh? Alfredo and Angelo Ferrari, above the law? Not a chance."

Viktor's expression darkened. He stepped closer, menace radiating from his calm demeanor. "I don't know what you're implying. Mr. Ferrari is simply concerned that one of his employees was attacked, and he wants justice. What's wrong with that?"

"Framing the wrong man. That's what's wrong," Silver Fox growled.

"Easy now, Mr. D.A. Those are serious accusations."

Silver Fox clicked his tongue and pointed a firm finger at Viktor. "We'll see about that." Without another word, he turned and walked away, his steps heavy with resolve.

Silver Fox suddenly felt a searing pain that shot from his back through to his chest. The next shot tore through his shoulder, twisting him before he hit the pavement hard.

Viktor fired another shot into District Attorney Calvin Wilcox's stomach as he lay on the ground. Agony, unlike anything he'd ever known surged through Silver Fox, crashing over him in relentless waves. His mouth, flooded with blood, stifled the scream clawing its way up his throat. He tried to crawl toward the house, but his limbs betrayed him, paralyzed, trembling. All he could do was lie there, gasping, whimpering, his breath ragged as life drained from him and his blood pooled across the cold concrete.

Through pain-blurred eyes, he saw Viktor approach, the gun steady, aimed at his head. Silver Fox closed his eyes, surrendering to the inevitable.

Then, a scream tore through the night, raw, chilling, and unmistakably human. It erupted from the house, slicing through the silence, echoing from one home to the next like a siren of doom.

It was the last sound Silver Fox heard before darkness swallowed him whole.

Across town, Demarcus lay propped on his mother's bed, elbow under his chin, facing her.

"I'm still a little upset with you," he said quietly.

Naomi reached out, brushing his cheek with gentle fingers. "You have every right to be. I'm upset with myself, too, for how I handled things back then."

Demarcus shrugged. "He seemed okay."

Naomi studied him. "And you're curious. Especially after your talk this morning."

"He seemed okay," Demarcus repeated, his tone casual, but the spark in his green eyes betrayed his interest.

"Uh-huh." Naomi took his hand. "It's okay to want to know your father. He wants to know you too."

"That's what he said. We'll—"

Her phone rang. She reached for it on the bedside table, glanced at the screen, and answered. "Hi, Carrick."

As she listened, her hand began to tremble. "What? When?"

Demarcus sat up, alarmed. "Mom, what's going on?"

Naomi held up a finger, her face pale. "Is he . . .?" Her voice cracked. "Lord have mercy. I'll . . . I'll tell him. Thank you for letting us know."

Demarcus stared at her, heart pounding. “What?”

Tears welled in Naomi’s eyes. “Calvin. He was shot tonight.”

Demarcus blinked, stunned. His mouth opened, but no words came.

Naomi reached for him, but he pulled away, springing to his feet. “Is he—” His voice broke as tears streamed down his face.

“Carrick said he’s in critical condition. It doesn’t look good.”

Demarcus turned away in anguish. “Why am I not surprised, Mom?” His voice was low, bitter. “Nothing ever goes right. Just when it seems like things are going to get better, everything falls apart. Does God hate me that much?”

“Oh, no, baby.” Naomi rose and walked over to him, wrapping her arms gently around his waist. She rested her head against his broad chest, her voice soft but steady. “God’s going to turn this around for your good. He doesn’t hate you. He loves you.”

Demarcus let out a low grunt, but he pulled his mother close, her quiet strength seeping into him like warmth on a cold day. “I still have a lot of mixed feelings about him,” he said, referring to his father. “But now I’ll never get the chance to know him.” Tears welled up and slipped down his cheeks. He wiped them away, frustrated.

“Shhh, don’t talk like that,” Naomi said to him. “He’s still alive, and God is still in the healing business. We’ll pray for him.”

“You can pray,” Demarcus muttered, gently loosening her embrace. He walked into the living room and sank into the couch, his shoulders heavy with weariness.

Moments later he felt his mother join him, settling beside him with quiet grace.

“Go see him,” she urged. “I can see how deeply this is affecting you.”

"Sure, and run into his family?" he scoffed.

"Your father said they want to meet you. It'll be okay."

"I'm not in the mood for more drama, Mom. I'm tired. Really tired." Demarcus dragged his hands down his face, the exhaustion etched into every movement.

"I know, sweetheart." Naomi leaned her head against his arm. "You've been through so much these past few weeks. But you're still standing."

"I'm also still facing prison time for something I didn't do."

"God won't let that happen," she said firmly, lifting her head to meet his eyes. "I don't want you speaking defeat over your life. Proverbs 18:21 reminds us death and life are in the power of the tongue. Speak freedom. Speak vindication and justice. Because I believe, with all my heart, that the truth is about to come out. The real criminal will be caught. I declare and decree it will happen very soon, in Jesus' name."

Chapter Thirty-four

"He's in a coma."

Carrick slammed his fist onto Lieutenant Mulligan's desk. "They tried to kill him. And do you know why?" His eyes swept from Mulligan to Detectives Hanes and Rich. "Because they found out he's Demarcus's father. Because he's helping his son. Because he's on our side now."

Carrick's face burned red, his eyes blazing with fury.

"I'm with you on that, Counselor," Mulligan growled, his own anger rising. "Someone went after Silver Fox last night, and I'm convinced it's tied to Demarcus's case."

"The same people trying to frame him," Carrick remarked. "They're getting more desperate and dangerous."

"Where do we stand with the investigation?" Mulligan asked, turning to the detectives. Two officers had initially responded to the 911 call, but when Mulligan discovered the victim's identity, Rich and Hanes were reassigned to take over.

"When we got there," Hanes reported, "the ambulance had already rushed Silver Fox to the hospital. His wife was hysterical. It took some time before she could even speak. She'd been in the kitchen when she heard his car pull into the driveway. She waited, expecting him to walk in, but when he didn't, she went out to check."

Rich stepped in, his tone edged with frustration. "She didn't see the shooter's face. Just the outline of a tall figure looming over the DA as he lay on the ground. She screamed, and the guy bolted, vanishing into the night. She ran back inside and called 911."

"That's horrific," Mulligan exclaimed. "What about their son?"

"Thankfully, he was at a sleepover," Rich replied. "After speaking with the wife and realizing she didn't know much, we left the forensic team at the scene and rushed to the hospital. But Silver Fox was already in surgery, and then he slipped into a coma."

"Right now, we've got nothing," Hanes said through clenched teeth. "Absolutely nothing."

"The other detectives canvassed the neighborhood last night," Rich said, shaking his head. "No one saw or heard a thing."

"Probably used a silencer," Mulligan speculated. "Until Silver Fox wakes up and tells us who shot him, all we've got is the back of a tall man."

"*If* he wakes up," Carrick snapped. "Father dies, son goes to prison, and the real culprit walks free, but not on my watch." He stormed out of the office.

Outside, Carrick pulled out his cell phone as he strode toward his car parked in front of the precinct.

"Babe," he said, voice low and urgent. "Do I have a story for you."

BRONX DISTRICT ATTORNEY SHOT IN COVER-UP CONSPIRACY blared across the front page of the *New York Post* the following morning. Two commanding images anchored the spread: Silver Fox, crisp in a pinstriped suit, his gaze cool and unyielding; and Demarcus, suspended mid-leap, muscles taut as he launched toward the rim in a thunderous dunk.

The article, penned by Simone O'Connor, read:

Bronx District Attorney Calvin Wilcox, known as Silver Fox, was gunned down last night and left for dead in his driveway. He now lies in a coma. Sources suggest this was a calculated move in a conspiracy to frame Demarcus Jones. Wilcox, who initially led the prosecution against Jones, had recently recused himself, citing personal reasons. He had since been vocal about Jones's innocence.

Investigators say new suspects have surfaced, and the police are actively piecing the puzzle together. Who orchestrated this brutal attack? Was the shooter targeting the DA to silence him? And when will the charges against Demarcus Jones—an innocent young man—finally be dropped? These are just a few of the questions swirling as the conspiracy unravels.

"He's alive," Alfredo murmured, eyes fixed on the newspaper spread across his desk. "He saw your face." His gaze lifted slowly to Viktor, who stood silently before him.

"I don't know how he made it," Viktor replied in a low voice. "I shot him point-blank. He looked dead."

"Looked dead but wasn't." Alfredo sprang to his feet, leaning in, his face flushed with fury. "He's not dead." He clutched his chest, breathing heavily through parted lips.

"Easy, sir," Viktor said, stepping forward. "Please sit down. I'll take care of it."

Alfredo sank back into his chair, his hand trembling as he reached for his now-cold coffee.

"They say he's in a coma," Viktor continued. "My contacts confirmed—"

"You and your contacts." Alfredo's voice faltered. He shut his eyes tightly, his breathing shallow.

"Sir, you're going to give yourself another heart attack," Viktor warned, concern splashed across his face. "Please, take it easy."

Alfredo opened his eyes just long enough to glare at him, then closed them again, struggling to steady his breath.

"I'll handle it," Viktor vowed. "He won't wake up." With that, he stormed out, determined to finish what he had started and silence Silver Fox for good.

Outside Silver Fox's hospital room, Detective Rich approached Detective Hanes. "Anything new?" he asked.

Hanes shook her head. "Doctor just checked in. He's still in a coma. No telling when, or if, he'll wake up."

Rich sighed. "It's been four days. I was hoping he'd come to and tell us who shot him. By the way, where's the guard who's supposed to be here?"

Since the shooting, Lieutenant Mulligan had ordered round-the-clock protection for Silver Fox. A uniformed officer was always stationed outside his room.

"I told him to grab some coffee. I'm covering until he gets back."

"All right," Rich said. "We can't risk the shooter coming back to finish the job."

"I asked the guard and his relief if they'd noticed anything suspicious. Both said no."

"That's something." Rich nodded.

"What now?" Hanes asked. "Where do we go from here until Silver Fox wakes up?"

"I say we take another pass at Bridget," Rich said firmly. "That girl's hiding something, and we need to find out what."

Just then, the police officer guarding Silver Fox approached, sipping from a steaming cup of coffee. "Thanks," he said to Hanes.

"No problem. Just remember to call us if anything comes up. You've got our cell numbers."

"Or if you spot anyone suspicious hanging around," Rich added.

The officer nodded, then lowered his voice. "Speaking of suspicious . . . don't look now, but I've seen that tall guy near the nurses' station a few times."

Hanes, standing sideways to the direction the officer indicated, tried to sneak a glance from the corner of her eye. Rich, whose back was to the man, stayed still.

"I didn't think much of it until now," the officer continued, casting a quick glance at Hanes. "I figured he was just visiting someone."

"When did you first notice him?" Rich asked.

"I think it was the day the prosecutor was moved from ICU to this floor."

"Two days ago," Hanes said. "I can't get a clear look. His baseball cap's pulled low, and he's wearing sunglasses."

"That's what makes him stand out," the officer said. "He's always got that red cap and shades. Plus, he's huge."

"I need to talk to him," Rich said, locking eyes with Hanes.

"Let's just say goodbye and head out," Hanes suggested. "We'll pass him on the way to the elevators. It won't look suspicious."

"Good idea," Rich agreed.

"We'll catch you later," Hanes said loudly to the officer.

They walked toward the elevators. As they neared the nurses' station, the tall man glanced at them, then abruptly turned and walked away.

Hanes and Rich quickened their pace. The man was already nearing the elevator bank. Without warning, Hanes broke into a sprint, Rich close behind. They reached the elevators just as one of the doors began to close.

"Wait!" Hanes shouted, racing forward. "Police. Stop!" She caught a fleeting glimpse of the man's face before the doors shut. She cursed under her breath.

"Let's take the next one and follow him down," Rich said, rushing into the adjacent elevator. Hanes jumped in beside him.

"How do we know he's headed to the lobby?" she asked as Rich pressed the button.

"We don't. But we'll find out."

"We were so close," Hanes muttered as the elevator descended.

They arrived in the lobby, now bustling with people moving in every direction.

"Do you see him?" Rich scanned the crowd.

"No," Hanes said, turning rapidly, eyes darting. "Maybe he got off on another floor to throw us off."

Rich hurried to the security desk near the entrance. "Excuse me. Did a very tall man wearing a red baseball cap and sunglasses just pass through here?"

The security guard hesitated.

Hanes flashed her badge. "Police."

"No," the guard replied. "I saw him come in earlier but not leave. He's hard to miss. Huge guy."

"Sounds like him," Rich said. "Have you seen him before?"

"Yes. I started seeing him about three or four days ago," the security guard replied. "You don't forget someone who looks like that."

"He probably got off on another floor," Hanes said, her eyes sweeping the crowd, scanning every moving figure.

Rich handed the guard his business card. "If you see him again, call me. It's urgent."

"Will do." The guard nodded.

Rich and Hanes exited the building through different doors, each hoping for one last glimpse of the elusive man. Minutes later, they reconvened at the car, their faces shadowed with disappointment.

"We could call in some backup," Hanes suggested. "Station an officer at every exit. He has to leave eventually."

"Maybe," Rich said, rubbing the back of his neck. "But right now, all we've got is that he was seen near Silver Fox's room a few times."

"You're right. Still, I can't shake the feeling we just let Silver Fox's attempted killer slip through our fingers."

Rich exhaled sharply. "I know. It feels like we're right on the edge of something, but still so far from the truth."

They drove back to the precinct in silence, each lost in thought.

A week later, Naomi sat in a patio chair in the backyard, the late-afternoon sun casting long shadows across the grass. Demarcus sat beside her, arms folded, his gaze distant.

"It's been a week since Calvin's attack," she said gently. "You still haven't gone to see him."

"He's still in a coma, far as I know," Demarcus replied. "What difference would it make if I did?"

Naomi studied him. "Is that really the reason?"

Before he could answer, her phone rang. She glanced at the screen. "It's the lieutenant." She answered quickly. "Hello?"

"Great news!" Lieutenant Mulligan's voice crackled with excitement. "Is Demarcus with you?"

"Yes, he's right here. What's going on?"

"Silver Fox is awake."

Naomi's eyes widened. "That *is* wonderful news."

Demarcus leaned forward, gripping her hand. "What is it?"

She turned to him, her voice trembling. "Your father's awake."

Naomi returned to the call. "Now he can tell us who shot him."

"That's the hope," Mulligan said. "And if he does, we can finally clear Demarcus. The charges will be dropped."

Naomi raised a hand skyward. "Thank you, Lord. I knew this day would come."

Demarcus sat still, silent.

"The detectives are heading to the hospital soon," Mulligan added before ending the call.

Naomi turned to her son. "You're awfully quiet. This is good news, Demarcus."

He nodded slowly.

"So why don't you seem happier?"

Demarcus's voice quivered as he spoke. "Maybe I'm scared to get my hopes up, only to find out Silver Fox doesn't remember who shot him. Don't get me wrong, I'm relieved he's going to be okay. Truly. But when it comes to getting these charges dropped, I—"

"Don't you dare finish that sentence," Naomi cut in, wrapping her arms around her son. "Just sit back and watch God work."

"Yes. Yes." Detective Rich punched the air triumphantly. "Now we're getting somewhere. Silver Fox is awake."

"It's on now," Hanes said, slapping him a high five.

Lieutenant Mulligan grinned. "Hold on. We were just told we've only got a short window to speak with him."

The three were gathered in Mulligan's office, deep in discussion about the case, when the call came in from the officer stationed outside Silver Fox's hospital room. Mulligan immediately phoned Naomi with the news. But just as Hanes and Rich were preparing to head out, the officer had called again, this time with a warning. The doctor was only allowing police a minute or two with the patient.

"That's fine," Rich replied. "We just need a name. He can give us the full story later."

A knock interrupted the moment.

"Come in," Mulligan called.

The door opened, and Carrick stepped inside. "Perfect. The crew's all here. I'd like to know what's going on while we—" He stopped mid-sentence, scanning the room full of grinning faces. "Wait. What's happening?"

"Silver Fox is awake," Mulligan announced.

Carrick's eyes widened. "Say what? And no one told me?"

"You were next on my list," Mulligan said with a chuckle. "I already called Naomi and Demarcus."

"Well, what are we waiting for?" Carrick asked. "Let's get to the hospital."

"We're heading there now," Hanes replied. "But aside from immediate family, the doctor's only giving the police a few minutes."

Carrick's face fell. He muttered, "I can at least wait outside his room."

The officers exchanged a knowing glance.

Another knock came at the door.

"Come in," Mulligan said again.

An officer stepped in. "Sorry to interrupt. There's a young woman here insisting she speak with Detectives Hanes and Rich." The officer moved aside, and they saw the woman.

"Bridget," Hanes and Rich exclaimed in unison. All four stared in stunned silence as Bridget Walsh stepped into the room.

She cleared her throat, her posture stiff with determination. "I'm ready to talk. This time, I'll tell you the truth."

"And only the truth, so help me God," Mulligan murmured under his breath.

"All right," Rich said warmly. "Please, have a seat." He gestured to an empty chair.

Bridget sat down. Hanes and Mulligan quickly followed, while Rich and Carrick remained standing, their eyes locked on her.

"Demarcus Jones didn't rape me," Bridget said, her voice steady but trembling. "And he didn't try to kill me." Her lips quivered, and tears welled in her eyes. "It was my boss, Angelo Ferrari."

Chapter Thirty-five

The music thundered through the club, pulsing off the walls illuminated by a kaleidoscope of flashing lights. Bodies moved in hypnotic unison, swaying, grinding, and gyrating to the beat, their energy electric. Drinks flowed freely as bartenders worked with swift precision, pouring liquor into eager hands. Nearly everyone was drinking, the air thick with celebration. Wisps of smoke curled upward—cigars, cigarettes, and the unmistakable scent of marijuana mingling with the warmth and rhythm of the night. It was Saturday, and the party was in full swing at Music Vibes Club on Madison Avenue in Manhattan.

Angelo Ferrari lounged on a sleek black leather couch tucked inside one of six semi-private booths reserved for the club's elite regulars. A sultry blonde perched on his right leg, a fiery redhead on his left. He took a slow sip of Hennessy, then leaned into the blonde's generous cleavage, drawing a delighted giggle from her lips. The redhead, unwilling to be outshone, leaned in and traced Angelo's earlobe with her teeth. He let out a low moan, savoring the sensation.

For the next few minutes, Angelo indulged in his favorite cigar and sipped from his glass, the rich aroma of smoke curling around him. The women stayed close, refilling their drinks, kissing him, their hands roaming freely. He was in his zone, confident, adored, untouchable.

"Angelo Ferrari?" A deep voice cut through the music.

Angelo looked up, frowning at the tall figure looming over him.

"Who's asking?"

"I'm Detective Rich," the man replied, gesturing to the officer beside him. "This is my partner, Detective Hanes. We're with the 47th Precinct in the Bronx. Behind us are officers from Manhattan."

Angelo's eyes darted between Rich and Hanes, wide with alarm. His hands quivered. "What do you want?" he asked, trying to sound defiant, though the tremor in his voice betrayed him.

Detective Rich turned to the women. "Ladies, if you'll excuse us."

They didn't hesitate. With drinks in hand, they slid off Angelo's lap and hurried away.

Angelo's trembling intensified as Rich and Hanes settled in on either side of him, their presence heavy and deliberate.

Rich leaned in close, his voice low and strong. "You have one chance to stand up and come with us quietly," he said in Angelo's ear. "Mr. Ferrari, you're under arrest for the rape and attempted murder of Bridget Walsh."

"What?" Angelo shot to his feet.

Hanes and Rich sprang up as well, their bodies closing in, forming a wall around him.

"I don't know what you're talking about," Angelo shouted, voice cracking with panic. "Leave me alone."

He lunged forward, trying to shove past them, but Hanes seized his arm and twisted it behind his back.

"Hey! What are you doing?" Angelo struggled, thrashing against Hanes's grip.

Rich grabbed his other arm and yanked it behind him. In one swift motion, Hanes snapped on the handcuffs.

"Mr. Ferrari, you have the right to remain silent," Rich said loudly in Angelo's ear. "Anything you say can and will be used against you in a court of law. You have the right to an attorney. If you don't have one, one will be appointed to you. Do you understand your rights?"

Angelo exploded with a string of expletives.

"Let's go," Rich said, unfazed by the outburst.

Hanes led the way, carving a path through the crowd. Rich gave Angelo a firm nudge, steering him toward the exit. The Manhattan officers followed closely behind.

"I'm going to have your badges," Angelo snarled, his face flushed crimson with rage and humiliation.

Heads turned. A few clubgoers whispered, others pointed. Some simply stared in disbelief. Angelo was a familiar face, wealthy, flamboyant, a regular fixture in the nightlife scene. Seeing him escorted out in cuffs was a spectacle.

"Do you know who I am?" Angelo suddenly stopped and twisted, trying to face Detective Rich.

Rich shoved him forward. "Keep walking."

"You'll regret this. My father will hear about this." Angelo kept ranting until they reached the street.

The detectives guided him to their car, double-parked in front of the club.

Rich swung open the back door. "Watch your head," he said as Angelo climbed in, then he shut the door and joined Hanes in the front seat.

The ride to the Bronx passed in silence. Angelo sat slumped, his head bowed, the fire in him extinguished.

Meanwhile, across town on the Upper East Side, two detectives stepped into the gleaming lobby of a luxury apartment building and approached the doorman.

"Detective Marley, NYPD," Marley said, flashing her badge. "This is Detective Trebek. Is Mr. Alfredo Ferrari upstairs?"

The doorman hesitated, his mouth opening and closing, eyes darting between the two men.

"This is serious police business," Marley said sharply. "Is he upstairs?"

The doorman nodded.

"What about his driver? Big guy, blond?"

"No," the doorman replied, voice trembling. He cleared his throat. "He left earlier this evening. I haven't seen him return. The girlfriend went out too."

"You've been here all day?" Marley asked.

"Yes. My coworker called in sick, so I'm covering a double shift."

"Excuse me." Marley turned and walked out, leaving Trebek with the doorman. Outside, she approached a plain white van, opened the rear door, and climbed in. Inside, a six-man SWAT team waited.

"Doorman says Ferrari's upstairs," Marley reported. "Viktor left earlier and hasn't come back."

"What's the move?" asked Duncan, the SWAT leader. "Sounds like the dangerous one's missing."

"Yes, but just to be safe, maybe two of you should come with me and Trebek upstairs," Marley suggested. "The doorman said he's working a double shift, so who knows if Viktor slipped past while he was . . . occupied. I mean, the guy had to use the bathroom at some point."

"You've got a point. Let's not take any chances with this guy," Duncan replied.

Marley gave a quick nod of agreement.

"Allen and I will go up," Duncan continued, gesturing toward a short Black man. "Cliff and Dyke will stay in the lobby for backup. Barnes and Glutton will cover the front entrance in case Viktor circles back."

With the plan set, the four SWAT officers and Marley moved into the building's lobby to join Trebek. Once everyone was in position, the doorman led them to the elevator. He inserted a key, granting them a direct ride to the penthouse.

"Thank you," Marley whispered as they stepped out. "You can head back down now."

The doorman nodded, his face filled with curiosity, though he said nothing.

The penthouse floor was silent. Thick, plush carpet muffled their footsteps as the SWAT team took positions on either side of Alfredo's door, weapons drawn and bodies pressed against the walls, hidden from view.

Marley and Trebek approached the door. Marley rang the bell. No answer. She pressed it again. Still nothing.

"Maybe he's not home," she murmured.

"Or already in bed," Trebek replied, keeping his voice low. He held the button down.

A voice finally called out from inside. "Okay, okay. Who is it?"

"NYPD, sir. Please open the door," Marley said clearly.

"What do you want?" Alfredo snapped from the other side.

"Mr. Ferrari, we're police officers. We need to speak with you. Please open the door." Marley held her badge up to the peephole.

Silence.

"Mr. Ferrari, please don't make this difficult. Open the door."

After a tense pause, the lock clicked. The door swung open to reveal Alfredo standing in the doorway, wearing pristine white silk pajamas, his eyes blazing with irritation.

Just then, the SWAT team appeared, silent, sudden, and armed. Their rifles locked onto Alfredo.

"Wait a minute." Alfredo stumbled back, hands shooting into the air, eyes wide with alarm.

In a flash, Duncan, the SWAT leader, seized Alfredo's wrist and yanked him into the hallway. Another officer slammed the apartment door shut behind them.

"Is anyone else inside?" Duncan's weapon hovered inches from Alfredo's face.

"N–no," Alfredo stammered, glancing nervously between the gun and Duncan's steely expression. "I . . . I'm alone."

Without a word, two officers slipped inside the apartment. The detectives remained in the hallway with Alfredo. Moments later, the SWAT team returned.

"Clear. He's alone," Duncan confirmed, his gaze drilling into Alfredo.

"What's going on?" Alfredo barked, his confidence creeping back.

"Mr. Ferrari, you're under arrest," Detective Marley said calmly. "Turn around and place your hands behind your back."

"What?" Alfredo's voice cracked. "For what? This is insane."

"You're being charged with attempted murder, conspiracy to commit murder—"

"Murder?" Alfredo's face turned crimson. "You people are out of your minds."

"Obstruction of justice. Witness tampering. Aiding and abetting," Marley continued. "Hands behind your back."

Trebek stepped forward as Alfredo spun around, shouting, "I need my lawyers."

Marley cuffed him swiftly. "Anything you say can and will be used against you. You have the right to an attorney."

"I need my lawyers," Alfredo shouted again, stomping his bare feet on the carpet. "I don't even know what this is about."

"Calm down, Mr. Ferrari," Marley said. "You'll get your call at the precinct."

"I need to change and call my lawyers," Alfredo snapped, glaring at them.

Marley exhaled sharply. "Fine. We'll come with you. Make it quick, or we're hauling you out like this."

Marley and Trebek followed Alfredo into the bedroom. Marley removed the cuffs while Trebek stood guard in the doorway.

Alfredo muttered curses as he rummaged through his closet. "Do you know who I am? Arresting me, Alfredo Ferrari?" He switched between Italian and English, his fury boiling over.

"Mr. Ferrari, get dressed. Now," Trebek warned.

Alfredo shot back something in Italian. Neither detective understood it, but the tone was unmistakably rude.

"One minute," Trebek said coldly, his patience thinning.

Alfredo glared at him, then pulled on a red-and-white Adidas tracksuit and matching Nike sneakers, which would be more appropriate for someone half his age. Once he was dressed, Marley cuffed him again. Without another word, they led Alfredo out of the apartment. Trebek closed the door behind them.

On the elevator ride down, Alfredo cursed relentlessly. The detectives and SWAT officers paid him no mind, their silence a wall he couldn't penetrate.

"George, I'll be back in a little while," Alfredo shouted confidently as the group marched him past the stunned doorman.

Outside, the night air buzzed with tension. The officers guided him toward a waiting police car. Marley swung the back door open and motioned with a firm hand.

"Watch your head."

Alfredo bent to enter, then paused, straightening up with theatrical flair. He scanned their faces, his voice rising with pride. "Do you know I have former President George H. W. Bush's cell phone number?" He lifted his chin like a peacock in full display. "I'll be calling him very soon." His chest puffed out, but the unimpressed stares around him deflated the moment. With a final glance, he climbed into the car.

Marley's grin stretched wide. "What about President Bill Clinton?" she teased. "Don't you have his number too?"

Laughter erupted from the officers.

Alfredo's face was as red as a tomato, his chest rising and falling in anger. If looks could kill, they would all be dead.

"After all, *he* is the current president," Marley added, twisting the knife.

Their laughter washed over Alfredo as he sat rigid in the back seat, eyes locked forward, his body trembling with fury.

Chapter Thirty-six

It was nearly midnight. North Broadway in Yonkers lay quiet, blanketed in sleep—except for Ms. Lopez. She curled up on her couch, wrapped in a blanket despite the eighty-degree heat. To her, it felt like eight degrees. A loud yawn escaped her lips as she shifted to her right side, rubbing her tired, reddened eyes before rolling to the left.

"*Estoy cansada*" she murmured, her voice soft and weary. "I am tired," she repeated silently.

Today had been the first day the thugs, as she called them, hadn't parked outside her home. Relief should have come easily, but instead, unease crept in. Her thoughts lingered on the kind young man who had helped her with her bags. When she did fall asleep, she had nightmares of him handcuffed and being led to jail, or the judge sentencing him to life in prison while he screamed at Ms. Lopez to help him. But she couldn't. She had to look out for herself and Juan.

Ms. Lopez turned onto her stomach, her face buried in the pillow. Tears slipped out, soaking the fabric as she cried quietly, eventually drifting into a restless sleep. Almost an hour later, she jolted awake. Sniffing the air, her nose twitched. Smoke.

She sprang to her feet and rushed toward the stairs. But just as she placed her foot on the first step, a ball of fire rolled toward her. Screaming, she spun around and dashed back into the living room. A loud whoosh roared above her. She looked up. Flames devoured the ceiling, slithering down the wall like a furious serpent.

"Juan!" Ms. Lopez called out, her voice cracking with urgency. She hadn't seen him in days, probably off getting high somewhere, but deep down, she knew he had something to do with the fire.

"Juan!" she shouted again, her throat tightening as thick smoke filled the living room.

Tears streamed from her burning eyes, mingling with the mucus dripping from her nose. The fire crept closer, its heat now so intense it singed the hair on her arms and legs. The house, mostly vinyl with brick corners, was a tinderbox. Flames raced across the walls and now encircled the front door.

With no other option, Ms. Lopez lunged for the doorknob. A searing pain shot up her arm. It felt like grabbing a piece of burning coal. She spun toward the back door, but it was already engulfed in flames. She had to escape.

A chunk of the blazing roof crashed at her feet. Screaming, she grabbed the doorknob again, her hand aflame as she wrenched the door open. Coughing and gasping, she staggered down the driveway, reached the street, and collapsed to her knees. Her eyes lifted to the inferno devouring her home, thick gray smoke curling skyward.

"No, no, no," she sobbed, over and over.

Sirens wailed in the distance. Within moments, five fire trucks roared up to the curb. Ms. Lopez remained on the ground, hacking and gulping clean air into her smoke-choked lungs.

"Ma'am, are you okay?" a firefighter asked, kneeling beside her.

"Juan. Juan," she cried, pointing toward the burning house. "My son."

"There's someone inside," the firefighter yelled, sprinting toward the flames.

Ms. Lopez felt an arm wrap around her, lifting her to her feet. She looked up. It was her next-door neighbor, the one she'd barely acknowledged since moving in.

"I saw the fire and called 911," the woman said gently. "Are you hurt?"

"My son . . . I think he's still inside." Ms. Lopez leaned into the woman's shoulder and wept.

"She says her son is trapped," the neighbor called out to others gathering nearby. The street quickly filled with concerned onlookers, their faces tense as firefighters battled the blaze. The tension surged as word spread that Juan was still inside, and panic began to ripple through the crowd.

Two ambulances screeched to a halt beside Ms. Lopez. Her neighbor guided her toward one.

"No. I'm . . . I'm fine," Ms. Lopez murmured, though her dazed expression said otherwise.

"Let them check your hand," the woman urged.

Ms. Lopez glanced down, suddenly aware of the burn. She had forgotten all about it. Shaking her head, she whispered, "Not now. Juan. They have to get my boy out."

A deafening explosion shattered the air. Glass burst from the windows as the fire raged on.

"Step back, please!" a firefighter shouted to the crowd. "Everyone, move back."

Ms. Lopez stood frozen, her limbs useless. If not for her neighbor's support, she would have collapsed. Her sobs had quieted to a low, guttural moan as she stared at the inferno.

Time seemed to stretch endlessly as firefighters fought the roaring blaze that had swallowed her home whole.

"In here," someone shouted from inside the house, the voice slicing through the night and reaching the crowd gathered on the street.

"I think they've found him," another cried out.

A fireman burst through the doorway, cradling a limp bundle over his shoulder. He sprinted toward the waiting ambulance, where EMTs stood ready. With swift precision, they transferred the body onto the gurney and hoisted it into the back of the vehicle.

Suddenly, a piercing scream shattered the tense silence, startling several bystanders. It was Ms. Lopez. Her eyes rolled back, and she collapsed, her body crumpling to the ground.

Moments later, she stirred. "Where am I?" she whispered, blinking at the unfamiliar surroundings and the two concerned faces hovering above her.

"You're in the ambulance, ma'am," one EMT replied gently. "Glad to have you back."

"Juan?" Her voice was raspy, barely audible.

"You mean the person they pulled from your burning house?"

Ms. Lopez nodded, fear tightening around her chest like a vice.

"He's been rushed to St. John's Riverside Hospital," the EMT said. "How are you feeling?"

"I need to see my son."

"Your blood pressure's stabilizing," he assured her. "You'll be fine, but we'd like to take you in for a full checkup."

"No, I'm fine," she insisted. "I don't need an ambulance."

"All right, that's your choice. But first, let me take a quick look at your hand."

Ms. Lopez opened her mouth to protest, then hesitated. Pain throbbed through her hand, and her heart. She nodded.

Once her hand was bandaged, the EMT helped her down from the ambulance. Outside, the kind neighbor who had called 911 was waiting.

"Can you take me to the hospital?" Ms. Lopez asked, her eyes pleading.

"Of course. Come on. I'll get my husband to drive us."

The neighbor gently took her arm and guided her away. As they approached the crowd, Ms. Lopez paused. Her gaze lifted to the charred remains of her home, and she gasped. The fire was out. Smoke curled from the ruins. The top floor had collapsed, and most of the lower level was gone. Only the four scorched brick walls remained.

"For what?" she murmured.

"Excuse me?" the neighbor asked.

"I did what I did . . . and for what?" Ms. Lopez gestured toward the wreckage. Her voice trembled. She wanted to cry, but the tears wouldn't come.

"What do you mean? What did you do?"

Ms. Lopez didn't answer. She was speaking to herself now. "Now my son has paid the price for my sins." Her body began to shake.

"Maybe we should take you back to the ambulance," the neighbor suggested. "Let them check you out properly."

"No," Ms. Lopez said firmly. "Please, just take me to my son."

The neighbors drove her up the street to St. John's Riverside Hospital.

"Thank you," she said softly before stepping out of the car and hurrying into the emergency ward.

"I'm looking for my son," she said urgently to the first nurse she spotted. "He was in a fire. They brought him here."

The nurse's expression shifted, softened with concern, shadowed by something unspoken. "Oh . . . I see."

Ms. Lopez's knees buckled, her legs suddenly limp, like overcooked spaghetti. "Please, no. Please."

"He was just rushed into surgery," the nurse said gently. "His condition is extremely critical. Come with me. Let's get you seated." The woman guided Ms. Lopez to a nearby chair, and she collapsed into it, grateful for the support.

"When will we know something?" Ms. Lopez asked, her voice trembling.

"We'll have to wait for the doctor," the nurse replied, placing a reassuring hand on her shoulder. "In the meantime, pray for your son." With a final glance, she hurried off.

Pray, Ms. Lopez thought. *Just like that boy's mother must have prayed day and night. I have to fix this. Lord, if it's not too late, please give me a chance to make it right.*

She rose and walked over to a small reception desk. "Hi. Could you please make a call for me? It's important."

The young man behind the desk looked up, saw the anguish on her face, and nodded. "Of course. What's the number?"

"It's the 47th Precinct in the Bronx. I don't know the number, but I remember one of the detectives. His name is Rich."

"Got it. Let me find it." He flipped through a directory, fingers moving quickly.

Ms. Lopez watched him, her heart pounding. Reaching the detective felt like the only lifeline left—for her son, for herself.

"Here it is," he said, dialing. "Yes, may I speak to Detective Rich?" He glanced at her. "I'm on hold. They're trying to locate him."

She nodded, barely breathing.

"Hello? Detective Rich? One moment, please." He handed Ms. Lopez the phone.

"Detective Rich," she said, her voice steadying with resolve. "This is Carmen Lopez. I need to speak with you urgently." She paused, listening. "I'm at St. John's Hospital, but I can come to the precinct in the morning."

Another pause. Then she said, "Okay. I'll be here, in the emergency waiting area. This time I'll tell you what I should've said long ago. That young man didn't attack that girl. He's innocent."

Chapter Thirty-seven

The next morning, Viktor stood restlessly in the long, winding line at United Airlines inside Newark Liberty International Airport. Just hours earlier, he had been en route to Alfredo's apartment to warn him about Angelo's arrest, only to spot a SWAT team storming the building. The moment he saw them, he knew it was over.

He bolted up the street, flagged down a yellow cab, and raced back to his apartment in Lower Manhattan. He barely stepped inside, grabbing only the duffle bag he kept packed for emergencies. Another cab took him to Penn Station, where he bought a ticket and boarded the PATH train to Newark. At the Hilton Newark Airport Hotel, he checked in under one of his many aliases using a fake passport.

Viktor had already booked the earliest flight to Mexico City. His plan was simple; disappear for a few days to the furnished apartment he'd purchased years ago under another name, withdraw funds from his offshore account, then catch a flight to Tolyatti—the impoverished Russian city where he was born and raised before fleeing to the United States. He would stay there until the dust settled, then return to the country he now called home.

"Come on," he muttered, towering over the crowd, eyes locked on the counter ahead. "Let's go." He checked his watch.

Viktor had timed his arrival precisely, just an hour before departure. With only a carry-on bag containing a passport, a change of clothes, and a modest stash of cash, he thought he'd breeze through. But now, stuck in line, he felt time slipping away. Every passing minute brought him closer to either escape or capture.

"Unbelievable," he said louder, drawing a glance from the woman in front.

He checked his watch again. That's when he felt a presence at his side. He turned and saw a face he'd only seen once but could never forget.

"Hello, Viktor," said Detective Rich. "Going somewhere?"

"Don't move," hissed Detective Hanes from the other side.

Viktor felt the unmistakable pressure of a gun against his ribs.

"Behind you are four Newark officers," Hanes added. "And more waiting outside."

Viktor turned slightly. The line behind him had vanished, replaced by three men and a woman with steely expressions, each with a hand tucked inside their jackets. He had been so focused on the counter that he hadn't noticed the trap closing in.

"Drop the bag," Rich ordered. "Slowly. No sudden moves."

Viktor obeyed. He had left his gun behind, knowing it wouldn't make it past security. He was defenseless.

"Hands behind your back," Hanes barked, snapping the cuffs on with practiced speed.

Flanked by officers, Viktor was led out of the terminal and into a waiting police car bound for New York. His flight to Mexico City would depart without him. His escape was over.

Two days later, Carrick and his wife, Simone, sat at their modest dining room table, sipping coffee and reflecting on the latest developments in Demarcus's case.

"That little Jezebel, Ms. Lopez, finally told the truth, huh?" Simone's face twisted with disdain. "She could've spared so many people so much heartache."

"I know," Carrick replied gently. "But we have to be grateful she finally came forward."

"Only after the house she sold her soul for went up in flames. Thank you, Lord."

Carrick nodded. "I agree. I'm sorry to hear about her son, though. He's still in a coma."

Simone's expression softened. "Yes, that's heartbreaking. I truly hope he pulls through. His mother may be wicked, and from what I've heard, he's battling his own demons, but I wouldn't wish that on anyone."

"We'll keep praying for him."

Just then, Carrick's cell phone rang. He answered quickly. "Hello?"

"Mr. O'Connor, this is ADA Carter."

Carrick's eyes lit up. "ADA Carter, what a pleasure." He winked at Simone, who responded with a thumbs-up.

"I was wondering if you could stop by the office," Carter said.

"I'm on my way," Carrick exclaimed, ending the call. He leaned in and kissed Simone deeply. "That's the call I've been waiting for." Another kiss. "I think this might be the end of Demarcus's nightmare." One more kiss.

Simone laughed, though her eyes shimmered with emotion. "After Bridget's and Ms. Lopez's statements, what else is there?"

Carrick took her hand. "Thank you for everything, baby." He touched a finger to her lips before she could speak. "I know you're going to say you didn't do anything, but you kept Demarcus's story on the front page of the *New York Post*. That coverage spread nationwide. You knew there was a conspiracy to frame him, and you never backed down."

"Neither did you," Simone said. "You've fought for him from the start."

"We make a great team."

"In more ways than one."

They high fived.

"I'm out of here," Carrick said, rising from his chair. "I've got an ADA to see."

Minutes later, Carrick was ushered into ADA Clark's cramped office.

"Have a seat," she said, settling into her chair. "Judging by the look on your face, I'd say you think you know what I'm about to say."

Carrick smiled. "Let's just say I know what you should say. You've got Angelo Ferrari, Bridget's attacker, in custody. His father and the hitman who tried to frame my client and kill the district attorney are both behind bars. Demarcus Jones is innocent," he continued, his tone firm. "And now, you need to drop all charges. Publicly."

ADA Clark let out a long sigh. "This case has been insane. Everything about it feels surreal. Sometimes I wonder if it's a movie or a dream."

"It's neither," Carrick said sharply. "For Demarcus and Naomi Jones, it was a living nightmare. This was their reality because some rich, lowlife, racist—"

"Okay, I get it," Clark interrupted. "Trust me, I do. I'll do everything I can to make this right, starting with dropping all charges."

Carrick nodded.

"I'll also hold a press conference to publicly declare his innocence."

Carrick nodded again, this time with quiet satisfaction.

"I'll also notify them about the arrests and charges filed against Angelo Ferrari, Alfredo Ferrari, and Viktor Sokolov," ADA Clark said.

"Thank you," Carrick replied.

Clark's tone sharpened. "The Ferraris' expensive lawyers are already scrambling for a deal. Meanwhile, Mr. Sokolov has sent word he's ready to flip on his former employers, who seem to have abandoned him." Her eyes narrowed. "Let me make you another promise. The Ferraris and Sokolov will pay for what they did to Bridget, DA Wilcox, and his son. They're going down."

Carrick stood, and Clark mirrored him. "We'll get them," he said with quiet conviction. "Thanks again."

"One more thing," Clark added. "The press conference is in about four hours. Want to stand beside me?"

"Absolutely. But first, I've got places to be and people to see."

Clark smiled. "Go on then. I'll see you soon."

They shook hands, and Carrick jogged to his car. Moments later, he was outside Naomi's apartment, ringing the bell.

Naomi opened the door, her face lighting up. "I'm so glad you're here," she said, lowering her voice. "Lieutenant Mulligan stopped by earlier. He told us Bridget finally came forward and told the truth."

Carrick nodded. "Yes."

"Demarcus is in the living room," she whispered. "He's very emotional right now."

Carrick gave a solemn nod. "I can imagine."

Together, they walked into the living room. Demarcus sat on the couch, his eyes red and fixed on the wall, unmoving.

Naomi sat beside him, gently taking his hand. Carrick took the opposite seat.

"Did the lieutenant also mention that Ms. Lopez finally confessed to what really happened that night? Carrick asked, his gaze steady on Demarcus.

Naomi's lips trembled. "Yes."

"The house Alfredo Ferrari gave her as payment for lying burned down, and her son's in the hospital fighting for his life. That shook her conscience."

Naomi nodded, while Demarcus remained silent, staring ahead.

"I come bearing better news." Carrick leaned forward, his eyes bright. "I just left ADA Clark's office. She's dropping all charges against Demarcus."

Naomi gasped, then leapt to her feet, clapping her hands. "Hallelujah! Glory be to God." She raised her arms and marched around the room, tears streaming as she praised. "Lord, I knew You'd come through. Thank You."

Carrick turned to Demarcus, who sat frozen, blinking slowly.

"Demarcus?" Carrick moved to the seat Naomi vacated. "Did you hear me?"

Demarcus turned his head, robotic and slow, but said nothing.

"It's over," Carrick said gently. "You're a free man."

Demarcus finally spoke, his voice barely above a whisper. "But I wasn't guilty. What am I being freed from?" His eyes welled up again. "What did I do to deserve all that happened to me?"

Carrick's voice softened. "You didn't deserve any of it. It's the evil that men do. But this time, good wins. The ones who hurt you are behind bars, and they'll pay. Trust me, Demarcus, it's their turn now."

As if pulled by invisible strings, Demarcus slid off the couch and onto his knees. A deep, guttural wail erupted from him, echoing through the room like a wounded animal.

Carrick recoiled in shock. Naomi rushed to her son, cradling him against her chest. Together, mother and son wept—loudly, painfully—for the injustice they had endured, for the nightmare that seemed to be ending, and for the hope of healing.

For justice, finally, for Demarcus Jones.

Chapter Thirty-eight

Demarcus stood before the grand house in Riverdale, his gaze sweeping over it as if it were a spacecraft freshly landed from another world. His heart thudded in his chest. He inhaled deeply, trying to steady himself.

Maybe this isn't such a good idea, he thought. *I should just leave.* He turned to go.

"Hello there," a bright voice called out behind him.

Demarcus spun around. A beautiful blonde woman stood smiling warmly.

"Come on in, Demarcus. We've been waiting for you."

He hesitated, then slowly walked up the driveway. As he approached, unsure of what to say, she extended her hand.

"I'm Mindy, your stepmother," she said, smiling, her blue eyes sparkling with welcome.

"Uh . . . hello." His voice came out rough. He cleared his throat. "Hi, I'm Demarcus." He shook her hand firmly. "Nice to meet you, Ms. Mindy."

"We're waiting," came a commanding voice from inside the house.

Mindy laughed. "That's your feisty grandmother. Come on." She kept hold of his hand and led him through the front door.

"Hello, baby." A petite woman with a crown of white Shirley Temple curls greeted him as they entered the spacious, elegant living room. "Come give your nana a hug."

Before Demarcus could process the word "nana," small arms wrapped around his legs. He bent awkwardly to return the embrace.

"Your grandfather is here too," said a gravelly voice.

Demarcus turned to see an older version of his father seated in a wheelchair. Thick white hair framed his head, and a neatly trimmed beard gave him a dignified air.

"Hello, sir." Demarcus extended his hand, but his grandfather opened his arms wide. After a brief pause, Demarcus leaned in for a firm, heartfelt hug.

"I'm so happy to meet you," his grandfather whispered. "I'm very sorry for all you've been through."

Demarcus nodded, emotion rising in his chest.

"Welcome to the family, son."

Tears welled in his eyes. He blinked rapidly and murmured, "Thank you, sir."

A throat cleared behind him.

Demarcus straightened and turned to find himself face-to-face with a tall young man.

"What's up, big brother?"

He stared at the pale hand extended toward him, then looked up at the handsome face framed by thick, curly blond hair. Green eyes, just like his own, met his gaze. The nose was straight, the lips sharp and pink.

They stood there, two young men from different worlds, black and white by society's standards, yet undeniably connected. Brothers. Blood brothers.

The room had gone silent. Demarcus glanced down and saw the hand still waiting. He grasped it quickly. "Sorry. You must be Samuel. Nice to meet you."

"No problem." Samuel grinned and pulled him into a man hug. "Hey, I heard you're going to Stanford. Guess where I'm planning to go?"

Before Demarcus could answer, Samuel beamed. "Stanford! Just like you."

"Oh. Okay," Demarcus replied, a bit stunned.

Samuel bounced with excitement. "It's going to be awesome having my big brother on campus. I can't wait." He hugged Demarcus again, and the room erupted in laughter.

Demarcus chuckled. Samuel was a whirlwind of energy.

"Don't forget me," called a voice from the corner. District Attorney Calvin Wilcox lounged on a couch, feet propped on an ottoman.

Demarcus walked over and embraced him. "How are you feeling?"

"Better every day," Silver Fox replied. Just over two months had passed since the shooting. Thanks to the skilled surgeons at Montefiore Medical Center, he'd survived, awakened from a coma, and was now steadily recovering.

"God is good," Silver Fox said, locking eyes with his older son. "I don't know what I've done to deserve His goodness."

"Now that's something I'm wondering myself," his mother said, and everyone laughed.

The next few minutes for Demarcus were filled with more hugs and kisses from his grandmother, Samuel animatedly telling him about his favorite NBA basketball team and requesting some pointers from his brother later. Everyone was talking to Demarcus, trying to make him feel welcome as they got to know him.

Finally, everyone settled down, and they all sat around the dining table to have dinner.

"Demarcus, my grandson," his grandfather began, "I know it's going to take some time to adjust to all this." He waved his hand. "But I want you to know from the moment my son told me about you, I couldn't wait to meet you. You're my flesh and blood, my first grandchild, and a huge part of this family now."

"And you never forget it," his grandmother added.

"We're so sorry about what you have been through," Mindy said, her eyes clouded with sadness. "What both you and your father have gone through. I'm glad that through it all, you have found each other. Now we have the pleasure of welcoming you into our lives."

Unshed tears glittered in Demarcus's eyes, his lips quivering. This wasn't what he was expecting when he finally accepted his father's invitation to dinner and to meet the rest of the family. How would he fit into this prestigious white family? He had wondered. Would they even accept him as his father had done? It seemed like they did.

"Thank you all. The last few months have been hard for me, and it will take a long time for me to get over this, if ever," Demarcus said. "But I'm hoping with time I can move on with my life as planned."

"You will," Silver Fox said firmly. "I am going to do everything I can to help you, and you have a very strong mother in your corner."

Demarcus nodded in agreement.

Demarcus's grandmother said, "I know it doesn't seem like it now, but one day, you will realize everything works together for your good."

"It was through the heartache you were able to connect with the father you never knew, and vice versa," Mindy added.

"Now you got yourself another family," his grandfather told him. "Who, from this day, will always love and care about you."

"And don't forget the coolest brother in the world," Samuel exclaimed, and everyone laughed.

"See? That wasn't so bad," Silver Fox said, turning to Demarcus with a satisfied smile. "I told you they were going to love you."

They sat together on the screened-in porch, the soft hum of conversation and television drifting from inside where the rest of the family had gathered.

"They were very nice," Demarcus admitted, his voice quiet but sincere.

"I sent a letter to Stanford to confirm your scholarship for next spring."

"You did?" Demarcus blinked, surprised.

"I sure did. You were falsely accused, and the charges were dropped. None of that was your fault, and it shouldn't cost you the scholarship you worked so hard for."

"If it doesn't work out, that's okay," Demarcus said solemnly. "I can go to CUNY part-time and work the rest."

Silver Fox shook his head. "If they don't honor it, I'll sue them. But either way, you're going to Stanford. I told you I'll pay your tuition."

Demarcus looked at him, eyes searching.

"Please don't say no," Silver Fox said gently. "Let me do this for you. I can't change the eighteen years we lost, but I can do right by you now."

Demarcus saw the sincerity in his father's eyes. "Okay," he said, nodding slowly. "Thank you. I'll make the most of it."

"I know you will," Silver Fox said, his voice full of pride. "You've got a bright future ahead. This didn't stop you. It just slowed you down a little."

"Thanks. I appreciate you saying that." Demarcus hesitated, then added, "I'm sorry you had to drop out of the attorney general race."

Silver Fox waved it off. "Right now, I'm focused on healing and getting to know you better. There's always next time. Who knows? Maybe you'll help me with my campaign, huh?"

Demarcus smiled. "I'd like that very much."

"One more thing," Silver Fox said, leaning forward. "I've assigned Salaam Alihammad's case to an ADA for immediate review."

"Really?"

"The justice system has its flaws, but this one's beyond me. He was arrested for armed robbery, no weapon, no witnesses, and still sat in jail for almost two years without a bail hearing or trial? That's not justice. As DA for Bronx County, it's my job to find out how that happened and fix it. And I will."

"That means a lot," Demarcus said softly.

"He was there for you when you needed him."

Demarcus shuddered. "I hate to think what would've happened if he hadn't been. He saved my life."

"Then I'll do everything I can to give him his life back. That's a promise."

"Thank you." Demarcus leaned back in his chair, studying his father's face. "It's really going to be all right now, isn't it, Father?"

Silver Fox reached out his hand, and Demarcus took it. "Yes, my son," he responded with measured assurance. "You're going to be all right. We all are."

I have told you these things, so that in me you may have peace. In this world, you will have trouble. But take heart! I have overcome the world.

John 16:33

Epilogue

"Ready?" Jerry's eyes gleamed as he waved the letter overhead, rocking eagerly on his heels. "One, two—"

"Boy, if you don't read that letter right now . . ." Naomi shot him a warning look, though her eyes sparkled with just as much excitement.

Demarcus watched the exchange with a quiet smile, sinking deeper into the couch as he studied his best friend.

"Okay, okay," Jerry relented. "Dear Mr. Jones, Congratulations! It—"

Naomi squealed and sprang to her feet.

"Ms. Naomi, I'm not finished," Jerry said, trying to hold back a grin.

Demarcus chuckled.

"My bad. Please, continue." Naomi began pacing between the two young men, rubbing her hands together as if she were warming up for a race.

" . . . is with great pleasure that I offer you admission to Stanford University," Jerry read on. "Your award provides full tuition, basic health insurance and fees through the university, and a stipend—"

"Thank you, Lord," Naomi burst out, unable to contain herself. "Glory be to God."

Demarcus watched her break into a joyful jig around the living room, praising the Lord with every step. His eyes welled up as he looked at Jerry. "Can you believe it?" he asked, voice thick with emotion.

Jerry nodded. "You can read the whole thing later. But listen to the last line." He cleared his throat. "We look forward to your athletic and academic accomplishments here with us at Stanford University."

The two friends threw their heads back and howled like they would when they won a basketball game.

"Full scholarship to Stanford," Jerry shouted, pumping his fists in the air.

Demarcus jumped up and wrapped his best friend in a bear hug, his grin stretching wide.

"Don't forget about me." Naomi joined the embrace, then pulled back and looked up at her son. "What did I tell you, baby? Jeremiah 29:11 says, 'For I know the plans I have for you,' declares the Lord, 'plans to prosper you and not to harm you. Plans to give you hope and a future.'"

Demarcus hugged her tight and whispered, "Thank you, Mom. You're the best. I love you."

"I love you too, my son. And remember, God loves you even more."

Just then, the doorbell rang. Jerry dashed to answer it.

Demarcus and Naomi turned as he returned, Silver Fox trailing behind him.

"Father?" Demarcus stepped forward, concern etched across his face. He gave him a careful hug. "You should be resting."

"I'm feeling stronger every day," Silver Fox replied, then kissed Naomi's cheek. "Sorry I didn't call first."

"That's okay," Naomi said warmly. "We were just celebrating." She winked at Demarcus.

"What's the occasion?" Silver Fox asked, glancing at his son. "I've got some good news myself."

"You first," Naomi offered.

"Salaam Alihammad was released from jail," Silver Fox announced.

"Really?" Demarcus's face lit up as the news sank in. The man who had saved him in jail was finally free. "That's just awesome."

"Thank you for helping him, Calvin," Naomi said, her smile stretching wide. "He never should've been there in the first place."

"I got a judge to approve his release on his own recognizance," Silver Fox explained. "I've assigned one of my top ADAs to the case. I'm confident we'll get the charges dropped."

"That calls for a celebration," Jerry declared with a grin.

Naomi's eyes sparkled as she turned to Silver Fox, then glanced at Jerry. "Speaking of celebration . . ."

Jerry stepped over to the coffee table, picked up the envelope, and handed it to Silver Fox. As Silver Fox read the letter, his smile widened with each passing line. The news was clear--his son's full scholarship to Stanford had been reinstated for the spring.

Without a moment's pause, he pulled Demarcus into a proud, heartfelt embrace. "This is incredible," he said, joy radiating through every word. "Everything's finally falling into place."

"Amen," Naomi agreed warmly. "The blood that gives us strength, day after day, will *never* lose its power."